solomon
and the queen
of sheba

solomon and the queen of sheba

BY CZENZI ORMONDE

farrar, straus and young

NEW YORK

*Where there is no vision, the people perish:
but he that keepeth the law, happy is he.*
PROVERBS XXIX:18

It was a time of waiting. Lifted by winds that come before the winter rains, the sighs of Jerusalem were carried far. They cooled the tents and hearts of those who still dwelt in the desert; the ardor of lovers in distant fields. They shamed into silence the haggling in the market-places and pressed the gentle hands of the old, who remembered, against the laughing mouths of those too young to remember that David the King had been a mighty warrior in the days of his glory.

Now he was old and stricken in years. . . .

The sadness moved across the Jordan into Gilead and whined mournfully back through dark mountain passes, even to the going down of the sun in the great sea; for it was whispered over crossroad supper fires along the caravan routes from Dan to Beersheba that the sweet singer out of Bethlehem, the one who had united twelve war-torn tribes into a time of peace, was now burdened with his years and for two moons had not crossed the threshold of his bedchamber.

While the austere doors closed off the King from the rest of the palace rooms, there were those who waited in the great hall below. Each evening the servants placed extra portions of bread and meat before the growing number of guests who sat at the low table by the hearth. As firelight burnished the sword and shield on the wall of stone, the newly arrived ruler of a tribe east of the Dead Sea bent his chilled nose over a cup of heated wine and spoke his thoughts to ancient Omri who had traveled far from the coastal plain to represent his people of Issachar. Since all was still well with the King's mind, if not his body—they both wanted to know—then how was it he had not yet called his son, Adonijah, to his bedside for the blessing of the firstborn?

Neither of the old men absently picking over last crumbs at the King's bounteous board was aware that he asked and answered in tones that assumed each was as deaf as the other. Nor did the two elders look up at the sudden whisper of fine linen as a stately, still beautiful woman rose suddenly from her place by the fire and left the room. A handmaiden quickly gathered the soft cushions which had eased the hours of Bathsheba's impatient waiting, and scurried after her.

When Bathsheba, the last of David's wives, left to spend more restless hours in her own apartments, the uneasiness in the room departed with her. The cool current of air from the unseen door, opening and closing in the deep shadows beyond the pillars, stirred the embers of a brazier in one of the dim alcoves and disclosed the triumph on the face of Adonijah's mother.

"I'll go now to the home of my son." Drawing a faded shawl over hair no less faded, she stood tall and thick-waisted beside the priest, Abiathar, who sat much closer to the glowing coals. She raised a square hand in protest when he started to rise. With a careful look at the yawning guards, the groups of court attendants and the elders, she lowered her voice. "The council with Joab and the others must be over by now. I have done my part. I was told to appear at the evening board—to wait until Bathsheba could have no suspicions of my son's absence, and had retired for the night." The glare of red-hot eyes in the brazier mingled with the dark anger straining upward into the loose folds of flesh beneath her chin. "As much as I loathe stepping into this house of David, and looking upon the woman who lords over it, there is a certain pleasure. Did you see her grow pale and snap the threads of her handwork when the name of Adonijah was spoken as the next king of Israel—"

"Hush now, Haggith! It is too soon to speak of this." Abiathar's thin fingers moved through the white and meager beard. His mind had strayed from her woman talk but with the first sound of conspiracy on her lips his thoughts struggled past the pale film of worry in his eyes. "The lady Bathsheba is unsettled by her concern over David. Nothing more."

Haggith looked down with kindly contempt. "A priest is after all only a man, with the blindness of a man. The most lowly woman in the king's household can tell you Bathsheba has not bothered to enter the rooms of our lord and husband since he laid himself on his bed of sickness."

The old man seemed to shrink inside his priestly vestments, and his head moved back and forth as if to escape an unwelcome truth.

"Let it be so, then," he murmured. "It would not be seemly for a wife of David to linger in his rooms and witness the more intimate ministrations given her lord by the maiden from Shunam."

Haggith suppressed a snort of derision at the old priest's implication. The blindness of the male, then, was equal only to the reluctance of parting with the legend of his vain and insatiable appetites of the flesh. There was no need to answer him. The truth hung between them and cut off the need for words. It was common knowledge.

The fairest maiden in the land had been sought to bring the purity and warmth of her body to the ailing king. But not even the lovely Abishag from Shunam could restore a vigor that had died long ago, followed soon by the last vestige of desire. The warm afternoon of her arrival at the palace had brought no twinge of envy to the women who had loved and been loved by the King. They watched her cross the main courtyard, escorted by guards. A demure flower, blooming in the late spring garden tended by hands of women who lived in the years of autumn. And those who were sitting in the great hall fell silent as the suppleness of youth and beauty was guided up the great stairs and taken into the chambers of the King. Bathsheba, sitting with Nathan the Prophet, had scarcely glanced at the girl before turning back to speak intensely to the righteous man of God who had once risen in a terrible anger to denounce Bathsheba's marriage to David. The one whom he had called adulteress had been there again that night when the girl finally emerged. The bloom of honored privilege at serving the King was now a stain of defeat and humiliation upon her smooth cheeks; it was written plainly on the face of Abishag the Shunammite. Her message to the guard outside David's doors had drifted down to those who gathered below. In a thin but surprisingly firm voice, she said, "My devotion to the king is now my greater honor. Not as a concubine to her master but as sister to brother, as a child brings the close breath of life to her father, for the rest of his days." And when she had made a request for more covers of goat-hair and more braziers to warm the bones of the King, she withdrew once more into the royal bedchamber and closed the doors softly behind her. Someone had broken the long silence then and murmured, "Poor David," and a mischievous young matron leaned toward the wife of an officer and whispered slyly, "Poor Abishag."

The nodding of Haggith's head affirmed the female knowledge that the heart of a woman could only be truly read by another.

"Make no mistake," she said to Abiathar. "The one who holds her head so high in this house will never bow it before the altar of honesty."

Abiathar sighed and cupped his hands to the warmth of the coals. "What is it then you read in the heart of Bathsheba?"

"Fear." Haggith savored the word and said it again, closer to the yellow-white lock of hair that hung over the priest's ear. "Fear for the day when Adonijah will sit on the throne. Fear for the death of all ambition that will die when she dies. Fear for the life of her precious Solomon."

Abiathar looked up sharply. "Solomon? Why should Bathsheba fear for the life of her son?"

"Have you lived so long, honored priest, that you forget the rules of all the kings that ever lived? Isn't it his first duty to secure his crown by banishing all possible claims to the throne?"

The old man's mouth sagged with despair. "Banishment perhaps," he conceded.

"The proud one does not know the meaning of the word. Given a choice she would rather die!" Haggith bowed to Abiathar and took her leave.

Bearing herself with conscious pride in being mother to the eldest living son of David, she crossed the great hall and the doors to the outer corridor were opened for her. Once outside and unobserved, she walked too swiftly through the labyrinth of gardens, bleak and burned by the forgotten heat of summer. She fastened her cloak against the chill in the air and hurried toward the palace gates. As she walked through, a startled look of pain distorted her face. She steadied herself against the rough stone until the pain had gone. A sentry recognized the mother of Israel's next king, and assisted her to a place of rest outside the walls.

[3]

She thanked him and sat in the recess, away from the light of torches that illumined the Horse Gate.

The silver glow of the night sky washed over the rooftops of Jerusalem below. The sound and shapes of people walking or standing in the shadowed streets changed abruptly at the clatter of iron-rimmed wheels and hoofs rumbling in the distance over the broken stones of the narrow lanes. The crack of a whip brought the chariot into sight, rounding a corner on one wheel. Cries of caution broke the soft gossip of the evening, huddles of darkness in the middle of the road seemed to shatter at the approach of Adonijah's chariot and the sound of running feet was swallowed by the thunder of his splendid carriage.

His mantle billowed behind him as he cracked the reins over the horses' rumps. His heavy-muscled arms, banded with the seal of David's army, pulled back with strength powerfully controlled and brought the chariot to a halt at the gate before the guards could run out and reach for the bridles.

His mouth broke in a proud smile and he spoke with patronizing exuberance to the younger man whose eyes, on a level with his own, glowed dark with admiration.

"Now tell me there have been no changes in the city all the while you were gone!" Adonijah tossed the reins to a groom and leaped to the ground. "You would still be riding that stallion of yours through the outer gates of the city if you hadn't first stopped at my house. Come then—" He broke off, seeing his mother had come forward with a smile on her face that faded as she looked beyond him and raised her eyes to the tall, broad-shouldered figure still standing in the chariot.

He seemed to loom larger than life-size against the glare of flickering torchlight behind him; and illusion of dark prophesy in the silhouette of a man. When the figure moved, smiled down at her and spoke the gentle salutation, "Peace be with you, Haggith," the woman seemed to breathe once more. Adonijah wondered suddenly that the flaming glow left her face untouched and still gray with something close to fright.

She moved away from his grip and said it was nothing at all. It was the evening light and imagination, nothing more. As she was about to walk through the city, to the house of her son which she preferred to any other, she knew the joy of seeing him sooner than she expected. As to this other one now. . . .

She came closer and peered up at him. This strange one had not been a stranger when he left to visit the fine cities of far lands, she said. He had been Solomon, the last seed of David's loins, the son of Bathsheba. First a child whose eyes opened wide with candor one moment, withdrew in secret thought the next; then a raven-haired youth who often wandered away by himself but more often could be found hovering on the fringe of his older brother's robust soldier life, making no secret of his good-natured envy of Adonijah. But now—here was Solomon the grown man. She could not understand it. He had not been away so many moons that this was a sudden growing, away from those who had heard only his first cries at birth and nothing but the sound of his name in the years between. She spoke out these things the best she could and Solomon chuckled at her amazement.

"Even a sapling grows into a tree, unnoticed," he said, "when you watch it every day." As he looked down at her from the chariot he read something on her face which he had seen up and down the land in the faces of strangers who looked at him, then turned to look once more and perhaps stutter an apology for staring.

One ancient pilgrim to the sanctuary ruin at Shiloh—in the hills of Ephraim where Joshua had cast the lots and assigned the territory to the tribes—the pilgrim had fallen to the ground defaming its sanctity to the Almighty by uttering long forgotten, long forbidden incantations to the alien gods of Canaan. He stopped only when Solomon touched him with a hand that was mortal and warm with living blood.

"Look closer, old one," Solomon told him, repressing his irritation at the man's stupidity. "I am no shade out of Sheol, or a vision come to haunt you from your youth. How do you remember David when he was strong and fought the Philistines?"

"The same height, the same bones," whispered the old man, peering at him as Haggith was this very moment. "The same eyes, gray as the sea and changing with the wind from gentle blue to the green of fury—"

"Mine are black as the tents of Kedar. See for yourself. And the color of his hair?"

The pilgrim studied the glossy darkness of Solomon's hair and he wagged his head with infantile chagrin. He was old and must be forgiven, he said, for age played tricks with eyes that had looked too long upon the world. He remembered now that the sun could find its own gold hidden in the mass of David's hair.

And so it was the same with Haggith. She was staring at him, remembering, and wondering how she could have made such a mistake.

Solomon had known Haggith better than the others who were the mothers of David's children. Ahinoam now, the mother of Amnon, the first of David's sons, was a wraith in Solomon's memory; a soft-spoken voice without a body, a work-worn hand clutched in grief at the news of Amnon's murder. Solomon could not remember the untamed Maacah, who had left her beautiful twins, Absalom and Tamar, and gone back to her father's people in Geshur. And of the others, pale shadows still living somewhere in the many rooms of the palace, there was only Haggith who was real, grown large and comfortably awkward with her love of sweets, still fiddling senselessly with the loops of noisy bangles she wore about one arm.

Solomon waited as Adonijah and Haggith spoke in low voices, then he leaped from the chariot and because she was the mother of the only brother he had known well and long enough to love, he kissed her gently on the cheek and was surprised to find it cold and unwilling to his touch.

[5]

"And how is it with my father?" Adonijah asked.

It seemed to Solomon that the answer was held for an instant behind Haggith's eyes before she said there was no change. A silent communication between mother and son touched Solomon's hungry need for something akin to its intimacy. They mistook his interest for curiosity and he laughed and told them it was a rare thing to possess, the communion with another through the language of spirit and the eyes. Something like apprehension flashed between the two, was gone as swiftly as the strange hardness in Adonijah's eyes.

"That is the greatest falsehood you ever told!" Adonijah laughed, too heartily. "You talk of being close to another person, beyond need for words. You," he scoffed as he dug an elbow into Solomon's ribs, "you with a different woman for each different mood—"

There was no use in explaining to Adonijah that his jest held more truth than he realized. There was no time to pursue the words to express the vague searching within him with no purpose in the searching.

Adonijah smacked Solomon in the stomach with the back of his hand and raised his eyebrows in mock surprise. "Look at him, mother. The one who used to lie flat on a rock and dream all day in the sun has a belly harder than my own."

With Adonijah's arm about his shoulder, Solomon walked with him to the gate. As Adonijah passed through ahead of him, Solomon turned to wave a farewell and was chilled to the bone by the stare of malevolence, gray and hard as the stone wall, that was quickly erased from Haggith's face as she turned her back and started down the sloping road into the town.

Solomon shook off the caul of foreboding, saw Adonijah striding ahead and hurried to overtake him.

He stumbled over a stone that marked the edge of the path and he thought, have I been away from my home too long to remember the way in safety? And from somewhere in the dimness of latticed windows and an upper door, opened for a moment to the clear air that drifted from the sea beyond the mountains, he heard soft whispers of welcome. A smile flashed in the passing light of a lamp carried by a sentry and Solomon felt the warmth of remembrance surging through him, dispelling the unhappiness on the face of Haggith. Long absence demanded a gallantry he had no time to indulge. Still he moved closer to the vine-covered walls of the women's quarters and to each pair of eyes, to the silken ripple of golden hair unbound and black coils still gracing some delicate oval of ivory, and he paid tribute in one all-embracing phrase: "How beautiful are the daughters of Jerusalem!" But to old Eglah who had heard his voice and peered out of sightless eyes to search for the one she had helped bring into the world, he felt the special need and touched his lips reverently to the hand on the window sill. And he pressed it with deep affection for the old nurse who had scolded his transgressions, and even now was demanding that he get out of the cold night air.

As he hurried once more to Adonijah the impatience that had informed each gesture since he heard of his father's illness now burst through the shell of his brother's small, inconsequential talk.

"I am most anxious to see our father," Solomon said.

Adonijah smiled with indulgence. "Now I *know* you have been away close to a year." He deliberately veered from the direct path crossing the main courtyard and sat down on a bench night-streaked by shadows of a terebinth tree. He continued, as if speaking to a stranger. "The King sees no one but his nurse, Abishag, and the High Priest Zadok. The rest of us, including his sons, must wait until we are summoned."

"Then why were you in such a hurry to arrive here tonight?"

Adonijah's shrug of worldly disdain seemed out of tune, somehow, with some unspoken concern. "Perhaps I have a feeling that tonight he wishes to speak with me."

"How long has it been since you entered his rooms?"

"Before the Passover, when he knew that he could not rise from his bed, let alone walk with Zadok and all his people to the high place for worship." Adonijah fastidiously brushed the dust from his mantle and lifted the hem free from the dew on the ground. "He asked to have me stand in his place."

"It is your right," Solomon said, looking down at his brother. "The king can look to you to carry his sword."

Adonijah's bitterness filled Solomon with an unnamed disappointment.

"If he ever drops it!" He snapped a twig from the tree and broke it into small pieces. "He lingers up there in his rooms that might as well be his burial cave. Ambassadors come for audience and go away disgruntled. Petitioners stop me in the streets as I ride through, pleading with me to hear their complaints—and there is no one to judge them."

This was a grave situation for Israel. He had not known that the king was too feeble to sit at the gates in judgment, or receive the homage of foreign emissaries in his Audience Room.

"I am less concerned about the people of Jerusalem," said Adonijah. "Let them settle their own troubles. But if the King does not sanction my succession—before he dies—there will *be* no kingdom!"

"I traveled into Damascus," said Solomon, "I skirted the borders to the east and to the sea—and the borders were quiet and peaceful."

"Peaceful! Have you no foresight, no vision, no wisdom?" He threw away the handful of twigs in disgust. Then he leaned forward, rested elbows on knees and his forehead was creased with lines of worry. "I have tried time and again to tell him. But he listens with eyes closed and then answers by asking for a cup of wine! He wanders in a dream of the past but forgets that he didn't conquer the Philistines by playing his harp! He refuses to see that the army's strength has been sapped by long years of inaction—and he peers at me through half-closed lids and says, 'Inaction—is that your name for peace?'"

Solomon sat beside him then, on the damp garden bench. "I would call that a wise reply."

"Yes," Adonijah said slowly. "I believe you would. But inaction invites invasion."

"Where is the danger?" Solomon was thinking that his father had conquered the Philistines, subdued the Canaanites. What now? "Surely the people deserve a time of peace."

Adonijah looked at him with eyes heavy with contempt. "Those were his very words when I last talked to him!"

"Tell me—what would you do to allay this evasive danger?"

"Increase the army tenfold. Raise it to wartime strength and march against Gezer. It has stubbornly remained a Canaanite city and should be destroyed!"

"A stronghold such as that?" This was strange reasoning. Gezer controlled the passage to the sea, it was true. But when Solomon had passed through, he found it a hub of commerce, not seething with unrest, and he told this to Adonijah.

"It is no concern of yours, Solomon. The affairs of Israel will soon be on my shoulders."

Strong ones, Solomon had to admit.

"Mark me," Adonijah went on, "David our father prattles of peace. Because the wars were about him, on every side. But he forgets they will be again—if our enemies know the King is weak and incapable." His eyes shone with eagerness to lead the kingdom to new triumphs. "I'll crush the Syrians to the north, expand our boundaries and the name of Adonijah will be one of glory!"

A silence fell between the brothers and Solomon saw the picture, not with horror at the blood that would be shed in further conquest, for that was inevitable. It was the way of conquering warrior kings. But he wondered if Adonijah had given thought to an army of defense, or considered another way of turning the eyes of Egypt's Pharaoh away from the possible siege of Gezer—which meant an unobstructed road to the capture of Jerusalem itself—

As he pondered these questions which Adonijah rightly said were none of his concern, Adonijah rose suddenly and looked toward the King's roof-terrace, partially visible beyond the trees and outdoor staircase leading to the royal rooms.

The heavy curtains against the embrasure of the bedchamber were being drawn aside. For a moment the figure of a young woman was outlined against the feeble light within. She stepped out onto the roof-terrace, letting the curtains fall back, blotting out the lonely light of the room behind it.

"His nurse?" he asked.

Adonijah did not answer. He was looking up, intently watching the white robe of the girl come closer to the parapet. The pale light of the sky enveloped her, made deep shadows of her eyes and Solomon looked swiftly at his brother and away again, unwilling to intrude on the almost tangible bond that held these two transfixed in an instant of secret desire.

This then was Abishag, he knew. And he studied the ground at his sandaled feet, not entirely prompted by finer sensibilities. Without shaping his thoughts into precise recalling of the law, he hoped that no one but himself had ever seen this naked look of love between the son of the King, and the King's concubine. Whether in name or fact, Abishag was the property of the King. And if a man laid eyes upon her and joined her body to his, he was guilty of treason. To claim the property of the King, in any form, was to claim the throne and was punishable by death. Nathan and Zadok had schooled him well in the law as it was written and the law as precedent. And now the dim and wonderfully kind figure of Saul's captain, the Abner who lived long before Solomon could remember, came to his mind from out of history. He was cast aside by Saul's son, Ishbosheth who succeeded to a throne already usurped by David. And Abner went down in shame for having coveted the concubine, Rizpah, who had belonged to Saul. And then again, when Solomon's brother Absalom, the comely, treacherous one who lifted the swords of an army against David, knew that the King had reluctantly been led into exile across the Jordan to Mahanaim, Absalom rode into Jerusalem at the head of his troops. And the first act of sealing his right to the throne was enacted in the rooms of the women left behind by David to tend his household.

"What are you sitting here for?" Adonijah shook Solomon's shoulder and Solomon was startled to find that the girl had disappeared from the parapet and the curtain was closing once more against the opening to David's bedchamber. "Go to your rooms, Solomon. Sleep well—and in the morning I'll give you the news of my father."

"How do you know he will see you? I heard no call—"

Adonijah's expression was evasive. "It is a good time to settle things. Once and for all." He glanced briefly toward the King's roof. "Abishag is an excellent handmaiden to the King. She tends him well. A most capable and efficient nurse." As he continued to extol the virtues of Abishag— only as a nurse—Solomon winced at the useless but necessary deceit. Surely Adonijah knew he could trust his brother. This was not an act of conspiracy against the throne. How could it be? Adonijah was the rightful heir. And when he inherited the crown he would also inherit the household of women: The court attendants, the musicians, the refugee slaves who had fled to Jerusalem for asylum, the old wives, the old nurses including Eglah with the blue ridges of veins swelling in her hands, and the young nurse—Abishag. Where was the crime?

"Will you tell him that I have returned and long to see him?"

"He will rejoice." Adonijah walked purposefully toward the courtyard entrance of the palace—and Solomon stood leaning against the terebinth tree, and looked up at his father's windows. Adonijah, the firstborn and favored son, would soon be in that room. Solomon harbored the hope that the girl Abishag would come running out, soon after, and call to him and say: "Prince Solomon, your father asks for you!"

The hope was instantly dispelled. Very faintly, from the room of his father, came the mournful sound of David's lute. Then it was silent and the grieving cry of an old man, an old father who could still embrace the memory if not the body of his favorite son, carried down into the garden where Solomon stood; and the wail drew itself thin—"O my son Absalom, my son, my son Absalom!"—

And then the querulous voice—was this from the throat of the once-mighty David?—asking who was there, who was it, Abishag, who whispered with her at the far door of the adjoining room? And because Abishag was calling to an old man lying petulantly in his bed, Solomon heard her say that Prince Adonijah had arrived and begged to see him. Then the murmur of male voices, one young and arrogant, the other a fading thread of affection. . . .

Solomon ran his fingers through his hair. If he could not see his father immediately then he would go to the apartments of his mother and dutifully say the correct things.

He walked along shadowed paths to the garden of his mother's house. It was in darkness but he rapped at the door, and if no one answered he could always say to her, "You were the first I wanted to see," and she would be pleased.

The door opened a crack and a vaguely familiar face, drowsy-eyed and flushed with the rosiness of disturbed sleep, looked out at him and her lips parted with the same moist invitation he had seen on the faces of the lovemaidens in the groves of Astarte in the remote hills of the pagan country.

"It is Leah," he said with surprise for when he had left she was little more than a child. "Are you now my mother's handmaiden?"

She stifled a yawn and smiled. "This is the house of your wife, Naamah." As she started to open the door, Solomon hastily raised a hand.

It was too late in the night to disturb the sleep of his wife. He would wait till morning. And he wanted to know where the Lady Bathsheba now had her quarters.

"Where indeed," the girl began, then added respectfully, "these rooms were too damp in the winter for your mother, too—distasteful to her comfort. She has taken apartments at the far end of the palace. They say the rooms of the Lady Bathsheba are the most luxurious in all the land. . . ."

Solomon, in one expert glance, appraised the slender hips, the imperceptible movement of the born harlot. No robe was sewn or ever would be that would disguise the badge of her nature if not her profession. Well, it was good to know that there was a Leah close at hand. Being in the service of the wife he scarcely knew, presented no difficulties. He took his leave, knowing that one night he would send for this girl and she would come to him—there was no hurry. . . .

He found his mother's rooms spacious, furnished with an exquisite sense of luxury not shared by the more austere women of the palace. And Bathsheba, after she had embraced him with tears of welcome in her eyes, was beautiful, trim and compact, with the clever brightness in her eyes he remembered so well.

"What an anxious heart you have given me all these months," she said, and led him to a place near the fire where a table was heaped with delicacies. She begged him to eat his fill, she herself resisted the temptation when she remembered her figure. But whenever Nathan the Prophet called on her he was ravenous and ate with the appetite of ten men—so she saw to it that her servants fed him well.

Solomon bit into a honeycake. Then he wrinkled his nose, sniffing the air with an exaggeration which brought laughter to his mother's taut features.

"He hasn't been here within the past hour at least," Solomon said.

"Now, now," Bathsheba said with mild rebuke, seating herself beside him. "I know the ancient one must have been born in the rags he wears. But he was your teacher, remember, even before Zadok. And he still calls you Jedidiah, Beloved of God."

Solomon slowly put the remains of the cake on the table. "I would like nothing more this night than to know I am loved by my own father."

He felt the fingers of his mother press into his knee with impatient urgency. "You know as well as I," she said, "that *you are* his favored son."

Solomon regarded her with an understanding smile. His mother would think that. She was forever seeking perfection in him, where it did not exist; bestowing virtues on him that were beyond the reach of any man.

He shook his head. "Not I."

His mother drew away from him then and he could feel the anger rising slowly within her.

"Never think for a moment it is Adonijah!"

"I had in my thoughts David's undying love for Absalom—"

"A traitor!"

"Even so," Solomon said, "his favored son." And his heart ached for the old man who cried out in his dying loneliness for the one who hung by his hair in a tree and writhed to his death in Ephraim with the arrows of Joab in his side.

What violence stalked the earth in the guise of justice, he thought. Son against father, brother against brother. From out of childhood memory he recalled the Feast of the Sheep-Shearing in Absalom's house at Baal-hazor, and in the midst of song the death cry of Amnon that left blood on the hands of Absalom. And he wondered why he was thinking of this now. Was it because he had never asked the question locked inside him? He knew what happened but never why. Was it truly to avenge the lustful abuse of Tamar that Absalom slew his older brother? Does a

[11]

man carry hatred on the point of his sword for two years before he plunges it into the ribs of his brother? Or was it because David's throne, the rightful inheritance of Amnon, lured the wild and lovable Absalom to his deed of evil. . . .

"You have not heard one word I said!" Bathsheba stood at the square latticed window at the far side of her room. She let the edge of the curtain drop from her hand and came toward him. "Scarcely home an hour and already you sit dreaming! Did my words strike no fear within you at all?"

He was puzzled and smiled at her through his guilty inattention.

"Hear me well." She spoke her warning in tones that commanded his full attention. "I looked down into the courtyard just now. Two of the elders came out of the great hall and walked toward the palace gates!"

Solomon touched a lock of her hair. "You are still too young to let silver shine in your hair—"

She grasped his hand with irritation. "It means something—I feel it strongly. Where would they be going this time of night except to the house outside the city walls?"

"To Adonijah? Why should they? Anyway, he is not at home."

"How do you know?" she asked sharply. "You've seen him! You searched him out—before you came to the palace—!"

He saw no need for this hysteria. He had hoped to return and find his mother a friend to the one who had been both father and brother to his growing years.

"I went to his house, yes. He was there with Joab—and they greeted me warmly. We talked of many things—"

"Of his eagerness to sit on the throne?"

Solomon got to his feet and slowly walked to the window where he could look down on the gardens and paths he knew so well. And because he was close to anger at his mother's petty suspicions, he spoke of the gardens he had seen in Jericho where the almond blossoms lay thick on the trees in the budding of the year.

Bathsheba's footsteps sounded behind him and she laid a softer hand on his arm. "Forgive my sharp tongue." He turned and smiled once more and she brushed an imaginary bit of dust from the shoulder of his tunic. "I think only of your good," she said quietly. "I have heard rumors—now, Solomon! Surely this girdle binding your waist is too faded for the son of a king! You were born a prince. Try to dress like one—and Solomon, my son, be patient with my words. I promise to make them brief."

"I want to hear no slander against Adonijah," he said with a firmness he knew she understood. And often feared.

She assumed the pose he found so familiar. Her feelings were injured. She would smile sadly—yes, there was the smile, wan and touched with the beauty of self-sacrifice; and she would say in the most tender of voices that she had failed as a mother, oh yes she had! And she would go to her bedchamber now—

When he was younger, the thought of bringing sadness to anyone, particularly his mother, filled him with remorse and he would plead with her to understand, and to Bathsheba the word meant to forgive. And she was well-practiced in forgiving gracefully, all the while speaking out her thoughts and opinions which had caused the unpleasantness in the first place.

But that was long ago—when he knew less about the subtle and various ways of women. She did not leave the room this time, but searched the folds of her robe for a piece of linen to dry tears still unshed.

"I heard rumors," she repeated, "and I feared for my life. And for yours."

What nonsense now was she speaking!

The quietness remained in her voice but the words were hard and struck him with the force of spears forged in her jealousy. "If Adonijah becomes king after David, he will have us banished—or murdered!"

"Have you taken to listening with open ears to idle talk!"

"Not idle!" She was Bathsheba once more. Direct and incisive. "You have forgotten that your father made a vow to me—when you were still a child."

"A man in the years of his love makes many vows. Now I bid you peaceful sleep—"

She clutched his arm. With burning pride she said, "It is a secret only Nathan knows—and you."

"Let it remain so."

"Your father David promised me that you would be the one to succeed him. 'Your son, Solomon, shall reign after me.'" She made herself straight and tall to impress him with the honor. "Those were his very words!"

Solomon rubbed the ache at the back of his neck, and hoped his sigh was a patient one.

"Words to a very old story. It no longer amuses me," he said. "I don't wish to hear it again."

"It was a promise, I tell you!"

"Then forget it. Once and for all time!" He lowered his voice and put his hands on her narrow, firm shoulders. "Look elsewhere for your ambition, I beg you. It doesn't lie with me. If Adonijah were not the rightful heir, the eldest—do you hear me, mother?—if he had no true claim to the throne, he would still be welcome to it! With my blessing. And my pity. What man in his right mind would wish to be a king!"

A secretive smile moved Bathsheba's lips and she caught his hand, for an instant gently, between her shoulder and her cheek.

"What man knows his right mind?" Then she smiled openly at him and wished him a night of pleasant dreams. "I have kept your rooms as they were—" a slight frown puckered her forehead "—I forgot. You may possibly find one of the alcoves filled with the clutter of Ahiah's scribbling. I gave him permission to use part of the room in your absence. He craved a time of quiet in order to write down the events of the days—"

Solomon grinned at the thought of Ahiah, the scribe, needing a quiet place to do his work. It was only an excuse for him to escape the shrillness of his wife's tongue. He kissed his mother's forehead and at the open door she said gently, "You are a good son. You are impulsive, unpredictable— you have looked on the wine when it was red and you have been found singing with joy on feast days of lamentation—but you have always honored your mother."

"And my father," he added and chided her with good humor: "Or has my strong-minded mother also changed the Commandments while I was away?"

He blew her a light kiss and hurried down to the courtyard as if suddenly released from intangible threads being woven to capture him in a net.

In the courtyard he saw Adonijah striding out of the great hall. His brother's face was set and mottled with angry determination. He did not turn when Solomon called to him. Nor did he stop in his purposeful walk to the Horse Gate.

"Did you tell our father that I had returned?" And instantly, Solomon was annoyed at his blindness for not seeing that Adonijah must have great troubles of his own. "What is the matter, Adonijah?"

Staring straight ahead of him, his face grim in the darkening night, Adonijah spat out the reasons for his anger.

"I told him of my plans. I told him of the dangers that were stirring from the Syrians, from Damascus, Edom and Egypt! When I told him Gezer should be taken and made a citadel of protection—he almost wept and said the greatest of tyrannies were wrought in the name of protection!" Adonijah suddenly halted, swung around and stood looking up at the roof-terrace of his father's rooms. And for a moment Solomon heard nothing but the soft night sounds in the garden and the rush of air as his brother breathed deeply of his disappointment. "Up there! There lies a king who sheds tears at the mention of conquest! When I informed him that some of the elders had gathered from the far tribes out of concern for the lack of justice and leadership in the land—when I said they looked to me for the answer—" Adonijah's great fists closed tightly at his sides. "He struggled to rise from his pillows and he said, 'I will give them the answer. Tell them that David the King is not yet dead!'"

Then Adonijah swung his mantle about him and without another backward glance, walked to the gate where his chariot was waiting.

Solomon looked after him until he disappeared and he doubted that Adonijah, in his fury, would remember that he had spoken to his brother at all. And Solomon knew then what he had always known—that he had no brother—that to Adonijah he was a pleasant and unimportant member of the family. There would always be ten years of living between them, with Solomon yearning to bridge the gap, to call out his brother's name in affection and hear it returned to him on some warm and friendly breeze.

He walked long hours, an alien in the place where he was born.

Passing the darkened house where the girl Leah was now servant to his wife, Solomon felt no urge to go within and stir Naamah from her bed. It was the house of a strange woman he scarcely remembered. A spare and twig-hard face, narrow and pointed as the faces of the high-born Ammonites. Yet in his animal days, when his father urged upon his sons the need to marry quickly that the sons and daughters of his sons might also bring forth in their own time—in those animal days it was a blind and advantageous marriage. But Solomon was relieved to remember that the ungainly Naamah who had seemed fair in her bridal clothes, was content to be the first of his wives and not be called upon to fill her days or nights with thoughts of her husband. She was a busy shadow in his past. Such a short time ago, he thought, and still it was his past. Perhaps tomorrow he would come upon her here in the shade of the trees, talking endlessly of her household duties, exchanging the secret of her excellently preserved figs with the women who sat with her and if she looked up and saw the figure of her husband, returned from his journey, she would bow in obedience and quiver with resentment at the shadow of a male intruding into her comfortable and undemanding woman's world. It was better so.

He found himself at the door of his own quarters and still did not enter for no light burned within. If Ahiah had already rolled up his scrolls and absent-mindedly walked out with his reed pen still over his ear—then who was there to greet him and say, "Solomon, you have come home," and he walked away from the door.

Then he heard the voice of Ahiah calling to him and he rushed forward to meet him. Here was certainly one unchanged. They clasped each other in affection and stood at arm's length ridiculing the mark of absence on the other's face.

"It is time you returned," said the scribe and his eyes warmed at the sight of Solomon. "I have had no one to talk to. Not that you'll be much good to me, now that the dissipation of high living has grooved horrible lines in your face."

"You are an old tree, Ahiah, beginning to bend with age. Soon you can walk with Abiathar or Nathan the Prophet."

"May that day never come. I walk as a scribe who writes down what he sees. I am neither priest nor prophet. I have no desire to bring the people to God and it is certainly not my destiny to bring God to the people!"

It was good to walk again with Ahiah. To look down and see the cap of hair clinging to his round skull like a flock of tiny, frightened sheep huddled tightly together on a steep hillside.

He had bought a present for Ahiah, but in his haste to come home, it was left for Benaiah and Zabud to pack into the bundles of his caravan.

"They are following me as quickly as the camels and horses will allow," Solomon said. "I could not wait."

"You traveled alone?" Ahiah sat down on a bench and looked up with neither surprise nor censure. He was a searcher of facts and accepted them for what they were.

Solomon could tell him. And no one else. He could pull back the sleeve of his tunic and show the spear wound, still fresh, won in a struggle against bandits who ambushed him in the narrow pass near the Beth-horon that rose over the Shephelah. He had killed three of them before he escaped and under other circumstances he would be brooding now over the act of violence—even against bandits and in his own defense—but the worry of his father drove everything else from his mind.

"I regret one thing," Solomon said, "in the fighting I broke the dagger I was bringing home as a gift to Adonijah. The hilt was a lion's head with eyes of ruby—do you think he would have liked it?"

Ahiah shrugged and the expression on his face was lost in the mist that had gathered thickly in the night around them.

"The design of the hilt would not matter," he said. "If the blade was sharp, Adonijah would delight in—owning it."

Solomon felt a twinge of regret. Had Ahiah been about to say "using" instead of owning it? Let the maligning of his brother come from Bath-sheba if it must. She had a woman's reason for her animosity. But not Ahiah. Not the cool mind, the deep-searching fairness, the warmth of his friend Ahiah.

The bleakness within spread out before him. As he had turned away to talk of other things at the window of his mother's room, he spoke now of the broken walls he had noticed outside the city, the stench of poverty in the back streets and the barren look of the housetops that would blister in the sun.

"Jerusalem was pleasing enough to your eyes before you visited strange lands," said Ahiah.

"I know. Perhaps it was a mistake to leave. We are a strange people, Ahiah, crying out to a stern God who punishes us with days of famine and drought. Yet we obey His commands like obedient children turning with no protest to the whips at our backs."

Somewhere in the grayness hovering about the bench was the breathing shadow of Ahiah who listened well. Solomon paced back and forth and then, with a remembered sense of well-being and delight, he spoke of the groves and hills, the lush yield of the fields and the festivals in the land of Canaan where the pagans were conquered in all but their secret worship of Baal and Chemosh, Astarte, Milcom, Moloch—

"We are told they are an abomination," said Solomon. "I believe they are. Still, I wonder."

"It is a good thing to see both sides," Ahiah said gently. "But may I suggest that you keep these opinions—half-formed as they are—to yourself?"

Solomon laughed. This was Ahiah once more. Taking no stand. Living on a mental mountain where the sight below was vast and varied, ugly and beautiful, and not saying which was good and which was evil.

"I should not be surprised to hear one day that you have left Jerusalem forever and gone to live with the pagans." There was a chuckle in Ahiah's voice.

"They eat better food, live in finer houses and sleep on softer beds," said Solomon. "Yes, I would journey far, Ahiah. There is much to see. I learned that in the court of Hiram. I sailed on his ships and I believe there is no end to the sea or to the land around it. In Cilicia I found steeds of such power and beauty—I'd like to own hundreds of them! But in my travels I heard of a land far to the south, past the desert and the meeting-place of the caravans at Petra in the red rocks of Edom. Beyond these, Ahiah, is a land of treasure. Spices and gold beyond your wildest dreams. And I have passed the glittering camel trains from this land, burdened with riches that dazzled my eyes! Yes—I'd go there, Ahiah. To the land of Sheba—a jewel of fertile hills and torrents of water and—" He broke off with a gesture of futility. "I talk without sense. I have no desire to go anywhere but up there—" And he looked up at the heavy curtains moving with the night wind against the shutters of his father's rooms.

"Then go," Ahiah said simply.

"Since I was a child—and scolded for it—I have never gone to my father without being summoned."

"You have been summoned," Ahiah said quietly. "He summons you in his sleep—"

"You are trying to spare my feelings," Solomon said. "It is the shade of Absalom that hears his cries in the night."

"I have heard another cry," Ahiah continued. "I walk in these gardens alone, night after night when my thoughts are full of questions not to be answered—I tiptoe from my quarters in the east end of the palace houses, barefooted because my sandals are not of the best and squeak at every step—and I walk in the night and hear David call out for Solomon, his 'Little Solomon.' "

Solomon came close, until the face of Ahiah was clear before his own. And unswerving truth was written over the sun-bronzed skin and the brown eyes that saw the happenings of the days and the nights in the city of Jerusalem.

As he searched the face of the older man, the brown eyes moved in warning to the side. Solomon stepped back and into the shadows. Coming silently down the outer steps of the King's rooms was the girl Abishag. She walked without sound and wore a cloak over her head and shoulders. Her movements were swift but furtive. She looked about her, then ran past in the shadows and disappeared.

In the flash of weak light reflected from a lamp in a garden wall, the girl's face was clear to Solomon and he detected an unpleasant slyness in her eyes.

"Now you can go up to your father," Ahiah said.

Solomon was angry and wanted to call the girl from her flight toward the palace gates, but Ahiah stopped him.

"This is nothing unusual," he said.

"She leaves my father sick and unattended!"

Ahiah nodded. "Often."

"Where does she go?" Solomon demanded and in the same instant Ahiah's silence joined his, for they both knew where Abishag must be found many evenings—in the arms of Adonijah.

After a moment, Solomon said, "I will go up then. Quietly. I'll look on him while he sleeps and if he needs me—I'll be with him."

When he entered the room of his father, Solomon stood for a moment by the embrasure, trying to pierce the gloom of the vast room so full of shadows and memory.

The essence of fragrant life-restoring spices, the ointments and salves to comfort the gnawing at brittle bones, the sound of an old man breathing in the distant alcove behind curtains drawn to protect him from the chill of an everlasting night—these things would haunt his nostrils and his ears for the rest of his days.

His eyes grew accustomed to the few changes that had taken place in the room. The boughs of fragrant trees had been laid across the clothes chest to soften the less pleasant odors of approaching death. And the shape of David's lute outlined itself on the wall, over the niche in which the father David had kept the crude wine cups of all his sons. Without looking closely, Solomon knew they would be covered with a film of dust, all except the wine cup of Adonijah, perhaps, for the girl would surely keep that one bright with her love. . . .

A chill pervaded the room and Solomon moved softly and with anxious heart toward the bed alcove. The coals in the braziers had burned low. And he pulled aside only the curtain at the foot of the wide dais—at the foot of the bed—and first tended the coals and brought them to new life. A murmur of gratitude for the added warmth came from the mound of pillows at the head of the bed and Solomon looked upon his father's face.

David lay with his eyes closed, the glow of the renewed fire touching his gleaming white hair. It hollowed the sunken cheeks and Solomon grieved deeply at the sight and could not recall, for a moment, the face of David as he once was. This was a stranger, dearly beloved stranger with a pellet of moisture in the corner of an eye that had looked on the suffering and bloodshed of conquest and the wrongs of others and the grievous sins of his own committing; this eye had also seen the building of order and justice and had danced in joy before the Lord.

Without opening his eyes, David's mouth moved in its fitful sleep and the words faltered faint and broken across the coverlets that were scarcely raised by the body beneath.

"Have mercy on me, O God, according to thy steadfast love;
According to thy abundant mercy blot out my transgressions—"

Solomon's hands gripped the curtain post of the dais and fought back a protest forming on his lips. Out of dark memory of sin, David was lamenting the long-forgiven crime that laid Bathsheba by his side in unholy love while she was still the spouse of Uriah the Hittite. Why now, Solomon cried to himself, must I hear him utter the same lament—but for *all* the days of his wrongs, for he surely has forgotten in his age the sins of his youth—

> "—Against thee, thee only, have I sinned,
> And done that which is evil in thy sight—"

The fruit of that union had sickened and died and Solomon had been born and was a symbol of God's forgiveness—and his name meant peace and days of rest—

Solomon moved closer, arranging the coverlet, pulling up a fur skin that had slipped to the floor and he covered David and saw the eyelids flutter like the transparent wings of a newborn dove.

Solomon bent over him and very softly, hoping his voice would move into the old man's dreams and quiet his soul, he reached into his memory and brought forth the only comfort in the sadness of his father's pleading:

> "Cast me not away from thy presence,
> And take not thy holy Spirit from me.
> Restore to me the joy of thy salvation—"

The eyes opened suddenly and full of a light that Solomon remembered well—the glow of hope and the closeness of David's God.

> "—And uphold me with a willing spirit . . ."

Solomon knelt on the dais then, bowed his head and felt the hand of his father groping over his head with disbelief, then with growing joy assuring himself that this was indeed the son of Bathsheba.

"My little Solomon," whispered David and as he touched his son's face the voice kept repeating in wonder: "You have come home—my little Solomon—you are here and with the dimness of my eyes I behold your face again and hear you sing my songs. You remember them. . . ."

"They are sung from the great sea to the plains beyond Jordan," Solomon said. "But they are songs of David when he rejoiced in the knowledge that the Lord was with him and walked by his side and by the side of all his people—'The law of the Lord is perfect, reviving the soul; the testimony of the Lord is sure, making wise the simple'—those are the songs you have written as firmly in the hearts of your people as His words are written on the gateposts of the believers. . . ."

Solomon fell suddenly quiet. He stared down at the fleshless hand of his father and held it gently within his own, as if it were a dry leaf close to breaking. He had spoken out of his heart and had said too much, for he felt his father's eyes, burning now, boring into the shadows by the bedside as if a shade and not a man of blood and substance knelt by his side.

Solomon raised his head and, with a lighter tone, assured David the King that he was loved by his people as none had been before him.

He felt a deep need to speak the words freely and it saddened him to know that in all the years of his growing there had been so few times that David was the father and he the son. They were busy years, filled with the fire and smoke of pillage, the purifying of God's land, the scorching of pagan land that raised its pillar symbols of the staff and its swollen obscenities to the gods of fertility. But now, though the secret groves still held their sacred serpents, the most flagrant abominations stayed beyond the borders of David's land. The man who had slain Goliath had also slain the greater menace of those who would not believe in the Nameless One too sacred in the hearts of his people to be profaned by an image. David had done all this. And Yahweh had blessed his name and his house and would lighten now his darkness, for had He not said He had made a covenant with His chosen one and would establish his descendants forever that his line should endure like the moon and stand firm so long as the skies endure?

He tried to say these things, and wondered, in his heart if he truly spoke them out—for surely this man, David the King if not the father, deserved to hear the triumph of his life and not the defeats he conjured up in his soul.

"Since your people were led out of Egypt," Solomon said quietly, "and wandered in the desert, there was never a time of peace until you gave it to them. You gathered the twelve and made them one—"

"At what a cost," David sighed. "At what a terrible cost! I took men out of their vineyards and put swords in their hands—"

"What else could you do?"

"I made widows to weep in deserted fields, and children grew up without looking upon their fathers. . . ."

I looked upon mine, Solomon thought, but did I have a father? He tenderly smoothed a lock of his father's hair but the King seemed unaware of this gentle attention.

"I have caused much bloodshed in my life," said David. "And I wept for Saul and Jonathan and their deaths that made me King, and I weep today, for the wound is fresh on me as the day they were buried in Jabesh-Gilead—the mighty who have fallen! What right had I to look on their faces and call myself the anointed one. . . ."

"You were chosen, my father. The elders sanctioned the holy oil that made you King." The words were lifeless and devoid of the comfort he wanted to give. How did one tell a man of greatness that in his simplicity he beheld only his particular sins, but in the eyes of his son they were the natural cruelties in all days of war?

The old man raised his head from the rumpled pillow and coughed, and his coughing was like the tearing of cloth on a blade dull with rust. Solomon supported him with one arm and reached for the bowl of water with the other. As the King drank from the bowl, Solomon thought: he has no substance, not the weight of his own shadow on the wall.

Once more sinking into his pillows, the King closed his eyes and for a moment Solomon feared they were closed forever, he was so still. But a hand moved on the covers. A dribble of water strayed from his mouth into the whiteness of his beard, and Solomon reached for a square of linen at the bedside and dried his father's mouth.

He sat and waited, and he spoke aloud the thoughts that formed in his mind:

"To everything there is a season, and a time to every purpose under the heavens. A time to be born, and a time to die. A time to keep silence and a time to speak; a time to love, and a time to hate. A time for war—and a time for peace . . ."

He looked up to find his father's eyes searching him, as if probing into a dim and forgotten past.

"You see," he mumbled, "my mind wanders like a lost lamb in the wilderness of my life. I cannot remember writing those words—" His face slowly brightened. "—I did not write them! They are yours!"

Words spoken out of dreaming thought meant nothing, Solomon wanted to say. Where his father's mighty power had swept through the land, his songs had soared like an eagle in the sky. What were the dragging sounds that came from his own lips but the ponderous efforts of thoughts, earthbound, that were trying to fly?

"Solomon," David said. His voice was tender and it had a familiar ring. Even now, this moment recaptured a windswept hill in Bethlehem and brought father and son to its terraced vineyards on a forgotten day when both were very young and the father dug into the soft damp earth and planted a young vine deep, and covered the son's hands with his own and guided them in heaping the soil about the roots, so tender. "Solomon, my youngest," David said again. "I remember you as a child sitting on my knees, as if it were only yesterday. But now I see a grown man—and I cry for the lost years in between. Where did they go? Where is a man's life when he can remember the terrible wars that raged about him, his triumphs and his defeats—and cannot remember the years of his son's growing—" He reached out and grasped Solomon's arm. It gripped the wound of the bandit's spear and Solomon's face gathered tight to withhold the cry of pain.

"Tell me," said David, with surprising strength, "tell me that I am not entirely a stranger to your thoughts." He released his hold and muttered, "As I was stranger to the dark thoughts of Absalom . . . !"

His father's head had turned away in remembered grief and Solomon rubbed the wounded arm until his father turned back to him once more.

David lifted his unsteady hands, turned them this way and that, letting the light of the coals mark the high places, the ridges of veins that were like the treeless mountain tops he had once conquered, watching the shadows move into the ravines through which his armies moved soundlessly through the night. . . .

"I am withered like grass," David said, "that cannot remember the dew. Adonijah spoke the truth. He came to me this night—though I did not call him—"

Solomon did not look at his father then, but knew they were not strangers to each other's thoughts. Abishag had come out onto the roof-terrace to give Adonijah a prearranged signal that this was the time—and Solomon turned his eyes slowly to watch the King, fearing in his heart that David, with one word, could name the crime of Adonijah.

But the King's eyes revealed nothing but reflection on the truth.

"Adonijah fears for the nation. He says the flock is without a shepherd. What do you say?"

"My brother is a strong and worthy leader. Perhaps if you gave him authority—"

"You speak of authority," the King said. His brows came together in a knot of concern. "I speak of my people. Is my flock without a shepherd?"

Solomon could answer truthfully: "It will not wander away. Your people love you."

"But I leave them an inheritance they cannot see. It cannot be stored in the granaries, or weighed on the scales of measure. They will receive from me nothing they can hold in their hands—"

Solomon studied his father, and offered the bowl of water once more for he feared the old man's thoughts were wandering after all.

David pushed aside the bowl and it clattered to the floor.

"Can you not understand what I say?" he thundered the words clearly and with vigor, then let his anger spend itself in sighs against the pillow.

"You must see, *someone* must see—" he murmured. "I have sinned and plundered and killed to set the boundaries of my land. My people are safe within the stone landmarks of their fields and vineyards of their home —but who will fortify the boundaries of their faith? Who will let them know that David the King left his people the only inheritance which can never be squandered? The never-ending road, the bottomless well of purest water, the finest gold which cannot be carried in the hand but in the heart—"

The old man was sobbing faintly. "Who will tell them?" over and over, and Solomon smoothed the mountains of veins, the ridges of triumph on the old man's hands and the shadows of defeat.

"I know nothing of other men's hearts," Solomon said soothingly. "But you have already given each man his rightful inheritance on earth: the right to sit beneath his vine and his fig tree."

The answer seemed to please and revive David. And Solomon was glad of that.

"I was told this night," David said quietly, "that a nation is only as strong as the sword of its leader. What do you think, Solomon?"

This then was the end of life for a gallant and mighty warrior. Solomon gave his father the only assurance he could.

"You have been valiant," he said. "You no longer need to prove your might by the sword."

David seemed to draw together, his spare and ravaged body grew taut and the cords in his neck throbbed and pulsed with the effort of speaking.

"I was not thinking of myself," he said. Then after taking a deep breath he continued: "It is a strange truth I have learned this day. That I have two sons, each in his own way a likeness of his father. Yet the father was both. I was a soldier. And I was a man of dreams and visions—with words that sang in my heart—" He looked at Solomon a long while. "Are you the poet, Solomon? Are you my loneliness?"

There was earnest pleading in the questions and Solomon grew uneasy at the weight of them hanging there suspended between them.

He eased the answer with a chuckle. "I am not a poet, my father. Your son Solomon has been called many things. A spendthrift, a fool, even a scoundrel—but never a poet."

"That is good," David said solemnly. "Nor have you been called a soldier." He waved his hand with a gesture of fatigue. "Leave me now. I want to think. . . ."

Solomon looked about the room with covert anxiety. He could not leave his father without an attendant.

The old man, with his eyes closed, seemed to sense his thought. "You may leave me with good conscience, my son."

"But you are alone—"

"Am I?" He opened his eyes and for the first time Solomon saw a new tranquillity in his face. "The little Shunammite is gone, it is true, but I am not alone. I am never alone, Solomon—"

Solomon looked down on his father, kissed him gently on the forehead. "God be with you," he said.

He stepped down off the dais, and walked to the door which led to the inner rooms of the palace. He believed he could sleep now. He had seen his father, and he believed he could sleep. David's voice came to him with a final request.

"Find me Zadok the priest," he said. "I would speak with him—and the others. . . ."

Solomon promised. He closed the door and moved into the corridor where the sentry was dozing near the wall. The great hall below was a vast shadow, a chamber of massive shapes strange in the dying light of the fire. He smiled when he saw the two figures sprawled out on the hearth, snoring loudly in their sleep. The livid scar on Benaiah's warrior face seemed the only thing alive in the room. He would let Benaiah sleep. The valiant man out of Kabzeel had earned many years of sleep. Let the commander of David's army lie there like the lions he had slain in his youth. The younger face of Zabud, who was Solomon's friend, was dark with fatigue. Let them both sleep until morning. Their journey had been long. And he had no desire to rouse them and talk until morning of their interrupted journey, so full of zest and the meeting of kindred appetites.

Solomon wished to speak to no one, least of all the self-righteous and thundering man of God who seemed more the prophet than Nathan. No, he had no wish to see Zadok the High Priest. Tomorrow perhaps, but not this night.

He prodded the sentry with his foot, gave him the message and waited until the soldier hurried away toward the rooms of the priest. He listened a moment at his father's door and heard only the murmurs of an old man —talking to himself. Then he walked quietly down the stone steps. He would walk as quietly past the sleeping figures of Benaiah and Zabud, and go to his own quarters—and sleep.

David lay in his bed, the strong bones of his nose and cheeks catching the last light of the coals and he knotted his hands in prayer.

"O Lord my God, my rock and my strength—hear your servant—mark my iniquities tenfold and remember well my sins and errors—for my lips must soon speak not for myself or my children, but for all the children, living and still unborn, who are God's peculiar treasure. Guide then the judgment of my will, O Lord, and make it Thine. Let me know which it shall be. . . ."

With the first glow of dawn filtering into his rooms came the muffled sounds of activity in the courtyard. It was much too early for the servants to be about. Solomon pulled the coverlet over his ears and shut out the stirring of soft footsteps and whispers past his window. Had it always been like this—the muted voices, the call of an order urgently given and as quickly obeyed, the braying of a mule somewhere back near the stables and the clash of metal as if swords and breastplates were being hastily donned!

He leaped out of bed and across the room to the window.

Benaiah stood in full uniform, his breastplate catching the first ray of sun, and with him were David's men, the Cherethites and Pelethites, and they were running to him, still fastening their glistening armor as they ran. As Solomon watched, they formed a guard of honor and his first thought was one of alarm.

He called his servants and they ran in to him, still rubbing their eyes with sleep and knew no more than he why the courtyard was alive at this strange hour of the day.

"My father!" He threw on his clothes as he ran out of the room and along the corridor that led from his apartments to the great court.

Something had happened to his father!

A servant passed and Solomon grabbed his arm.

"What is it, what is the confusion?"

The servant was puzzled. "I know only that through the night there was strange news from outside the city gates." ·

Now whatever could that mean! Solomon rushed out and found Ahiah hurrying toward him from his own gardens.

The courtyard was now filling with the palace attendants. Merchants who had arrived early to spread their wares at the first light of day, stood immobile and subdued in the shopping square. Grooms were leading the finest horses of the guard toward the gates and from the far end of the palace grounds, the royal mule, white and garlanded with flowers, was being led by soldiers.

"What does it mean, Ahiah?"

"Perhaps Nathan the Prophet can tell us."

Solomon followed the scribe's glance and saw the ancient and crooked figure of Nathan leaning heavily on the gnarled staff he had carried through his life. He was walking out of David's rooms, above, and when the crowd in the courtyard saw the prophet they fell silent and bowed in reverence.

Nathan stood there, and as Solomon ran across the damp grasses of the garden and leaped over the low wall between him and the King's outer staircase, he called up to Nathan and asked for the King.

"The King, Jedidiah, is well," said Nathan. His voice rang out with the same fiery power it had held in the days when he was honored more than a king.

Someone called to Solomon and he turned quickly to see his mother and Zadok come out of the great hall. Bathsheba ran toward him and even in this moment Solomon knew that whatever had occurred was important enough to bring Bathsheba from her rooms with the crusts of sleep still nestled in the corners of her eyes.

She made obeisance before him and Solomon was angry and embarrassed, feeling the tension of the crowds behind him mount as he lifted his mother to her feet.

"What is the meaning of this!" He held her arm fast, as if it held the secret of the morning and could be made to divulge it. "When does a mother make royal obeisance before her son!"

Bathsheba straightened, looked up at him with smiling triumph. "I made obeisance before the new King of Israel!"

Behind him there was a stifled gasp among the courtiers and Solomon, in angry irritation, drew back from his mother as if fearing his impulse to strike her.

Zadok bowed his head. "It is true, Solomon. She is not jesting."

Then Solomon saw that Zadok wore his priestly vestments and the ephod of his office. On his breast he wore the plate of twelve jewels. His robes of gold and purple, blue and scarlet were colored as the signets, each the memory and name of a son of Israel; each treasured and held as symbolic authority in the High Priest.

"It is seen and told to us that Adonijah has gathered the elders at his house," said Zadok. "And through the night his supporters have gathered secretly and have slain oxen, sheep and fatlings in abundance—"

"It is no offense to feast and drink in one's own house!"

"Wait!" Zadok raised his hand and Solomon tightened his mouth against the sounds of disgust that pressed against it. "He has joined with him Joab and his guards and is preparing to call himself King. When the sun moves to En Rogel, then Abiathar the priest will anoint him—without your father's consent!"

"I can talk to him," Solomon said hurriedly. "I can tell him his impatience is unworthy. He will listen to me—I'll make him listen!"

"Even so," said Zadok. "It is not the wish of the King that Adonijah succeed him. While he lives, or after death."

Solomon stared at him with disbelief.

Zadok, reading it, extended his arm and thundered up to the ancient one at the head of the stairs. "Hear it then from Nathan the Prophet!"

Solomon moved up to the stairs and Nathan spoke out: "David said unto us, 'Have Solomon my son ride down upon my own mule. Bring him down to the spring of Gihon; and let Zadok the priest and Nathan the Prophet anoint him king over Israel. . . .'"

Solomon stood on the lower step, staring transfixed at the one whose word had never been questioned.

"It was told to us by David," Nathan went on, "to let the trumpets blow and let there be piping of the pipes and rejoicing for 'Solomon shall sit upon my throne,' said David, 'and be King in my stead while my eyes still see it!'" Nathan stared fiercely down the layers of stone no harder than his eyes. "David has appointed you to be ruler over Israel and over Judah!"

This was nightmare, the fancy of whirling drunken sleep and the cheers that filled the air were the sounds of dreams and had no reality. His fists beat into his thighs. He turned in fury on Bathsheba who had followed at his heels.

"What manner of treachery is this," he whispered between his teeth. "Have you shaken an old man's wits with your jealousy and your lies?"

He recoiled from the conciliatory touch of her hand, pushed her away and ran up the stairs, past Nathan and the personal guards, past David's equerry and the huddled, crying figure of Abishag. She was ugly with tears and her face turned away from him in sullen resentment.

The curtains were drawn back from the bed and Solomon plunged toward it, burning with anger, shouting at the placid face of David against the pillows.

"Take back the promise you made my mother!"

David opened his eyes and said gently, "Calm yourself, Solomon. I made no promise I would not gladly break for the welfare of my people. My fondest hopes, my deepest fear for them, found an echo on your own lips—"

"I have no wish to be King!" Solomon's voice was hoarse with tension. "I have no right!"

David continued as if Solomon had not spoken.

"If each man is to live in peace beneath his vine and his fig tree, it is you, Solomon, who must bring this to pass." His eyes dimmed with sadness. "In doing this, your own happiness must be denied. And for this cruel inheritance, my heart bleeds for you. I give you my crown, Solomon, now while I live. But my tears have already been shed for the years you will wear it."

"Then spare me its burden!"

"The Lord guided my choice. Your brother would only lead my people back to the time of wars. They must have a time to build their faith, my son. A tower of strength in God. A rock beneath their feet in times of adversity and a refuge that will never fail them."

As his father spoke, Solomon saw the shadow of Nathan at his side.

"You are to build a Temple to the Lord, Solomon," Nathan said. "You must fulfill the dream of your father."

"A dream denied me for my sins." David paused for breath. "I have been evil in my days of strength and weak against the evil of others. Be strong, therefore, and show yourself a man—"

Solomon bent closer and pleaded to be heard.

"It is Adonijah who should be King—"

David's voice came weakly from the shadows of morning at his bed. "Kneel, Solomon. I must give you the blessing of the firstborn."

"I am not the firstborn!"

David's eyes glowed with stern authority.

"Before there were kings in Israel—there was the law! First there was Saul, but the law was greater too than Saul. And greater than David. It will be greater than you, Solomon. But in this moment I am still King, and I have the power of command!"

For a moment their eyes held. The eyes that were like the sea, the pilgrim had said, were now green in anger.

"Kneel!"

The intensity of the voice, the eyes, made Solomon fear for his father's strength. The old man was laboriously raising his head, supporting himself on one wavering elbow.

Solomon lowered himself on one knee at his father's bedside but as he did, a whisper of desperation came from him.

"Consider—remember that Isaac in his blindness rejected his son Esau who was the eldest and blessed the head of Jacob without knowing what he did. . . ."

David was unmoved. "And Jacob was named Israel, and we are all sons of his sons."

Solomon felt the trembling touch of his father's hands on his bowed head and he heard the solemn and irrevocable words that formed the Blessing of the Firstborn.

"God make thee as Ephraim and Manasseh—" David spoke the words with sonorous fidelity to the law, and Solomon, searching desperately into his early learning under Nathan and Zadok, remembered it was Jacob, in his turn, who blessed Joseph's children in Egypt, and placed his hand on the younger Ephraim instead of the older brother; but when he spoke this protest, David continued: "—The Lord bless thee and keep thee. The Lord make his face to shine upon thee and be gracious unto thee. . . ."

"My father, my lord and King!" Solomon looked up and spoke with the birth of open defiance. "I beg you not to do this—"

"The Lord turn his face unto thee and give thee peace—" David's voice intoned. He was spent with the effort and Solomon's protests became an anguished, almost inaudible suffering in his throat.

He found himself standing then, looking down at his father whom he loved. But he loved justice in all things more than he loved any human and gathered his strength and said, "I cannot obey you."

David's eyes grew stormy. He struggled and sat upright with a powerful lurch of his wasted body. All the remnants of his past glory seemed to rise up and give his feeble body fresh vigor.

"You defy me! My voice has grown weak with the flesh, but my word is still the word of a King!" His wrath was terrible to behold, and Solomon knew its power. "Get you to Gihon! Nathan! Zadok! Benaiah! Take my son, Solomon, to the spring of Gihon—!" His chest sank, hollowed between the bones of his shoulders, and as he sat propped on his elbows he stared at Solomon with his head thrust forward, every muscle in his body rigid with authority not to be denied, and he gasped, "It is a command!"

Solomon felt then the touch of Zadok's hand on his shoulder, and he looked up into waiting, immutable faces. Worn by the conflict, he lowered his eyes before the law of the land and the word of the King.

He got to his feet and with leaden steps walked toward the embrasure, glowing now with the light of the morning. He heard his name and turned to see David's wrinkled face, resting against the pillows, soften with an infinite compassion.

"Solomon," David said again, softly, and his whisper held tears and sorrow. "God be with you!"

The burden of this new responsibility weighed down the corners of Solomon's mouth, still he looked with understanding on his father for he was the King and he had spoken; and he hoped in his heart that some tenderness and forgiveness came to his eyes and his lips to ease the sadness of his father. . . .

All through the day, from the first paling of the morning stars over the land of Sheba, secret looks were swiftly withdrawn when they met the eyes of the Princess Makada.

She had not been deceived by this so-called "journey of inspection" along these eastern shores of the Red Sea. She had long ago woven a subtle pattern of warning from the loose threads of gossip back in the great stone palace where, about this time, old Belkis would be screaming for her chamber windows to be smothered with hangings against the demons of the night. The evil spirits that slid on moonbeams through the smallest of cracks, she believed, wanted to steal the amulet which held her soul.

Such a beautiful amulet Belkis wore—to house such a mad and foolish soul. At night the old Queen screamed in raucous fear for its safety. The halls would be echoing at this very moment with her cries of suspicion and desertion. Someone would tell her—Sami, the soothsayer, most likely —that the soundless palace was her own doing. She had ordered silence— and there was silence. The absence of her daughter, Makada, was also an order. Sami would remind old Belkis that she had sent the girl who was a princess on her first tour of the land of Sheba—which she would one day rule. And with the girl had gone a suitable retinue of slaves and servants, the Grand Vizier Tamrin, whose advice was as sage as it was smooth, and Bashir, the huge ebony giant who commanded the Queen's army. The old Queen would be lulled into forgetfulness and whine like an obese infant until sleep came, and her jowls would slacken in sweating oblivion, completely concealing the amulet locked about her soft fat neck.

Makada stretched full length on the silken mat before her crimson tent with its saffron tassels and its cords of tiny golden bells that were moved by the breeze from the sea. She filled her body deep with the clean air and her eyes opened with defiant joy to the moon that was meant to be evil for the one who slept in its light. They knew a secret, she and the silver one in the sky—a sly sharing that watched and was unmoved by the emotions of those about her. It informed her through the movement of leaves in the treetops and the still-warm sand beneath the amber sheen of her outstretched leg—why Tamrin and Bashir had so cleverly maneuvered her presence on this journey.

It was past the time for their telling—yet she had been well-schooled in disguising curiosity, restlessness and contempt. She would wait until dawn —when the small caravan would start homeward. If then Tamrin's elegant long nostrils could not sense her impatience at this useless delay, she would devise some punishment for him which would ease the boredom of the short journey eastward.

Her thoughts of appropriate revenge wandered in an evil circle of mischief. She could bribe one of the slaves to fill the Grand Vizier's waterbag with sea water. Or place rocks in the folds of his camel saddle. Imagination drew her body into curves of unsmiling glee knowing the Grand Vizier Tamrin, once seated, would prefer to die in agony rather than dismount. He was like that in all that he did—lending his bearded dignity to a decision or a cause, never yielding to its loss.

She sat up abruptly. There had been a sound—unfamiliar to ears attuned to the usual rustlings of a desert night camp. Her serving women snored lightly in the shadow of the tent. A horse arched its neck into the stream and was noisily gulping water. Beyond the trees a sentry, yawning loudly, shifted his spear; camels snuffled in the stockade, and from somewhere far in the distance a nightbird's cry faded on the wind. With an animal's wariness but without its fear, Makada rose without sound. Her hair was a mass of black fire. Tawny limbs, struck with moonlight, were quickly covered by the folds of her robe. Leaving her sandals where she had kicked them at sundown, she moved into the shadows, skirted the carts of baggage already prepared for early departure, and looked sharply at the entrance flap of Tamrin's tent. The glow of an oil lamp flickered within and there was a muted sound of greetings exchanged and the low rumble of male voices.

Her eyes circled the small camp. Two horses, steaming from a swift ride, were being cared for by a slave. When he led them away, she moved closer to the tent—and listened. The secret rendezvous would either assure her first instincts of conspiracy or warn her in time of danger to herself. Tamrin was an enemy of the Queen, but to be an enemy of the Queen's daughter was a more serious matter.

Now she listened and the listening brought a faint smile to her lips—for she heard the hated name of Solomon—and when she heard it spoken in fear and the hoarseness of true anger, she tore aside the flap of the tent and entered.

Two strangers sat with Tamrin and Bashir around the ornate brazier of glowing coals. The Commander of the Sabaean army, half again the size of Tamrin, sprang to his feet and assisted the slower bones of the Grand Vizier to stand and make obeisance.

"Emissaries of Israel," Tamrin said to the two strangers who were startled by her entrance, "Makada, Princess of Sheba, honors us with a visit"—his eyes rebuked her presence even as he smiled—"sooner than I expected . . ." He made an elaborate ceremony of introduction, as if they were all back in the vast throne room in Mareb instead of gathered in a tent on the high ground near the sea.

She looked at each one carefully. The first one was grizzled and far beyond his youth yet his height scarcely cleared the top of the tent. A still-vigorous fighter, this Joab, who had once been Commander of the Host in the time of King David. These two who rode in darkness and whispered of Solomon over coals in strange tents, had traveled far from their home. Now why?

She stepped closer to the second man who had moved swiftly into the shadows when she entered. He still gripped the hilt of the sword at his waist, as if ready for attack. He was a big-boned, suspicious man. The light from below cast deep shadows into the lines of bitterness that framed his mouth. A handsome mouth, if one didn't look too closely and see that its firmness was but a mark of unswerving petulance.

His voice, even in formal greeting, was brusque with the long habit of caution. Makada thought it unwise of this Prince of Israel, brother of the one who was called All-Wise, not to disguise his deep resentment with more subtlety; for she had heard rumors of his self-exile from the land beyond the stretches of desert and mountains to the north: The place that was called Jerusalem—where David the King had died after leaving his crown to Solomon the young, denying the older Adonijah his birthright. . . .

Her interest in him was beyond speech and her eyes moved down to his sword hand. He seemed to read her mockery, slapped the scabbard with the flat of his hand and in his irritation forgot he was in the presence of the Princess of Sheba.

"My lord Tamrin," he said, "have I been invited all this distance to hear news of importance, or to be stared at like a freak of nature?"

Foolish man, Makada told herself. He should not antagonize me, risk the support of power I will one day hold over Sheba—my powerful, rich and indomitable Sheba. . . .

She eased the dilemma written on Tamrin's hawk-like face by lowering her eyes with demure acceptance and seating herself on a low bench away from the fire, to be still and listen. The bones of all these men were cold with anxiety, lust for power, bitterness. If they only knew the warming exultation of supreme confidence—as she did.

"Let us sit once more, Prince Adonijah." Tamrin waited until the guests were seated. He indicated the bowls of food and the pitchers of wine at their disposal and apologized for the absence of servants. "But on an occasion such as this, it is wiser to speak with care—and only before those who recognize danger and the need for action."

Makada felt the wariness of Adonijah's glance on her and Tamrin answered the question in the mind of the Prince.

"We may all speak freely, Prince Adonijah. All here are of the same mind—or I would never have brought the daughter of our Queen to this meeting arranged so many moons ago. The Princess Makada has good reason to hear what we have to say for it concerns her future. Still, I would have wished for a word with you alone before summoning her—" He lifted his richly embroidered shoulders in a gesture of resignation. "—But since she is here—"

"We have little time for talk," said Adonijah, and the older one with the grizzled beard touched him with a restraining hand.

"Let us hear out the Grand Vizier of Sheba."

"What is it you want of me then?" Adonijah demanded.

"It could well be that you want something from *us*, Prince of Israel." Tamrin poured wine into the drinking bowls and as they were passed from hand to hand he spoke of the glory that once was Sheba's—its fertile burgeoning gardens, its fields of golden grain watered by dikes and reservoirs that were the envy of all kings. He spoke of the fragrance of spices that perfumed its air. Its fabulous merchant fleet that sailed the seas surpassed the navy of Tyre and the wealth of all the Phoenicians who commerced in gold and precious stones that spilled from the jewel boxes of Tarshish and Ophir. . . .

"No more," Joab's eyebrows met darkly over the strong bridge of his nose.

"Precisely," said Tamrin. He leaned forward and his eyes pierced flame-light and shadow to reach the face of Adonijah. "The power of Solomon is the death rattle of our country! It will reach out and squeeze the life-blood of our prosperity."

"I am not concerned with prosperity or the lack of it." Adonijah drained his wine cup and wiped his mouth with the back of his hand.

"You should be, my friend," Tamrin said with soft emphasis. "For you would be *Sheba's* friend—if we helped you gain the throne of Israel."

A dull film covered Adonijah's eyes, red-rimmed from fatigue and the sting of desert wind. He said this had been an idle journey, a useless journey, if Tamrin wished only to offer him support in a revolt against Solomon.

"We offer you a thousand horsemen, skilled with arrow, spear and javelin. A mounted army of warriors—"

Adonijah waved a weary hand. "Your words are empty—"

Bashir's fists flexed at his side, prepared to choke the insult from the Prince's throat. But Joab leaned across the fire, unmindful of the heat, and laid his huge hand against the glistening black chest.

"My lord speaks of Solomon's power," said Joab, "not of doubt that your warriors are among the best."

"I feel the need of sleep," said Adonijah and got to his feet. "Come, Joab, I promise your bones good rest before we leave in the coolness of the day that is breaking."

"But you mustn't leave!" The rings on Tamrin's fingers glittered as he gripped Adonijah's wrist. "You must accompany us to Mareb, to the city of the Queen, and hope she looks upon your cause with as much favor as does the Princess!"

Adonijah studied Makada and could scarcely suppress a yawn of extinguished hope. "The Princess is very beautiful, but she is not the Queen," he said. "And if she were, I could only express my pity for the impoverished country she will one day inherit. There is nothing *she* can do to help me." He started toward the entrance of the tent, where Joab already held back the hanging of camel's hair.

"Wait!" Tamrin lifted the hem of his robe and his sandals whispered hastily across the floor. Makada looked at the sharp bones jutting beneath the dry skin of his ankles and the memory of once watching an Egyptian mummy peeled free of its ancient wrappings crossed her mind. . . .

Tamrin pleaded with Adonijah to reconsider, to travel to the east and an audience with the Queen where "you will learn there is profit for you and for us—if we join forces!"

"I bid you good night," said Adonijah. He walked out to call orders to his servants that they would camp for the night and move on with the day that was dawning.

Tamrin flung his robed arms outward like a great and angry bird about to take flight.

"Bashir, arouse the camp! We must lose no time." Tamrin turned to her. "Prepare at once! We must beseech the Queen to listen to us, before Adonijah leaves the country—"

Makada hurried away, not out of obedience but with the first stirrings of fear. The camp was already moving with noiseless urgency. Her garments flattened against her body as she ran and she felt she was running now and would be forever if Tamrin failed in his plea with old Belkis.

The Grand Vizier had spoken the truth to the man who was the brother of the upstart king whose power and greed threatened to swallow the glory of Sheba. As she ran to her tent she wished that this time there would be something she could do. But she could not remember a time in her life when her mother listened to her with anything but contempt. So the daughter whose eyes slanted with arrogance, who held her chin proudly, whose ripe lips closed over secret thoughts had become known among the courtiers and the slaves as "The One Who Speaks Only To The Gods." When her serving women heard her crying sharp orders as she ran to them they stood for a moment staring at her, then flew in all directions to obey her commands and one of them muttered to another, "Can it be that we have served this one since she was left by the gods at the chamber door of the Virgin Queen, and thought her too weak and submissive to be worthy of the great throne . . . ?" And an older woman bent low to roll up the finely woven mat that covered the floor of Makada's tent and whispered, "I have seen in my time a placid field of grain begin to make the sounds of anger hidden deep beneath its roots and at sundown we ran to our tents and covered our faces in fear. And through the terrible night the earth was torn asunder and where the field of grain once stood, there —in the morning—was a mountain of smoke and fire."

Through narrow canyons that were the dry beds of forgotten rivers the caravan climbed up from the shores of the sea to the mountains of red rock and wind-tortured shrubs. Some hours before, when the rim of the sun was still blurred by the curtain of mist in the distance, Tamrin had apologized for the rough and unfamiliar road back to the city. But it was shorter, he said, much shorter. Soon after, at the first sheltered water hole where fresh horses were awaiting them, Bashir came riding in to join them.

Makada had been too deep in thought to notice his absence.

"It is done," he said to Tamrin, and in one unbroken motion he leaped off his lathered stallion onto another. Before he raced ahead to lead the caravan through a more treacherous pass he called out: "The reluctant prince cannot travel too far—too soon. Unless he rides a limping horse. . . ."

"Bashir is a man of resource," Tamrin said with quiet admiration. And he rode beside Makada's palanquin until the daylight faded and renewed itself on the high and sudden vista of the City of the Queen.

Its thick walls followed the contour of golden hills moving with flocks and beyond the green tangle of wilderness there rose the shining watchtowers of the palace.

Makada's breath was not captured, as it usually was, with pride at the first sight of the gleaming city. For this was a strange returning.

As she looked upon the magnificence of all that would one day be her own, a cloud passed over the sun, trivial and transient, yet it cast a great shadow on the walls, the towers, and her heart.

She felt Tamrin's eyes on her, watching her closely as the caravan slowly threaded its way through the guarded gates. When she looked at him a gleam of satisfaction hid itself in the hollows beneath his polished cheekbones and he courteously reined in his horse and waited for her to be carried into the city.

"You will find it—expedient—" Tamrin advised as they walked through the lofty halls of the palace, "to allow yourself the privilege of haste. At a time such as this—a long bath could very well be your last one."

He bowed and stepped into one of the small audience chambers where his appearance brought forth a chorus of complaints. Makada recognized one of the voices. It drifted after her as her feet moved lightly along the mosaic floor and she thought it odd that with all the honey and oil in his words the voice of the Phoenician envoy still grated like the stone hinge on the gate of the leopard pits. Not only the envoy was weary with waiting. Another voice—perhaps it was the King of Edom's—thundered with indignation. He had been here three days, pacing like a servant in an anteroom, while the Queen spent her time inspecting her royal burial tomb!

Tamrin then was right. This was no time to step into the luxurious bath adjoining her chamber and dream away precious time while her body gave itself over to the handmaidens with their endless jars of ointments and perfumes.

She whirled about, dismissed the personal servants who were following her, then walked into the inner courtyard, through still another flowering garden, and entered the throne room.

Even at this hour of the day the great ceiling, supported by vast pillars, was lost in shadow. Deeds of glory carved on the columns rose from base to capital, telling the ancient history of the kings and queens of Sheba since before the time of Joktan. Before time itself. The last of these was Makada and she was determined not to be the last.

She walked toward the dais and stood for a moment staring at the ebony throne with its backrest of the sun symbol bisected by a crescent moon of sapphires and rubies. The chair's emptiness was no less formidable than when it overflowed with the royal mountain of the Queen's bejeweled flesh.

The eyes of courtiers and attendants peered at the princess with curiosity.

Following the thick-set King of Edom, Tamrin closed the door of the small audience chamber on the resigned envoy out of Phoenicia, and walked with great dignity into the throne room. He paused, distressed to see Makada seated so calmly on the top step of the civet-covered dais. He knew she was well aware of the forbidden desire in the dark eyes of the younger courtiers. Her indifference, all the lure of her unselfconscious postures, her very presence alone in this room was always a disturbing distraction. And a danger. He feared that one day—any day—Makada's eyes would look upon one of these men of mortal heritage, and if that moment held the full awakening of her senses, they would be spent as fully and with rich abandon on the unworthy one. And nothing could be done. In all things she was completely dedicated. The slightest spark would indiscreetly enflame her. This was to be avoided at all cost. Tamrin wished he were the court sculptor instead of Grand Vizier. Then he could carve the image he wished in the hardness of diorite. But he still worked with human clay, to be kept swathed in a cautious covering of moisture each day to delay the fixed and unalterable portrait until the moment of its greatest perfection. Eventually she must have lovers, he knew, but not now. She was too vital to his plan. All her emotions and vital energies must be channeled to the highest good of the land. By subtly and patiently molding her sense of duty he had shaped her mind into noble purpose, a flawless form but—the gods be merciful!—with its immutable cast as yet untested.

He struck his hands together. The court attendants bowed and moved away. Guards closed the doors on the last whispers of the courtiers' bright-colored robes and the last faint clash of bangles worn by the women, and the jingling anklets of the dancing priestesses who served Wadd, the god of love, in the sacred temple.

Makada inclined her head as Hadad, King of Edom, bowed before her. Then she turned away to pet the leopard cub that had strayed in from the compound. Tamrin knew that her preoccupation with the fat little cat was a disguise to cover her intensity. She would miss no word, not the slightest inflection.

The aging potentate shivered with impatience and the Egyptian cut of his beard bobbed up and down as he spoke in a fierce whisper.

"I'll wait no longer, Lord Tamrin!" He paced before the throne. "I came a long way to seek help—"

"You need it," Tamrin answered. "But pray be seated, King Hadad."

"King!" Hadad snorted and rolled his eyes to the ceiling. "A king of what! A slave nation. A vassal ground beneath the heel of Solomon!"

Tamrin nodded slowly, with sympathy. "First David, now the son of David—crushes the might and glory of Edom. You waited too long in exile, my friend. You should have left Egypt the moment you knew King David was dead—before Solomon could gather his defenses against your rebellion."

"You may well talk!" Hadad came close and Tamrin looked down at the puppet king who had no kingdom. "Take care, Tamrin. You too may soon feel the long reach of Solomon's ambition. Isn't it true that the trade of your own country is already touched? That the caravans you send to the far places are taxed for crossing through *his* country?"

Tamrin was more than alarmed by the current situation, but it was not part of his nature, nor of his position, to admit Sheba's weakness. "It is customary," he said, "to pay a levy. We can well afford it."

Hadad snorted again. "You are as blind as your ruler—whose tomb is more important to her than the growing danger of King Solomon!"

At this instant a door at the far end of the room was flung open by an armed guard and a gong was struck. Its sound vibrated through the halls and the room filled once more with attendants and courtiers who came from the side doors and the gardens. Among them Tamrin saw Bashir and Sami, the temple priest. His painted, half-naked body—a weird collection of skin and bones—moved with a stilted gait toward the shallow brazier of coals near the throne chair and two of his priests accompanied him with the plaques and urns filled with the secret powders of divination.

All faces turned toward the open door of the corridor leading to the Queen's quarters. Even as a seneschal thumped the floor with a staff and announced: "Her Majesty, Queen Belkis of Sheba!"—the heavy footsteps of the Queen could be heard. A moment later her gigantic body seemed to fill the doorway. She passed though it, followed by servants carrying platters of sweetmeats and pitchers of wine. A crown of exquisite beauty rested on an orange-red wig of wiry hair and as she strode into the room one eyelid drooped over a lunatic stare which she flicked at all corners of the room. Her court made obeisance. Tamrin, by raising an eyebrow, reminded Makada that the Queen was present.

The girl who was the Princess, lazily uncoiled her legs, stood up and made a reluctant gesture of respect. Belkis heaved her weight up the steps and squirmed her flesh into a comfortable position in the throne chair. No one spoke until the Queen's old serving woman had supervised the arrangement of the food platters and had tested the wine for poison. Satisfied that she could eat and drink without fear, Belkis speared the sweetmeats with a long-handled prong in one hand and held out her goblet for wine with the other. All this while she glared at Hadad with suspicion.

"A royal visitor, my lady," Tamrin said quickly. "King Hadad of Edom."

Hadad offered her an ornate box and as it was taken from his hands by an aide, he bowed low. "A gift of friendship, Your Majesty."

"Take it, Vashi," Tamrin said to the granite-faced woman who was the wine-taster. "Open it for your Queen—"

Vashi obeyed and produced a pair of jeweled armbands that would better have fitted the Queen's powerful wrists. Belkis took them in her hands and, examining them with an expert eye, she asked Hadad why he was here and to kindly state his business with the utmost speed for she was engaged in a project which required much supervision: the building of a mortuary temple. The most splendid structure! It would surpass anything the world had seen, even Queen Hatshepsut's puny effort to insure her immortality at Deir el-Bahri. Now what did he think of that?

"Your Majesty," Tamrin interposed smoothly, "your royal visitor has no wish to disclaim the superior beauty of your final resting place, even though his loyalties and his wife are Egyptian." To better impress her with what he hoped eventually to say, Tamrin added: "King Hadad is married to the sister of Tahpenes—" And as the ruler of Sheba continued to chew her food— "—Tahpenes, Your Majesty, is the Queen of Egypt, the wife of the Pharaoh. . . ."

Belkis swallowed her food, was silent a moment. She seemed to be waiting, gathering some inner forces before committing herself to words. Then, as her court waited—she produced a rolling, rumbling belch.

"This latest shipment," she complained to Vashi and indicated the food, "is seasoned beyond my taste. Now then, Tamrin." And he recognized the genuine shrewdness underlying her gross behavior. She had diverted the issue by gastronomic thunder and preoccupation. "What precisely is on your mind? Another scheme to frighten away my soul?" She touched the blood-red ruby amulet set in the flat collar of jewels around her neck. "You, Sami—tell our Grand Vizier that you are not named after the God of Hearing without good cause. Stir the embers now —while I listen to what mortals have to say—and when I have finished you will tell us all what the *gods* say. . . ." Satisfied, she turned to Hadad. "I listen with infinite patience and courtesy to your every word." She folded her fat hands across her stomach and leaned back against the sun and moon that were set with precious stones; the royal ring on her forefinger, capturing an errant shaft of sunlight, winked and flashed like an evil eye set in the middle of some grotesque image.

Tamrin wondered if after all these years of probing the sly workings of the Queen's mind she was still able to deceive him; for she was remaining true to her word, listening with inordinate courtesy to all that Hadad spoke.

"I came to warn Your Majesty. My kingdom was once strong and rich— even as Sheba is today. Yet we are in bondage since Solomon sits on the throne of Israel. The fate of my land will soon be the fate of yours! To expand his power he will reach beyond Edom—hear me well!—and unless we join forces and destroy him, all of us are lost! I have journeyed to Damascus and found there the one who is a thorn in Solomon's side, Rezon. But when Rezon of Damascus gathered an army Solomon did not bother to meet force with force. He fortified all the cities round and about the city of Damascus!"

"A clever man," murmured the Queen.

"But Rezon was defeated before he could lift a sword! That is the way and the power of Solomon!"

"The fate of Damascus is no concern of mine," said the Queen calmly. "Nor is the fate of Edom. Or the crown you do not wear. . . ."

"But the fate of Sheba—" Tamrin began.

"Sheba is an ancient land. My ancestors were kings and queens when Solomon's were slaves in Egypt!" Belkis reached for a pomegranate, bit into it. "He is the son of a goatherd!"

Tamrin felt the long length of his body crawl, as if someone had dipped a hawk's wing in the ice of a mountain lake and traced its tip over his spine. "It would be well, my lady, to give heed. What has happened to others—can happen to us. Sheba will go down into the dust—"

Belkis spit out a mouthful of fruit.

"A worm!"

Her fury centered on Makada who sat near her feet. The Princess was dangling a string of pearls teasingly before the cub in her lap and in the same instant that she picked up the animal and held it close, Belkis threw the fork, sharp-pronged and long, at her daughter. As the baby cat screamed in pain the long handle quivered in its back. The writhing of its body turned its eyes, wide with shock, toward Tamrin and for an instant the eyes of Makada and those of the frightened leopard could not be told apart.

She did not take her gaze from her mother as the cub, still wailing and scratching, was removed from her arms.

Belkis continued as if nothing had happened. She wanted to know more from Tamrin, whose face was so ludicrous, so somber because her land was about to go down in the dust. . . .

"You have just shown that a single worm can spoil a fine piece of fruit," he said. "In such a way, Solomon's might can destroy your world. It is bitter fruit, your Majesty—"

"I'll hear no more," said the Queen. "Let Edom and Damascus look to their own past—then condemn the present. They were pirates on the seas and thieves in the wilderness!"

"No more than the companies of Sheba!" Hadad said. Then he quickly begged her forgiveness for he had a request to make: "I need the support of Sheba's army and the help of her Queen."

"You will have my help, honorable Hadad," Belkis said in the sweetest of tones. She got to her feet and her anger was terrible to behold. "Out of my country!"

Hadad quivered with rage. Then turned and fled.

The Queen sank back in her chair, muttering petulantly. "Why am I plagued by such jackals. Let him eat the scraps from Solomon's table and be content, but see that he does not come begging at mine! He is a swine, afraid of losing his power, his wealth, the trade he never had—"

"As we are gradually losing them," Tamrin said with emphasis. "Your daughter can tell you, I speak the truth. The Princess saw with her own eyes three of our galleys rotting in our ports for want of markets to trade our wares! She went with us to Ezion-geber where the arm of the sea always welcomed us with rich reward in copper and iron. She found there great houses of fire whipped by desert winds and out of these furnaces comes the rich metal to load on *his* ships that sail to Tarshish and all the far islands. . . ."

The Queen squirmed with irritation. Tamrin walked closer.

". . . He has built fine roads throughout all of his kingdom for commerce and, who knows, perhaps roads for war! There are fortresses on his boundaries, magnificent cities for his chariots and golden shields for his horsemen—"

The old Queen impaled him with her bad eye. "How do you know this?"

Tamrin paused a moment, catching his breath. "From his brother—Prince Adonijah!"

Belkis gripped the arms of her chair and demanded to know where he was, this renegade brother of the king!

"Here," said Tamrin with anxious pleasure. "Here in your own country. He will be an ally more powerful, more effective than a hundred Hadads and Rezons—a thousand kings. For he has a personal cause for revenge—"

"Clear the room!" shouted the Queen.

When it was cleared of servants and slaves, she called Tamrin a fool. A king of fools! Didn't he know that she'd rather pay any tribute on her caravans, see her fleet diminished, even her boundaries changed—rather than risk the wrath of Solomon by sheltering his brother. "It would mean war!" She would not hear of it. Not while she wore the crown!

"Solomon could decide to take that too," Tamrin said.

"Not so long as *I* live!" said Belkis. "I'll have peace for the rest of my days—"

"But Sheba will live after you have filled the number of your days," Tamrin insisted. "What then?"

A sly and evil smile spread over the Queen's face. Her body shook with a silent chuckle as she looked at Makada. "By that time—it will be *her* crown—if she ever wears it! But she'll not be a *rich* queen—" her face darkened as she stared at Tamrin and Bashir. "None of you will profit! In the endless chambers of my tomb I am burying my wealth. All of it! You'll never find it!" A bewildered film covered her eyes. Her face sagged and trembled as if she were about to weep. "And the gods curse you if you *do*. . . ."

As she started down the steps of the throne, Tamrin made a last plea. "You bury more with you than your wealth, Your Majesty. You bury the land of Sheba!"

She turned a face of bland indifference on him. "A fitting end then, when it comes. I was Sheba's greatest Queen—I deserve to be its last. . . ." and she mumbled on her way out of the room that Adonijah must be sent from the country at once—did they understand—at once! At the door she turned and called to Sami: "Priest! Come with me. . . ."

In the barbaric sumptuousness of the Queen's private chamber, Vashi stirred the air with great webs of brilliant plumage for Belkis was faint with worry, more perturbed than she had wished anyone in the throne room to know.

She watched Sami finish his rituals before a small image of the licentious Ashtoreth and the other precious-stoned but hideous replicas of the huge idols that loomed on top of the highest hill in the city, opening their gaping mouths of fire on feast days for the sacrificial taste of the newly born.

The spirit of the trees lived in the hungry jaws of Talab, and the one who was the Hearer wore a lion's head with a jeweled crown and the horns of a bull.

She must have the help of all these terrible powers. As she watched, Belkis chewed her lower lip with the few teeth the gods had left her.

The wizardry of Sami must bow in her behalf, work his magic powers before sharp-toothed Kawin the Sustainer—for she must be sustained! The priest was commanded to bring forth his secret potions for the Tidings-bearer and conjure, conjure! He must claw the flesh from his bones before the mighty Jaghuth. . . .

Like the fierce winds fanned by the dark wings of the vulture-headed god of seasons and of death, she trembled with fear because her tomb was still unfinished. She was sore with the burden of fright and interrupted Sami again and again, demanding words of reassurance. He alone could read the smoke that rose in the sickly green flame from the powdered skin of the cobra. He alone could discern the future by examining the kidney of a fresh-slain lamb.

"What do you see—what do you see?" she whispered.

Sami's reptilian eyes, closed in mystic communication, slowly opened.

"The ruler of Sheba," he intoned, "will live through many harvestings of the grain."

And the tautened bulk of the Queen loosened with relief and let itself spread and flow into the cushions of the mammoth couch.

"Then it is the same." Her voice seemed to come up out of her feet, so undersized they impaired the proper balance of her weight and she often stumbled through the palace halls. "Ah then, thirty and five more risings of the river!" She would have time to spare in which to complete her splendid resting place.

The amulets and rings that hung from Sami's bones jangled harshly as he turned to her. The indigo-stained sockets beneath jutting, hairless brows hollowed a deep bed for the snake-like glitter in each eye. There was doom in his voice. And authority.

"The spirits of Sheba's sky and fields, the powers that harvest the yield —threaten to destroy! The blood, the flesh, the rivers flow red—unless condoned—unless appeased!"

Belkis lurched forward, her mouth slack, the lower lids of her eyes drawn downward in fury.

"Go on!" she commanded.

"They say you will find no more peace this side of your tomb. And no rest on the other side!"

Terrified, she leaned toward him and clutched at his feathered wristband. "You have made some mistake—"

He shook his head slowly. "The gods are angry with you—you favor yourself more than you favor them. . . ."

Her words were broken with increasing fear. "I will do anything—anything! Only beg them to give me an after life, the spirit of a god that I may live with my fathers who are gods . . . !"

"Your soul will be reborn, have no fear." He pointed a dark-knuckled finger at the spirit-amulet about her neck. "Reborn in the body of a scorpion!"

She clutched the jewel and drew back from him. Her face broke into a mass of watery pellets that swelled and ran down her raddled cheeks. She felt them drop from her chin but when Vashi bent over to pat dry the moisture, Belkis pushed her aside with the violent power of a warrior.

She faced the indomitable priest as if her great size could overwhelm his soothsaying. But the tight skin over his skull-face remained unmoving. The gods had spoken through him.

Defeated, Belkis wilted with despair.

"Tell me what I must do—"

He consulted the embers and chanted over them and told her she must make sacrifice. "Blood," he intoned, "living blood . . ."

"They shall have it! A hundred oxen—ten newborn infants on the first turn of the moon—" and Sami said that was not enough. Then she would offer virgins from the temple! And when he said still not enough she grew rigid with terror and offered more and more and still it was not enough. Balefully she said what then would satisfy them, what would bring her immortality, what sacrifice must she make to be a goddess among gods?

"*Royal* blood," her priest intoned.

Belkis searched his face for the meaning and cowered before it. "Not mine," she whispered.

Sami did not answer. He drew the wicked knife of sacrifice from the scabbard at his waist and offered it to her. She shrank from it.

"Royal blood," he repeated, and the burning coils set deep in the painted hollows commanded her to take it.

Belkis stared at the hilt of the shining blade and her hand closed slowly around it.

"They shall have it," she whispered . . .

Sami started for the door and she called to him in a hoarse whisper: "First, I would ask time—"

The priest said the gods had given her time, and had now taken it away. If she wished to regain their favor in the life of the tomb—there must be royal blood.

Then she pleaded with him for a last moment in which to speak to her beloved daughter.

"I will send her to you," said the priest.

The moment he closed the door an evil delight filled the Queen's eyes. She touched the knife now and concealed the blade in the folds of her garment. "Royal blood," she repeated aloud and looked up suddenly to see the watchdog face of old Vashi, about to leave, looking at her with unconcealed loathing.

"Stay!" Belkis commanded her. "Come here." Vashi slowly obeyed. "You have no tongue, Vashi, I took care of that when you crossed my wishes many years ago. But I still do not trust you. You would find *some* way of warning her!"

The Queen sat waiting then, and smiled as she watched the door.

In the throne room Sami was triumphant. He strutted and posed with stiff-kneed importance as Makada, without a trace of emotion, silently obeyed his order and left the room.

He kept the Grand Vizier waiting before he answered the important questions.

"What is the meaning?" Tamrin wanted to know. And Bashir told the priest to stop speaking through smoke when he addressed the Grand Vizier and the Commander of the Sabaean Army.

With a triumphant leer Sami assured them that with the help of the gods *he* had accomplished what the great Vizier and the so-great Commander had failed to do.

Tamrin felt a surge of hope. "You persuaded her to receive Adonijah!"

Sami complacently savored his diplomatic excellence for another long moment.

"Belkis will not be here to receive him—or anyone else."

When Tamrin stared at him, probing the mystery of his meaning, Sami revealed that "at this very moment the Queen is speaking last words to her daughter"—for the gods had demanded the supreme sacrifice: royal blood.

Tamrin would have sprung on him, but there was no time.

"Fool priest!" he cried. "Assassin!" Followed closely by Bashir, he strode toward the door, flinging recriminations over his shoulder at the unperturbed priest. "The Queen will never kill *herself!*"

Sami groomed the dangling feathers of his regalia with proud hands. "I gave her the sacrificial knife. It is her duty to use it on herself. She knows it is written in our mystic law that ruler or priest must perish at the time of his greatest power—"

A piercing scream from the Queen's chamber froze Tamrin before he could reach the door, stopped Bashir in his tracks.

Now all is gone, thought Tamrin. All is finished. Our last hope lay in Makada—and now she is dead before her time. . . .

He could not tear his eyes away from the door leading to the Queen's chamber. He could not move his feet, make the first move, to walk down the corridor, open the Queen's door and face her cackling, obscene madness.

"Someone—" whispered Bashir.

Tamrin heard it then, too. The faint sound of footsteps approaching. The halting tread was about to enter this room. It was long in coming and Tamrin's ears pounded with the beat of his heart that drowned out all else.

Then Makada appeared in the open doorway.

Only her deep breathing revealed the plain story of struggle and a fight for life. She stood quietly beneath the lintel and was framed by the legends of Sabaean glory carved into its precious wood.

Now her name will be added to the dynasty of Sheba, Tamrin thought. The name of Makada will be the greatest of them all—because I will *make* it great! I have molded the clay into a thing of beauty and dedicated power. Those two hands, kissed by the sun to the hue of ripe and golden fruit, will hold the destiny of nations to come. . . .

He looked down at those hands and saw that she held the knife which Sami had given the old Queen. It was stained dark and left a red streak on the polished stones of the floor after Makada tossed it away. Behind her Vashi appeared, her face aglow with a new and loyal devotion. In her old hands she carried the crown that a few moments before rested on the flaming wig of Belkis. Now it was set on the shining darkness of Makada's hair. Then Vashi handed the royal ring to Tamrin.

He took it, placed it on Makada's finger and backed away two paces from the regal creature who stood before him.

Without reflection, with no surprise or belated shock to mar the dignity of her calm, she said slowly: "I am now the Queen of Sheba!"

Tamrin was aware of Bashir and Sami making willing and eager obeisance to their new sovereign. But he could only stare in disbelief.

But a few moments before, Makada had left this room bearing only the uncertain promise of fulfilling his consuming hopes. The marks of his fingerprints had shown plainly on the still-wet clay. But now she stood before him polished and without flaw, a creation beyond his wildest expectation. She was a true Queen. Her courage had been tested and not found wanting . . .

With a deep bow which made obeisance to his own good judgment as well as to her crown, he said, "Long live the Queen of Sheba!" And he led her to the throne.

The word went out and the doors were thrown open to the multitude of her people and the heralds sounded the trumpets of festival.

There was no sound of mourning for Belkis who sprawled in a heap on the floor of her chamber. In her eagerness to appease her gods she had lunged too quickly to plant the blade deep into Makada's throat. With her balance destroyed her own pampered flesh had been pierced. The amulet containing her soul had been torn from her neck. It lay broken on the embers of the fire—and like a monster washed up on a forsaken shore—her dead and hooded eye stared at it with an expression of bewildered surprise.

In the midst of raucous confusion, Makada saw the coronation was only an excuse for weak bodies to indulge in strong wine.

When the last rays of sunlight gave way to the soft glow of fires in copper bowls, she ordered the throne room cleared. When only the sounds of joyous cries came up to her from the streets, she saw the impatience on Tamrin's face and permitted him to speak his mind.

"The matter of Adonijah," he reminded her, "cannot remain for long, your Majesty, unsettled."

"Where is the little cat?" she asked. And as the servants and stewards scurried to find her one who was whole and uninjured by the old queen's vicious temper, Makada cast a sidelong glance at Tamrin and was amused.

He was pulling at his beard, opening his mouth to insist on action, closing it again when he remembered he was no longer speaking to a lump of unfinished clay. She knew his purpose when he had schooled her so relentlessly through the days that became years. It was her right to show him that once molded, once shaped and fired and smoothed to its ultimate form—there was no way it could be altered. He had made her in the image of a Queen, cold, imperious, arrogant and without heart. Then let the image sit here on the throne, look down on its creator, and laugh inwardly at the stricken look on his long hawk-face.

The little leopard was brought to her but she no longer wanted it. It seemed to her now that all her life she had craved something, and the moment it was placed in her hands she despised it for being there.

"Your Majesty," Tamrin began once more. "We must make plans—"

"Then we must not waste time, Tamrin." And she doused the expectancy in his eyes by asking that the notables be admitted, those who had been kept waiting so long for an audience with her dear mother.

The Babylonian delegation, richly turbaned, entered and bowed low. Their spokesman regretted that the exchange of trade between their lands had dwindled, this journey, to a caravan of only four and twenty camels.

"Give me the weight of spices you brought for exchange," she said.

"The value of a hundred weight, your Majesty."

"And the pannag?"

He cleared his throat. "A smaller quantity than usual," then he added quickly: "But all the lapis lazuli our poor caravan could bear."

"How fortunate for you," she murmured, and wondered how long he would stand there before her in his gaudy stripes and belled slippers, wringing his hands with gratitude.

"We hasten our return to our land," he singsonged, "that we may fill the air more abundantly with praises for the Queen of Sheba!"

"The Queen would wish," said Makada, "that your caravan had been filled as abundantly."

The emissary was mournful-eyed and obsequious. "The fault is not ours, your Majesty. We pay heavy tribute since the Wise One sits on the throne of—"

"Enough!" She dismissed him but the name of the Wise One named Solomon seemed to linger, echoing throughout the rooms. Would she ever be able to hear it without wishing he could be placed in her hands, that she might destroy him?

She bowed to the next emissary and the next and was not surprised to find her duties so easily discharged. One wave of her hand and an emissary departed, one lift of her chin and Tamrin hastily introduced the last visitor, the long-patient envoy out of Phoenicia.

She studied the rich clothes of the man before her, and graciously accepted the gift on behalf of her mother who, unfortunately, had been "stricken suddenly and carried away to the burial caves of her ancestors."

The delay in receiving him had been deliberate. She resented above all things the friendship rumored to have arisen between Hiram of Tyre, the richest city in Phoenicia, and the young King who lived in Jerusalem. As a consequence the roaring river of trade between Phoenicia and the land of Sheba had become an ominous trickle of unprofitable exchange.

The envoy redeemed the disagreeable effect of his voice by employing words of poetic grace. His restrained praise of her beauty caused her to wonder dispassionately if her appearance, too, had been created by one of Tamrin's many devious methods. She accepted the praise as her due, withholding any outward evidence of boredom. Beauty, she had been taught, was the richest of possessions—but only when cunningly assessed far beyond its actual value of exchange.

Disdainfully, she fingered a portion of the goods he had brought to the court of Sheba. There were partially unrolled woolens, soft as the fur of the little cat; delicately webbed cloth out of Gaza and linen, fine-patterned, from the bazaars of Damascus. A mesh of crimson shimmering with crescents of gold and stars of turquoise slipped through her hands and with a whispering sigh, fell at her feet. A pity, she told the envoy, that it was without substance, for the design was suitable enough for the saddlecloth of her sleek black stallion . . .

Tamrin cleared his throat again behind long interlocking fingers. Makada was pleased to know her Grand Vizier was increasingly distressed over her apparent neglect of state duties; mainly the business of immediately sending for Adonijah.

But Tamrin had better learn now, from this beginning of her reign, that she was not to be swayed, pulled on subtle threads of persuasion, or forced into matters of important decision.

She listened with unnatural patience to the envoy's monologue and ceased looking for its meaning. It had none. He was mouthing smooth words of no importance, hesitating, waiting for the right moment to break the polished shell that concealed something he had to say. Yet he was unable to bridge, with simple words, the short distance from the foot of the throne, to her jeweled earrings. She decided he was a highly educated idiot who could not cross to the other side of a road without traveling by way of Babylon.

"You will convey the sympathy of the Queen of Sheba," she said, "to your good King, Hiram of Tyre."

She had cracked the shell. For an instant the envoy's confusion threatened to spill over, beyond recapture.

"Sympathy, your Majesty?"

"He once enjoyed visiting this court in person. But then, it must have been that he was devoted to my mother's—beauty." She smiled disarmingly and he responded with a wary recognition. "Has he grown too soft and tender to sit on the hump of a camel?" She glanced at the list of merchandise in this latest shipment from out of the rich land of Phoenicia. "Or is it his memory that is affected?" And she waited, wondering which words would roll now off the tongue of this sly one to oil his caution.

"The gracious Queen of Sheba is most clever with riddles."

"The answer should be simple." She indicated the flaming folds of color half-draped over her knee. "Why does Hiram send me lengths of cloth from Damascus?"

Tamrin cautioned her lack of diplomacy. "Most expertly woven cloth, my Queen. Unexcelled."

"But unexpected! I bargained for lengths of cedarwood from Lebanon —not lengths of gaudy trash to clothe my camel-drivers."

It was Belkis who had bargained, she remembered now. But how natural it was to talk of trade and business as if she had worn the crown all her life. And how she enjoyed watching the stain of confusion deepen on the cheekbones that shone over such proud black beards.

The envoy's first effort to answer resulted in a squeak, a clearing of the throat and a fresh start.

"King Hiram begs your indulgence." He bowed low. "At the conclusion of my arduous journeys in the circle of eastern courts, when I am once more in the great palace of Tyre on the sea, my first duty will be to convey your displeasure to the King."

"It will be more than a year before you return to Hiram." She ignored Tamrin's small signals of censure. "Must I wait all that time for an explanation? Now tell me, honorable envoy of a King reputed to be also honorable, where is my shipment of cedars?"

"In—Jerusalem, your Majesty. A long-standing agreement with King Solomon who builds a house of worship in his great kingdom."

"An insignificant kingdom," said the Queen, kicking aside the tangle of colored cloth at her feet. "Ruled by the son of a goatherd!"

The envoy inclined his head at a discreet angle, ready to nod agreement if she spoke in earnest, as ready to shake from side to side if her remark was a sly test of his honesty, or a jest.

"He must be a very poor business man," she said.

"Some shrewd merchants agree with you—some just as shrewd change their minds after dealing with him." He shrugged. "It is a matter of opinion. In this case he underestimated. His demand for cedars to form beams and supports, has increased seven times. Unfortunately, to meet that demand, our supply was diminished." He raised a finger quickly. "But only for a short time! I can assure you the happy arrangement made between our country and the land of Sheba will be fulfilled—eventually." He permitted himself a wry smile. "The Queen must realize that trees still grow in Lebanon. We must give them time—and ask the Queen's pardon for the delay?"

"The Queen is most displeased!" said Tamrin. "The agreement with Phoenicia called for cedars now—not in the uncertain future—"

Makada remained calm. "It is all right, Tamrin. I am content to wait." Tamrin's eyebrows rose high on his forehead and she regarded his puzzlement with a faint smile.

The envoy had recovered all and more of his poise. He was once more the cultured diplomat, shining with success.

"Most gracious Queen! King Hiram will marvel once more at the bounty of Sheba's good will. Now, since we are in accord—"

All this time, thought the Queen, all this time to make known what he truly came to receive. . . .

"—Your Majesty will understand the king's anxiety to look upon the tusks of ivory that were promised him?"

"What a pity." The Queen sighed. "No ivory."

She looked upon the envoy's shocked disappointment and saw the color drain from his face.

"But the agreement—"

"Ivory for cedars," she reminded him gently. "Cedars for ivory."

He gestured to the array of cloth and she asked him if he had ever tried to build a house or a bridge with a bolt of cloth.

Submitting to defeat, the envoy inquired with a last hope: "No ivory —now what am I to tell King Hiram?"

"The same thing you told me," she said innocently. "It seems that when my merchants last traded with the land of the East, the demand for elephants exceeded the supply." She aped his manner and his words. "But only for a short time! I assure you, elephants still grow in the land of the East. We must give them time—and ask the King's pardon for the delay?"

The envoy regained his composure with a rueful smile.

"If you have so outwitted me in friendship," he said, "may you never be my enemy!"

He bowed low with respect, stepped back and withdrew from the room.

Makada felt no sense of triumph. Tamrin's praise annoyed her. From the far alcoves of the room groups of court attendants had gathered and now whispered of the new Queen's shrewdness, her wit, her cold and unrelenting sense of business. And Makada, sitting in silent thought, heard Sami the priest confide to Tamrin that Makada would surpass the ruthless authority that had been her mother's. It would be less obvious, therefore more dangerous, for it was disguised with soft-spoken cunning.

"The envoy from Phoenicia," said Tamrin, "can never again boast of his lively and unconquered tongue."

"There is little victory," she said quietly, "in outwitting a fool. I've learned new things on this day of days, Tamrin. Did you hear the men of Gath tell of Solomon's fame? They said kings and princes from far and near come to kneel at his feet—" she accused him with a sharp glance. "—Why haven't you told me this?"

Tamrin spread his hands.

"Would you have believed me?"

She regarded him and considered. "No," she said.

"He is low-born and thirsts for power," Tamrin reminded her. "Today you were a hope, a shining hope to my dreams for Sheba. You will not sit in comfort, as your mother did, and stuff your body while Sheba slowly sinks in the dust!"

"My land must *never* perish!" It was her oath and her creed. "Nothing, no one can take from the land of Sheba the glory that is hers!"

She saw the eyes of Tamrin brighten with triumph. If this stirring in her blood, this cold and dedicated purpose was of his making—then he had good reason to rejoice. She felt vaguely that doors which had never opened to the ordinary delights were closed forever to her. Not locked and forbidden. But passed by, in some dim corridor of her mind, without regret. She was now the Queen of Sheba—and she would make Sheba proud of its Queen.

"—He may already be far out of reach," Tamrin was saying, and she realized he had been talking again of the need to enlist Adonijah to their cause. "I would humbly suggest that my Queen summon Bashir and order him to send messengers to the camp of Adonijah before it is too late!"

"Tamrin," she said quietly, "I am no longer a child to be ordered about and told what to do and be reminded that duty to my country comes before all else."

"This is no time to remind me of *my* duty," Tamrin said sharply. "If you do not summon Bashir, have I your permission?"

She was weary but as she rose from the throne chair she smiled down at Tamrin. "How can you summon the commander of my armies—when by this time he is well on his way to the camp of Adonijah?" She descended the steps to allow Tamrin a moment to recover. "Did you think I could sit on that chair, in the midst of festival and eating and drinking —and forget for one moment that we have a dangerous enemy to conquer?" She pitied her Grand Vizier in this moment. She should have consulted him first perhaps, before ordering Bashir and two aides to fetch the brother of Solomon and bring him to her.

"My admiration is boundless," Tamrin said and made obeisance. A fresh concern furrowed his cheeks. "We are assuming, perhaps, too much. He could refuse to come with Bashir."

Makada yawned and quickly covered her mouth with her palm. The spirit of life was held in the breath. One must not let it escape. . . .

"Have no fear, Tamrin," she said, "Adonijah will be here."

When she left the room a shapeless shadow emerged from the dim anteroom and the big servant who had been loyal to the old Queen was now ready to serve the new.

"Come then, Vashi," said Makada. "Follow me, wherever I go. Stay with me for the rest of my life. . . ." And Vashi followed her like a huge and faithful dog.

When Adonijah and Joab were brought into the city, they were given the choice rooms in the palace of Sheba's capital city. Makada had made sure the sullen prince was treated like a king. And he accepted the attendance of all the servants, the luxurious baths and the willing love priestesses from the shrine of Wadd, with cold enjoyment.

From the start he did not hesitate to swallow the foods which were forbidden in his home country. He no longer called it home. If he could not live in Jerusalem as king he had no wish to live in it at all.

He looked across the low table of inlaid pearl and beaten gold and laughed at Joab's stubborn rejection of all things that had been an abomination in the land of his youth.

"I have lived longer than you, Adonijah," Joab said gruffly. "Closer to the days of carrying the Ark of the Covenant into battle. And I remember, too, the many times when my mother, Zeruiah, and her brother David who became king, gathered on the feast days and we ate at a table of plenty, eating only the meat of animals unblemished."

"What did it gain you!" Adonijah washed down his food with strong wine and threw the drinking vessel across the table. He was filled to bursting with long-smoldering anger and he beat his fist on the table. "You fought at my father's side, led his host into battle and killed his enemies —to protect him. As reward he looked on you with hatred and put Benaiah in your place as commander!"

"Abner was not his enemy," Joab growled. "I slew him out of fear that since he was a commander of Saul's army, he would become commander of David's."

Adonijah paced the floor and looked back in fury at the powerful general who for this first time had divulged the nightmare of his conscience.

"Put Abner and Amasa, too, behind you," Adonijah said. "And Absalom! Keep burning in your mind the memory of a feast that was to have been my coronation! See it clearly, Joab! The elders gathered to escort me in solemn procession to En Rogel. The singing and jubilation of those who cried, 'Long Live King Adonijah!' Hear the sound of trumpets and cymbals and singing from a distance, and remember how we looked into the distance, toward the road leading from the spring of Gihon to the city and were told by Jonathan that Solomon had already been anointed king! We saw the procession, Joab, heard the singing, the cries of 'Long Live King *Solomon*'—" his voice broke in remembered anger. "How can you forget the sight of him, dressed in the royal robes, wearing my father's crown, riding the royal white mule! See the elders rush away from me to bow to the will of David and join the treachery of my brother! Remember the horn of oil that was meant to anoint me, and see it tremble in Abiathar's hands and spill to the ground!" He looked at Joab, hairy arms resting heavily on the table top, staring with unseeing eyes at the strange walls of the room. Adonijah laughed with bitterness. "That is why I can eat the food of pagans, Joab, and look upon the beast-heads of their gods as we did last night and feel no horror when they belch fire and smoke over the sacrifice of screaming human flesh! Am I any less a sacrifice, thrown into the flames of Solomon's ambition and trickery?"

Joab got to his feet and Adonijah saw the deep-seamed face regard him with understanding of the bitterness they shared.

"I vow Solomon shall die knowing the fury of a brother's strife." It was a solemn pronouncement. "When you fled to the horns of the altar for sanctuary, and were torn from it and brought before Solomon at his orders, he should have slain us both. We will make him regret his weakness seven times seven!"

"I live only to see him dead!" Adonijah looked out into the courtyard of the palace, blind to the fountains and the lushness of strange blooms. He saw only the austere room where David had once sat, with a simple acacia-wood bench for a throne. And now Solmon sat there, receiving obeisance after his coronation. Adonijah remembered being dragged there by the soldiers who were told to take their hands off him and when they did this, his own hand had unsheathed his sword and he lunged at Solomon for a death thrust. Solomon had made no move to avoid it. It was Benaiah who thwarted the blow. And still Solomon came toward him, extending his hands in love and friendship, sparing his crime of treason and calling him a worthy man.

"I'll not do to Solomon as he did to me," Adonijah said grimly. "I'll not tell him to go to his house in peace and have no fear!"

"The time will come," Joab growled. "Perhaps this *is* the time."

Adonijah shook his head. "What can this girl-queen offer but spears and horsemen? What good are these without a holy cause to bring the people to my side!"

Disconsolate and resigned, they went out to meet Tamrin who had provided them a magnificent escort to the Field of Cavalry.

It was a waste of time for Adonijah. He could share Joab's admiration for the spectacular skill of the archers performing for them below the royal enclosure, but he could give the Queen of Sheba no reassurance that these men or a thousand like them were an answer to his problem.

He felt her eyes searching him covertly after each exhibition of skill.

Bashir's warriors, with wild cries, threw whistling javelins and spears into moving targets with simultaneous impact. He watched twelve half-naked horsemen wait motionless in the center of the field until birds were released from wooden cages. When the birds had reached the zenith of the sun and were outside the range of less skillful men, the archers drew their bowstrings and brought them down.

"Excellent," Adonijah admitted and saw a look of irritation pass over the Queen's face at his meager praise.

The men of the troops wheeled their horses, saluted her with spears and departed for the compound. And mounted swordsmen took their place, pairing off in a frenzy of fencing, a dangerously realistic sham battle.

"Are these warriors of Sheba not superior to those of Solomon's army of defense?" She seemed sure of his answer.

"Far superior in skill, your Majesty." He watched the glittering spears of the Sabaean soldiers disappear from sight, and he was filled with a brooding regret. "Against any other country or king they would know only victory. Against Solomon they would taste their first defeat."

"Our Queen numbers her warriors in the thousands," Tamrin said. "Solomon's horsemen and chariots number as many, but soldiers grow soft when there is no war to test their spears."

"You are well informed," Adonijah said, with a wry glance at Joab.

"I have made it my business," said Tamrin, "to learn everything possible, even to the number of his fortresses."

"Fortresses!" Joab said. "Chariot cities circle his land, like copper nails around a shield!"

The Queen looked sharply at Adonijah and Joab. "I was told you were eagles of war among men. And I find nothing but timid sparrows!"

Adonijah smarted with the challenge but swept it aside with an impatient gesture. "I am unwilling to engage in a war unless I am sure of winning. If a strong army were all I needed to defeat my dog of a brother I could have raised one with Rezon of Damascus, or the King of Edom!"

"What is it then you need?" she demanded. "Name it."

"Solomon's strength is beyond siege of men and weapons," he said. "His defense is not in his army alone, nor in fortresses, chariot cities and the vast network of roads. His power lies within. He has a loyalty from his subjects which surpasses that of David's time."

"Loyalty can be bought," she said. "Sheba is still rich. Take the gold in my treasury and with it buy the seeds of discontent to sow among his people."

Adonijah shook his head in silence. Joab muttered, "You cannot buy discontent among those who share a banquet of prosperity."

"But it is said he burdens the people with heavy taxes," said Tamrin.

Adonijah smiled with resignation. "For the first time in their lives they own something worth taxing. After my brother stole my throne he was shrewd enough to fatten not only his treasury, but the shrunken bellies of his people."

He saw the first flush of defeat deepen the sun-brown skin of the Sabaean queen.

"He must have some weakness," she said then.

"When he allowed me to live," said Adonijah, "that was his only weakness." And he told her Solomon's armaments defended him against invasion, his alliances placed him beyond fear and his wealth above corruption!

"No man is above corruption," said the Queen.

"There is no one left who would dare try," said Adonijah. "Kings who threatened to be his enemies now give him their trade, their gifts, their daughters in marriage. I tell you he wants for—"

"How many—daughters?" The Queen's voice was too calm.

Adonijah regarded this a useless question, a woman's curiosity.

"A hundred," he said, "perhaps three. Some say he has in his Palace of Women a thousand wives—"

He heard her then repeating it softly to herself:

"A thousand wives—"

An enigmatic smile touched her lips. Adonijah looked at her now as a beautiful and enchanting woman, but he cast the thought aside. He had no wish to involve himself in love with a woman such as this, who could drown a man's senses, perhaps even cause him to forget the burning desire of revenge. He felt the power of her nearness and he abruptly moved away from the fragrance of her body and the delicate sheen of her lips which were parted now with some slow and secret pleasure. It was better to take his own pleasure as he wanted, with the dark-eyed ones of the love temples, or the maidens in the courts of distant lands, the ones who were like Abishag, slavish in their love, tiresome in prolonged devotion. . . .

He made swift obeisance to the Queen, picked up his mantle and was preparing to leave when a soft statement from the Queen made him pause.

"There is a way to defeat Solomon."

It held all the impact of a sword thrust into the target of Adonijah's moving thoughts. He felt Joab and Tamrin grow tense with him. Still he felt no hope.

"He has a weakness, this King Solomon," said the Queen, looking at no one as she rose and signaled Vashi to come with her cloak.

Her Grand Vizier was also being cautious. "Prince Adonijah is brother to the King and knows him well—"

"Not well enough." The Queen smiled slowly and drew her cloak about her. "Perhaps a man who has known a thousand women—has never really known one . . ."

Adonijah watched her leave, seat herself in the carrying chair which awaited her beneath the canopy of red and gold, and long after she and her retinue disappeared he stood in silence and wondered.

That evening, after the heat had gone from the city, Makada lay on the flat polished stones of her roof garden, and the breeze from the far sea stirred the corded fringe of her skirt into slow-moving serpents of blue. She was vaguely aware of Vashi, piling many pillows on the hammock of cheetah skin, for the upper chambers of the palace still held the warmth of the sun and on such nights it was good to sleep beneath the light of the moon god.

A slow and warm tide of contentment moved through her body, turning it with feline undulation over on its side—a movement broken by the sounds of voices coming along the corridors. She sat up abruptly then, crossed her tawny legs and bent forward from the waist, eager to catch the first expression on the faces of Tamrin and Bashir when they entered through the curtained arch.

Before they made obeisance, the studied restraint of Tamrin, the glint in Bashir's eyes, gave her the answer. And she was assured.

They approached her with solemn respect and awe.

"Your Majesty," said Tamrin, "you have succeeded! Adonijah is most anxious to speak once more with you—"

"In the morning. Have him brought to me then. You will hear me now. Adonijah will gather what forces he can, establish a secret encampment within a day and a night of Jerusalem. Bashir, you will meet him there with my armies. The finest companies of Sheba. And you will also take an abundant supply of spears, javelins, shields and horses for the men of Adonijah and Joab."

Bashir bowed. "And when it is done, your Majesty, how many nights will elapse before we lay siege to the city of Solomon?"

"As many nights as it takes your Queen to know that once you breach the walls of Jerusalem, you will meet no opposition—from within. When that moment comes you will receive this." She touched the royal ring on her forefinger. "A token from your Queen. It will mean that the loyalty of Solomon's people has been divided."

Tamrin's lower lip protruded with deep concern.

"Have no fear, Tamrin." Makada was filled with growing confidence. "It can be done. And quickly!"

What manner of wedge could be driven into the solidarity of Solomon's growing power to scatter his people in confusion, create the fear and weakness that would open the gates to easy conquest?

Tamrin respectfully asked the Queen to make it clear to him.

"I am making a journey," she said. "To Jerusalem."

Tamrin was a competent vizier, and Makada admired his skill at specious debate. At the moment he obviously thought it wise to appear shocked.

"Not Jerusalem! Surely this is an idle wish, to leave your own land. It is not the custom!"

"It is now." She rose slowly and sat on the cushioned bench near the parapet.

"Would you trust the affairs of your kingdom to your thieving council of advisors?"

"Since you vouched for the loyalty of each appointment, Tamrin, are you now saying your own word is not to be trusted?"

Tamrin bowed to that but continued: "It is a long and difficult journey." He studied her from beneath jutting brows. "But if you insist on this foolish venture—which I discourage with all my being and will have it so inscribed in the records this night to preserve the honor of my name—what reason will you give Solomon for this journey?"

"A pilgrimage, Tamrin," she corrected him gently. "He will hear from my own lips that when the Queen of Sheba heard of his fame which has spread to the four winds, she came to sit at his feet and pay homage to his wisdom by proving him with hard questions."

"Ingenious," said Tamrin. "But not without great risk."

Bashir was less adept at gathering the reasoning of a woman's nature into his military mind. "Solomon is a grasping tyrant, a scoundrel who stole his brother's crown. Why should our illustrious Queen sit at *his* feet?"

With mockery, subdued by Bashir's blunt compliment and her respect for his skill as a warrior, Makada suggested that Tamrin should one day undertake to instruct Bashir as thoroughly as he had taught her the more subtle forms of successful conquest.

"The sharpest weapon," she told Bashir, "is not always a sword."

"Well spoken," Tamrin admitted, "but I would be remiss in my duty if I did not suggest this journey could be fraught with danger for your Majesty. What do the gods say?"

"Sami has already consulted them," she said.

Through the readings in the liver of a frog and the spleen of a swine, Jughuth, Talab and Ashtoreth had blessed the springs with pure water in the oases of the desert, promised to hold the harsh winds from Sheba's goddess-queen, and condoned the journey to the land with groves of olive and terraces of myrrh.

Tamrin was fretful. "You should know something of this land before you visit it. I shall instruct you. In my travels I have learned something of its fertile plains, its ranges of mountains, the rocky height which is the City of Jerusalem, the treeless wilderness and the sea that sinks deep in its precipices to the east and is filled with sour waters in which nothing lives—"

Makada was not listening. She clapped her hands. Handmaidens emerged from the shadowed greenery of the roof garden and she told them to go quickly. "Fetch the tailors and women who sew. I must have robes embroidered with pearls and rubies! Bring me craftsmen who will fashion new bracelets for my arms, anklets of gold, headbands and collars of ruby and amethyst!"

The serving maidens hurried away to do her bidding.

"Bashir! Order the store chambers thrown open. Bring forth casks of powdered gold, precious stones, and a hundred and twenty talents of gold—a special gift for the wise King Solomon!" Her eyes glowed, luminous with challenge, and she ordered Bashir to gather together their vast store of ivory and the finest spices for her royal caravan—

"A caravan?" Tamrin asked. "It is a long distance from the land of Sheba to the land of Solomon."

She whirled on him. "Has my mother's spirit possessed your tongue that it seeks safety and protection in the distance between our kingdoms? Your old Queen was content to eat and drink and turn her horrible eyes the other way while Solomon's power crept closer, down to the eastern gulf of our own Red Sea! Should I wait for him to appear at the gates? If vast stretches of desert and treacherous mountain passes are no hindrance to Solomon's plans, then neither are they to *mine!*" She recovered her breath and spoke with quiet authority. "You will arrange the details, Tamrin. By ship to the eastern arm of the sea. To Ezion-geber. Then to Jerusalem by caravan. Send out the word. Heap the backs of camels and mules and horses, Bashir. Heap them high with the treasures of my land and let the beasts of burden wear crown pieces to shame the one he wears with such pride. Let the coffers of topaz outnumber the bales of cinnamon to let him see how little we regard the jewels he treasures. Swathe ambergris in shawls of priceless silver thread. Let his royal nose be teased with perfumes and aromatic ointments he has never known. Bring spikenard, the civet from the cats of the forest, the balsam and frankincense—go now, Bashir, there is no time to lose."

Bashir bowed low and moved away with the noiseless tread of a black panther.

Makada looked steadily at Tamrin. "I see delight and approval reflected in your eyes. Have you any further suggestions?"

"You have anticipated every one!" He rubbed his hands together slowly.

"Then let the word be spoken: In the land of Sheba, until the day I depart, if a man drops hammer or needle at his work, another shall pick it up until he, too, falls from the need of sleep. Search the desert and the woods and the sea and all the lands about, and capture the rarest fragrances, the most delicate scents and have them carefully packed in jars of porcelain and alabaster—and on them all must be the seal of the Queen of Sheba! The sun and crescent moon will rise on a new and everlasting glory for us, Tamrin, one that will never be overshadowed by the Star of David!"

"There has never been, there will never be again, a camel train of riches to equal the caravan of the Queen of Sheba!" Tamrin spoke with great pride and it pleased her. "It will be a glittering, endless thread of jewels on the desert, as far as the eye can see—from this land to the heart of his wretched city!"

"When he beholds the splendor of it all," she said, breathless with the frenzy of conquest, "may his eyes be dazzled into blind defeat!"

It was the spring of the year when, in David's time, the kings went forth to battle. But the warrior-king now slept with his fathers, and his son had dominion over all the region west of the Euphrates from Tiphsah to Gaza and over all its kings and there was peace in the land.

For Solomon's kingdom was established greatly.

It was still the habit of Ahiah the scribe to rise occasionally before daybreak and, carrying his sandals, tiptoe through the sleeping ante-chambers and corridors of the palace. Solomon had insisted that Ahiah and his brother Elihoreph, both writers of history, be free to put down the records as Shisha their father had before them, and moved Ahiah's living quarters closer to his own. Part of Solomon's own rooms overflowed with records to be sorted and written down in their proper place and time, a wilderness of dates and places to be classified for the first time since the Exodus from Egypt, close to five hundred years ago.

This was a precious hour to Ahiah. One in which to think back and around and far into the events of time and even, perhaps, to find one's own place in a world that had so changed during his lifetime, changed under his bare feet as he walked softly through the palace.

He passed through one of the halls, dimly lit by wicks in cressets of oil niched in the colonnaded wall. The gloom of space concealed the elaborate carvings, the larger rectangular pillars and the gleaming ornamentation of frieze and sculpture along the architraves that framed the entrances to many rooms. Ahiah wondered if the shade of David ever walked these halls, once austere but familiar, and lost himself in their transformed splendor.

He passed the audience chambers, large and small, and the old throne room which was now a simple but richly built hall of judgment; and he passed the great curtains and doors that closed off the new room Solomon had ordered constructed, in which he could receive princes and kings from other courts in a surrounding more lavish than their own.

So much had changed, so much. . . .

A drowsy sentry opened one eye at the courtyard entrance of the great hall, recognized Ahiah, and settled back to wait for the relief of the morning watch. Ahiah walked out into the mist of graying darkness, sat on a bench in the courtyard and put on his sandals which could squeak now if they liked. With his robe caught close against the pre-dawn chill, he walked through the gardens. The sound of water dripping from the graceful fountains, the heavy perfume of flowers was still a recurring but delightful surprise to him; and he remembered the night when he had met Solomon wandering here in this misty courtyard when it stood bleak and neglected within thick walls built in haste to protect David's stronghold, hard won, hard kept in the days of war.

He passed through the palace gate toward the east and looked down on the sleeping rooftops of Zion. There, too, the touch of Solomon could be seen. There were new bushes and trees, planted in some more fertile region to the north, and transported here at great expense after they had grown tall; for Solomon had seemed obsessed with the need to quickly provide each man, after he had labored all morning in his own fields, the right to sit in the shade during the heat of the sun. Beyond, where the old city had been built round the Millo, Solomon had filled in the breach. New, flat-roofed houses of stone and sturdy wood were built on the gently sloping ground, before it fell away into the valley of the Kidron brook. And beyond that, the Mount of Olives rose dark and beautiful against the first streak of dawn.

These were things to behold, Ahiah thought, when one was alone with memory of the past and thoughts of the future. Without being aware of it, he turned northward and his footsteps led him up the ascent to the Temple area. He looked up, to the topmost level of Mount Moriah which David had purchased long ago from Araunah, the Jebusite landowner. And as if the dead king's dream had been long buried and had grown to power that could raise the rock that covered it, the flat stone threshing floor now held the dream of David magnificently outlined by the faint glow in the eastern sky.

He paused a moment to rest and thought that in a strange way, this thing of beauty, growing high, held the shape of Solomon's destiny. And still more, the destiny of Solomon's people. The foundation is made of solid stone, he thought, fine-hewn in the quarries and brought up in silence with margins squared. Three courses of solid stone. And from the rectangle of its walls there rises the first house of the Lord. A structure to draw the eyes and hearts of all men for all time, and bend the heads of kings and shepherds in humility. A magnificent structure, with walls of cedar and doors of olivewood to be overlaid with gold. A fine thing, Ahiah told himself, that it stood higher than the house of a king. But he wondered if, in this state, it was not the physical symbol of their faith itself. Deep-rooted in the heart, perhaps, but still half-obscured by the scaffolding of old superstitions still to be torn down. Rough remnants that still clung to the pure vision of desert wanderings, not quite destroyed after lingering in pagan cities outside the Promised Land.

Ahiah moved past the sleeping huddles of Phoenician artisans and stonemasons sent by King Hiram of Tyre. They would soon be stirring their bodies and superior talents, to pick up mauls and wedges and fine cutting tools to beautify a house for the God of those who had labored too long in the wandering to know anything of art and the crafts they yearned to acquire. But they were learning quickly. Just as they had shaken off their land-bound anchors and now sailed the seas in ships of the great merchant king, so they were gathering with the Sidonians in the forests of Lebanon in the north to cut cedars and firs and lash them into rafts that came down to the ports of Solomon's land. And they picked up the mauls and wedges and fine cutting tools and watched and learned with eagerness that became skill.

He reached the forecourt near the entrance and when he approached the two freestanding columns which Solomon had named Jachin and

Boaz, Ahiah peered close and saw a deeper shadow move and rise from the fine things that had been brought up the evening before and left for the king's inspection. Ahiah was not surprised to recognize the tall figure who not only wore the tunic of a workman but had developed the same broad, long sinews of the workman himself.

Solomon was estimating with rule and hands the span beneath the gigantic wings of the unfinished cherubim.

"It is wide enough," Ahiah said.

Solomon answered without turning around. "This entire Temple, Ahiah, is being erected with less noise than your sandals make. Now see here, why I'm not sure of the width. It must easily span the mercy seat of the Ark—" He stepped away from it then and turned his head this way and that. "I started thinking about it in the night and couldn't sleep. It's to be moved inside today—and I must know exactly—" He turned abruptly to Ahiah and the scribe saw faint shadows of strain beneath the king's eyes and cheekbones. "You know such things, Ahiah. Give me the answer."

Ahiah said it was an answer best suited to the knowledge of his brother.

"Elihoreph has a talent for two things," said Ahiah. "Filling his head with facts. And his ever-starved stomach with food. My food. Still, I remember his writing down the figures when your father moved the Ark from the house of Obededom and brought it into the city—" He paused and looked around, as if far below, the tabernacle of goat-hair which still housed the Ark of the Covenant could verify its dimensions. He remembered the length of two cubits and a half, and width one cubit and a half, the same as the height. And he allowed for the gold rings which held the staves by which it was to be carried, and he gave the number to Solomon without hesitation, but with a smile. "At least that is one thing I can't argue with my brother. The measure of the acacia-wood box covered with gold is something we can't dispute, nor the presence of the tablets of the law preserved within it. But last night he talked for three hours, by himself, over using the name Horeb or Sinai for the mountain where Moses received those tablets of the law—"

Solomon was not listening.

There were many times now, Ahiah thought, that the king's mind was elsewhere, searching out some new thought, pursuing a fresh dream to enlarge and beautify his land. He would talk about these things and keep others deeply hidden even from Ahiah. He would talk of the fine results of dividing the kingdom into districts governed by twelve administrators, the new roads of basalt that threaded the land and brought the trade of riches to remote Jerusalem; and he would speak with eagerness of the furnaces turning out copper at Ezion-geber to be loaded on his ships that were now as fine as anything in Phoenicia.

And all the while, when he spoke of these things he seemed to be asking: "Am I a worthy king, Ahiah? Was my father justified in naming me to take his place?"

"When the Temple is completed, Ahiah," Solomon was saying, "there will be a great Hall of Pillars to build. A house of Lebanon and a new palace for myself."

Ahiah watched his eyes, grown restless and unhappy these past few years, and he wondered what Solomon would do when the last palace was built, the last road finished, the last chariot city established as Megiddo and Hazor and Gezer now stood, in defense of the land. What new thing would claim his driving will and hold back the brooding thoughts of night that drove him out of his bed, up to a mountain top before dawn to ponder a span and measurement that would still be there for the measuring in the more reasonable light of day?

As Solomon's critical gaze swept over the terrain below, where laborers were emerging from their tents, he questioned small details of the landscaping which was already completed on many of the terraces. But he was delighted with the almug trees that patterned the ascent with the green lace of their leaves.

"Not even Hiram can boast of owning so many," he said, then turned to Ahiah with a quizzical smile. "Our royal guest has been sleeping late in the mornings."

"When I passed his rooms," said Ahiah, "I could hear him snoring like a whale."

With the suddenness of the sun, shimmering now in the full brilliance of dawn, Solomon shook with laughter deep in the bronzed bareness of his chest.

"I know why he sleeps late. From exhaustion. He stays up all night figuring new ways to cheat me—"

Ahiah grinned. "He was your father's good friend, and yours—"

The earth rumbled and they both turned, startled, toward the broad ramp built for carts and oxen to bring supplies to the temple site. Even as they watched, twenty of Solomon's horsemen appeared, led by Benaiah, and Zabud was also with them.

Solomon leaped over the gold basins and lavers piled in the forecourt, and ran out to meet his commander. The horses' hoofs of the guard came to a halt, while Benaiah and Zabud dismounted and came forward to greet Solomon.

Ahiah approached more slowly as Solomon was still flinging questions at the two without waiting for an answer.

"Now tell me, where did you find him—and did you give him my message? Was he in Baal-hazor tending his estates, or in Hebron, watching over his vineyards—well, speak up! When will my brother come to me in peace and sit at my right hand all the years I am King?"

Benaiah's face darkened as it always did when Solomon spoke in this manner about Adonijah.

"He is not to be found," the commander said and, after a slight hesitation, went on because he had known Solomon as a gay-hearted prince and did not always feel restraint toward him, although he was his King. "It is rumored over the campfires of other lands that he has gone to seek allies to rise up against you in revolt—"

Solomon's stern glance silenced him, but only for a moment. Benaiah rubbed the scars of his rugged and enduring face. "You will recall that on the day of your coronation I warned that his blood which you spared that day would eventually become a tide of insurrection!"

Solomon sighed heavily. "You forget he has no support, Benaiah. Where would he find it? Rezon of Damascus is no longer a thorn in my side, and Hadad of Edom is afraid to cross the shadow of his own door!"

"There could be others—" Benaiah began but a reminding look from Zabud stopped him. "I beg your indulgence, my lord," he said awkwardly. "We came on a different matter." And he told Solomon that while his patrol was searching the countryside and the desert regions for Adonijah they had seen a royal caravan approaching Jerusalem.

"It will arrive within another day," he said.

Solomon had long passed the time of enjoying the amazement in the eyes of royal visitors when they looked upon his city, glistening in the sun, his palace and his throne. He sighed and walked slowly back toward the temple where the workmen were already busy. Benaiah and Zabud walked on each side of him and Ahiah was content to follow.

Zabud was gesturing extravagantly as he described the caravan. He pictured a blazing desert sun, like a mammoth gong in the sky flashing a signal for carnival, whipping at the glittering palanquin of the potentate who traveled to Jerusalem. He spoke of musicians and acrobats, dancers and singers—nothing had ever been seen like it before in all of Israel—or anywhere else! Even the camels wore crowns and ornamental headpieces and there were glistening chariots of electrum, and pack animals bearing elaborate burdens and ornate litters that carried cages of peacocks, gibbons, screaming birds of outrageous colors and sleek panthers; and the vanguard of plumed stallions was led by giants whose dark muscles, even at the distance they were seen from the far hills, rippled in the sunlight—

Solomon was preoccupied with the placing of the sacrificial altar in the forecourt.

He narrowed his eyes, and with the accuracy of a plumb line ordered the foreman to realign the base.

"A hair's breadth to the left, Jeroboam!"

The young foreman carried out the order and as Solomon watched, he put his fists on his hips and said quietly: "What misbegotten royal son of Belial chooses the busiest season of my year to pay a visit!"

"Not a king," said Zabud. "When we saw the outriders dispatched for the city, we intercepted them and brought the message ourselves. The visitor is a queen—the Queen of Sheba."

It meant little to Solomon. He squatted on his heels, measured the level of the altar with his eye, approved it, then started down the hillside toward the palace.

"She comes with great riches, my lord," said Zabud.

Solomon paused, and looked long at Zabud.

"My friend," he said, "continue the search for my brother. If you cannot find him in the spring of the year, then search through the summer —and don't return without news of him."

Zabud bowed and left.

"And you, Benaiah," Solomon said, wearily putting a hand on his commander's shoulder, "take the royal guard, polish your shields and see that the uniforms are as resplendent as always, and escort this king or queen of whatever it is—into Jerusalem with the usual ceremony."

Benaiah hurried away. Ahiah walked beside Solomon in silence. They descended the terraced slope and not until they were walking through the courtyard toward Solomon's rooms did Ahaih remind the king that Sheba was the jewel in the desert, the fabulous oasis he wanted to visit— in his youth.

He smiled at Solomon's startled reaction. "My youth, Ahiah? I've scarcely begun to live. I've not been King long enough to know the meaning of age."

"Age is less a matter of time, than responsibility."

Solomon looked at him wryly. "I understand. I carry the burden with conscience—and I'll soon be losing my hair, as you are." He was silent a moment, pausing at the foot of the outer stairway leading up to the rooms which were once David's and now his. "I still have the dagger I bought on my early travels as a present for Adonijah. Broken as it is. I keep it wrapped in linen in my clothes chest—do you think I'll ever have an opportunity to give it to him? Will he ever reach out his hand to me in a gesture of love and friendship?" He turned, without waiting for an answer and started up the steps. Then he called down to Ahiah: "Did I ever say I wanted to visit this land called Sheba?"

Ahiah smiled up at him and nodded his head. Solomon shook his head and smiled. "How quickly one forgets all the wild foolishness of earlier days—and remembers only the grief." He lifted his chin and said brusquely, "Sit at the table in the great hall this morning, Ahiah. With your pens ready. Hiram is bound to talk business even as he eats." Then Solomon ran up the stairs.

A few moments later he reappeared in the great hall. He wore a fresh linen tunic with a girdle of blue and gold about his waist and his hair was still glistening with the water from his bathing.

He had been right. Hiram was anxious, in a friendly manner, to close the deal of exchange that brought him to Jerusalem. He was well-fleshed, rosy-cheeked and was heartily enjoying his morning meal. Only his long upper lip with the fine seam down the middle told of his shrewdness which he never compromised for even the dearest of friendships.

For the cedarwood now on its way out of Lebanon to this city he was asking only twenty-two thousand kors of wheat in addition to the fine-beaten oil—each year for a specified time.

Solomon broke his bread and ate it with figs and honey. "Twenty-*two*? My dear friend, the wheat multiplies more quickly in your mind than in my fields. I originally agreed to only *twenty*."

Ahiah dipped his face low over his wax tablets to smile at Hiram's annoyance.

"My cedarwood is not harvested as easily as your wheat, *King* Solomon!"

"True, *King* Hiram. But have you ever tried feeding your people with cedarwood?"

Hiram spread his hands, patronizingly. "For only twenty thousand kors of wheat I naturally could not deliver cedars of the best size and quality."

Solomon's smile did not reach his eyes, for in this he was serious and firm: "No matter what compromises we make between ourselves, Hiram, none but the finest materials go into the house of my Lord."

"In Tyre, now, we build a shrine to the god Melkarth. And I'll admit to you and no one else that he is worshiped just as ardently as if he were made of the finest stone and the choice trees—" He began to chuckle at his own bad jest but saw the look of restrained anger on Solomon's face. He cleared his throat and got back to business. Solomon's good humor was quickly restored and the bargaining continued. Solomon had to concede, at last, but was unwilling to admit it.

As he was about to agree that twenty-two thousand kors of wheat it would be, Bathsheba hurried in with as much dignity as possible and when the amenities were over she said anxiously, "Why are we wasting time when there is so much to be done! The steward of the household is in a frenzy and the cooks are throwing up their hands at the number of people to be served—"

"What's this, what's this?" Hiram asked. "Another royal visitor? Good. I do enjoy meeting my rivals—especially at another's court—where the expense of entertaining is not mine."

"You might have told me, Solomon," Bathsheba wailed. "What a task it will be. Hundreds of servants, musicians, slaves, heaven knows what—"

"We've accommodated that number of people before," Solomon said calmly.

"But the visitor was a king, a potentate from an eastern land—a *man!*" said Bathsheba. "And men never notice the finer details of the appointments in a palace. But this is a woman! One glance, and all the gold and precious stones and all your fine buildings and inlaid floors will mean nothing if she sees one unpolished goblet! Have I your permission to oversee the appointments of the rooms she will occupy and the food that will be served—"

"Yes, yes," said Solomon. As she hurried away he smiled at Hiram. "Such a fuss over the visit of the Queen of Sheba."

Hiram, with his mouth full of food, began to laugh heartily, then his face turned purple and he choked and washed down his food. The color drained from his face as quickly as it appeared.

"The Queen of Sheba!" He got to his feet and looked around frantically, like a fat trapped animal. "By my gods!"

"What is the trouble, my friend?" Solomon rose from the table but Hiram had already started from the room, speaking as he walked. "I must leave, Solomon. Quickly!" Solomon hurried after him, pulled at his arm. "But what of our business, we haven't finished—"

Hiram's big hairless head bobbed up and down.

"We have finished! Twenty thousand kors of wheat it is! I'm being robbed but I haven't time to stay and defend myself!"

Solomon gripped his arm, preventing his exit.

"Why all this suddenness?"

Hiram took a deep breath and tried to speak calmly.

"Solomon, my good friend. What is shaped like a camel, croaks like a frog and devours living men—I should ask such an easy riddle!"

Solomon lifted his eyebrows and questioned wryly: "The Queen of Sheba?"

"Old Belkis herself!" Hiram mopped the sweat on his forehead with the sleeve of his robe. "I had a double purpose in visiting your city, my friend. Business. And postponing the result of my envoy's last visit to the Queen's court. The cedarwood I promised her is holding up the ceiling in the vestibule of your temple. Goodbye." Nearing the door, he turned back to grip Solomon's arm in consolation. "May my gods and your God protect you! Now I must gather my servants—"

He was gone. With bewildered amusement Solomon lifted his shoulders and returned to his meal.

"What do you make of it, Ahiah? Whenever Hiram of Tyre sacrifices two thousand kors of wheat—" Solomon chuckled. "She must be even worse than her reputation. I wonder—are we being visited or invaded?"

Ahiah was noncommittal, still he added a bit of information that had come his way some time ago: that the Queen of Sheba was a behemoth of a female with the appetite of ten men.

"Never mind that," said Solomon, and indicated the tablets on which Ahiah had been writing. "Just make sure a record is made of Hiram's transaction. It isn't every day I get the best of him in a bargain."

Escorted by Benaiah and twenty of Solomon's horsemen carrying golden shields that glistened in the sun, the Queen's caravan entered the city.

The townspeople were accustomed to the sight of rich royal caravans, but nothing like this had been seen before!

They lined the streets, strewn now with flowers for the occasion, and gaped with amazement at the bizarre but majestic parade making its way through the streets leading to the palace on the hillside. The Sabaean vanguard carried long standards bearing the sun-and-crescent-moon emblem of the Queen's mystery domain in the unknown south. Musicians and dancers swayed to the barbaric, muted beat of drums and the sound of tambourines. Acrobats, tumbling at the sides of bedecked camels, and conjurers wearing painted masks with brilliant feathers, brought shy smiles from soft-eyed mothers who stood in humble doorways and heard the laughter of the little children who peered, wide-eyed, from behind their skirts.

The peacefulness of Jerusalem stirred to the promise of holiday spirit with slow reluctance; for the years of devout wandering moved through the blood of its people, if not in their memory, and such revelry as this— on any day but a festival of praise to Yahweh—was to be looked upon with courteous but solemn reservation.

Tamrin, and the high dignitaries of Makada's court, rode camels adorned with amulets of gold and saddle coverings of shimmering cloth from Damascus. They were followed by the shrouded litters of the Queen's personal attendants and necks craned above the growing crowd of onlookers to speculate which carrying chair held the Queen of Sheba. And then, as the endless skein threaded its brilliance through the streets, there was no doubt. For the palanquin of the Queen, escorted by a human rectangle of slaves holding a length of gold chain, was a spacious jewel box curtained with gossamer veils that sparkled in the sun. Its ebony handles were balanced on the massive shoulders of six dark-skinned Samsons whose gliding precision assured their royal burden she rode on a cloud.

Singers of Jerusalem raised their voices to chant a welcome to the royal visitor and in the market-place two old merchants paused in their bargaining to observe that Solomon would surely levy another tax to cover the expense of *this* one's entertainment.

The singers followed the Queen's palanquin to the gates of the palace where, as far as the eye could see, the walls were lined with camels and horses being relieved of their burdens and taken away.

The chanting at the gates drifted through the open doorways of the throne room and a quiver of anticipation moved through the crowd of resplendent dignitaries.

At the far end of the vast room were six steps, each flanked by carved lions, and the treads of the steps were broad enough to hold costly seats of honor near the great throne of ivory and gold. And the back of the throne was round and there were stays on either side of the place of the seat where Solomon, in kingly robes of crimson, purple and gold, sat in all his glory.

He sat with one hand cupped over his brow as if pondering the riddle Ahiah had asked a moment ago, but actually kneading the ache of a sleepless night behind his eyes. His duties had absorbed him far into the night. Two of his officers over the districts, the one from Makaz and Ben-hesed who was over Arubboth, had traveled far and long to hear his judgment of disputes which had arisen between landowners in their territories. It had been dawn of this morning before the governors and the litigants had departed, each content with his rightful measure of justice.

The murmur of courtiers, officers and the ambassadors of many lands came up to him with unreality more meaningless and kindly than the dreams which had disturbed his sleep.

"May I inquire," said Jehoshaphat his recorder, "if the salutations I hear being sung to the visiting Queen are of King Solomon's invention?"

He heard Ahiah answering for him.

"Without a doubt," said Ahiah.

Jehoshaphat's puzzlement brought a fine smile to Solomon's half-hidden lips. Why then, the recorder wanted to know, was she called "Lily of the Morning" and hailed as "Rose of the Dawn" when it was common gossip that she more resembled an overgrown and repulsive weed?

Solomon removed the hand that covered his face.

"Now that is a riddle for you, Ahiah."

"With a simple answer. The eyes of the ugliest woman never believe what they see in the mirror."

"Which makes a tribute to her beauty roll smoothly from the tongue, Jehoshaphat. Because it is so gratefully received." Solomon sighed with impatience. "So much to be done at the Temple, and this monster of Sheba keeps me waiting!"

The blare of trumpets from the courtyard drowned his comment to all but Ahiah. "An ancient privilege of all women," he whispered in Solomon's ear.

"True." Solomon sighed again. "But when I think of what she must look like, I wish that Eve had kept Adam waiting a little longer." He beckoned Jehoshaphat closer. "Now remember. Interrupt me as soon as you can without too much discourtesy. Tell me that you have arranged for her immediate tour of the palace, the orchards, best seen in the light of the moment—or perhaps the palace kitchens would delight her more, it makes no difference what you say, *anything*."

And then the flourish of trumpets was loud and deafening at the door and with the first silence, Benaiah and the guard formed a path to the throne. Benaiah's captain called out the name of Tamrin, His Excellency, Grand Vizier of Sheba!

Preceded by seneschals who carried scrolls of the finest papyrus, Tamrin walked slowly toward the throne and Solomon thought, "He walks with too soft a step, this one," and when the guards stood aside and Tamrin looked up to speak his greetings to the King he reminded Solomon of a lean bird of prey, dressed in the plumage of authority but thirsting for more.

"May the Great King of Israel and Judah live forever," said Tamrin, bowing low, "in peace and prosperity."

A message right from the heart, Solomon thought, and lifted one hand in a gesture of welcome.

"Wish me only peace, Grand Vizier," he said. "Prosperity will then take care of itself."

Tamrin moved to one side and with the practiced gestures of formal protocol he indicated the gifts being carried in from all entrances to the throne room.

"In the name of my Queen we beg your Majesty to accept these humble tokens of our esteem, affection and friendship."

The stewards of the palace were already bewildered by the abundance of goods being carried in and had drawn aside the curtains beyond the colonnade of pillars to reveal that the adjoining rooms were also being filled with costly treasure.

Solomon looked back to find Tamrin's eyes filled with a lofty contempt, quickly dispelled by a smooth deference in his manner. He then thumped the floor with the end of his staff and ordered the lists on the scrolls read before the King.

The gifts collecting in the other rooms were nothing, Tamrin explained. The attendants would now name the presents to be personally offered to the illustrious court of Solomon.

As the seneschal unrolled the scroll and started to read, the gifts were borne in. First to appear were six dancers from the temples of Sheba, whose anklets jangled softly as bare feet moved in unison along the length of carpet leading to the throne. Their arms were laden with open coffers of gems that brought whispers of astonishment from the crowded room. The casks of powdered gold, the amethyst and turquoise were brought to Solomon's throne that he might look down on the boxes of alabaster and the jars filled to overflowing with precious stones. The priestesses moved away and the procession continued, each treasure surpassed by the next.

Slaves bore a basket toward him and he looked down at one hundred and twenty shining talents of gold. His eyebrows lifted with appreciation for the Queen's excellent gesture of generosity. Servants appeared carrying perches and cages of exotic, screaming birds; and as a giant Sabaean entered with a lion on a jeweled leash, the women of the court drew back with soft murmurs of fear until the animal had been taken away. The impressive pause which followed caused Solomon to brace himself. With a whisper to Ahiah, Solomon expressed his knowledge. Now that they had seen the "King" of Beasts, he said, it must be time to look upon the Queen—

Tamrin's voice stilled the room into respectful expectancy.

"Her Supreme Majesty—the Queen of Sheba!"

She was borne in then on her carrying chair, now unveiled. And her face, too, was uncovered for all to see.

The salutations of obeisance to the Queen came up to Solomon as in a dream and were lost in the tumult of his heart, suddenly alien, pounding like an angry stranger at the gates of his ears. And he thought surely, in this sudden silence it can be heard. . . .

He rose slowly from his chair and because he was aware of moving at his usual pace, it seemed that he must be a man divided: one who wore a crown of self-possession never yet disturbed, who calmly stood outside measuring the other within whose whole being, like some wild, long-captured bird abruptly unfettered, soars with beating wings into the infinite mystery of its home.

He stepped down from the throne and on the middle landing of the stairs he waited and forced his guarded gaze over the assembly. No one was watching him. Not even Zadok the High Priest, usually so eager to seek out the secret thoughts of the King. Not Naamah, grown thin-lipped and spare, who was the first; nor the patrician daughter of the Pharaoh who was the last.

A mist seemed to rise from nowhere, a burnished radiance blotting familiar faces into shadow, leaving only the one. She stepped from her carrying chair and all the elusive dust motes of forgotten dreams now became warm and golden substance moving toward him, forming for the first time the nameless longing all the nights of his years. . . .

She stood at the foot of the stairs and her eyes, slanting like dark and luminous almonds, held an instant of promise that reached out to him even as it was veiled and withdrawn. With the slightest inclination of her head she addressed him as he descended the last of the stairs—and he knew the sound of her voice before she spoke:

"May the great King whose fame encompasses the earth live forever. And may it always be so that rulers of strange lands visit yours in trust and friendship."

The low, soft cadence crept like the shadow of a vine round the stone barriers of formal greeting.

"We had not expected the Queen of Queens to be so—" he looked away abruptly from her beauty and indicated the lavish gifts "—so generous!"

"I am sure you are accustomed to even greater—generosity." The polite turn of her smile which included the lovely women of his household, added his respect for her tact. But with it a fleeting sense of caution.

He extended his hand and the light touch of her fingers held the impact of a close embrace. As if the sensation were tangible and emanating into every corner of the room, he escorted her up the stairs with less than his usual gallantry. Choral groups now formed near the colonnade and as the Queen was seated in the place of honor at Solomon's right, she listened for a moment to the antiphonal song. Fruit and wine and honeycakes were carried in on platters of gold and after she had sipped the wine, the guests of the court moved in small groups and spoke softly as the servants passed among them.

Solomon said it was known to him that Sheba was a land of untold wealth and far-reaching commerce. But it was not reported that it was ruled by so young a Queen.

"What *was* reported of Sheba's Queen?"

Solomon sensed that Ahiah had taken a step closer and was waiting for the answer.

"I had heard of the Queen's enormous—loyalty," Solomon said quickly. "Her prodigious appetite for—learning and knowledge."

He heard Ahiah's muffled cough moving away, into the crowd.

"My mother," said the Queen of Sheba with a sad smile. "The gods took her from us—with the swiftness of a dagger, leaving me a child among monarchs. And so I came to your land, to learn the wisdom of its King, and to see its wonders—that I may better rule my own."

He looked at her a long time, searching out the mystery—whatever it was—that lay behind her eyes.

"Extravagant gifts," he murmured. "Extravagant praise."

"In my foolish eagerness to sit at your feet," she said simply, "I have blundered. You distrust my humility. And my gifts—I had hoped some of them would be a rarity in your palace. But I have carried trees to the forest and fish to the sea. I brought you gold, and I am chagrined for having brought grains of sand to the desert—"

"May those sands of the desert measure the days you remain here."

She lifted her face with the slow and graceful movement of a sun-weary flower to a gentle rain. And Solomon knew with stirring awareness that he looked upon flower and child, as well as woman. He knew beyond question that he would never have any desire beyond her.

She was looking at him with grave speculation. In any other woman it would be an expression to cool the blood into something less than the wish to touch her hand once more; but he found himself fascinated. He had seen the eyes of many ripe-mouthed women in the lamplight of half-forgotten hours; the accusing silent gaze of the undesired, and the questioning possessive eyes of those he quickly learned to leave alone. But in this moment of her measuring silence there was no boldness, no injury or desire to dominate—there was no trace of guile. And it came to him with the shock of plunging into the waters of a cool spring, that this woman called the Queen of Sheba had never loved. Yet he could be mistaken, for there was deep hurt, thinly masked by graciousness and an aloof response, and what had brought these things to pass—it was too soon to tell.

The proud lift of her chin recalled him to the moment. He realized she had propounded some riddles which he had answered too readily for her pleasure.

"Forgive me for having heard them before," he lied and could see she did not believe the lie. "Perhaps you can answer one which was asked me only before you arrived. And I gave the wrong answer. Would you like to hear it?" When she nodded her head, he said: "What is it that cannot lift the weakest man against his will, yet is stronger than a thousand oxen and can be carried by a child?"

"What was your answer?"

"I thought it was life itself. A man on his way to the grave cannot be revived, and envies the child who lives so lightly. But Ahiah says I am wrong."

"Which is Ahiah?" she asked, looking about the room. "One of your priests, one of your gods?"

Solomon saw Ahiah not far away. All the lines in his face were pyramided into strained patience as he argued some point with Jehoshaphat, whose loose-limbed body, bent with gaunt resistance, would not yield.

"Ahiah is my scribe." Solomon pointed him out. "A man of great wisdom."

"Greater than your own?"

He laughed. "I'd have none at all if I were sure I knew all there is to know. Only boys of sixteen are beyond learning. After that, it is a constant seeking and in the end one learns there is no end to the seeking."

"Then I have much to learn," she said, and he could not tell whether her eyes were veiled by more secret thoughts, or by the light-fingered shadows reaching into the room.

The wicks were now being lighted in the burnished bowls of oil. Solomon heard the determined stride of Jehoshaphat coming toward the throne. Ahiah had lost the argument then, and Jehoshaphat's solemn sense of duty had triumphed.

"My lord," he said, "it was your wish that your royal guest be escorted to the palace roofs to look down upon the King's orchards while their blossoms are a sea of flame in the dying sun."

Good Jehoshaphat. Poor, brilliant, devoted—stupid Jehoshaphat! Solomon sighed softly for all rigidly literal minds. Still, a "sea of flame in a dying sun" suggested a pale shred of imagery had somehow become caught on the sharp-edged facts that filled his recorder's bony skull.

"As the Queen wishes," Solomon said, hoping to see reluctance in her eyes.

When she rose so quickly he felt a pang of disappointment. Was she eager to be gone from his side?

Her rising brought the line of guards to attention, the attendants into silent waiting.

"Another time?" she asked, as he stood close to her. "There are other borders between your land and mine, a very long journey. I am a poor guest to find myself too weary to look upon more beauty than I have already seen this day." She glanced briefly at Tamrin who had emerged from his social wanderings to await her orders. "We are filled with wonder at the splendor of your city, and with the joy in the faces of the servants who stand before you. I came to see it with my own eyes and I know now that all I heard about you in my own land was but half the truth."

"And you came here to discover the other half?" He spoke it softly, almost against his will. Was the swift curve of her breath caught and held in anger, or surprise? In the dusky half-light the ruby pendants hanging from her wide collar of topaz, rose and fell in swift flashes of warning, like beacon fires he had once seen years ago, kindled and quickly smothered on the crests of enemy hillsides. "I mean only that there is still much to be seen," he said quickly and was pleased by her smile. As they descended the steps he suggested a royal feast in her honor. "Tonight? After you are rested. . . ."

"I beg your indulgence," she said graciously. "I am most eager to learn the ways of your kingdom, but after the tedious journey—" she made a small gesture of fatigue "—I am afraid a crowded banquet hall—"

"Then let the banquet be served you in your own apartments. But what a pity to spend your first evening alone in my kingdom."

She turned and studied his face a moment. "I regret that less than denying myself the pleasure of sitting near its King."

The words were a bold invitation, disarmed by the candor of her smile. She was waiting for his answer and he gave it with a formal nod of his head.

"This evening," he said, then he brusquely signaled to Benaiah. "You will escort the Queen of Sheba to her quarters."

She turned then and, followed by Tamrin and her personal attendants, she walked past the guards and bowing courtiers toward the doors. Solomon looked after her with impersonal courtesy but his thoughts raced to overtake her, bring her back into his vision; for now that she had turned away and was moving from his sight he searched his mind and could not recall the color of her eyes, whether her hair was the darkness of night or held the light of the moon. . . .

She had reached the doors and before she stepped into the corridor, Solomon spoke into his memory and said I must remember this, that she wore golden sandals and a sheath of golden cloth and on her head —and the words were flat sounds that circumscribed a sun by saying it was round and bright. He listened instead, as the others talked, to the song that lay within him, waiting and nameless.

She was gone. And with her leaving he could not remember that she wore golden sandals, or the color of her gown. He saw the eyes of doves by the rivers of waters, beds of spice and sweet-smelling myrrh, a fountain of gardens, goats that appear from Gilead, pomegranates and a heap of wheat set about with lilies, young roes as twins, towers of ivory and the fruit of the vine—

And he looked up into the face of the Pharaoh's daughter, as if she divined his thoughts and understood. She was waiting near the column of pillars. He had not been aware of walking away from Ahiah and Zadok and the others, and he smiled, calling himself a lovesick shepherd howling at the moon on some deserted hill.

"My lord is thoughtful," said Tanis and he read sad resignation in her eyes. Their serenity alone, he thought, redeemed the sharp intelligence of her aquiline features.

"Relieved that it is over," he said.

She smoothed one hand with the other, avoiding his gaze. She meant to ease his torment, he knew, and he was shamed and grateful.

"One day," he said, knowing this was not the time to say it, "I will build a palace worthy of you."

"I am content in the house my lord has provided me," she said.

"It is not fine enough for the daughter of a Pharaoh, or the wife of a King."

The throne room was clearing. The stewards at the far end were gathering the gifts from Sheba, moving them to the store chambers to be weighed —that his return gifts should exceed the measure of what she brought with her. And the thought of her leaving the land, as she had just now left the room, flung his arm in a sweeping gesture of denial. . . .

"Such ostentation," he said, and walked with Tanis to the courtyard. She was silent and waited for him to speak. "You are much too good for me, Tanis. You ask no questions. Make no demands." He touched her hand with warm affection. "Perhaps you possess all that is most worthwhile in me because you are not possessive. Is that it?"

"I possess nothing of you, my lord," she said gently. "I have known that from the first."

"Yet you listen patiently and without bitterness, knowing my thoughts are of another."

"I claim no virtue for that," she said. "I have no choice."

"There would be more stillness within me," he said, "if it were otherwise. I wish it were."

She straightened and moved away from his touch, perhaps out of some inner shyness, or because Zadok and Ahiah were coming toward them across the stepping stones from the garden of fountains.

"With my lord's permission—" she started to withdraw.

He touched her cheek lightly with the palm of his hand. It was smooth and dry and he thought it would be like this even after many years, unchangeable and timeless as the Nile itself. She disappeared down the path which led to her private garden, and he walked to meet his scribe and high priest. As he walked he called servants to him and handed them his outer robes.

Ahiah said, "I regret that Jehoshaphat has never learned that a King's order can sometimes lose significance in the face of such compelling beauty."

"Never mind that," said Solomon. "We still have much to do. There is still time to see the master mason before sunset. Then, Zadok, will you supervise the placing of the lampstands in the Holy Place?"

"It is not only my duty but my intention." His eyes glowed in the dying light with unspoken condemnation.

"Will you speak what is on your mind, Zadok?" The three of them now moved toward the palace gates. Ahiah assisted Zadok around a heap of crushed stone being used to repair a wall.

Zadok pulled his arm from Ahiah's protection.

"I still have the power of my sight! And there are many things I would rather not see. Even a heap of stone that will change still another wall of the palace."

"You are filled with fear, High Priest," said Solomon. "Of things seen or unseen. You protest over change. Yet you say we must move with the times—"

"He is unhappy," Ahiah explained, "because you are host to a pagan Queen."

"We also gave hospitality to a pagan King," Solomon reminded Zadok. "Or is King Hiram's worship to be condoned because he helps us build the Temple?"

"Hiram is not beautiful," Ahiah said with a gentle smile. "He is not lovely to look upon. And the Queen of Sheba—ah! There is one who could breathe life into a dead man!"

"Or evil into a good one!" Zadok cried.

Solomon looked around quickly, but Zadok had not directed the imprecation on anything but the rocky ascent of the road up to the Temple. . . .

Now that he was through giving instructions to the one who would supervise the feast in the great hall for his visiting princes and ambassadors, Solomon was eager to be finished with his dressing and out of his rooms. The servile tottering of old Benjamin, solemnly performing his one duty of the day, was straining the King's patience. He could find the girdle of scarlet and blue thread in half the time it took David's feeble manservant to cross the floor, sometimes pausing in bewilderment in the rooms so transformed since his former master had lived out the number of his days. But it was a tacit understanding between the king and his younger personal stewards that the one who had grown old faithfully serving David, should be allowed the delusion of believing he was still indispensable.

The curtains of the embrasure had been drawn back and the glow of evening, meeting the lamplight within, provided Solomon's excuse to dismiss the stewards before their time. He told them to take out all but one lamp, and as they obeyed he leaped up from his seat on the clothes chest, and hurried across the room.

"This one will do, Benjamin!" He preferred to fasten it himself, but the hands of the old man already held a belt of soft doeskin and it made no difference to Solomon that the watering, weak eyes had selected leather and thought it the scarlet thread the King had ordered. He stood with arms uplifted while Benjamin put it around his waist.

"Now, Benjamin, go to your bed." Solomon touched the bent shoulder.

Benjamin bowed his head and hesitated. "I am too slow and feeble to serve the King any longer."

Solomon had frequently tightened his lips against the pressure of speaking this truth. But now it was the whispered apology of the last leaf that clings for its life to the new and vigorous branch of an ancient tree. For all Solomon's impatience to be gone, he could not bring the softest breath of cruelty close to the brittle stem, causing it to die and fall to the ground for the want of being needed.

Benjamin blinked mottled eyelids as he listened to the King's words of reassurance. Solomon watched the dry, down-curved mouth quiver. Captured like a shriveled fish into a fine network of lines, it was drawn upward to the surface of a grateful smile.

"How can you ever be too old to serve one you once held as a child?" Solomon asked. He could remember that, and also a dim recollection of seeing a younger, black-haired Benjamin kneel before David as a bondsman who had served out the years required for his freedom. And he vaguely recalled Benjamin pressing the side of his own head against the door, waiting for David to pierce his ear. Then, as now, Benjamin wore a loop of metal through the lobe, to call attention to his proud status of being a free man who chose to remain a servant to his master, the King.

The moment Benjamin had disappeared into the shadows of the corridor, Solomon picked up his mantle from the bed. Even as he hurried toward the waiting moonlight beyond the opening to the roof-terrace, he paused, wondering at the sudden bloom of lamp glow in the room he was leaving. He turned. A steward stood at the threshold of the small hallway leading to the room in which Solomon often met with his officials to settle the minor problems of the day.

"My lord," said the steward, holding the lamp high, "as I carried out the light bowls of your writing room I was met in the halls by Benaiah, the Commander of the King's Host, and also by the Lady Bathsheba. They beg an audience with the King."

First the delay with Benjamin. Now this!

Solomon threw his mantle aside and started toward the small audience room. This was surely conspiracy against his first evening alone with the Queen. If he had been less anxious to be with her, he would have found it easier to deal with interruptions. Quickly. But his various and subtle sensations, like soft shoots of new green, were to be guarded against footsteps that might blunder into the secret paths of his yearning. And his brusque dismissal of Benaiah and Bathsheba would lend too much importance, in their minds, to his appointment with the Queen of Sheba.

He had many times asked his mother not to rise and make obeisance when he entered a room. But she rose now, as always, with the inevitable persistence of the sun and Solomon subdued his irritation with the certainty that Joshua himself could not have commanded her to stand still.

"Well now," he said, "what matter of importance takes you away from the feast below?"

"Let Benaiah speak first," said Bathsheba.

As the powerful bulk of his commander moved a step closer to the light of the single lamp on the table, Solomon knew that Benaiah spoke first in order that he should be dismissed first. And he sighed, wondering what pattern of suspicion was to be confided to him later, after Benaiah had gone.

Benaiah's request was straight as the sheathed sword at the belt of his leather tunic. He begged the King's permission to join Zabud who had already formed his patrol and was waiting this moment in the guard rooms over the armory for the King's last word.

"Zabud *has* my last word." Solomon braced himself for what he knew must be coming. There had been subtle words of warning over many supper tables, glances exchanged between those who strove to probe the secret of his last moments with David. "He will go without you this time, Benaiah. You are commander of the standing army and your duties have multiplied since you were permitted to head the search for my brother in the early part of this year. The new conscription list must be made. It is overdue—" He spoke of all that Benaiah had done, and well, to bring the army to wartime strength, to maintain its discipline, keep the soldiers strong in mind and body, a difficult task in times of peace. But beneath the praise and under the orders to continue, to prevent his men from becoming lax and disorderly, there was the unspoken barrier between king and commander. One word from Solomon, one moment of fear for himself and the throne, and Benaiah's search for Adonijah would surely end in death. "I want my brother found and brought to me, alive."

Benaiah's hairy brows met over his direct gaze of unswerving loyalty. "Does my King doubt that I would obey his orders?"

Solomon smiled and patted Benaiah's iron-sinewed shoulder. "Have no concern about that, my friend." Still, he thought, my father trusted Joab as I trust Benaiah. My father said to Joab: I have crossed over the Jordan into Gilead and my heart is burdened for my poor Absalom, my son who has gone into my house and calls himself king in my place; and he has gathered mighty men and pursues us to the point of battle, and I must muster up the mighty men to go forth and they must meet their swords with the spears of Absalom's army; but I charge you, Joab, Abishai, and Ittai—commanders over the thousands—I charge you, deal gently for my sake with the young man Absalom. . . .

And Joab, out of loyalty to his king, killed Absalom as he hung by his hair. . . .

No, Solomon thought. I can trust Benaiah's loyalty but who can say what crimes are committed in the *name* of loyalty?

"You have no cause for fear or suspicion, Benaiah."

"I have no fear of enemies I can see." And the color rose up into Benaiah's brown and ravaged face, paling the angry scar of the lion he had fought in a snowy pit. "I ask only that I go with Zabud to seek Adonijah and Joab and assure the King that their absence from the wilderness of Judea or the plains of Esdraelon is a harmless one."

"I need no assurance." His tone dismissed Benaiah and the commander bowed and left the room.

With the opening and closing of the door the laughter and sounds of the feast rose up from below for a moment, and were as quickly muffled into silence once more.

Finally, Bathsheba said, "The son of Jehoida shares my own fear."

Solomon could not meet her eyes without hostility. Her solicitude for his safety was more untenable for disguising the hard core of her hatred for the son of Haggith.

"On the day of your coronation," she reminded him, "he uttered words that still ring in my ears, strike me cold with terror in the middle of the night that could be sheltering his treachery. He will appear with a terrible army and you will be slain on the throne of your father—then you will know that when he cried out that there could never be peace between rivals for that throne, he spoke the truth!"

"Then for the love of all that's holy," Solomon spoke softly between closed teeth, "let there be peace between brothers!"

He heard her slight gasp of realization. She had said too much. Her voice would now come forth soft as the blue robe she wore, especially woven for her on the looms of Lachish; and the transparent veil of her headdress would seem to conceal in its folds the sharp murex shells that dyed it purple-red in the great vats of some seacoast city of Canaan.

"Then you will not listen," she said with self-pity. "You would refuse to hear what Adonijah asked of me one night before he left this city. And if you knew his request—you would be forced by law to abandon your misplaced trust in him—"

"I'll listen to no more!" Did she think that he lived in ignorance of Adonijah's request for the concubine-nurse of old David? What evil motive now did she place on his brother's love for Abishag? She would laugh at the word and name it only as an open defiance of the King. He would not let her speak further about this. At any time!

Bathsheba smiled sadly and paused on her way to the door. "Let my son the King forgive his anxious mother, but grant her a small lenience."

"Anything you wish," Solomon said with courtesy.

"It concerns the girl Abishag." His mother looked at him with wide eyes and then away, as if to spare him the warning burning behind his eyes. "It has nothing whatever to do with your dear brother. Or did you think perhaps there was some connection—?"

Too innocently spoken. Too adroit.

"I would ask the King," she said, "to relieve me of this handmaiden who sulks and whimpers and often stares at me with malevolence from some corner of the room."

"You asked for her services," he reminded Bathsheba.

"That was before, when I thought it wise for the object of Adonijah's affection—" she broke off and smoothed her error quickly: "—But you sent her down to the house of your brother to care for poor Haggith."

"Why do you consider her less worthy of watching now?"

"No one would look at her a second time. You have not seen her since the coronation."

Solomon had seen her many times at a distance. A thin and sallow little wretch, stewing in sullen rebellion, chided in the women's quarters because the King had never called her to him, scolded by the gaunt and maddened Haggith who roamed the rooms of Adonijah's deserted house until the day she died. Poor Abishag, he thought, and saw again the sour lines of bitterness on her face the one time he spoke to her and offered to send her back to the house and fields of her father in Shunam. David should have done that, he often thought, sent the girl away before he died, giving her a bounty to offer some shepherd while she still possessed the bloom of her youth. And he struggled uselessly against the bonds of law that limited his authority to cast off or bestow on another his inheritance.

The truth, he suspected, was that Bathsheba favored people with beauty. She liked to have them around her, to look into comely faces and see admiration returned.

"A place can be found for Abishag," he said slowly.

She thanked him with a kiss on his cheek and quietly left the room.

For a moment he stared into the bowl of light and leaned his weight on fists that would dig deep into the polished wood of the tabletop. Would there never be an end to the uneasiness in his thoughts? Could he ever lie in peace in these rooms without seeing the shade of his father watching him, waiting for him to carry out the charges that would brand him a murderer? He swung away from the table and the light behind him threw the shadow of his terror on the floor and up the walls to the place where David's lute hung in ghostly silence. Beneath it, in the niche, was the waiting wine cup of Adonijah. Solomon had removed all the others when he transferred the harp from the bedchamber. And he remembered that at the time Ahiah had looked at him with understanding eyes and said, "Solomon, one day when more than wearing the crown has made you King, you will place the lute of your father and your brother's wine cup back in your bedchamber." And Solomon had wondered if the scribe had guessed at the torment of waking suddenly in the moonless nights, as if a dead finger had plucked one of the sagging strings, filling the air with its mournful note that shattered the peace of dreamless sleep. Just as Benaiah and Bathsheba, by their coming, had cast a shadow over his eagerness to be near the Queen of Sheba. Now as he hurried to his bedchamber, picked up his mantle and walked out onto the roof, his desire to go to her was quickened by the urgent need to leave the shadows behind.

He paused for a moment near the parapet, perhaps to recapture his earlier mood by finding it in the thick fragrance of flowers blooming in the moon-washed garden. Squares of light from the open doors of the great hall below framed bushes of olive and willow into brilliant, unreal green, and voices, merry with his finest wines, floated out over juniper and mulberry and the tallest fronds of the date-palm trees. He looked past these, to the half-hidden rooftops of palace wings and the large houses of fine stone. Far beyond, he saw the watchtowers of the Horse Gate, heard the cry of sentry to sentry and the faint sound of horses' hoofs as Zabud led his patrol out into the stretches of desert and mountain—and Solomon's silent cry went with them—to find his brother.

He shook off the last remnant of his somber mood and hurried down the wide steps of gleaming stone.

The servants of Solomon carried in immense golden platters holding delicacies from all parts of his land and those of the lands and islands beyond his borders.

He watched the Queen, sitting at the low table of her dining quarters and when he saw her surreptitiously move her head closer to sniff the strange and exciting essences of each new dish, he looked away and was delighted by her childlike amazement. The steaming partridge had been stuffed with mushroom and sprinkled with the seeds of coriander and its breast gleamed with spiced oil. The roasted lamb with a touch of anise, the leban which she savored with the wide-eyed greed of a polite peasant, the sweetmeats and cakes of fig dripping with honey, all the fatted fowls and flawless fruits brought exclamations of wonder from her lips.

"And I heard long ago, in my own land," she said, "that there were often famines in this land of milk and honey."

"May there never be again," Solomon said. "Even your servants are well cared for, in their own quarters—"

She was sipping the wines of Hebron and Baal-hamon and seemed not in the least concerned for the welfare of her attendants. Still, he noted with amusement that an old watchdog of a woman stood nearby and tasted everything before allowing the Queen to eat it.

"Why are you laughing?" she asked.

He hadn't known that he could laugh and was filled with a lightness of spirit he hadn't felt for a long time. An hour with her had done this to him and he longed to tell her of it, but there was always the old one at her side, or Tamrin, the Grand Vizier, who had gone to join the guests in the great hall.

"She tastes your food before you touch it," Solomon said, "and she sips your wine."

"I inherited her from my mother, who believed that Queens live longer than their wine tasters."

"You are in Jerusalem now," Solomon said. "I assure you we have lost only one guest that I remember. From overeating—not poison!"

"Then King Solomon has no fears?" She gave him a sidelong glance which, but for the question, might have been amorous. He wondered, idly, if she knew that her eyes spoke a different language than her tongue. . . .

"I have found fear useless and a burden. And it accomplishes nothing. It only insults your friends, and flatters your enemies."

She looked at him so intently he found himself wondering once more what secret thought lurked in the corner of her mind; and he smiled, seeing her pass the delicately crusted sweet over her shoulder to Vashi. Meeting his glance with awareness, she arrested the gesture with an apologetic smile.

"I am pleased." Solomon drained the last of his wine. "You have decided to trust me."

"Completely," she said, and for a moment their eyes held the same intimacy that had so quickly eluded him in the throne room.

She rose suddenly and dismissed his servants with her own, then she asked Vashi to take fruit and wine up to the roof of her house.

"It is very beautiful, all this." She indicated the spacious room and the halls leading to rooms beyond, and she moved past the luxurious couches Solomon had introduced into his own land after one of his trips to Egypt. She stood at the open doorway to her gardens and the evening breeze blew the saffron layers of her skirt close to her hips and the length of one leg was exposed to the glow of lamplight. Solomon had seen more immodest costumes in Egypt and yet this display of jeweled flesh held all the blandishments of the groves in Canaan. What was it she wanted of him then? Surely a Queen had no need to use the artifice of a serving maid.

Perhaps the answer was less complicated than he thought. Employing the lure of a sensuous serving wench could imply she wished to be treated as one.

As she spoke of the beauties of his land and the luxurious quarters he had provided her, he approached her as she stood looking out at the fountain in the leaf-shadowed garden. Her shoulders were soft beneath his hands. The scent of her hair held the sun that had burnished her skin. The heartbeat at her throat leaped to the touch of his lips and raced with his own. She turned slowly in his arms. Her lips parted as she raised them to his, but he stood transfixed by the eyes, inscrutable and opaque with studied caution.

With the pain of discovery he felt a sudden anger and his kiss became a harsh need to share the pain. She did not withdraw.

He held her at arm's length, searching her face as if it held the answer to her strange passivity. Far more puzzled by his own reluctance to accept her yielding, he walked away from her and stood near a shadowed recess of the wall, waiting. The scathing rebuke expected was not spoken. He could feel her eyes on him, drawing him back to some dark depths of their own design. He reached for a small object in the niched corner of the wall and idly fingered its stone surface.

He did not take his eyes off the figurine as he turned and said, "The King humbles himself before the Queen's displeasure." He wished he could say more—that he had turned away from submissive offering because he demanded, for the first time in his life, more than the offering. . . .

When he looked up she was standing quite close to him and if there was anger in her eyes it was hidden in the faint smile with which she took the figurine from his hands and replaced it in the niche. He noticed then that the carving was exquisite in craftsmanship, ugly in design. Eyes of sapphire gleamed in a hideous face and the body, unlike the grotesque symbols of fertility in the images of the Moabite goddesses or the local

Baals of the Canaanite hill country, was a writhing contortion of evil.

"This image of Ashtoreth belonged to my mother," she said. "And now she guides the destiny of Queen Makada as she foretold the last days of Queen Belkis."

Solomon heard nothing but the name Makada.

As if she had never known the intimate touch of his hands or the kiss meant to shame the wanton movements of her body, she was self-possessed and regal. She walked to the open door of the garden and looked back at him with guileless invitation.

He followed her out into the garden and up the broad stairs to the roof of her house. And up here he looked at the broad couch covered with a gleaming coverlet of costly cloth, at the canopy which she had somehow transformed from a rich awning to one of rioting color.

"I took the liberty," she said softly, "of making a corner of your beautiful house into the semblance of my home in Sheba."

She had brought hangings and covers, and carpets of richly dyed camel's hair. Cushions of unbelievable softness were thrown against the parapet but she ignored all the signs of comfort and stood like some image incapable of deeper feeling than the polite exchange of their talk. She professed an intense interest in his pools. What was the length of these reservoirs and how did they bring the water supply to Jerusalem?

The starlight on her hair, he thought, is silver dust on a desert night. . . . "The longest is almost six hundred feet," he said, and told her of the waters it held from the winter rains and the channels built underground to the springs and pools which made a garden of these hills in the wilderness of Judah. He answered her questions about the flues in the copper furnaces and the obstacles overcome to build the roads of basalt and he thought her lips had been sweet to the touch and were now a remote shadow of scarlet. . . .

And all the while she was looking over the parapet to the housetops beyond the trees and he was sure her questions were idle stepping stones to something more important.

"You are either a devoted ruler," he said, "or a most unusual woman."

She glanced at him with polite curiosity.

"You have shown no curiosity about my wives," he said.

"I had given them no thought," she said. "I must make amends for such an oversight. Now, where do they live?"

He pointed to the palace beyond, where even at this hour the figure of a woman, young or old, passed across the lamplight of a latticed window. Some could be heard singing softly in the court garden and beneath the porticos of adjoining apartments groups had gathered to gossip softly through the spring night. And he told her that some were called wives or concubines when they were neither, but musicians or servants, old retainers or young refugees from the slave marts, each worthy of his kindest regard.

"I have heard it said you have a thousand wives."

"A great exaggeration." He laughed. "Like my reputation for riches and wisdom, it grows each time in the telling."

She shook her head slowly. "No, it is no exaggeration to speak of your wealth and your power. I came to see it with my own eyes. And I have seen."

He came closer to her and made a move to cover her hand with his own but she withdrew it upward in a graceful arc to smooth the wild fringe of hair blown across her forehead by the sharpening wind.

"Surely not all your wives were inherited or acquired in their need of protection," she said.

"No," he answered slowly and with honesty. "Some held the promise of happiness."

"Not the fulfillment?"

"That is more the question of a woman, than of one monarch to another."

She raised her shoulders in a light shrug of indifference. "To understand a country one must first know all about its king."

"Then I can tell you the King is like all other men. That is all."

"Other men do not have a thousand wives."

That was true, he agreed. "But most men seek a different woman for each different virtue—as I did. Without knowing that it is possible to find one who has the power to be all women, and banish the loneliness in which he lives."

She was silent a moment. He wished it were possible to fill the silence with his thoughts. How could he say that Naamah was the pitiable one who had no love to give and none to receive? He could not tell Makada that Mara's singing made it possible to love her silence; that Sara and Deborah were made for his wilder moods when he'd thought too much and drunk too much and needed the earthy laughter of their untutored minds; and he could not explain that the drowsy charm of the one named Leah languished after one night; for in the light of morning when she broke her bread he had been saddened to observe that she not only had the beautiful eyes of a calf, but also its eating habits. She had chewed herself out of his affections completely. . . .

"The house apart from the others," asked the Queen, "is that, too, a house of loneliness?"

He followed her glance, to the large house with the tree-shrouded garden. "It is the house of Lady Tanis," he said. "The daughter of the Pharaoh."

"You speak of her differently than the others."

"Perhaps I respect all of them, but the Lady Tanis has my highest regard."

"Doesn't this 'regard' relieve your loneliness?"

Solomon looked down on the house of the Egyptian woman and thought of the solace he had received there in the soft accents of her advice, the sympathetic listening to his aching moments of despair. . . .

[80]

"Immeasurably," he said and knew instantly by the sharp intake of the Queen's breath that she was nettled by this praise which she mistook for passion. But he did not qualify his statement. It was truth and he let it stand between them, seeing it liven her curiosity and flash across her eyes with annoyance—before it was controlled by an enigmatic good night.

Now it was ending, this first day of her coming into the land of Solomon. As surely as the moon still existed sharp and clear behind the pale shreds of cloud, so did her purpose brighten, cold and unmoving, beyond the gathering uncertainty of things unknown.

After Solomon had left the rooftop of her house, she had looked down into the garden, waiting for him to reappear and cross its pattern of light and shadow on the way up to his palace. And her eyes, like those of a jungle cat, fixed on the tall and unmistakable figure of Tamrin pressed close into the deep shrubbery of the arbor wall, away from the stepping stones which led to the gate. She saw that one of his hands covered the jeweled emblem of Sheba in his turban and the other had drawn a fold of his cape over the metallic emblazonment of the robes he had worn to the feast. Now that Solomon had passed by, paused at the gate a moment as if in deep thought, then resolutely closed it behind him, she saw Tamrin free his hands. The sun and crescent emblem shone in the moonlight as Tamrin waited for the footfalls of the King to fade into silence. The cape of the Grand Vizier swung back as he walked toward the house, allowing the glitter of his identity to stare back into the night.

"Vashi." Without turning, Makada knew the bulk of mute animal devotion stirred out of some far corner and with soundless speed was moving closer to receive orders. "Tamrin is approaching my garden door. Anything he has to say can wait until the morning. Go below and try to tell him this with the movement of your hands."

She turned and watched Vashi disappear into the shadows of the stairway. Then she heard the voice of Tamrin below, heard it grow louder as he ascended the steps. She threw a veil about her shoulders and sighed. Clumsy Vashi! Still, perhaps no sign language had yet been invented that would stop Tamrin from any predetermined course.

He appeared like a tall and shining eagle and as he made a swift obeisance she hoped his departure would be equally as swift.

"You will be pleased to hear the comments whispered in the great hall this evening," Tamrin said. "Those who are close to the king say he has never looked upon any woman as he looked on you."

"I need no one to tell me that! What else did you learn?"

"The truth of Adonijah's warnings. Everywhere is complete adulation for Solomon. Everywhere is the smell of his power!" Tamrin's face hardened. "You must walk softly, arouse no suspicions—"

"See that you do the same! An ill-timed move could destroy us instead of Solomon."

He stepped closer and she looked away from his narrowed gaze.

"You seem less certain than when you awaited the King's presence at the evening meal." The questions he did not ask hung for a moment unanswered.

She walked slowly to the safe shadows of the couch beneath the canopy, away from his probing eyes.

"Perhaps you found Solomon's wisdom great enough," he suggested softly, "to see the true reason for your visit."

This, at least, she could refute with scorn. "His wisdom! Only another name for cleverness and a quick wit. The most common serving girl holds more wisdom in her than the wisest of men—" And more knowledge of men, she thought ruefully, than the great Queen of Sheba!

She heard the Grand Vizier sigh with satisfaction.

"That is well," he said. "Now I must have your royal approval. If it please your Majesty, you will answer any inquiries of my absence for the next few days with a suitable excuse—"

"Your absence?"

"A most urgent one." He spoke quickly. "You must have heard or observed a patrol leave the palace grounds?"

She nodded. Did he think she had no servants to keep her informed, no jugglers who amused the sentries at the gates and then stole into the Sabaean guard room and whispered what they had seen and heard?

"Under the command of one named Zabud," she said, "who is known as the King's friend."

"He searches for Adonijah."

"I know." Makada smiled and contemplated the star-fired rounds of pomegranates glowing crimson in a bowl of dark leaves. "But he searches first in the wrong direction. Adonijah and his men are safe enough in their mountain camp. By the time Zabud circles the land and crosses paths with Solomon's brother, it will be too late—for Solomon."

To insure that end, Tamrin told her, he was leaving at dawn. "It can be said that my admiration of Solomon's kingdom was overwhelming and that I sought to see its wonders for myself. I'll meet with Bashir who is now approaching the borders. He will be told to gather his men of Sheba, encamp with your armies beyond any roving patrol of Solomon's. When the danger is past, he will proceed to the camp of Adonijah and make no further move until he receives the order from his Queen."

Makada agreed. "Return in two days' time," she said. She was relieved to have him out of the way, hoping her resentment of him would withdraw during his short absence. A courier could have traveled in his place, but she knew Tamrin's answer to that would be his usual one: "Trust me to trust no one."

She was alone now with her thoughts, muttering them with reproach into the deepening shadows: "Tamrin the superb tutor, the sculptor who fashioned my mind, voice and manners; who skillfully polished my knowledge, and—blundered! He caused me to be obvious with the man I would defeat, to be submissive as any priestess of Ashtoreth! Tamrin the wise one of Sheba who knows all—" Her laugh was filled less with bitterness than shame. "—He taught me all I know, still he blundered because he forgot to teach me how to be a woman!"

In a quiet rage she seized a pomegranate and was startled as the bowl of fruit floated toward her, supported by the almost invisible hands of Vashi who had once more become a shadow among shadows. Makada's eyes flashed, she hurled the pomegranate from her and it cracked against the parapet. The stain of anger showed red as blood against the white stone. She stretched out on the couch, closed her eyes and felt the old serving woman's fingers smooth the damp tendrils of hair from her forehead. Makada grew taut against the touch, fearing the gesture of tenderness she had never known would weaken the bars against the growing uncertainty within her.

"We must steal out at nights, Vashi, learn all we can, quickly," she murmured. "You and I must discover for ourselves what makes the people of this land look on their King as a friend, not as a god." She was calm now and allowed Vashi to bring a coverlet of fine wool against the coolness penetrating the canopy above. She knew sleep would never come to her in the alien rooms below. Her fingertips crept to the hollow between her shoulder and throat, moved away instantly from the bewildering, quickening recollection of Solomon's kiss. She crossed an arm over her eyes, knowing that Vashi was making signs of warning against sleeping in the open, in a strange land, where the demons of night were more evil than in Sheba.

"Have no fear, Vashi. There is only one evil spirit in this city. He lies in his lordly bed and plots to make a vassal state of my land, a humble subject of its Queen."

She uncovered her eyes and turned her head to the serving woman.

"You are the perfect slave. You are my ear, Vashi. If you had a tongue to repeat my weak and whimpering thoughts—I should have to kill you." She stifled a yawn and as Vashi nodded in slow agreement, Makada moved restlessly beneath the cover. "I wonder," she murmured, as her eyes closed once more, "if she is very beautiful—this Egyptian woman he married. . . ."

In the late hours of that night, sentries of the star-time watch bowed silently as the tall, familiar figure of their king moved out of shadow into the light of their torches and passed into shadow again, walking alone, through the streets and byways of the sleeping town.

It was not an unusual sight. A kindly fable was repeated with chuckling respect over wine cups and games of draughts that a most clever thief had turned his superstitious back forever on Jerusalem, complaining as he rode away: "How can my business prosper when the King walks at ungodly hours, day or night, and is everywhere at the most unexpected times and places?"

At the sound of footfalls, the light-sleeping eyes of an old, crippled beggar opened in slits of wariness beneath his hood of deep-rooted fear.

He stroked the landowner's two nervous lambs, cautioned the ox into silence. Then he crept noiselessly from the manger to peer through the gate of the street wall that enclosed the inner courtyard of his master's house at the edge of the town. When he saw who was passing by on a nocturnal stroll, he blessed him for lifting a useless old man from the shame of a beggar's odorous mat into the straw of self-respect, warm with the sweetness of young wool and the breath of the animals he was hired to tend. Yet even as he drowsily blessed Yahweh, the One True God, for the dignity of his late years, faint images of forgotten gods floated on the fringe of somnolence, too pale to be recalled in the light of dawn, but beckoning now for recognition, demanding the propitiation of long-forbidden worship; and as he drifted into sleep once more, his dry mouth shaped words of obeisance to the names of the Baalim who had been the lordly deities in stones and trees in the towns of his confused and wandering early youth.

And a physician emerged, gaunt-eyed, from a limestone house lovingly built by the hands of a young husband who had lived without fault yet was bowed low in the room within, rending his clothes with grief; for the lusty cries of his firstborn were drowned by the shrill wailing of old women who mourned. It was not surprising to the physician that he had been summoned too late to assist. He was looked upon as a magician of last resort—and no wonder. The leather pouch at his waist carried only the surgical instruments he had learned to use in Egypt and he had released the demons of aching pressure from the skulls of a hundred grateful warriors, wounded in the battles between David and the Philistines. The balm of Gilead was his to use, potions to be brewed with steaming figs and the hot poultices of oil, barley and cassia had drawn words of blessing along with the burst of poison from the bodies of men. He stood at the gate, the knuckles of his clenched fist showing angry ridges of white in the starlight. What good, he wondered, to carry all the prescriptions from the days of Imhotep himself, if the One who had said let there be light had neglected to say, "Let there be light in the minds of men." He spat on the ground and walked from the gate, carrying only his unlighted lamp and his ignorance of knowledge which the Lord, if He were full of mercy and justice, would have revealed to those of His children who would heal the sick and the poor. He pulled his cloak about him against the chilling memory of the house he had just left. All the while he worked by the light of wicks sputtering in their saucers of oil, he had felt the accusing eyes on him, peering with fear and superstition from dark corners of the room. An errant drifting of smoke from the clay oven had borne to his ears a sinful beseeching, a rocking, wailing prayer to the Babylonian god of healing, and the name of Ea was quickly stifled by someone who said hush now, hush and fear the wrath of Yahweh for sounding any name other than His. . . . But the voice of righteousness had drifted into wavering admonitions and was silent when the goddess of childbearing was implored by the old voice that found it sinless to pray to Ishtar when the God who spoke the word of light was speaking now the word of eternal darkness.

And when the young mother's head had fallen back and remained motionless against the sweat-streaked linen of her bed, the doctor had looked down at her with more pity than the Almighty had shown. In the immobile instant before the members of her family swarmed toward the dead in body and fell to the floor with grief, an unholy cry moved behind his set lips, asking those kneeling forms to mourn for the physician whose spirit was slowly dying within him. He had been taught to believe that no rain could quench the fire before God's altar. Before the words had been spoken by the son of David that a child, trained up in the way he should go, would never depart from it when he was old—long before these words had been spoken, the physician had been that child. He was trained in the ways he should walk. And now that his years were growing full, he wandered for days and moons at a time, and never had he strayed so far as on this night, walking the familiar streets of his city. The toes of his leather sandals appeared and disappeared with each soft whisper of his robes and he was bemused, watching them, remembering that as a child he had passed idle moments in a game of his own invention. He would pass through a room, noting a table and bench and whirl about suddenly, expecting to find that the moment his eyes were turned away, the table and bench had vanished—that all things vanished and returned only as the eyes accepted them once more.

Many years ago he had walked with his father through the fog-bound streets of a seacoast town. And he had told him of his secret game. His father grew silent and listened to the child's mixture of fear and delight as a potter materialized in front of his shop to carry his wheel inside, out of the damp air. And the child turned back quickly and found that the swirling layers of fog had swallowed the potter and since he couldn't be seen, he no longer existed. And it seemed then to the child that his father was a long time in speaking, but the words were gentle. "My son, I wonder if the potter also knows the little game?" The thought was a puzzling one and a tremor of fear came over the child, for if the potter looked upon a child as he passed by with his father, and saw them disappear into the fog, could it be that he thought the child and father did not exist? The little boy started to cry and his father carried him the rest of the way, soothing him, telling him not to see with his eyes alone. . . .

The physician's long-handled lamp clattered to the street and he looked up suddenly, shocked by the impact of a body already stooping to retrieve the lamp. "I beg your indulgence," muttered the physician, "my thoughts blinded me. . . ." He looked into the face of his King.

The son of David smiled his apologies, even as the physician made a hasty obeisance.

"Eli the physician works long past the hours of the laborer in his fields." Solomon looked about him, then said quickly, "Allow me to light your foot lamp for the path to your home—"

He moved swiftly, parted the curtains hanging at the entrance of a large goat-hair tent and disappeared inside. Only then did the physician realize he had met his King in front of the tabernacle. An ironic smile turned his thin lips and he sat down on a low stone bench near the forecourt. The foot lamp of one who wanted to believe yet found belief dying within him, was being kindled at the menorah in the Holy Place itself. In his younger days this would have been a sign, a warning that he must not cast off the covenant with the Lord. He shook his head slowly, for in his younger years that would not have been the need, for his faith was as strong as his body.

He looked toward the entrance as Solomon emerged, carrying the lamp close to his own feet as he came into the forecourt. And Eli looked at this man who was his King. He had heard Zadok's priestly blessing over that dark unruly hair. "See ye him whom the Lord hath chosen," came the words, ringing out at the spring of Gihon, "that there is none like him among all the people! Behold the King of Israel and Judah!" And Eli's heart leaped with a fresh joy at sight of the one who had stood there in the pure waters for it was a certainty, a substance as tangible as flesh, that the Lord had made His face to shine upon the son of David. And he knew a moment of hope for himself and all the others who had their secret weakness, that with a King such as this one, he had nothing to fear. He wondered if Solomon himself realized what his presence meant to a man whose mantle of faith had grown too small and worn to cover his expanding knowledge; this was a king who did not charge into battle to fight his problems, did not pace his rooftop as David had, high above the streets of the town. Solomon came down to his people and walked among them and when he spoke it was with the speech of one who shared their experiences and his words were a guide through the troubles that beset their living days. . . .

"Now then, Eli." Solomon was standing over him, handing him the lamp. "Your face is grave and the hour is late." His face brightened. "You could have avoided worry all these years and been able to sleep through the night—if you had accepted my offer."

Eli rose and sighed. He made a disparaging gesture with his hand. "You already have too many court physicians. All growing fat from lack of exercise." He took the lamp from Solomon's hand and thanked him. "You have lightened the darkness at my feet." That was all he meant to say before bidding the King good night, but he found himself telling Solomon of the young woman who had died and the hundreds of innocents he had seen perish while the wicked lived and prospered. And how was it now, that man and woman were cut down and thrust into the pit without mercy . . . and why was he, a well-educated physician, denied a fuller knowledge when it was spoken that God made us in His image. . . .

He waited for an answer, and knew there was none. There was a silent meeting of thoughts between him and the King who had said no wisdom, no counsel can avail against the Lord.

"You are a wise man, Eli," said Solomon. "Doesn't wisdom bring more vexation than ignorance? We both know that when you increase your knowledge, you increase sorrow—and your doubt."

Eli slowly turned the handle of the lamp in his long fingers. "She was only eighteen," he said. "And for all my learning I could not save her."

"Perhaps we have grown too comfortable with the knowledge we already possess," Solomon said. "Or in seeking to enlarge it, we go to teachers who have forgotten the True Source. Can it be, Eli, that we learn only in proportion to our willingness to learn? Is our history of miracles coming to a close because we are apt to close our hearts to God?"

Eli glanced swiftly at Solomon. Was the King being clever, challenging him with these simple questions unworthy of his time? But in Solomon's face there was no hint of taunting superiority. There was earnest interest, a shade too polite, and Eli smiled and knew that the King had no great problems on his mind this night and was impatient to be gone.

"You must forgive me," said Eli. "I grow old and sad, but you are still young enough to seek the answers to your own questions. Peace be with you."

Eli turned and walked down the narrow street. Solomon watched him for a moment and pitied the man who prayed for the perfect understanding which was the Lord's. "We are only men," Solomon thought, "and the disc of illumination, growing larger and brighter, creates a larger arc of encompassing darkness. . . ." He turned toward the palace walls in the distance. Need the arc of darkness bury the face of God? The contrary was true. Eli had no more learning than the King. And the King never for a moment forgot that he was but a servant of Yahweh . . . not for a moment. . . .

He quickened his pace, avoiding the streets where he could possibly be detained. He had never known an evening when his need for solitude had tolerated such persistent invasion. First the cringing man unaware of the damp stones about the cistern on which he sat, with his hands and head drooping between his outspread knees. Now there was a pitiable sight, the man who sorrowed over his fate, the one he had married. She was now screaming vile words at him from the high windows of their house, barred to his defections as husband and provider. Solomon would have walked away but the man looked up and, recognizing him, fell at his feet.

"My lord," he cried, even as doorways opened and cries of neighbors filled the street, protesting their disturbed sleep. "My lord, I am a laborer in the King's service and have willingly served my month of time in the forests of the Lebanon—for the better part of two years. And each time that I return to my house and my wife I am beset with agony which I must endure, by law, for the two months of tending my field, my house and my marriage duties . . ."

"Would you change the law?" Solomon asked.

The man clutched the hem of the King's tunic and seeing he had soiled the garment with his grimy hands he muttered an apology, swiftly abandoned in his passionate plea. "I would change the law, my King—"

Solomon frowned. Could this fool not understand that the King was no despot, no tyrant sending his strong and able men to labor in the forests, cutting trees one month out of every three? Was it cruel to enforce labor among his people when the cedars for the Temple were building their own salvation? He thought not—and made the mistake of looking deeply into the hopeless eyes of the one at his feet.

"Get up, man, and go into your house in peace," he said. "Your wife will cause you no more trouble."

"In my house there is no peace." The eyes were level with the King's now. "I married a shy one who had known nothing but her father's tent and the labor of the fields. I built her a house and she cooks now on a good stove—but she has grown vain and quarrelsome with such great wealth and treats me like the pariah dogs that eat the scraps of our table."

"Hear me," Solomon's voice grew sharp with impatience. "Tell her the King has absolved you from further labor in a far country. From this moment she has no cause to bewail your absence from the hearth one month out of three." Now, he thought, why does the fool stand gaping at me as if I had thrust a sword in his bowels?

"My lord." The man's voice became hoarse with urgency. "When I said I would change the law—it was an idle wish, a wagging of my foolish tongue. I beg forgiveness for the offense, and plead my ignorance that you may lift your words of punishment. . . ."

"Are you without your senses! Can you not know a blessing when you hear one?"

"To be forced to live three months out of three and twelve out of twelve with a contentious woman—in all humility, my lord, can it be called a blessing?"

"What would you have me say?"

The man lifted his shoulders high and spread out his hands in such a gesture of hopelessness, Solomon repressed a smile.

"Is it possible, my King, to be sent—somewhere, anywhere—"

The trembling request became a mute expression of despair. As Solomon told him to make his plea in proper order in the hall of judgment, the strident screeching of the wife assailed his ears with such force, he felt an overwhelming sympathy for anyone who must live with it.

"Have you children?" he asked, and looked toward the substantial but ill-kept dwelling.

The man had neither children nor a moment of quiet in his house, he told Solomon. His wife was barren, her hands idle, but her tongue was wicked and knew no shame—and he wept for her lost beauty that had trapped him like a fowler's snare.

Solomon searched the face for sly deceit or lust that yearned to be satisfied at a fresher well, and finding nothing but naked misery standing before him he said, "Go to the overseer of the mines in the Arabah. You will fill out your two months carrying ore to the fires of smelting—then return to your house. Your wife will work at a public loom and learn how to be a crown of pride to her husband and she will find no joy in working and returning to an empty house. You will find her soft-spoken when you return."

The man knelt in gratitude but Solomon was already moving away, followed by the echo of shrill and incoherent abuse. And at the sound, the King wondered if even Zadok, the High Priest, would not have been tempted, as the King was, to decree a sweeping law against the rights of women who brawled in their homes. He would have to report the incident to avoid confusion on the list of conscription. But he would not be criticized this time for altering a law to a circumstance. The law of labor was inviolate. It remained intact. He had merely solved a working man's dilemma—and what use was a King unable to do so?

Now, perhaps, he too could have a few moments of quiet, for the man at the cistern had been only the first of other distractions before Solomon had met the physician. He feared his words to Eli held neither logic nor comfort and he was certain those old eyes had not been deceived by the gesture of lighting a subject's lamp. It was prompted only by anxiety to shorten the accidental meeting. But under the sun of false praise in the morning bazaars, it was likely to become an incident of royal humility. It would swell in the telling until it burst like an overripe melon and many mouths would savor it as further proof of righteousness in their King.

A nagging sense of guilt turned Solomon's footsteps from the marketplace and into the ornate Street of the Silversmiths. The shop fronts were shuttered and the soft silence evoked once more the inscrutable smile of Makada as she bade him good night a few hours earlier. It had been beyond his power to close his thoughts to her as resolutely as he had closed her garden gate. And so he had avoided the sounds of long-feasting still coming from the great hall, and had gone aimlessly into the town to walk.

The interruptions tonight had been, in fact, fewer than usual. Still, it seemed that by the time he met Eli, each informal petition, each complaint lost its worthy cause and merged into gigantic conspiracy, stealing away his secret thoughts of the Queen.

His head seemed full of dew and scent of the night blooms spilling over brick walls and hanging from the rooftops. The cloth of scarlet and gold that hung over a narrow window became the breeze-driven movement of her skirts as she had stood at the garden door; the pleasing curve of an ivory vase high on a rooftop became the throat he had touched with his lips and it shone in the pallid light like the tower of David that was built on terraces, a thousand shields hanging upon it with all the quivers of the mighty men. But what woman, even a sovereign, could rise above him so strong and unassailable? He paused, breathed deeply to steady the pounding of his heart, and studied the sky above which held less mystery for him now than the woman who had entered his throne room only this day.

He was annoyed at his quick exaltation and puzzled by his own help-lessness to put aside the tremor of limbs and the beads of dampness on his forehead. It was an illness. *She* was an illness—invading his body as if it were a citadel without walls. Now that was something he might have asked old Eli. Instead of rushing into the tent and lighting the lamp from the branched candlestand before the Ark, instead of politely revealing his impatience, why had he not asked the physician a question: My heart leaps like a lame goat in the mountains, not as a sure-footed hart among the hills—and I would know if your excellent training has probed into the effects of deep emotion upon the body? Now Eli, my friend, he should have said, is there an antidote for such an affliction, for it warns me that the embrace I long for could be the end of all desire, and without desire unfulfilled, I would lose all my will and strength and joy in ac-complishment. You doubt me, Eli? Then look to your ancient scrolls and name me a man who could love without restraint and still, with his ex-cesses heavy in his limbs, lead an army to victory, create a poem in his heart, or rise to magnificence with a Holy Temple in his outstretched hand. Still, to turn one's back on pleasure was for the prophets who thrived on renunciation and fed the purity of divine vision with the foolish light of self-denial. And I, Solomon thought, am far from being a prophet.

He felt that now he had regained his sense of balance which no woman had ever succeeded, for long, in destroying. How young he had been a moment ago, to see the rich pallor of her throat in the ivory vase—

His eyes fastened on the vase, visible now through a shadow of foliage that half-obscured the edge of the newly built roof; and Solomon's voice roared down the length of the street like an angry lion's. The high window of the house framed a mat of hair, and eyes glittered down at him out of their puffed lids. The shopkeeper wanted to know who destroyed the rest of an honest man who had toiled all day in rooms below and was sleeping the sleep of righteousness . . .

Solomon bellowed at the face in the window, and the voice brought recognition and silence to all the doors ajar in the neighborhood.

"You toil *too* long in the rooms below among your silver and fine pot-tery! You leave your house unfinished above to count your profits below." He pointed a finger to the shopkeeper's rooftop. "There is a law of this land that commands every man to build a parapet of safety on the roof of his house!"

"The morning will find the bricks and mortar prepared, my lord."

"So be it," Solomon said more quietly. "And until your rooftop is safe, and the wall built to prevent the falling of innocent feet over its edge, you will hire a watchman to guard your family and neighbors from its danger."

A sigh of complaint drifted down to him. A watchman's hire was more than a shekel-weight of silver for the day!

"Pay it and gladly," Solomon warned. "Or risk the blood of anyone who plunges to death because of your neglect. Would you be a murderer?"

The word hung in the air with all the fear of its punishment. And Solomon walked away from it, angry at the peril caused by the good people, the devout and humble who prayed and slept in righteousness and pleaded innocent to the crime of carelessness.

He walked swiftly through the palace gates and not until he crossed the courtyard to the staircase of his rooms did a chuckle break through the grimness of his thoughts.

There would be no need to hold further sessions in his mind with Eli. One healthy burst of fury had swept everything from his mind, restored the balance of his emotions. All was well. The bands of sleep would fall easily upon him this night. He raced up the stairs, entered his rooms and yawned with a great sense of well-being as he threw off his cloak.

Sleep did come easily and swiftly, before he had finished muttering the prayer of his lifetime ". . . The Lord is my refuge and my fortress— His truth shall be a shield and a buckler. Thou shalt not be afraid of the terror by night, nor of the arrow that flieth by day— He shall cover thee with His pinions and under His wings shalt thou take . . ."

The bedchamber filled with deep shadow. And the King of Israel slept without dreams.

Coming up out of slumber he felt the light touch of a hand against his shoulder and his mouth parted in fragments of tender speech as he pressed it into the pillow beside him. "O that you would kiss me with the kisses of your mouth, for your love is better than wine . . . I slept, but my heart was awake . . . arise, my beloved, let us go forth, early to the vineyards and see whether the vines have budded. . . ." His eyes opened to the first canescent light of day and the coolness of the linen against his face swiftly stilled the fear that his lips, drugged in sleep, had betrayed him to anyone but old Benjamin whose hearing had waned long before his usefulness.

Solomon stretched, looked up at the old man bending over him with lightly folded hands, and he made his voice of morning prayer in a stronger tone than usual. Its volume, he hoped, would banish the shame of putting words of carnal love into the brightness of a new day, ahead of the reverence due the Eternal. "Blessed art Thou, O Lord our God, King of the universe, who hast sanctified us by Thy commandments." Only then was Benjamin free to speak and he said he had laid out the garments of blue and white for the king's audience in the hall of judgment, and the water in the basin of gold was warm for the King to wash himself.

He dressed and walked out onto the roof terrace to finish his morning fruit and to lure the birds with crumbs from the fresh loaf of his table. Bathed in the aureate glow of a rising sun the small beaks pecked at the rim of the parapet and the hollow of his hand and the wings were soft beneath his touch. He could not remember a morning such as this, when things familiar became touched with a special beauty. Perhaps, he thought, it is the first time I have opened my eyes to a day free of burden.

A strange and wondrous lightness filled him as if this time, this trembling moment were the first springtime of his life and he wondered what had become of the others; for surely yesterday was as today. The winter was long past, the rain over and gone. The earliest flowers had bloomed and disappeared without notice, for hardier blossoms appeared on the earth and would soon fade in the fierce light of summer. He realized with a touch of sadness that many days had passed since the first cutting of the barley harvest and soon the Feast of Weeks would bring in the sheaves for the holy festival; and the words of Moses and Joshua and the Levites under Zadok would be spoken without change, enjoining the children of God to gather in solemn assembly fifty days from the first cut of the scythe in the standing grain. . . .

He brushed his hands clean of the crumbs and laughed at the wild beating of wings at his feet. It was a good time of the year, when singing has come, he thought, and the voice of the turtledove is heard in our land.

He turned swiftly at a sudden sound. "And the snoring of Benaiah. . . ." he muttered, and crossed the roof to where his commander slept crouched in a corner with his mouth moving ludicrously against the approach of a bee. Stirred awake by the King's foot, Benaiah snorted, reached for his sword and was on his feet before he was awake.

As he sheathed his sword he muttered the words of obeisance to Yahweh, and then bowed to the King.

"I wanted to give you news before you go to the judgment hall, my lord."

"Have you thought of some new reason, my friend, to follow Zabud and his men?" They descended the stairs together and as they walked Benaiah told him of Tamrin's departure from the city the night before.

"I saw him leave," Solomon said. "I was near the eastern gate when he rode through with two of his aides."

"Did his leaving not strike you as strange?"

Solomon shrugged. "He's a Sabaean. And all Sabaeans are strange."

"His word to the guards filled me with suspicion."

Solomon patted the hammered gold band on the thick-muscled forearm of his commander. "I wonder how you so often narrowly escaped enemy arrows in my father's wars, with all that weight of distrust you carry in your soul."

"Perhaps that's why I survived."

The King's mood was too light to sustain the darkness of Benaiah's warning. What manner of visitor left the city gates to explore the wonders of a strange kingdom without a guide, he wanted to know, and had Solomon been informed that the two Sabaean aides had been left to camp in a mountain cave three miles away while the Grand Vizier Tamrin proceeded—alone?

"No," Solomon admitted. "I had not heard, but have no fear. The Grand Vizier has the dark look of a cormorant, to say nothing of the nose.

It sits high between his eyes and will sniff the right wind to bring him back in good time."

"I am not concerned about *his* safety."

They had reached the courtyard entrance of the judgment hall and Solomon, seeing Zadok the High Priest pause before entering to wait for him, whispered confidentially to Benaiah. "Since you are burning for an order to keep watch on a Sabaean, let your ambition be assuaged with more distinction." His mouth twitched with amusement at Benaiah's side look of wariness. "Keep an eye on the Queen," Solomon whispered. "Go to her house and escort her into the hall of judgment." As Benaiah's lips tightened with disapproval, Solomon lifted an eyebrow. "Now don't tell me you would rather pursue a voracious cormorant than walk by the side of a beautiful woman!"

Benaiah muttered, "As you wish, my lord," and Solomon watched him cross the courtyard, raising his hand sharply to right and left as he selected splendidly uniformed captains of the guard to accompany him.

Then, as if casting off a cloak, Solomon abandoned his wry amusement and greeted Zadok with great respect. The High Priest's shining white beard moved gently against his robes of blue as he spoke: "Give the King Thy justice, O God, and Thy righteousness to the royal son!"

And together they entered the large antechamber where court attendants waited with the sleeveless mantle of judgment and the ring of David on a cushion of finely woven linen with fringe of gold. As Solomon slipped the ring on his finger he looked down at the lion of Judah wrought in gold and onyx on a field of sapphire and it brought to his mind, for the first time in many hours, the thought of Adonijah. Solomon saw a lion's head with ruby eyes on the hilt of a broken dagger wrapped in linen, waiting in the bottom of his clothes chest for the brother who had turned from him, and he felt the blade touch him with sharp, swift guilt. Not a day of his reign had passed, till this, that he had not thought of Adonijah again and again, and he recalled with small comfort that the sight of his brother's wine cup—was it only last night?—had reminded him that there was still an ugly breach to be mended in the walls of the King's splendor . . .

There was something more than the usual silence of preparation as he felt the mantle being laid upon his shoulders. He could feel Zadok studying him as if he would break the solemnity of this moment with a troubling question.

On these days when the court of hearing was open to any and all petitions, Solomon put aside the differences between him and Zadok. He saw in the magnificent figure, in the brow turbaned with dignity and assurance, all the fire and zeal that coursed through the veins of Abraham's children. He was a leashed power, whose eyes burned with an authority possessed only by permission of the King. The King could argue loudly with Zadok, forgetting that the High Priest had been one of his teachers; he could scoff at the pillar of stubbornness who glumly approved the building of the new Temple, but declared with reverberating protest that the *Hekal* of the structure was desecrated by the worldly ostentation of the ten candlesticks of branched gold. Before the *Debir* as it now stood in the humble goat-hair tabernacle, before the Holy of Holies which separated the Ark from the rooms which approached it, there was only one candlestand. And the assisting Levites tended its light with a devotion not to be increased tenfold by increasing the duty in the same number. . . .

Whatever it was this time, if not the tiresome haggling over a trivial detail, Solomon knew it must wait.

The doors of the hall were thrown open and the buzzing voices of spectators, litigants, accusers and accused, visiting ambassadors and richly robed princes, fell into silence as Solomon entered.

He was not a King rising to his throne in glistening raiment on these days. He looked neither to the left nor to the right as he came into the room which had remained more as it was in his father's day. Concessions had been reluctantly agreed upon which would alter the austere and unembellished throne room of the son of Jesse. To the singer out of Bethlehem and the conqueror of the Philistines this had been a roofed and pillared symbol of his own greatness and his own humility. Solomon could not let the stature of his father be diminished in the eyes of those who inherited the thrones of David's one-time enemies. They came as vassals, it was true, but vassals had eyes to see and minds to calculate the worth and power of David's son—and so Solomon pleased their eyes and dazzled their minds with rich appointments, to divert their attention from the one object in the room which seemed not to belong: the simple acacia-wood bench on a low dais. David's throne. Only by keeping his eyes on that symbol of a King's mortality, could Solomon walk slowly across the length of the room and speak his thoughts in silence: "May the king judge Thy people with righteousness, and Thy poor with justice. Let the mountains bear prosperity. . . . May he defend the cause of the poor, give deliverance to the needy and crush the oppressor. May he live while the sun endures and throughout all generations. May he be like rain that falls on the mown grass, like showers that water the earth and let peace abound, till the moon be no more. . . ."

And when he had spoken to the King within himself, he sat and faced his people as a man. He looked about then, as the room settled into the business of the day. There seemed to be more than the usual number of spectators. He wondered at that, particularly when he saw Eli the physician sitting on a low bench. The old man sat with his fingers spread out, the tips of each hand meeting the tips of the other and his morose eyes met Solomon's smile of silent greeting with a questioning sadness. And he saw the face of Tanis, inconspicuous and serene in the background of a babbling group who bent their heads together in last minute consultation. When Zadok was seated nearby, and the officers of Solomon's court had taken their places, Ahiah looked up from his collection of wax tablets and tapped his lower lip with the point of the stylus. The scribe seemed to have lost, for the moment, his customary detachment.

"What is it, Ahiah?" Solomon leaned toward the bench on which Ahiah sat with his brother, the gaunt Elihoreph, and Jehoshaphat the recorder. "Has some foreknowledge of the day's petitions finally pierced your shell of unfeeling intellect?"

The frank surprise on Ahiah's face brought a smile to Solomon's. Then it was only curiosity intensified that had altered Ahiah's expression. He was a cool river that flowed into small inlets, explored the fissures that threatened to undermine the steep and rocky shores, and moved on, over and around the reeds and rocks that would capture his pity and beg it to linger past the time of exploring.

Solomon heard the first petitions with patience, and angry accusations were tempered by his demands for equal regard. Cattle and goats were restored to their rightful owners. A claim of inheritance between a long-absent brother and a poor man who had stayed at home to cultivate the fields of his father, promised difficulties until the smooth-tongued brother fell into his own pit of lies. . . .

Solomon, without taking his eyes from a master defending himself against charges of a laborer, knew the moment the Queen of Sheba entered the room. It was not the soft, restrained murmur among the spectators as they parted for the royal escort. Nor did he need to see Zadok's hands become rocks of angry stone. Solomon listened intently to the oil of righteousness pouring from the lips of the man who stood before him and, missing no detail, he was acutely aware of the tension that stirred his senses when the whispering stopped and he knew that somewhere—he had only to lift his eyes and mark the spot—she was standing quietly, observing him from the edge of the crowd. When Benaiah and his men took up their customary positions near the seat of judgment, Solomon knew that the Queen was seated in a place of honor and he anticipated the moment when his eyes would be free to look upon her. The voice of the accused was silent.

"You have spoken all that is in your mind and heart," Solomon asked, "and find yourself innocent of the charge?"

"I am without guilt, my lord."

Solomon turned to the servant who stood near his master, and the servant had nothing further to say. He had labored for this man two days and had received payment for only one. That was his charge and he waited for the King's decision.

Solomon asked the master: "Why did you pay him one day's wages when he labored for two days?"

"He was incompetent!"

"You must have known that by the end of the first day, yet you permitted him to work the second." Solomon fixed a stern eye on the defendant. "He is worthy of his hire. Pay him his wages for two days—before sundown."

Now, in this moment while records were being written down, while the petitioner and defendant were withdrawing to make room for the next case, Solomon could look out over the crowd. He must be casual, as if his mind and his whole being were not being turned to the woman who sat so regally on his far right. He smiled and inclined his head in her direction and the faintest of bows, with a gracious smile, was his reward. In the instant that he caught her image it was whole and complete and remained a picture of shimmering gown, jewels and deceiving stillness that faded long after the rich merchant had mumbled his quavering dilemma. Solomon willed from his thoughts the discovery that the Queen had a mole just above the pearl and coral ornament she wore above her left elbow. Yet as the merchant stood before him, elaborating on his troubles, Solomon was caressing that arm, removing the jeweled band. . . .

"As I understand it," Solomon said slowly, "if you ride at the head of your camel caravan, your servants who follow in the long and valuable train, steal your goods."

The merchant nodded solemnly.

"And—if you ride at the rear, your goods are safe, but you lose your servants' respect and obedience because it is a lowly position for such a rich and honorable merchant."

The merchant sighed heavily and his narrow face drooped in a grimace of despair. Laughter, quickly smothered, moved through the crowd. And Solomon was grateful that no more serious problem had come before him when his thoughts had been so curvaceously divided by the outlines of a woman.

"Have you tried riding at the head of your caravan, with your face turned to the rear?"

A burst of quick laughter broke from the crowd, and it was quickly silenced by the unsmiling survey made by the King.

The merchant seemed to be turning a sickly color, and he swallowed hard. "The very thought, my lord, loosens the food within me."

"So what are you to do?" Solomon considered, restraining a smile. "If you ride at the head, you lose your goods. At the rear, you lose your dignity. A difficult decision. I daresay your camels are as all other camels?"

"They are of the finest breed!"

Solomon asked: "Does that mean they carry the fragrance of pleasing odors in their breath and skin?"

The merchant shrugged. "A camel is a camel, my King."

"Then the solution is simple. If you cannot decide whether to ride at the head or at the rear—then by all means, let the *wind* decide."

The merchant stared at the floor a moment, then beamed with satisfaction and the hall of judgment rocked with the merriment of the spectators —a merriment in which Solomon noted the still-somber face of Eli, the solemn demeanor of Zadok and Ahiah. All three were looking at the old woman and young man being brought before him by irate townspeople—and the room hushed to hear the complaint.

The defendants wore rent garments of recent mourning. The man was the husband of a young woman who had died during the night in childbirth. The old woman was her mother.

Solomon glanced quickly at Eli and saw the physician leaning forward intently. So this was it. The young woman referred to was the patient Eli had attended only last night.

Each of the old woman's neighbors, in turn, condemned her and the young husband. Their wails of mourning had carried through the night air into the sleeping rooms of honest, God-fearing people, and on the breeze of lamentation there had come the unmistakable names of heathen gods!

"And more!" A red-faced man took a step forward and, pointing a finger at the bewildered old woman, shouted that her neighbors had banded together and gone into her house of mourning—

"To mourn for the lost daughter of this woman?" Solomon asked.

"To search the house for *teraphim!* And we found them! Small figurines of wood and clay. God-images!" The man took a deep breath, his eyes glittered with satisfaction at the gasp of astonishment from the spectators.

Solomon frowned. "*Teraphim* are forbidden, I admit. Still, they are the harmless household gods which our ancestors carried in their tents of wandering without offending the Eternal One."

Zadok spoke for the first time. Solomon turned in astonishment, for in all his days of hearing petitions the High Priest had kept his silence during the session.

"To keep household gods is a great sin!" Zadok thundered. He turned his fierce gaze on the old woman whose eyes were rolling with fear. "They should have been thrown out with all your pagan superstitions many long years ago!"

A shocked silence fell upon the room. Solomon spoke into it with quiet anger.

"Let me rise," he said, and got to his feet. "Take the seat of judgment, High Priest?" He turned to Zadok and made a polite gesture to the bench of David. The priest sat rigidly in his own chair and stared at the accused pair in front of the throne.

"Well then," Solomon continued calmly and turned to the accusers of the trembling woman. "Which one of you cares to wear the mantle of justice while he hurls charges against these two?"

There was no answer, only a shuffling of sandals as the townspeople gathered instinctively closer to one another, still determined and defiant.

"She's an idolatress!" said one.

The word ran through the crowd like a wind that would rise and shake the treetops of a forest.

"My lord!" The young man stepped closer to the seat of judgment. "Last night my wife died. This is her old mother who might have cried to a thousand gods with her lips but to only One in her heart—"

"Idolater!" someone cried. And still another.

Solomon silenced the room with a glance. He stepped down from the dais and as he approached the old woman, her accusers moved back reluctantly. The creature who looked up at him with the dumb eyes of a work animal still wore a huge square of coarse linen about her waist and when she lifted a corner of it to wipe her twitching, grief-lined face, a streak of flour from the apron remained beneath her eyes.

He spoke gently. "Your good neighbors took you away from the baking of your morning bread?"

Her eyes sought her son-in-law and he came to her side.

"She is ignorant of everything but her grief," he said. "She has forgotten that she called on the deities of her youth. I swear that they were as hidden in her memory as the images uncovered by these—as you called them, my lord—these *good* neighbors."

"Where were they hidden?" Solomon asked, and a chorus of voices rose to tell him they were found in a camel saddle-bag. "You all bear witness against this woman?" And again they answered that they did bear witness. "Is there anyone else in this room who would charge this woman with idolatry?" And he looked straight into the eyes of old Eli. The level gaze of the physician revealed nothing but polite interest, but Solomon knew now that Eli had come to hear his answer. Could this old woman be punished for grieving over a lost daughter, for returning to the little images of her own girlhood, the unique and family patrons which cooled the fevers of children and helped the bread to rise on a day of rain?

"Was the saddle-bag clean and polished?" he asked.

It was filthy, one of them said. It was hidden in a dark corner, another cried, and dust rose from it in a choking cloud.

The young widower said, "It is true, my lord. But in such a clean house, scrubbed to brightness every night of the year, who remembers to clean an old thing forgotten and thrown aside? What use is a saddle-bag when one does not own a camel?"

"The punishment for idolatry," Solomon said slowly, "is stoning to death. It is so written in the law."

Zadok, hearing the King's words, repeated them: "It is so written." And Solomon looked carefully into the faces of these people who accused the old woman. He saw the eyes of a woman waver and look away from him, and one of the men rubbed his chin to cover the blush of shame rising from his throat. The other two still bore the stamp of self-righteousness and it was to these two that Solomon spoke.

"You," he said to the man who had spoken loudly, "are a Benjamite?"

The man was puzzled. "It is true that I come from the tribe of Benjamin, my lord."

"You speak with pride, and rightly so. A noble tribe." Solomon saw the man swell with pleasure, then turning back to the seat of judgment, Solomon continued: "But if the youngest of Jacob's sons, if Benjamin had never been born and there had been eleven sons instead of the twelve

—what then would you be?" He took his time, seating himself slowly, drawing the long rectangle of the mantle across one knee. He looked up to find all eyes fastened on him with puzzled inquiry and he was most of all surprised that Zadok was as bewildered as the others. Only Ahiah guessed what was in the King's mind. And the scribe turned his stylus over and over in his fingers and smiled to himself with malicious glee.

"I could add," Solomon went on, "*where* would you be, righteous man of Benjamin. I can tell you. You would be nothing. Because you would not exist."

"I fail to see—"

"You will. The mother of Benjamin was the woman Rachel. When she and her husband Jacob and the sons of Leah her sister fled from the greed of Laban who was Rachel's father—what did Rachel steal and conceal in the saddle of her camel?"

The whisper moving in the crowd became a soft chant as one word *teraphim* was passed from mouth to mouth.

"Was Rachel stoned? Was our beloved Rachel accused of idolatry for carrying away the little images as she would have carried away her favorite playthings as a child?" Solomon asked the questions calmly. "Or did she live in mercy that she could die giving birth to the last of the twelve sons of Jacob?"

The head of the Benjamite was lowered and there was no voice against the old woman, not even Zadok's.

The bereaved young husband was looking at Solomon in a strange way and his face seemed to lose its bitterness. "I called the child Benoni," he whispered, "as Rachel did. 'Son of sorrow.' "

"Call him Benjamin," Solomon said, "as Jacob did. He will be the son of your right hand and bring you joy." He lifted a hand to one of the stewards and ordered a cruse of fresh drinking water. It was brought in silence to his side.

"I must refresh myself," the King said to the petitioners and the accused. "And when I have drunk I will hear the charges repeated—from the beginning, as they were spoken word for word. . . ."

He turned to the side then and, waving away the offered hands of servants, poured water into a drinking bowl and slowly drained it. He wiped his mouth with slow deliberation on a square of fine linen, folded it with precision and when he had put it aside he turned to see what he expected to see. The accusing townspeople had quietly disappeared. Only the young man, supporting the old woman, waited for his words.

"Now why are you here?" Solomon asked quietly. "Where are those who would accuse you?"

"They have gone." The young man grinned and his smile was good to see.

"Then go also," said Solomon.

Their leaving, unpunished, gave rise to a murmur of dissatisfaction.

And for a moment the room was alive with the whispers of those who defended Solomon's decision.

Petitions were concluded for the day, and still the crowd did not leave the hall of judgment. They moved in small groups, arguing among themselves. Solomon ignored them all.

He walked toward the Queen who was looking about her with a strange eagerness, listening carefully to all that she heard and when Solomon stood before her she started, and a faint color stained the amber pallor of her face.

"The King of Kings has shown great wisdom," she said. "Still, he seems troubled."

Solomon glanced over his shoulder and saw the unrelenting back of Zadok disappearing from the room.

"My High Priest and some of my officers—even the visiting elders— were not pleased with my leniency."

"What do they matter, or their opinions?" She asked the question with the candor of a child who would be instructed. "*You* are the King."

He smiled down at her. "You will learn that in my kingdom there is a force even greater than the King."

"I feel that it was my presence which so disturbed your High Priest—"

"No, no, no!" Solomon said quickly and changed the subject to the pleasanter diversions offered by the rest of the day. He must leave now to receive administrators from the northern provinces. And a problem of levies had arisen which would consume the early hours of the afternoon. But later, when his daily work at the Temple site was finished, then they would feast and the evening would be long. . . .

"Perhaps it would be well to postpone the feast." A pretty concern widened her eyes. "I should not be cause of further discord between the King and his advisors."

"I have no advisors," Solomon assured her with a tinge of impatience. "I *am* the King."

"You have made me very happy, Solomon." She spoke softly and her eyes held a promise. "Still, let me eat at your board without festivity until I am sure your priests know that I wish you no harm."

They could have been alone in this vast room. At the sound of his name on her lips, Solomon was filled with an ecstatic yearning. Forcing his eyes from the Queen, he sought the only one who could restore him to himself. And he sent a steward to hurry quickly, and bring the Lady Tanis to him before she stepped out of the side archway and disappeared.

When he looked back at Makada he was surprised to see dark anger on her face, but it was so fleeting, so quickly transformed into a soft radiance that he knew he must be mistaken.

"You showed an interest last evening," he said.

"In meeting the Pharaoh's daughter?" She seemed to rebuke her failing memory. "Naturally. I am most eager."

Tanis stood beside him, with her lady-in-waiting at a discreet distance from the royal group.

Two women, so unlike. The one gracious and understanding with a breeding of endless centuries in her veins. He could look at Tanis and feel the cares of his office fall away as into a quiet pool, unruffled—undisturbed and undisturbing. She was acknowledging the introduction with an invitation to the Queen of Sheba.

"I should like very much to see your garden and your house," responded Makada.

And Solomon saw them leave together, the narrow sheath of Tanis' gown, her angular headdress and erect bearing contrasting—so cruelly—with the creature of indefinable allure who walked beside her: The unknown woman that he would give his kingdom to know! And he wondered if David in the stifling heat of a summer's night had gone out to his rooftop and looked down on the house of Uriah where Bathsheba was bathing and felt as strongly the urge to lie down with such beauty and to completely know it. . . .

Behind him the main doors were flung open by soldiers and in the instant of shrill cries and shrieks he saw that Tanis and Makada, arrested by the brawling sounds of fighting women and the rough voices of guards, had turned at the archway to watch the cause of the commotion.

Solomon scowled and was glad to see Benaiah rushing forward to take charge. It was not seemly to bring such coarse and vile women into a calm court of justice. They were being restrained from scratching at each other's eyes and their clothing was torn and stained from fighting in the streets. A group of people from the town followed as the women spat: "Pig!" "Harlot!" "Thief!" And someone cried, "Let the King judge who is mother of the child!"

Solomon moved out into the center of the room and only then did the room become quiet.

He looked at the bedraggled slatterns who screamed in strident voices and they, too, lowered their voices and stared at him with sullen faces. The dark-haired wench mumbled, "She says I stole her child!"

One of the soldiers brought an infant in swaddling clothes before the King and the eyes of the other woman were terrified. She blew a ragged stream of hair from her face and cried out: "The child is *mine!*" And before the soldiers could restrain the dark-haired one she had clawed the arm of the other and blood flowed, unheeded, to her elbow and dripped on the floor.

The spectators, aware of a growing crisis, were subdued and looked on with silence. A soldier said he had arrested the women for disturbing the peace. The dark-haired woman had run out of a house with the child in her arms and the other woman had catapulted from the door in pursuit and they fought over the child.

"We live in the same house, that lying woman and I!" The dark-haired one thrust out her chin and spoke clearly. "Each of us, but three days apart, gave birth to a son—"

The other broke in: "Her child died in the night! She stole my baby as it slept by my side and claims it as her own. She laid her dead child in my bosom and when I rose at dawn to feed my child—it was dead—but it was not *my* child!"

Solomon raised his hands to quiet their shrieks as each flung the epithets of the streets in the other's face.

Solomon wished to be spared this decision. He could look into each face and find nothing which revealed the truth to him and his uneasiness grew within him. For the first time in many months he was confronted with a dilemma beyond solving. And the hush of the room, the complete silence added to his deep concern. Then the faces around him merged and flowed into an indistinct pattern as he withdrew his mind, but not his eyes, from them. And it seemed that he knocked at a massive gate of gold which opened silently to his touch and he heard a gasp of horror and astonishment rise from the crowd as his lips opened and commanded Benaiah to draw his sword.

There was no movement in the room and he saw it clearly now, the reproachful eyes upon him, the anxiety and fear—and he grew angry to think the words that had come to his mouth and were spoken, fell like pebbles lost in a pool.

"Benaiah! You heard my command! Unsheath your sword and quickly! Or have you suffered the fate of Lot's wife and are nothing but a pillar of salt!"

The sword was drawn.

"Now look at me," Solomon said to the two women. "I cannot tell which one of you speaks the truth."

"I speak the truth!" screamed the dark-haired woman.

The other was silent. Her eyes were on the child at Solomon's feet.

"Pick up the child, Benaiah. Remove its swaddling clothes—and divide it with your sword!"

The eyes of the silent woman filled with panic and she pressed a hand over her mouth. The dark-haired woman watched impassively as the child was freed of its clothes and its small hands reached up to the point of the sword above its head.

"The living child shall be divided. Give one half to one woman, and half to the other."

Benaiah hesitated only a second, then he raised his hand for the thrust and the blade gleamed as the terror-stricken woman wrenched free from the soldier's grip and flung her body protectively over the child's. Her hair streamed on the floor and she pushed it back from her face as she looked up at the King.

"My lord," she gasped, "give this woman the living child. But do not slay it. Let no harm come to it!"

The dark-haired one laughed bitterly. "Let the child be neither mine nor hers—but divide it according to the King's judgment!"

Solomon felt the hard core of uncertainty dissolve within him.

"Sheath your sword, Benaiah," he said quietly. "Let the rightful mother pick up the body of her child she defended for she is the real mother."

The woman, sobbing with relief, clutched the infant to her and the crowd burst into cheers. Solomon sat very still for a long moment and his mouth was dry and he scarcely heard the approval of the people as they dispersed, nor the quiet words of Ahiah speaking to him.

"Wisdom is a treasure above all riches, Solomon," he whispered. "Take care that it is not taken from you."

And after he had gone, Solomon wondered how he had spoken the words to slay the child and how he knew that only the true mother would sacrifice her living child to another, rather than see it die. . . .

The mother of Solomon rose at a late hour from her comfortable bed that morning. A weariness had overtaken her at the feast in the great hall the night before. Whenever her son was absent from the royal board Bathsheba felt obliged to mingle with the guests until the last envoy or ambassador had sipped the wine remaining in his bowl and had retired to his rooms.

She never admitted to herself that her stately presence on these occasions was more a habit of vigilance than hospitality. Beneath the unhurried dignity with which she listened to the most tiresome visitor, she dispatched an army of sensory tentacles into the bright glow of talk at the table, and into the shadowed corners of the vast room. Even as she responded to a compliment from a vassal prince out of Moab, or inquired after the family of a distinguished viceroy from the north, her invisible sentries hovered over the sudden merriment of a group beyond her sight until assured that the laughter did not disguise a hidden conspiracy. Then they moved on to search out the words muffled in an alien beard and to probe the silences that lingered past the time required to select another morsel of meat or to refill a wine cup. At the close of the evening, after such a day of splendor, she had been content and slept well.

When the curtains of her bedchamber were parted the few but choice jars of fine glaze and silver on her dressing table were struck by the brilliance of the sun.

Having dressed and eaten with an extraordinary sense of well-being, she allowed herself to smile at the sullen handmaiden who would soon be urgently needed in some other part of the palace—if Solomon had not forgotten his promise.

"The day is touched with the light of summer," Bathsheba said, and looked quickly away from the younger face with its lines of wintry bitterness. "Come up to the roof with me, Abishag. You may help me spin out the new thread. . . ."

She was sorry now that she asked the girl to pick up the spindle and whorl and sit with her in the warmth of the sun. A thousand suns could not melt that droop of Abishag's lower lip. In some remote corner of her impatience, Bathsheba wished to advise the girl. She told herself it was the kind thing to do; but as she paused in her deft handling of the thread and spoke words of comfort, they were balm to her own conscience. She could say with a sigh that it was a pity about poor Abishag but could one do more than tell the child she was being foolish and for the love of all that is beautiful and glorious in a garden, why bury one's youth by walking in the weeds?

It was no use. The girl, Bathsheba told herself, was beyond help. She sat there at the feet of the Queen Mother and dutifully manipulated the length of thread growing beneath Bathsheba's fingers. She appeared to be listening, but with an irritating civility.

"Does it mean nothing to you," Bathsheba asked, "to know that the King and I have your welfare at heart? Or is it that you prefer to continue as a mere handmaiden?"

"My wishes are of no importance, my lady," said Abishag, smoothing the skeins lying soft against her palm.

The beautiful day was becoming chilled for Bathsheba by the presence of this dull lump of ingratitude at her feet. She looked down at the pale eyelids of the boneless little Shunammite. They were lowered over eyes that swam in a pool of hatred.

Exasperated, Bathsheba ordered Abishag to go below and care for the saffron veil which had been stained the night before by careless wine. Abishag obeyed, and hearing her soft footsteps moving toward the stairs, Bathsheba grew taut, opened her lips and resolutely refrained from calling the girl back to her. She had been on the point of spitting out her resentment of the Shunammite's thinly veiled insolence. But asperity would only convince the little fool that she was justified in loathing Solomon and his mother.

Her words would have named a day shortly after Solomon's coronation. They would have evoked the very image of Adonijah and a daring request. Even now, the hands of Bathsheba trembled on the spindle as she recalled the cold light in the eyes of Haggith's son on the day he had begged to speak with Bathsheba. And he had assured her he came peaceably.

"My lady knows that the kingdom was rightfully mine and that all Israel set their faces on me, that I should reign." How cleverly, how calmly he spoke the words that disguised the swords' points of a threat. "But the kingdom is turned about and is become my brother's," and he added hastily: "—for it was his from the Lord. . . ."

He would ask a petition of the King's mother, and she had looked at the height of him from head to toe and said, "Say on."

"I pray that your son—who denies you nothing—will grant me Abishag the Shunammite to wife."

A fierce tumult had beaten in Bathsheba's breast and through it she saw the cruel line of Adonijah's mouth, the direct gaze that spoke outright and eloquently for the throne while his lips mouthed lies of an emotion he did not possess. To covet a woman who held the name of concubine to the King! The meaning of his request was clear to her and she restrained an impulse to shriek out this subtle treachery. "I will speak for you," she said quietly, "unto the King." And when he had bowed and withdrawn she hurried to find Solomon, to warn him that Adonijah must be slain! She had searched everywhere, had heard a rumor that her son was sitting with Ahiah, but he was not in the house of the scribe; neither was he walking in solitude on the Mount of Olives, where he so often walked. Her messengers returned with no news and she had dismissed them and gone with Benaiah down into the streets of the town itself, protecting her fine skirts from the touch of beggars' hands as she searched for a man who must be told that a king belittled himself by treading the same stones as common men.

The passing of hours brought a reasoning light. She sat at the right hand of her son who wore the crown with such sadness in his eyes. She meant to tell him, as if with understanding and genuine sympathy for the plight of lovers, that Adonijah had made a reasonable request. Once spoken then, in the face of his court, Solomon would have no alternative to the law. And the veiled threat of Adonijah would find its end before it sprang into life. Solomon had failed to hear her out—that day. And soon after, Adonijah had disappeared and the need to reveal his devious plot against the throne diminished with the days, but did not expire. A moment such as this—with the Shunammite's sour mouth closed against all speech but the inanities of servitude—brought the full blast of recollection dangerously before her.

Bathsheba released a pent-up breath and put away her weaving to clear her mind. She walked to the parapet to examine the small white blossoms springing from a potted bush. To reveal Adonijah's daring request would only inflame the girl's bitterness. The lovesick little fool could not possibly know that above his desire for any woman, Adonijah loved himself. Abishag was not even a great desire. She was a forbidden name. To ask for it in love was a ruse to force Solomon's sword against his brother's. To kill the King in self-defense would assure his favor with the people, for the support of Adonijah was secret but strong at that time. And if Solomon, out of kindness, relinquished Abishag to his brother, the people would have turned from their new King and named his softness of heart a moral weakness in the face of the law. The High Priest and the elders would have risen in protest. Either way, Solomon would have forfeited his throne.

She saw it now as Solomon must have seen it—when he had so cleverly avoided listening to her on that day. And she marveled again at the son she had borne who held such wisdom within him.

The air was sweet and silent—unusually silent.

She gazed over the parapet. The gardens were partly visible and through the trees, near the courtyard entrance to the hall of judgment she saw soldiers of the guard gathered close, craning their necks to see into the room. She smiled to herself. Solomon, her son, was once more drawing forth the admiration of his people. The high and the lowly were warmed and exalted by the child she had given to David and a great pride engulfed her. On such occasions she could look far across the courts and burgeoning gardens to a corner of a palace rooftop. The roof of David's captain, Uriah the Hittite. The house had been glorified with new stone work and stout cedars and was occupied by Benaiah and the King's guard. But it was still the rooftop where a slender, seductive young Bathsheba had boldly looked into the King's eyes as she bathed; and her Hittite husband, who was cold to her embraces, had died where David had sent him—into the forefront of hot battle with the Ammonites. The siege of Rabbah was now long past, but it had been many years before Bathsheba, as David's wife, could look at the rooftop that witnessed her naked allure and not see the guilty finger of Nathan the Prophet accusing David of murder and naming her an adulteress. . . .

Now the doors of the judgment hall spewed forth an excited throng and the guard resumed their positions as a slattern held a child close to her torn dress and crooned over it as she disappeared down the path to the palace gates. Snatches of talk came up to the parapet, murmurs of awe and amazement. And then a side door opened for a unique procession. It moved through the gardens and past the fountain near the joining of paths. And it turned into the road leading to the house of the Pharaoh's daughter.

Bathsheba looked down at the sedate princess who was Solomon's wife and she was pleased, for she admired humility—in other women. The Egyptian servants of Tanis walked before and behind, clothed decorously for their appearance at the King's hall of judgment. The color of their raiment was subdued, as the King preferred it to be on such an occasion, but out of further respect to his wishes, Tanis had ordered that no robe should be drawn at the waist with the crossing of the girdle cloth looped at the top to signify the sacred *ankh* emblem of life in their native land. Later, they would reappear in the fine linen garments of Egypt. Tanis herself would put aside the modesty of her turban, adorn her head with the golden serpent and put jeweled slippers upon her feet.

But this other one now, this woman from Sheba who carried herself with such easy arrogance . . .

She was trailed by soft-stepping servants with a savage beat sleeping in each naked foot, as if at any moment all of them—even the huge woman who followed her—would break into some Canaanite screams and leap with madness into the air. . . .

She was conjuring up fears which did not exist. The Queen of Sheba was a strange and bewitching creature, it was true. A lesser man than Solomon could possibly find her completely enchanting. But one had only to pause a moment and see beyond the smooth walk, the studied grace of each gesture . . . A woman to fear.

As the little procession disappeared, Bathsheba's fingers closed around one of the blossoms and it fell at her feet. She had not meant to destroy the flower and it made her sad to see its whiteness crushed. She picked it up and smoothed the petals as she eased her thoughts. She must conquer this urge to see evil in the shadows of a room, the innocent laughter of the King's guests, or to look upon the visit of a foreign queen with a shudder of misgiving.

A thick wall of green vines surrounded the house of the Pharaoh's daughter. Rows of palm trees thrust their gaunt necks through the tangle of leaves, like wild-haired sentinels captured on their own battlements. Their hungry shadows stole across the garden to reach the table where sweetmeats and cooling drinks had been abandoned by Tanis and her guest.

Makada had been shown the rooms of the house. Lofty pillars fashioned by craftsmen from Egypt, finely embroidered hangings, luxurious couches and soft rugs told her Solomon had transported all that was familiar to the princess in her homeland. And she wondered why. Her first cool appraisal of the Egyptian woman had been subtly altered in these past few hours. There was no beauty here to envy, nothing to be seen in the fine-boned face with its chin thrust forward as she walked. The voice was soft and soothing, still Makada had heard other voices more pleasing to the ear. Why was she the favored one? As they walked now through the gardens, Makada listened to the voice at her side, explaining the symbol of reincarnation held in the seeds of the lotus. Here were her pools of water lilies and the cyclamen had been planted by her own hands. Makada felt a moment of disdain for royal fingers that dug into the earth, and she wondered at anyone looking down into the sea of pink and white blossoms with such tenderness. Blooms such as these covered the slopes in the land of Sheba, yet she had never stooped this way to study the petals with a concentration due only an improved blade for the weapons of her warriors.

She was aware that she had withheld her murmurs of interest too long. They were passing one of the inner gates and Makada spoke of the carving on the glazed tiles. Tanis answered with such alacrity, Makada knew the Pharaoh's daughter was only being courteous, covering her silent, pleasing thoughts with harmless talk. Since leaving the hall of judgment she had moved as one in a dream and her eyes held the memory of a wondrous vision. Makada could not understand it and her curiosity stirred with unbearable intensity. Had anything so momentous happened? If there had been great wisdom in the matter of the two women claiming the same child, she failed to see it. Why was the dividing of the child received with such horror, and the ultimate decision with such awe? The reverence had shone in Tanis' eyes too. And Tanis had whispered, as if to herself: "He is the head of all nations, people who have not known him will bow and kiss his feet. Foreigners come crying to him and those who have lost heart. . . ." Makada had spoken without thinking: "Is he a demon or a god?" And Tanis had lowered her eyes to the path under her feet. "A god—as every man is a god to the woman who loves him." Makada had not answered. Blinded by Solomon's cleverness, for it was nothing more. If there was greatness in him, it was evil magic. And anyone who had watched him in that moment of indecision before he ordered Benaiah to slay the child—anyone could have seen that his soul communed with spirits. And she had noticed something else. He had touched and turned the ring upon his finger. Anyone who stole the ring from him, would steal his power. The conviction was strong and found words. Tanis had come out of her reverie then and her eyes danced with polite amusement.

"His ring?" She shook her head slowly. "No, my lady. There is another source for Solomon's—magic." But she had said no more and now the hours of small things stood between them and not until they approached a roofed work-shed, almost hidden by high foliage, did Tanis lose something of her abstract manner.

One of the Egyptian craftsmen working within, escorted them to an inner room where a portrait bust of limestone was being fashioned on a pedestal of white-flecked granite. Tanis looked at the replica of her own features.

"My father ordered this," she said with a wry smile. "The sculptor is not as gifted as Thutmose of El Amarna—but then, neither is the subject as inspiring as Queen Nofretete. Her beauty still lives in the image he made of her."

Restraining her lack of interest in dead queens, Makada murmured politely: "She was the queen who journeyed to the land of Punt?"

"You speak of Hatshepsut."

The name vaguely recalled old Belkis, rolling her hooded eye at the King of Edom as she boasted her burial tomb was vastly superior to the ancient Egyptian queen's. With an imperceptible shudder, Makada closed her thoughts on the memory and the fleeting glimpse of eternal darkness that shadowed it; for beyond that abyss voices long unborn spoke the name of the Queen of Sheba who visited Jerusalem many ages ago with a caravan that glittered with precious jewels for the King. . . .

As they left the workrooms Tanis told her Nofretete was the wife of Ikhnaton.

"And who was he?" Makada sighed and sat beside the Pharaoh's daughter on a bench in the seclusion of an arbor.

"The King of Egypt who worshiped only one god. He believed the sun was Aton and ruled the universe—"

Was it possible, Makada wondered, that Solomon could listen to such idle talk as this?

"—I have often wondered," Tanis said, "why this belief died when the

King died. And why the God of Moses did not expire with his great prophet in the mountains of Moab. . . ."

"How she rambles on," Makada thought. "She speaks of monotheism while I wish to speak of Solomon." There was an indefinable mystery in this garden somewhere. Her eyes had seen everything, even the crown of Isis on the basalt image in the altar grove. The incense spiraled from the burnished bowls beyond the trees that made a hidden, secret thing of the Egyptian woman's worship. Not even the falcon head of Horus, or the image of Osiris surrounded by painted birds and apes of obsidian could be seen unless one knew the devious path which led to them. . . .

Time was growing short, and she had learned nothing. She would be blunt.

"Did your father as Pharaoh also order your marriage to King Solomon?"

Makada saw a fleeting expression of pained embarrassment cross the face of Tanis. Makada boldly cast away the knowledge that the embarrassment was for her own lack of sensibility.

Tanis answered quietly. "It is part of my heritage to accept authority." Her long fingers laced themselves placidly in her lap. "Perhaps it is a blessing to have such a training, especially when one has been born without beauty?"

Makada suspected such cultured manners. Realizing her own had suffered by comparison, she met the other woman's urbanity with equal ease.

"A Pharaoh's daughter has no need for beauty—if she is the favored one of the King."

A look passed between them which Makada could not identify. "The Queen is most gracious," Tanis whispered. "I was happy to come here and if I seem to have the confidence of the King it is flattering."

"Then it isn't true that you share his innermost thoughts?"

"No one does," Tanis said and her face grew thoughtful with a hint of concern. "He has no advisers. No prophet's lips foam in his presence since the death of Nathan who formerly pointed the way. The King listens well, even to fools. There is wisdom in that, too, for in the listening he has sometimes caught a gem of common sense overlooked by most men. No, the King has given many of those close to him an impression he fosters wisely. To close the door on free speech Solomon would be closing the door to his own power. He listens, as I said. But he acts as his conscience dictates."

His conscience. She would not ask the meaning of that from the Pharaoh's daughter. At the moment there were other meanings to probe with caution.

"You are content, then, to be one wife among many?" Makada looked at this strange woman who must be made of stone.

"I am more than his wife." Tanis spoke with trembling pride. "I am his friend."

"My Grand Vizier once told me that friendship was an end to marriage." Perhaps she was overstepping herself, but there was no turning back now. "What was the beginning?"

Tanis smiled. Makada had seen expressions such as this on the faces of mothers who indulged the foolish questions of their children. She had never seen it on the bloated flesh of Queen Belkis, still it was to be recognized. She straightened and rose from the bench, prepared to leave. Tanis took a step quickly at her side. "Forgive me," she said. "I am not offended, nor should you be. I smiled out of amusement at your directness—and perhaps out of envy. You are so young—so very beautiful—" For an instant a wistful shadow clouded the eyes of the princess. "The beginning? I will answer you plainly." As they walked toward the outer gate, Tanis said that the Pharaoh of Egypt had gone up and captured a strategic fortress that lay between his land and Solomon's. He had burnt it with fire and had slain the Canaanites who dwelt in the city and had given it as a dowry to her when she became Solomon's wife. . . . "So you see," she said, since Solomon's army was not yet strong enough for wars he could not capture and subdue the stubborn people of Gezer. The city was necessary to the peace of his country. So he married it."

Makada was beginning to see. "A political alliance."

Tanis nodded.

"Were there many—others?" How many times had this powerful leader made peace with hard kings by whispering soft words to their daughters?

"Many others," Tanis said. "And you are wondering how Solomon made peace outside his nation and risked the endless bickering of female rivalry within his own walls."

"Perhaps he has found some magic potion to quiet their jealousies."

Tanis laughed. "Not even Solomon could do that."

"Why not?" Makada asked with sharp eagerness. She had been told that Solomon sat like a fat spider in a web of alliances. Why could he not control the rivalry among his wives? She waited anxiously for the answer.

Tanis shrugged slightly. "They are women. With the weaknesses of all women. They are vain and spend hours before their mirrors—" her voice broke in a mocking warmth—"just as I do."

"You love him." It was only a word to Makada.

"I do not know," Tanis said. "Perhaps. I knew the reason for his marrying me—still when I learned what war would mean to his country—I did not resent being the instrument of peace. He needed time to bind together his people in a union that will defy time itself. And he will. If I felt close to that ideal—then perhaps that is love."

"You are a royal daughter," said Makada, "with the soul of a slave."

"The Queen of Sheba has never loved," Tanis said. "Or she would know the joy of being a slave."

The rebuke was lost on Makada. "You have no fear that the King will one day rule over your father's land?"

"No more fear than you have for the safety of your own kingdom, my lady."

Makada glanced at her swiftly to detect some hidden irony. There was none. Or perhaps Solomon had instructed her well, to put the Queen off guard, to throw an innocent smile over the King's dark schemes to conquer.

It was a game she could play. She praised the goodness of the King and wished that she might spend many days learning the secret of his wisdom.

She felt Tanis' eyes studying her as they walked through the late shadows of the garden.

"I am relieved to hear that," she said finally.

"Relieved?" Makada arched her brows.

"I am glad that you see his greatness and know you have nothing to fear —because you have the power to hurt him."

Makada paused and turned a bland face on the Pharaoh's daughter. "Now why should I wish to harm Solomon?"

"There is no reason—I beg your forgiveness. It was a moment's foolishness." She smiled. Her teeth were an even line of white in the growing dusk.

Seeing the slow approach of the women, the striped headcloths of Egyptian sentries bowed low. They opened the grilled doors of the gate and waited with arms crossed, like rigid figures of some ancient sovereign's cartouche. Somewhere from the hidden porticos of the house came the faint metallic jingle of a sistrum, and Makada wondered what manner of king was Solomon. He permitted an alien instrument to sound out the tears of Isis swelling the River of Egypt with her mourning for Osiris, who died each year with the cutting of the grain, and disappeared into the underworld with the coming of winter. Surely his gods would cast thunderbolts from the sky in jealousy.

She chose her words with care. "Are you content," she asked, "that I have no evil reasons for visiting your lord and King?"

"I am content."

Makada thanked her with a slight inclination of her head. She was pleased, she said, to have the confidence of the great Pharaoh's daughter. Since the ruler of Egypt was the incarnation of Amon-Ra, the approval of his daughter was in reality a blessing from the powerful sun deity himself. There was cold reason behind her flattery. She knew what her own deities could do to one who offended them. She had seen men pluck out their eyes at the order of Jaghuth, and Kawim, the powerful, had dried up the springs and wells of Sheba with a mighty blast of his hot breath—the year that Sami could not supply the fiery mouth with a hundred pieces of living human flesh.

"I have a thousand and one questions to ask the King." She spoke as one who wished above all things to be trusted. "If I am too constantly by his side, will it humiliate the daughter of the Pharaoh and Amon-Ra in the eyes of the court, or cause her a moment's vexation?"

"I was once told that to the hungry soul all things are sweet. I accept my portion without envy or fear—for I have nothing to fear," Tanis said, "—from any woman."

Makada suppressed a smile. How did such a spare and immaculate body harbor twice her weight in conceit? But aloud she said the Pharaoh's daughter was noble to rise above the blight that withered the hearts of ordinary women.

Tanis smiled. "I am jealous—but not of the Queen of Sheba."

Makada swallowed the sharp retort that had leaped to her tongue.

"Of what then?" she asked as if it were of no importance.

"Solomon will never belong completely to me or to anyone else." The Pharaoh's daughter seemed to be speaking softly to herself. "Because of his God."

"Which of his gods commands such loyalty from him?"

"There is only the One."

"Can the King's enormous wealth not afford more than one god?"

A trace of scorn had escaped her lips and Tanis smiled at her as Vashi had last night when she was curious to know if the Egyptian woman was so beautiful.

"His wealth *is* the One God."

"When you married Solomon why did you not also embrace his God?"

"He did not ask that of me."

With the shadow of tenderness soft on her wide thin mouth, the daughter of the Pharoah did possess something close to beauty, an inner shining that puzzled Makada.

"If he had?"

Tanis spoke with slow deliberation. "I don't know. It is not a simple thing, to relinquish the belief of your fathers. I have no wish to turn my back on the comfort and nourishment of my early years. I don't believe it is possible. I could stand before the Ark of his God, perhaps move my lips in the songs of his worship, still I would be fearful that when the time came for my lifeless heart to be weighed on the scales it would know the fury of Thoth. Still, I read the forbidden rolls that tell of the one deity of Ikhnaton. He was believed to have a loving heart that looked on men with mercy—the same as Solomon's God—so I sometimes wonder—" She paused to watch a servant kindle the first lamp of evening near an obelisk marked with the hours of the day. The light flickered across the gnomon and the shadow of the angular bar wavered between the markings. "You see?" Tanis indicated the pillar. "The light from the oil is coming from below. He will light another at the side—and still the reading will be false. I often look at this, when the shadows fall early in a walled-up garden—and I wonder if the blaze of seventy lamps placed all around by the hands of men could shed upon it the true brilliance of the sun above." She apologized with a swift smile. "Forgive me. You speak with such candor, such directness, and I answer you with wretched riddles."

Makada could not see what an inaccurate time-telling device had to do with light created by man or the light of the sun. But if anything was to be learned from this day with the Egyptian woman, there was need of restraint.

She remarked politely on the purity of the stone lines with their pointed top and Tanis said it was nothing. The flat rectangle of basalt that used to lie over there, where the iris now grew, had been a great work of art. The markings had been exquisitely carved. And she had brought with her from the Pharaoh's court a beautiful clepsydra with a delicately wrought vessel to catch the precise amount of water that dripped through a carefully calculated hole in the upper container. It gave her the hour and moment at any time of the day.

"I had them all removed," she said, "all but this pillar which is more ornament than timepiece. It seems to offend the King less than the others."

What had waterclocks and sundials to do with the King? Makada sighed inwardly as she asked the question, for she was surely wasting more of her time than all the clocks of Egypt could ever record. . . .

The passing of time, Tanis told her, assailed the King with the affliction of a disease. "He is blessed with outward composure," said Tanis, "but the burden of the crown weighs heavily within him. He would melt it down with an inner fever of impatience. . . ." She lifted her chin high and arched her long neck with a look of fleeting concern. Makada could not tell if it was caused by her thoughts or the sudden gust of wind that rattled the thick leaves of the vines against the east wall and moved the long earrings of the Pharaoh's daughter. For an instant, though the visiting air blew hot against the flesh, Tanis seemed chilled as if by a warning. She crossed her slender arms against the pectorals and amulets heavy-jeweled to compensate the meagerness of flesh beneath. "This is strange," she said, and brushed her arms slowly as if shedding the memory of the breeze that had come and vanished on such swift wings. "It is not the hour or the season—" She seemed to be smiling away some unknown fear. "They call it the wind of the Lord that blew out of the Wilderness and piled up the waters for them to pass safely through the Sea of Reeds—"

"You were telling me the King is consumed by some inner force—" Makada reminded her, and Tanis lost some of her tension as they resumed their walk.

"When his head is heavy with fatigue he often seeks out the quiet of this garden. He says every man is entitled to a garden of peace, an island of green that shuts out the turmoil of a sea. If he can't find it in his soul he can at least lie here without looking upon shadows that mark the shortness of our sojourn on earth."

Makada unconsciously quickened her steps. The people in this land, even the foreign woman here, spoke too much of their souls. As if someone held them to account for all their actions! Perhaps the low ones of the earth could indulge this fancy, after they had accounted to their kings and queens—but the King himself was above such foolishness.

"He feels," Tanis was saying, "that the task before him is greater than the one lifetime he can give to it."

They reached the gate and it was like stepping out of a room with drawn curtains into the rioting brilliance of another world. A coolness from the far sea seemed to soothe Tanis. Long spears of intense light cut through a crimson-streaked sky. They broke against the tops of stone towers and far walls and fell in fragments through the open door of the gate. The intricate pattern of the grillwork spread itself as a soft carpet beneath her feet. She turned abruptly, startled by a large and soundless shape emerging from a nearby angle in the wall.

Makada's brows came together. "It is only my serving woman." Her frown sent Vashi down the path to the shade of a sturdy terebinth and she stood beside it, waiting, motionless as the ancient oak itself.

"The poor woman," Tanis said. "Sitting in the hot sun all afternoon. If I had known, she would have been sheltered and given a cool drink—"

How could one value any opinion of the Pharaoh's daughter when she muttered senselessly over the comfort of a common slave!

Makada spoke polite words of leave-taking, but Tanis did not hear. She was looking beyond Makada's shoulder, into the high distance.

"It is so beautiful." There was wonder and awe in her voice.

Makada turned her head and looked up at the rough scaffolding defending Solomon's Temple from assault by the dying sun. The flaming crown of the hill seemed to be suspended. It had become in this moment part of the sky and was lifted up out of the earthbound shadows clinging to the lower slopes. The god of Tanis, thought Makada, has driven his fiery steeds across the heavens each day, charging first into the eastern face of his rival, soaring high and dipping low to whip fires of copper from the pillars, to reach down through the high narrow windows and lure the gold and silver from the vessels within the walls.

"A house that will endure for all time," Tanis whispered.

An ugly heap of stone and cedar overlaid with gold, thought Makada. That is how Adonijah had described this building to her. She remembered how bitterly his mouth had twisted, resenting the vast riches heaped upon this hill, wealth from all sources, trophies of war in the time of David, lavish gifts from the peaceful rich and heavy taxes from the poor.

"Wood rots," Makada said quietly. "Stone crumbles."

She had seen much with her eyes this day. Still, an uneasiness stirred within her for she had found no meaning in what she had learned. It was elusive. She reached out for it, grasping at each thin trail of smoke. It could not be held in the hand. She must search it out and hold fast before it eluded her completely and drifted away. For the first time she wished Tamrin were here. She needed him to clarify her thoughts and shape their meaning—for somewhere in the mist of her confusion was the tangible form of a weapon.

Adonijah had said the time would come when all the sheep who had been bled of their gold and labor would bleat with shame and protest against a house of worship. The army should have received this vast bounty, he said. But Makada had seen the hundreds and some of the thousands who wore the proud shields of Solomon's army and though they practiced in peace they were prepared for war. So the answer did not lie in that direction. . . .

"It will endure," Tanis said again.

"I must visit this house before long," Makada murmured and turned swiftly at Tanis' small gasp of astonishment.

"It would never be permitted." Her eyes were wide, her tone softened. "Women are not welcome—during the construction."

Unbelieving women, Makada said to herself, and waited for Tanis to continue.

"It is the High Priest and the Levites who object."

A sense of approaching revelation cautioned the Queen's tongue. "Surely the King would allow you."

"Perhaps," said Tanis. "But I have no wish to cause dissension."

The woman was bloodless, Makada thought. Had she no spirit at all?

"Then I, too, must refrain." Her smile, she hoped, was candid.

"Thank you. You must understand why I fear the slightest interruption in his work."

Makada's heartbeats raced to the brink of discovery.

"I am sure you have good reason," she said with a casual movement of her hand. When Tanis hesitated, the Queen caught her breath. Perhaps she had been too clever, too convincing in her pretense.

"He has permitted me to worship as I please—"

"But you keep your gods hidden."

"That is of no importance," Tanis said. "It is the freedom of belief which holds me grateful to my lord. He has never tried to change my views."

"Is the god who lives on the high hill made of more precious stone than yours?"

Tanis looked down, drawing the faintest of smiles from her face. She followed a square of moving shadow with her toe. "No," she said quietly. "My gods are made of finest wood and costly stone—but not his."

"Then what a pity it is you hide them from the sight of others."

"That is the last thing I could wish."

Makada wondered at the deep intensity that lay within the whispered words.

"If I did such a thing," Tanis went on, "it would undo everything the King must accomplish. He made a vow to his father—and a covenant with the people of his God—"

The word "people" echoed through Makada's head, drew the skin taut across her temples.

"—They would be confused and bewildered if their leader turned his back on them. For the first time they have brought their God of battle and desert wandering into the City of Peace. The sword of Solomon is one that would cut through ignorance—"

[115]

"An unfortunate word," Makada said more sharply than she intended. "Do you call your own belief ignorance and superstition?"

Tanis smiled. "Naturally not. But I and my people have not known the temptations of those who sometimes lost their way in strange lands"—she shook her head slowly—"no, I could not do such a cruel thing to the King of Israel."

But perhaps he will do it to himself, Makada thought, and she pondered over the thread of hope Tanis had unwittingly given her. She took her leave and when Vashi moved away from the tree to follow her, Makada glanced back at the gate. She saw Tanis study the fading pattern at her feet a moment, then turn slowly and disappear into the garden.

Makada looked up toward the ramparts of the scaffolding, now dark and strong against the paling sky. And she turned the thread of thought this way and that, for it was thin but inexpressibly bright. All the way to her house she forgot to scold Vashi. She was busy plucking skeins out of nowhere, examining them, watching them vanish without concern now, for others appeared in their place. She would choose them with care until they wove themselves into the perfection of the one she held fast. . . .

She bathed and lay in her bedchamber with her eyes closed. Vashi's heavy hands, dipped into the most subtle essence of oil, smoothed her back and arms with a light touch. A drowsy contentment drifted in with the evening breeze.

"It will not be long, Vashi," she murmured, and rested the side of her head in the crook of her naked arm. For the first time since her arrival she could allow herself a moment's languor. "Sheba will not go down in the dust—like Edom and Damascus—" Vashi's fingers no longer massaged the length of her back. They had stopped abruptly, but it did not matter. Nothing could disturb this warm sense of well-being. "—The brother of Solomon will bless the day he rises against the King—" The fingers of Vashi beat a warning on her back. Makada jerked the towels about her as she sat up and stared at the girl standing silently at the open door. "Who are you!"

The single lamp in the room revealed a young and bitter face, losing for an instant its withdrawn hostility. Was there a flash of pleasure in the dark eyes of the stranger?

"My name is Abishag, my lady." She bowed low. "It is the wish of the King that one who knows the palace acquaint you with every detail of its hospitality. I am to assist the Queen of Sheba in any way she desires."

He had sent someone to spy on her! "Come closer," she ordered, and studied Abishag carefully as she took a few steps into the room. "You do not appear to be a handmaiden."

"I waited upon David the King in his last days with the same devotion I give to his—rightful successor."

"How long did you stand at the door—listening?"

"I heard nothing, my lady." Abishag lowered her eyes and bowed once more. "Nothing."

She was lying. Makada swiftly recalled the words she might have over-heard and transposed them in her mind.

"It doesn't matter," she said. "If you wish to repeat my words to the King you have my permission. Tell him I said the mother of Solomon should bless the day she brought forth a king—"

Abishag's face remained immobile. "Yes, my lady."

"I have brought many servants with me—but you may remain. Go now." Abishag withdrew, softly closing the door behind her.

Because he deplored the eagerness with which he looked forward to the evening with Makada, Solomon found the vexations of the day an atone-ment and easier to bear.

The deputation of five out of Asher, Naphtali and Dan, would have tried the patience of ten kings.

Ahiah was not far wrong when he listened to the querulous group and whispered, "Give them little of your time, Solomon. They are like fussy partridge hens, ruffling their feathers to look important, cackling only be-cause they are too old to lay an egg."

"They have a right. Their provinces lie against the borders of Phoenicia," Solomon said, and wondered if old Benjamin had remembered to leave out one of the new robes that arrived this morning in the tribute caravan from Damascus. "What would it profit me to keep peace with those out-side my kingdom if it caused unrest within? I must put their minds at ease."

He had ceded twenty cities of their region to Hiram of Tyre and though he had the authority, it seemed to them an abuse of power. They de-manded an explanation. They admitted afterward among themselves that the King had heard them out with inordinate patience.

What had appeared to be a menace and arrogant extravagance, was in substance a reasonable transaction. The cities were a pledge to Hiram for goods and labor received, a loan to be paid in time. The towns would eventually be restored to them.

The spokesman of Naphtali stroked his beard with slow deliberation. "The master mason of Solomon's temple is also named Hiram, so called by his mother who comes from my province and his father is from Tyre."

The one from Dan waved a disgusted hand. "Always boasting!"

"How does a man's name carry weight," another wanted to know, "with the subject of the twenty cities?"

Solomon sat back, allowing them to argue a moment among themselves. The moment a delegation forgot its unity of purpose, he had learned, they had already lost the purpose of their unity.

Then he asked: "Has the honorable one from Naphtali something more than pride on his mind?"

"May I ask first, my lord, if I heard correctly. Did the King say the twenty cities are without worth?"

"That is what I said."

"Then why did King Hiram accept them in return for labor, timber and gold?"

"Twenty cities sounded as impressive to Hiram as they obviously did to you."

The five exchanged puzzled glances.

"Then he hasn't *seen* them?" one asked.

"Not yet," said Solomon.

One of the elders held his head in his hand and moaned: "Wars have been waged for less cause!"

"What will happen if the King of Tyre recalls his laborers from the King's temple?" asked the delegate out of Asher. And the one from Naphtali added dolefully: "Including Hiram, the finest stonemason on the face of the earth—whose mother came from the tents of Naphtali!"

Jehoshaphat, sitting on Solomon's right at the council table, was pained by such shallow foreboding. He rose, tall and gaunt in his official robe of recorder and with an eloquence that surprised Solomon, reminded the five worried men that the kings of Phoenicia and Israel were men of peace. They were bound not by treaty—for such words often were more fragile than the waxed tablets on which they were written—but by the stronger bond of friendship.

The gloomy one from Asher reminded Jehoshaphat of David's peaceful delegation of ambassadors to Hanun, King of the Ammonites. "And what happened? Their beards were cut off and they were sent into the streets wearing only the upper halves of their tunics! That was friendship?"

"Hanun was the son of Nahash," Jehoshaphat said coldly. "David's peace was with the father."

"As Hiram's friendship was first with David," answered the old man. He looked long and earnestly at Solomon. "My lord, when King Hiram looks upon cities and finds them equivalent of nothing—will he still be your friend?"

"You need have no fear for the length of your beard or your tunic." Solomon smiled. "Hiram will remember only that before I was well informed on the smelting of ore, he once traded the skill of his shipbuilders for twice their worth in copper. Then he wrote me a letter chiding me for not looking after my interests. He said it was all a priceless lesson in fair trade. Now I shall do the same."

This was something the delegation could understand. They nodded in thoughtful agreement and several of them whispered it was a shame the entire transaction was so small.

"Our ability to outwit each other is more than the basis for mutual respect," Solomon explained. "It is also the spice of our friendship. Now, if your fears are allayed—?" He looked at each in turn and received a quick nod of agreement. "—Then sit at my table this night and sleep well before journeying to your homes in the north."

They left, happily appeased. And other distractions moved before the table of council to plead, protest, make arrangements or ask favor of the King.

Several times, as he weighed a decision on taxes he stood at the sill of the window and looked out toward the tops of tall palms that marked the garden where *she* was visiting and his mind turned into the paths that were knowing the touch of her feet. He wished he walked beside her in the soft haze of day—the day that would never end.

The silence in the room told him Ben-geber was still waiting for his answer. He brought his thoughts back to the commissioner over sixty great cities with bronze gates in Ramoth-gilead and Bashan. The soft mouth irritated him. Good living had corrupted Ben-geber's body into rolls of hairless fat, simply clothed for the time being because he had come to beg indulgence. Solomon wagered to himself that he had not crossed the Jordan without a suitable supply of richly embroidered mantles in his baggage to be used on less humiliating occasions while he was at court. He had apologized to the King. The early harvest of his region had been stricken by an unseasonable storm. Therefore, he abjectedly repeated that his spirits were in a lower condition than the crop, for it meant a shortage in the grain he was due to supply one month out of twelve to the King's household . . .

Solomon had deliberately punished him by delaying to answer. Sweat rolled down the fat cheeks of Ben-geber and Solomon was unmoved. Let him sweat. If he had the wit of Hiram now, Solomon thought, I could excuse him with pleasure. The man was a shrewd commissioner, capable too. But his speech was monotonous, with the buzzing sound but never the sting of a bee. It is not to my credit, Solomon told himself, that I would rather listen to the lively lies of a scoundrel than the dull talk of an honest man.

"It will not be held against you!" Solomon spoke brusquely. He caught a look of self-satisfaction on the well-fed cheeks, now shining with relief. "Not if you make up the shortage with an equal measure of meat." And as the room began to clear he turned to Jehoshaphat. "Let it be so recorded." He drank some water and set down the cruse with a small thud of weariness. "Now, Ahiah. We can write the letter regarding the fortifications of Sheba—" He broke off abruptly. It was a simple slip of the tongue, yet he corrected the name to "Sharuhen" with a sense of guilt and glanced quickly to see if the scribe had noticed. One couldn't tell. Ahiah and his brother, Elihoreph, had been well schooled as *sopherim*. It seemed to Solomon that in every court, including his own, the scribes were the most scholarly, the best educated and—in this instance—the most discreet. Ahiah was dutifully bent over his tablets and he did not meet the King's eyes until all the letters were completed for the day.

But later, as they both climbed to the Temple site to examine the fine new stones of the forecourt, Solomon caught the eyes of his scribe studying him; not critically, nor with amusement, but with the interest Solomon himself might show for one of those weapons of stone or scraps of bones unearthed from an older age when the earth of Adam and Eve was young. It annoyed him to be studied as an artifact and he told Ahiah this.

Ahiah laughed. "You a relic of the past? On the contrary. That is my brother's pastime, not mine. His nose grows longer by the day poking into dusty records and he listens well only to stories of the past. I suppose that is our reason for constantly arguing. He thinks nothing of great importance is going on in the present. And I am interested in nothing else."

Solomon's eyes remained on the great table of stone being heaved into position by the husky men under Jeroboam's supervision. The table of the shewbread resisted their straining backs and Solomon moved toward it. "Which one of you is right, Ahiah?"

"Neither one of us." Ahiah moved along with him, and watched. Solomon put his shoulder to the table, adding his weight to that of the half naked Phoenicians. And the massive stone edged forward onto its roller. Solomon watched it move slowly into the building, and sighed.

"Neither one?"

"I tell him sometimes we should have had another brother. One in between, to link our thoughts more agreeably. One who would not forget that we who live are part of everything and everyone who *ever* lived. And we, in turn, are part of the future. But you see, I forget this. I find myself interested only in the living man."

"And do you judge him?" He felt, rather than saw Ahiah look at him long and carefully as they moved across the forecourt.

"Of course not. Do you draw a line under a man's life before that life is finished?"

"When it is, he is still appraised with falseness."

"How so?"

"Because he is viewed from a distance. The distance of eternity first of all. Then the measure of time as we know it—a day, a month, a hundred years; and worse—he is judged by a mind of different standards, someone who did not live in the same times, know the evil and good of that day, the circumstances that shaped his soul, the misfortunes he tried to overcome—"

"And the temptation," Ahiah said quietly. "And the loneliness, Solomon?"

Solomon ran his hand over the molten brim of the great basin cast on the backs of twelve molten oxen. It served his purpose for the moment, to divert the personal question.

"See here, Ahiah. You and I stand before this molten sea. It is a receptacle for water. Rain water, ablutions—whatever the need. There is no law against beauty, so I asked for a design of exquisite proportions. So here it is. Vast and magnificent, gleaming in the last rays of the sun. But will it be only that to some who look at the beasts it rests on? They will see three facing east, three to the west and to the north and south. And they'll say we regard oxen as sacred."

"But it will not be true."

"It isn't *now*. But it will seem true to the one who thinks it."

"You are leading me by the nose," Ahiah complained, "and I will not be led into an argument on the existence of truth."

"Only an example," Solomon said lightly and they started down the hillside. "Ask any ten men today the truth about my father. You'll get ten different answers. Tell me if your picture of Samuel or Joshua, even Moses is the same as mine?"

"History changes, the world changes, but human beings remain very much the same. That is the only comfort I take in this argument. So far as the past is concerned, go talk to Elihoreph. He knows more dead people than live ones! He can tell you a man said this, he did thus and so because he searched for the answers and even found some of them written down."

"And when a man's life is written down like that, Ahiah, who bothers to read between the lines?" He supposed his hands had been as roughened as this from the earliest days of the construction, but as he brushed them off now, he thought for the first time how harsh they might be to a softer skin. . . . "I am not a warrior as Saul was, nor can I leave the sword of a Goliath for my son as it was left for me. So I am not concerned about the opinions of unborn ages, for only the giants of war live forever in honor. I'll be a name, a small arc of time between the king who was before me and the son who will follow me—nothing but legend. So I sometimes wonder why I concern myself with right and wrong."

"You will be remembered because you do concern yourself. You once said a nation that throws off restraint and destroys its vision—destroys itself. So does a man." Ahiah turned his head toward the dying sun. "I am afraid, Solomon, in spite of all you do or don't do—you will be long remembered—"

"Stop burying me! I feel like something your brother drags home from his dreary excursions into moldy caves!" Solomon hurried down the slope, anxious to get to his rooms and bathe the dust of these reflective moments from his mind. He could hear Ahiah chuckling softly behind him and he looked back over his shoulder, waved a derisive hand at the old scribe and laughed with him.

Makada watched the singers of the evening follow the cymbalist from the banqueting room.

"There is a sadness in the songs of your people," she said.

Solomon wondered how a psalm of Asaph, joyfully exalting the One who demanded nothing but a loving heart, could fall with doleful sound on such a delicate ear.

"You must forgive us our lamentations." He smiled but was certain his irony was lost on her. "We have had little time or cause to rejoice."

Her words had been casual, without substance, yet they bothered him. He was sure they were not true. There was no merrier eye, or gustier laughter than he had found in his own people. They did nothing by half measure. When they mourned they tore their flesh and tore their clothes with mourning and poured ashes on their head; when they laughed and danced—the very earth seemed to rock with joy; and when they loved. . . .

"It is said that the subjects of a king carry on their faces the reflection of their master's heart." Her eyes moved around the room. "What do you see?"

"They may all be subjects—but all are not of our tribes." How could one find a similarity between the swarthy and the pale, the fine-boned with straight, sparse hair and the curly-headed ones from a region long cut off from its neighbors by the deep gorges that surrounded their mountains? Then, with the melody of the absent musicians still ringing in his ears he picked out the faces of those who were not vassals of alien blood and he looked closely. There were the five who had arrived full of complaint and now, full of food, were laughing softly among themselves; there were his ministers, richly robed, and the commissioners of regions he had created to administer the affairs of the nation; there was Ahiah, slyly pouring wine into the goblet of Elihoreph as the earnest scribe leaned far to the other side to convince Ben-geber that Sodom and Gomorrah and the other three cities of iniquity, doomed to brimstone and fire, now lay at the bottom of the Sea of Salt.

And beneath the lightness of mood about his table, he thought he saw an eternal loneliness in the eyes, or was it, even in the very young, an in-born memory of timeless wanderings—beyond actual experience? Then it must be changed! For the memory carried through the years, from generation to generation, was a joyous thing, a peculiar treasure: It was Balaam sent by Balak to curse the sons of Jacob and their son's sons, and Balaam returning with the words, "How can I curse whom God has not cursed?" It was the Song of Deborah and the Song of Moses, the Song of the Well and the singing to it when Moses and Aaron struck a rock in the wilderness where nothing grew, and water sprang forth at the touch of the rod and came forth abundantly. . . .

He turned to the Queen and found her studying him with intense curiosity. Out of courtesy, he did not tell her his thoughts. He agreed with her that the songs had a melancholy. "Perhaps I can now write them a song of joy—perhaps even fulfillment—"

Still, the shadow of her words fell on the pleasure of the evening. When she turned to the elegant ambassador from Thebes at her right side, Solomon's eyes moved down to the carnelian tips of her toes, beating the rhythm of tedium. His disappointment sharpened to an edge of pain. She was neither watching nor enjoying the performers who would entertain her. He hoped she was wearied of it only because it was foreign to her understanding, for that could be altered by time. But his need, which had sprung full-grown, now smote him with an angry fear that her impatience was born of indifference to him. It was a new and disturbing sensation. It towered over him and, like King Og of Bashan who roared for an iron couch nine cubits long to hold his giant body, it scorned the simple bed of reason.

Finding sadness in one of his favorite songs was a small thing, yet he had an impulse to grasp her shoulders, shake them until the force of his will raised or lowered every sensation within her, no matter how insignificant, to the level of his own. He sighed at his own foolishness. Because he was obsessed by her he was demanding the impossible: that her delight in all things should surpass the limitations of mere sharing and become fused, whole and complete, with his. And he knew such a thing could never be done. Joy, like pain, was a variable. Fruit of the vine from the same wineskin was more pleasing to one tongue than to another. For the first time he knew the bitterness of drinking from the larger cup. What he would savor to the last drop, she would perhaps set aside, or worse— taste with nothing more than fleeting desire. And he was touched with the wish to be forgiven by all those who thought he had shared the fullness of their love. He had taken it selfishly and in ignorance believing that no love held, for him, meaning beyond the moment.

Her sandal, still tapping the soundless carpet, mocked his intensity.

He sat at the head of the table which lined three sides of the rectangular room. It hummed with the talk of more than a hundred guests. He let his eyes wander down the heaped and gleaming board that followed the colonnade at the far side of the room and he surveyed the one set out from the length of wall at his left; and he watched the broad space between fill with wrestlers from his own ranks and squat-legged acrobats out of Gaza who pyramided, tumbled into intricate contortions and rolled away.

From both sides of the room the voices of his guests came up to him through the light of many lamps. He caught snatches of Ahiah's conversation with a viceroy of Egypt who had recently returned from the court of the Pharaoh. Ahiah was prodding him about the shortage of papyrus in Jerusalem.

"Can it be," he asked, "that because our great leader was found in the bulrushes your ruler punishes us by refusing to cut them for the manufacture of writing material?"

The viceroy was accustomed to Ahiah's good-natured abuse. "We send all we can. But I find it hard to understand—our scribes write many books, histories, records, documents, and you'll admit our land is more ancient and vast than Israel—still, they use less than you demand. What is the answer?"

"Perhaps we have more to say," said Ahiah. And when the viceroy threw up his hands in mock despair, Ahiah once more tipped the cruse and added to the remainder of wine in Elihoreph's cup. He waited till Elihoreph gave Ben-geber an opportunity to answer, and he watched his brother lean forward and take another big gulp of wine before turning back to his discussion. Ahiah grinned at the viceroy, who was now looking past him, at the fringe of lank hair on Elihoreph's head. Even from where he sat, Solomon could see that Elihoreph had dressed his ungainly bones in a fine-woven robe but he had left the dust of crumbled shards in his hair, the mementoes of an afternoon's exploring.

"My brother is a brilliant man," Ahiah was saying. "But he will not admit he is a glutton. He firmly believes that he is temperate in all things and never drinks more than one cup of wine with his dinner."

The moment the first stewards appeared to clear away the remnants of food, Solomon was distressed. The Queen had risen suddenly, pleading a headache and as Solomon rose to accompany her, she restrained him with a swift hand. He must not leave his guests, and she could find her way—her servants waited in the courtyard, and Vashi was an admirable bodyguard.

The bodyguard was spreading out the square of white linen that had touched the Queen's lips and hands during the meal and into it she was putting the scraps of food remaining on Makada's plate.

Solomon stared. "What are you doing?" he asked, forgetting the woman had no tongue to answer.

Makada was already nearing the door. She paused.

"It is the custom."

"Haven't my stewards provided a lavish table for you and your servants?"

"It is not being carried away for me or my servants." Makada's voice was icy with formality. "She will bury it."

"Now why should she do that?"

"She makes certain her Queen will not be harmed by evil incantations spoken over it." Someone at the table could not restrain a smothered burst of amusement. Makada glared at the offender and Solomon did likewise.

"My guest has forgotten that we, also, are enjoined on certain nights of festival to eat all and everything, and nothing remaining should be touched the next day!" He knew the smothered laugh was for the mention of magic and spells attending the Queen's haughty custom, but he begged her forgiveness. He went so far as to offer Vashi the beaten gold vessels and plates but Vashi tied the corners of her linen square and left the room, following the Queen with unruffled dignity.

Solomon could not leave immediately. He must stay for a moment or two with his guests, let them tease his wit. Forty riddles they asked and forty times he became an unwilling magician, a shade in rich garments who could reach beyond the disappointment of the evening and the somber tomb of his thoughts to somehow find the right answer.

When he rose from the table to leave, Benaiah came to his side with questions about the conscription of labor—questions that need not be asked at this moment. Solomon knew the vital question would somehow slide into the conversation—but it was not until he had left the banqueting room and stood in the courtyard that he ferreted the kernel of importance from the chaff. Benaiah had remarked on the absence of Zadok at the King's board.

"He is sulking no doubt," Solomon had answered. "He is chastising me for the judgment of the old woman. It will take at least another day for him to look on me with favor. In the meantime his heart is the stone pillow of Jacob."

"The Queen of Sheba remarked on his absence," Benaiah said slowly. "A strange thing—she called him the High Priest Abiathar."

Now, as he stood thinking about it in the garden, it was odd that the name of poor old Abiathar, long gone from the court, should come from the lips of a stranger. Perhaps she had heard it many years ago from her mother, or a visiting emissary. But if she had, it was also likely she knew Solomon had sent the faithful but misguided old man back to his fields in Anathoth. There were too many unkind rumors about the priest who had, with Zadok, once followed David with the Ark when he went into exile. They were sent back to guard it where it belonged, in Jerusalem. But when too many voices spoke against the old man for supporting Adonijah, Solomon called him and said no harm should be done to him; for this was the priest who had escaped the massacre of Nob and joined David on his flight from Saul's wrath, and he brought with him the ephod and the sacred lots, the *Urim* and *Thummin* to cast as oracles of guidance.

Solomon wandered slowly, aimlessly as he thought of Abiathar, and Shimei the son of Gera, who also had to be banished because of David's charges on his deathbed. But these were actions easier to accomplish in knowing that banishment for the old priest meant his safety; and casting out of Jerusalem the one who had so vilely cursed David was just punishment. But to carry out the rest, to raise his sword against Joab—to kill. . . .

His footsteps had taken him up the hillside. There was no moon. A powdery luminescence cast a silver veil over the sky and in the torchlight of the sentries at the Temple wall he saw a furtive shadow move. It wore the dark robes of a native woman and yet there was no disguising the grace of those movements, the light step as she drew her hood close and hurried away from the gate at the first chance of discovery.

So this was her impatience to be gone from the table. This was her "headache." He smiled to himself. She would never give up after only one attempt to see whatever she hoped to see. He would have to make it easier for her. Tomorrow night—at this hour—there would be no guards at the side gate leading to the Temple.

As he descended the leafy terraces of the mountainside his thoughts drifted across the reality of Makada's furtive attempt to pass through the walls. Her curiosity became a translucent image beyond the veil of fantasy in which she was seeking her one beloved, and he was the one she sought. The deception haunted him. He hurried up the outer stairs of his rooms, crossed the roof-terrace and went directly to the chamber where Ahiah sometimes worked.

A single light shone over the table and he pushed aside important documents waiting for his seal. He sat down to exorcise his longing with a reed pen. He would gild her motives with equal yearning and her words would come up to him as something beyond his power of imagining. . . .

He wrote quickly, but not quickly enough. Only fragments of the swelling song within him lingered on the point of his pen.

While the king sitteth at his table, my spikenard sends forth the smell thereof.

My beloved is to me a bag of myrrh that lies between my breasts. . . . *I am the rose of Sharon, and the lily of the valleys.*

As the lily among thorns, so is my love among the maidens.

As the apple tree among the trees of the wood, so is my beloved among the young men. . . . *He brought me to the banqueting house and his banner over me was love* . . .

His left hand is under my head, and his right hand doth embrace me. . . .

My beloved is like a roe or a young hart: behold there he stands behind our wall, gazing in at the windows, looking through the lattice.

My beloved speaks and says to me, "Arise, my love, my fair one, and come away; for lo, the winter is past, the rain is over and gone. The flowers appear on the earth, the time of singing is come and the voice of the turtledove is heard in our land. . . ."

Her words, coming from his pen, had leaped like a swift gazelle across a chasm of impatient time, had sprung beyond the searching of a bride to the bed of green boughs and the waiting arms of her bridegroom. He dipped his pen into the inkhorn and returned to the searching, seeing once more the lithe movement of her body quickly escaping the light of a guard's torch and darting into the shadow.

I would give her these thoughts, he told himself, these thoughts as she moves among those shadows . . .

My beloved is mine and I am his. . . . *Upon my bed by night I sought him whom my soul loveth. I sought him but found him not; I called him, but he gave no answer.*

I will rise now and go about the city, in the streets and in the open places; I will seek him . . . *and not let him go.* . . .

What is that coming up from the wilderness like a column of smoke, perfumed with myrrh and frankincense . . . *Behold, it is the litter of Solomon! About it are sixty mighty men of the mighty men of Israel, all girt with swords and expert in war, each with his sword at his thigh, against alarms by night.*

King Solomon made himself a palanquin from the wood of Lebanon. He made its posts of silver, its back of gold, its seat of purple. . . .

Awake, O north wind, and come, O south wind! Blow upon my garden, let its fragrance be wafted abroad. Let my beloved come to his garden and eat its choicest fruits. . . .

The flame in the bowl of oil sputtered with expiring. Solomon filled it carefully and found a fresh wick, to avoid calling a servant. But as he continued, the words of his song became the wings of poor, captured birds that struggled against the bars of ink lines that held them from soaring into a limitless sky.

He threw down the pen and sat with his elbows on the table, his head in his hands. Then he rose and walked through the rooms. They were very still, too still. He poured a drink and looked up at the lute of David, silent on the wall. No song remembered in its wood and strings could echo the plaintive sound in his heart. What she had said, then, was perhaps true. He had hoped to write something of his joy and it seemed to hold only the sadness she found in the songs of his people.

He drained the bowl and set it down with a clatter. Was the woman to be as elusive as wisdom, an illusory brightness moving always beyond reach of the constant searching? Surely other men were more fortunate than he: a warrior like Benaiah, for instance, with his vision sharpened by the edge of a sword sheathed in wariness; Eli the physician, who pondered perhaps over the injustices of a divine being, yet found comfort in the one wife of his youth and his age; the men from the northern provinces who had set their concerns on a single problem of this day and now slept with ease in their beds; all those who lived without climbing, stumbling, falling back to rise and climb again.

Ahiah was right. There were no caprices of the earth, no upheavals of its mountains or in the ways of its rivers that surpassed the sublime peaks and winding depths of a man's mind. . . .

The sound of laughter and wild shouts of men came up to him. He moved toward it, eager to escape the unmoving things that filled his rooms. He stepped out onto the roof terrace and looked below. The noise took form within the house of his commander. Benaiah had taken off the splendid mantle he had worn at the feast and his great arms glistened with moisture as he threw open more doors to the night air, and returned to compete with the rowdy antics of his officers. They moved in and out of the lamplight, testing their strength and skill with arms locked in the vise of adversaries. There were feats of balance with ten fine wine goblets balanced on chest and arched thighs, and when one of them dropped the great iron bar from over his head the sound of its falling was lost in the cries of mocking scorn and another picked it up to try his own skill.

Solomon had forgotten that this was the night. Before a company left with replacements for the labor crews in Lebanon, or took others down to the mines of the Arabah or to the copper furnaces of Ezion-geber, they gathered in the house of the commander for a night of celebration. He had always enjoyed the high good humor, even the coarse jokes, and he hurried down the stairs to join the festivity.

Still, when it was at its height, he felt the evening was over, and he left without being noticed.

It had been some time since he visited the rooms of Ahiah. Their low yellow walls and flat roof were connected with a far wing of the palace by a corridor open on one side to a garden of herbs that gave up a sweet scent to the night air.

Somewhere in the back of his mind there must be a reason for his coming here, instead of returning to his own quarters, but it was not worth the time to find it. He could say he longed for a stimulating game of draughts with either Ahiah or his brother. He was about to knock on the door, then hesitated. The voice of Ahiah's wife was raised, reprimanding Elihoreph for snoring, for lying on the couch with his sandals covered with dew. How could she keep a tidy house with such a lazy brother-in-law constantly dropping his reed pens underfoot, bringing in worthless pieces of broken pottery to clutter up the shelves.

Injured dignity drifted out the open window with Elihoreph's mumbled response. "Woman, shield your tongues—for I'm sure you possess more than one—from things you do not comprehend. I have honored your house with the prizes of rare ostraca that hold the history of ancient man in the curve of their clay—" He moaned, as if the effort of rising suddenly created thunderbolts in his head. And the woman's voice escaped through teeth closed in anger.

"You are a disgrace! You sit at the King's table and swallow enough for ten fat men and drink enough wine to float one of his ships to Tarshish and return! Still your bones show!"

"My brother's good wife feeds me too well." His voice was coated thinly with oil, enough to smooth the sharpness of her scolding.

"Sometimes I think a jackal gnaws at your liver. It is the animal inside who eats my raisin cakes faster than I can bring them from the oven— come now, I will steady your footsteps into your room." There was the sound of Elihoreph's sandals shuffling uncertainly across the stone floor and Ahiah's wife clucking with shame at the thought of how he must have staggered away from the King's board.

"I can't understand it." Elihoreph's voice grew faint as he moved toward his bedchamber. "It must have been wine of extraordinary strength —you know I confine my libation to one single bowl at the evening meal. . . ."

Solomon leaned against the vine-covered doorpost and smiled. He would wait a moment, allow the proud wife of Ahiah to tidy her room before entering. The night breeze moved a cool cylinder of metal against his cheek. He wondered that more people didn't hang a *mezuzah* of this kind at the entrance of their houses. He supposed Zadok would object to that, too, since the posts themselves, at the entrance of ancient tents had been lettered with the same words that were here enclosed in a sheath of copper. He wondered how long, and with what eyestrain, the brothers must have bent over the thin roll of lambskin to letter the words spoken to Moses by the Lord:

"Hear, O Israel: The Lord our God is one Lord and you shall love the Lord your God with all your heart, and with all your soul and with all your

might. And these words which I command you this day shall be upon your heart; and you shall teach them diligently to your children, and shall talk of them when you sit in your house, and when you walk by the way, and when you lie down, and when you rise. And you shall bind them as a sign upon your hand, and they shall be as frontlets between your eyes. And you shall write them on the doorposts of your house and on your gates. . . ."

"I have forgotten," Solomon said to himself, and felt a twinge of guilt ride up his spine, thinking of the child Rehoboam, born of Naamah. There had been no time—no time—to sit with the child who was a pale and grave-eyed stranger to him. He had not the time to be a father to one if he was to be a father to all his people, he argued, and knew he was deceiving himself. David had found time, at least for his first sons, those who had come before the one he called his "Little Solomon." With firm resolution, Solomon promised himself to teach the child—*diligently*—this child of his dutiful but passionless seed. Simultaneously he was relieved, for he recalled that it was a promise to be postponed. Naamah had asked his permission this morning to journey to her father's home in Ammon with the boy. It was an annual request, annually granted during the time of harvest when the winds blew the chaff of winnowing into the air. The child's eyes watered and grew red-rimmed and he made odd faces to dispel the running in his nose. It was high and clear in the palace of Ammon and surely it was more sensible to free the child's head in pagan air than allow him to suffer with the wind of the righteous.

This, too, was false reasoning, he knew. As if to assuage his conscience he remembered as best he could the admonition in the blessing:

". . . If you will obey my commandments—to love the Lord your God and to serve him . . . he will give the rain for your land in its season, the early rain and the later rain, that you may gather in your grain and your wine and your oil. And he will give grass in your fields for your cattle, and you shall eat and be full. Take heed lest your heart be deceived, and you turn aside and serve other gods and worship them, and the anger of the Lord be kindled against you and he shut up the heavens, so that there be no rain, and the land yield no fruit and you perish quickly off the good land which the Lord gives you. . . ."

How simple, how easy it was to find reasons for his weakness. He shook his head and sat down on the doorstep. I place my faults, he thought, on the faults of the days in which I live. I rush up to a mountain top at strange hours of the day and the night and find a thousand duties to excuse my neglect of one. It has been too long since I sat in the darkness and saw light. May it never be far from my thoughts again that I am responsible for my own actions—responsible to myself, my fellow man—and above all, to my God. . . .

The woman had returned from the other room. Her question now was petulant and held the expectancy of a negative answer. "I hope you remembered to bring me a new quern from the market-place, Ahiah?"

His response was vague and indistinct. It came reluctantly, as if from the great distance of concentration.

His wife sighed. "What a life I lead. You sit here poring over old records, writing new ones with your ears deaf to the sleeping noises of your brother. Not even helping him to his bed! Don't you love Elihoreph?"

"As my own brother," Ahiah mumbled. And the faint scratching of a stylus on a tablet could be heard.

"So be it," said his wife. "But what has that to do with forgetting to purchase my quern?"

The sound of writing stopped.

"Now that is a riddle Solomon himself couldn't answer," Ahiah said. "Nor I."

"Can I bake bread without flour? Can flour be made without grain? And how can I grind the grain for flour with no quern to grind the grain for the flour to bake the bread—"

"Enough, enough!" Ahiah said hastily. "You shall get it. But I fail to understand why a woman of your social standing does not send our flour to be baked in the public ovens."

"For the loaves of a holy festival?" Her voice rose with indignation. "My mother would rise out of her burial cave if I took our portion of the first cutting of wheat and did not bake the offering to our Lord with my own two hands."

The light from the window, falling across the herb garden, began to disappear.

"Now, woman!" Ahiah protested. "I still have work to do. Why do you take the lamp into the bedchamber?"

Her step resounded firmly, grew faint. "Because it is time to go to bed."

Ahiah chuckled and said he bowed to a superior mind. He would follow her in a moment, after he had taken a breath of air in the garden.

The door opened and he was startled to find someone sitting on his doorstep, but not surprised when he recognized the King. He closed the door and came closer. "Now why do I find you here, Solomon?"

"Only because my sudden urge to be gone was swifter than my feet."

"Well then, let us enjoy the moment."

Ahiah sat down beside Solomon and for a time neither spoke.

"The moon that walks in brightness is hiding from us once more. And in a few nights the lovely crescent will appear low in the west. Do you remember my instructions to you many years ago—about the stars and the theories of the old Babylonians? We should most certainly adopt their system of calculating the years." He studied the cloud of stars that stretched across the firmament. "Has it ever occurred to you that we have taken quick advantage of the skills and arts of other nations, without losing the unique quality which sets us apart from them?"

"Our belief," Solomon said. He plucked a blade of grass and twisted it idly around his finger.

"The ethics in our belief," Ahiah corrected him. "Without it we could still go astray on every high place of Canaan and you would be building a golden calf instead of a fine house to the Lord. Which reminds me—I looked everywhere for you tonight. You were not in our workroom, nor at the Temple. I didn't see you in the streets of the town—and the chamberlain of the house of women said you had been expected to spend the evening with the lovely one from Beth-shan, but you hadn't appeared."

He had forgotten this, too! During the day, when he rebelled against the complete capture of his sense and will by the Queen from the south, he had given instructions to the chamberlain that he would visit the quarters of the pale-haired one. . . . Now surely something had gone wrong within him when a fair creature out of Beth-shan did not stir his eagerness for an intimate hour, nor provoke a sense of loss over forgetting it. The name of her native city, instead, reminded him that the food depot there must be checked carefully for Beth-shan's location was strategic in the Valley of Jazreel and the Jordan land.

"Beth-shan," he mused. "I never journey that way without seeing in my mind poor King Saul and Jonathan killed and fastened to its walls and the head of Saul hanging in blood in the temple of the Philistine god."

Ahiah shuddered. Solomon apologized for the morbid memory and asked Ahiah to remind him in the morning to send the lady a suitable gem, a turquoise perhaps from his chest of jewels.

"It will please her vanity but not her pride."

"What of my pride? How many of them would come so meekly into my arms, so willingly, if I were not the King?" He twisted the grass tighter around his finger, paling the flesh until it throbbed in protest. "I am not *that* vain, Ahiah. When some of the officers boast of conquests won on battlefields of secret rooms they whisper darkly of their defeats and call reluctance in a virtuous woman the unnatural desire of Sodom. I wonder why."

Ahiah shrugged. "There are men who must constantly prove to themselves they are men—because they are ridden with uncertainty."

"Oh now, that is surely a wild thought. Why only tonight the strongest captain over the hundreds spoke in this fashion. He would run his sword through your soft middle, Ahiah, if you called him less than an irresistible man in the eyes of all women and a giant among men."

"Let him dream." Ahiah turned to Solomon. "So that's where you were —in Benaiah's house. Would you mind letting the blood flow back into your finger, before it drops dead on my doorstep? I passed the house without a thought that you were part of the revelry."

"The weight I lifted was six hin above the one Benaiah hoisted over his head."

"I detected the rattling of dice. Did you also distinguish yourself in this field?"

"Let us say it is fortunate I didn't wager my crown," Solomon said wryly. "Jeroboam would be wearing it."

"Jeroboam? The son of Nebat of Ephraim?" Ahiah was as surprised as he ever appeared to be.

"That is correct. The young foreman who gets so much accomplished without seeming to make the effort."

Ahiah leaned forward, resting his elbows on his knees. "How did a labor supervisor edge his way into the select group of officers? They usually discourage the invasion of an outsider."

Solomon laughed. "Jeroboam does not invade. He infiltrates. As to being an outsider—well, I was there."

"You fight a greater battle than any of those who brandish a sword, do not forget. The figure of peace should be draped in the wanton bangles of war—then perhaps it would win more favor from those who worship the conqueror's mighty stride." Ahiah creased his lower lip between two fingers and pulled it slowly back and forth. "Jeroboam is a young man of promise—"

"Men work willingly beneath his supervision. He's valuable."

"How valuable, once the Temple is completed?"

"I plan to put him in charge of all labor over the house of Joseph." He watched Ahiah's face. Nothing but a slight lift of one eyebrow betrayed his skepticism. "You think he has an ambitious light in his eye?"

Ahiah put his head to one side, and was silent.

Solomon answered his own question. "I do. That is why I intend to promote him. Give him a responsible position."

"I miss the subtleties of your reasoning," said Ahiah. "If he proves to be a potential enemy, why place him in a position of trust?"

"He will be content with a splendid uniform—at least for a time. And if he holds a position of trust—I'll always know where he is." He patted Ahiah's brown arm. "You worry too much. Now tell me, why did you look for me this evening?"

"There were dispatches to be sealed and sent to all directions. The couriers from Tyre are waiting to take Hiram the agreement on wheat and oil, and his caravan of merchants lingers to carry the portion of this harvest to Phoenicia."

"All in good time," said Solomon. "But I'll attend to the agreement first thing in the morning."

Ahiah cleared his throat. "For a moment, while I sat at the work table, my tired head thought you had sealed the document and I was about to slip it in a leather pouch and call the courier—a fortunate thing I took a second look."

Silence constrained them for a moment.

"I wonder what Hiram of Tyre would have thought," Ahiah said without a smile, "if he received a poem saying his love was better than wine, that honey and milk lay under his tongue, that he was a garden fountain, a well of living water and flowing streams from Lebanon. . . ."

Solomon was grateful for the darkening sky, the stars that disappeared and allowed his face to burn without being seen. Then suddenly, thinking of Hiram receiving such a message from the King of Israel, Solomon threw back his head and laughed until Ahiah cautioned him about disturbing his wife.

"It would be worth seeing," Solomon chuckled. "Hiram's face would fall into a thousand pieces. . . ." The laughter went out of him as suddenly as it came.

He rose to leave but Ahiah still sat on the step, a huddled shape of questioning silence.

"Some random thoughts, that is all—" Solomon was annoyed with himself for making an explanation.

"It is lyrical," said Ahiah softly. "A song of songs."

"It was meant for no eyes but my own!"

"How selfish of you." The scribe's voice was mild and full of sympathy. "I know it is a love song—or part of one—but I could not help wondering what Zadok would think if he read it."

"He would think the King of Israel was possessed."

"And is he, Solomon?"

Solomon kept his face in shadow and did not answer.

"You wrote the words of lovers," Ahiah went on, "but Zadok would say it transcends mortal love and becomes a marriage with the Eternal—between the Lord and his people . . ."

"It is strange to hear you speak like this, Ahiah. Is it because you grow older that you begin to speak of love greater than the love of man and woman?"

"Who am I to say? Before the first stirring of desire, a man is too young to think beyond his next meal. And when desire is the tender dust of half-forgotten years, he begins to wonder if all love is not part of the divine order—I weary you, Solomon." Ahiah rose and stood at his door, rubbing the stiffness out of his back. "Go in peace, Jedidiah—sleep well. . . ."

Solomon walked away and Ahiah stood for a moment looking after him, even as he disappeared into the corridor.

"A wise man is not meant to be a happy one," he whispered to the unhearing ears of the King. "The higher he goes, the wider becomes his horizon." For a moment his eyes shone with unshed tears of compassion. "You are reaching heights, Solomon, where others cannot follow. And it is lonely on the heights, Son of David. The wind blows colder and one yearns for human warmth—as you yearn for it now—but look to the top, Solomon, look to the top for it is closer to God."

The third hour after the midday sun they drove through the town. Makada stood behind Solomon in the royal chariot, balancing her body against the possible accident of touching his.

She asked why the crowd sang out the name of a foreign queen with the same joy they expressed toward their own monarch. That would never happen in her city of Mareb. And if, as he claimed, he was not a god, was it not risking his god-like prestige to leave his drivers to an idle afternoon in the compound of the palace armory? And how could his subjects respect a king who journeyed forth holding the reins of his own chariot and disdaining the trumpeting heralds and glitter of his splendid guard of horsemen?

In the next instant, without waiting for an answer, she was perplexed because he had stopped, here in the bustling market-place. To allow that man—so hideously deformed she could not restrain a shudder—to drag those twisted stumps of legs and swollen upper body across the street?

"His mind is not stunted!" Solomon cut short his swift anger, and acknowledged the cripple's smile with a casual wave of his hand. He quietly blessed him in the name of the "King of the Universe who has created variously formed creatures."

"The man is insolent!" she whispered. "He did not bow in obeisance or gratitude!"

"Why should he?" The fellow had been born too low in the body to bow before any man, he thought. It annoyed him to be reminded, in this way, that he often forgot how to be grateful. Not for his own sound limbs. But for the words of the Lord, spoken through the mouth of Samuel the Prophet, warning his people not to look on a man's height or his stature; for it was the weakness of men to look only on the outward appearance and not see as He sees—with the heart.

Goodly proportions and smooth bronzed skin, Solomon had too often observed, concealed leprous scabs of self-seeking.

"You needn't pity him," he said heartily. "He is whole and shining within. I know him well. He speaks as many forgotten tongues as Ahiah, and he's the finest silversmith in all of Jerusalem—"

"So you call yourself King of the Universe." The soft mockery in her voice turned his head sharply over his shoulder. Was there no end to the things she did not or would not understand! Then he sighed. Rather let her think him the king of conceit than to proselyte and spout an explanation from a chariot in the market-place. In this light her eyes were enormous. The blackness in them was finely rimmed by a delicate nimbus of grayish green. For an instant, out of some long-forgotten journey past pagan shrines, he was reminded of two strange cromlechs of stones guarding twin circles of dark and secret mounds.

He smiled in spite of his irritation. Her aloof bearing in the restricted space of the chariot was ridiculous and amusing, particularly when in his own mind she had been clinging close to him since the moment they started.

"You will say next that I command the four winds," he said, "and all the creatures of the sea."

"I heard that also. And that you speak with the eagle and hoopoe, the heron and owl of the sky and all things that spring from out of the earth."

She regarded him gravely. "Is this true, that you understand the language of the four-legged beast and all manner of crawling things?"

Surely she couldn't be serious!

"Those in particular!" he answered quickly. "It is the result of carefully studying the layers of sweet oil on the tongues of a common variety: the two-legged ambassador." She was still unsmiling. "Surely you believe," he went on, "that I possess a carpet that rises at my command and carries me through the air, wherever I wish to go?"

She tilted her head to one side, a gesture he had already come to recognize when she scrutinized him with reservation. "No," she said slowly. "I am not convinced of *that*." She stole a glance at the busy marketplace. "If you owned such a carpet we would not be standing here in a wheeled carriage. And all these uncivilized creatures would not be smiling behind their fingers at us—because the one who drags his feet crossed your path to safety long ago!"

Solomon could blame no one for staring at her. She was so beautiful in her pride and indignation! So cool and untouchable; as if his impetuous kiss had cast a spell over her. He had an urge to shatter this image she had built up around herself. He wanted to snatch off the turban draped around her head, shake out the golden pins in her hair and let it fall loose and wild to her shoulders. . . .

She began to fidget beneath his gaze. He turned his back on her suddenly and over the noises of the street, his laughter rose in a spiral of exuberance. He flicked the whip over the backs of the stallions. They lurched forward and Makada was thrown against him. He quickly freed one hand at a time from the reins and firmly fastened her arms around his waist.

As they passed through the gate they were forced to slow down. Crowds were coming from all directions. The glittering headbands of visiting princes could not outshine the eyes of maidens who boldly rode in carts heaped high with produce or walked demurely beside the mules of their parents. And the young men, elaborately idle against the city walls, appraised them with heavy-lidded indolence. These were the serious-minded young men, hoping to find their future wives among the early arrivals, yet withholding their final judgment until others would arrive from villages and towns to wait for the Feast of Weeks. During this festival, many marriages would be arranged.

When he told Makada this, she was only interested in knowing if *he* had ever waited like this.

"Never," he lied.

And he studied the very young ones, imitating the worldly postures of the taller, full-grown men; leaning against the wall between the gates, assuming the attitudes of weary experience while their hearts were leaping like fish in a wild sea. Ahiah had caught him here more than once, a refugee from the dull lessons with Zadok and Nathan. He knew so well what they must be thinking and feeling, these very young ones down from tending the household sheep in surrounding hills, or fresh from the barley fields of their fathers. He didn't envy them.

Then the arms of Makada instinctively tightened about him as the wheels hit a rut in the road and he put a hand over hers. Her body swayed lightly against his as the chariot moved slowly and he laughed at himself for thinking he was beyond the experience of the heart that leaped like a fish in the sea. Perhaps the mature years did not change the symptoms after all, only the ability to hide them.

Sentries ran forward when they saw the royal chariot unescorted. Before they could spring into the crowd to clear the path, Solomon shook his head vigorously. There was no hurry—no hurry at all. So long as she kept her arms where they were.

Many people had come to pay their tithes to the tax collectors who sat at the gates marking down the weight of silver received, the number of sheep, the fruit and the grain, nuts, honey and oil. A delicately boned, officious young collector was pained when an odorous ram with wicked-looking horns fixed him with a baleful eye, stopped in his tracks and refused to move. He could not be coaxed, led or jerked by the rope into the animal pens. A crowd began to gather and a ripple of giggles passed through the young women who watched. The fastidious nose of the collector caused him to close his eyes with distaste and turn his back on the ram. It was an error. The animal lowered its head and charged. With a surprised and womanish scream, the collector sprawled face down in the dust, and the crowd rocked with laughter. An old farmer leaned against his mule and doubled up with the pain of laughing.

Solomon sighed. "I'm afraid the animal proved himself to be the better man." Seeing an opening now ahead, he drove down the side path of the valley. He asked her again if she would not prefer to visit Bethlehem-Ephrath. It was only a short distance from Jerusalem.

"No!" Her unaccountable vehemence seemed to embarrass her. "I have no wish to travel south of the city—" She changed the subject, a bit lamely he thought, and they rode in silence toward the brook, already finding the dry rocks of its summer bed. As they dismounted, Makada slipped easily out of his arms, looked up from the valley to the high walls of Jerusalem. "Soldiers!" she whispered with a note of fear. "Why are there so many? Do you expect an attack?"

Solomon followed her gaze. She had seen only the companies of the host emerging from the gates. She had no way of knowing that only a small number of the men were needed for the task of the day.

"Look beyond," he said. "And in the far distance—"

He pointed to the struggling lines of men, burdened mules, camels and baggage wagons converging outside the city walls. The helmets and sword hilts of guards flashed in the sun. Officers rode their horses up and down, shouting until order was created in the ranks of the working men.

"You can see it all better from the top," Solomon said with a heavy heart, for this was one of his reasons for wishing to travel a greater distance from the city; it depressed him to witness this sight. "When the Temple is finished," he explained to her, "and our debts are satisfied there will be less need for this forced labor." Inwardly he wondered how long his people would take such a condition with good grace. It was not in their hearts to be anything but free men, powerful and strong in their freedom. They understood, he hoped, that all real freedom is exercised within walls of sound law. And their law as a nation was based on God's word. But sending them away to work in far places could be called an order of a high-handed King.

They crossed the Kidron and started up the hills east of the city. He doubted if she had heard his explanation of the conscription. Once satisfied that his soldiers were on a peaceful mission, she lost all interest. She asked him how it happened that his great city had been established so out of the way. No rivers for shipping lay at its door and the sea was many miles away; even the great caravan routes passed it by. "And still, all the rivers and seas and roads heap their wealth at your door," she said. "It is an unlikely place to hold such power."

"I have often thought the same thing." Solomon parted the heavy branches, hanging low over the path, and held them till she passed. "My father once said Jerusalem was like this tough and beautiful olive tree. It grows in stony land and before it becomes too gnarled and old to flourish it sends forth a new family of seeds and the strongest of them grows to take the old one's place."

"Perhaps he was speaking of the kingdom itself," she said, walking quickly ahead. "It is similar then to the law in Sheba. Only when the old tree has not the grace to know it is old and useless, and clings stubbornly to life, it is cut down." She looked about her on the level of the mountain which gave her a direct view of the city across the valley. Then she looked up to the next summit and said, "I must stop for a breath or two—why are you staring at me?"

"Was the Queen of Sheba before you—cut down?"

A faint smile touched her lips. "You think I killed her."

"You couldn't have," he said quickly.

She reached up and plucked a leaf from the tree, smoothed it tenderly against the palm of her hand.

"Yes I could. Easily. She threw a sharp-pronged meat fork into the back of my baby leopard. Since then I have had no liking for leopards." She looked up, wide-eyed. "But I like very much to hunt. Have you speared many lions, and where in your country are the best waterfowl?"

"You were there when she died?" he asked, unable to banish the picture of suggested violence from his mind. "Your mother—Queen Belkis—"

Thinking of her mother seemed to be an unemotional business.

"If I hadn't been there," she said casually, "she wouldn't have died." And she told Solomon in spare, cold words how the old Queen had heaved her gross weight across the room, trying to kill her. "She lost her balance. She had small feet but always wore shoes much too tight. So you could say she was killed by vanity—not her own dagger—I like the color and form of this leaf." She touched it softly, then slowly tore it in two, then four parts and finally scattered all the small pieces on the ground. She looked at Solomon, smiling, and dusted off her hands.

Curiosity swept through him like fire over a dry field. "What did you do—after the period of mourning had passed?"

A puzzled expression leveled her brows. "Mourning?"

He explained the time of sorrow after a loved one had died. Surely she must have felt the shadow over her life.

"No," she said with disarming frankness. "I rejoiced because the shadow was finally gone." She moved slowly, as if in rhythm to some inner music, toward the ancient olive press with its great wheel that stood in the middle of a cleared space. Birds passed from the fringe of trees with a rustling noise. "I danced," she said, moving one arm in a strange, symbolic gesture and following it with her body into a sinuous pattern. Her anklets jingled as her feet scarcely seemed to move from the ground and the thin layers of skirts whipped back and forth as she turned. She moved in shadow and light and the sun pierced the groves of fruitful boughs to dance on the gold of her bracelets.

Solomon caught his breath, not without a sense of guilt. He was looking on some pagan goddess breathing life into all his old memories of careless lingering near the pillars of vine-covered shrines in Canaan where Astarte dwelt with the serpent at her thigh. . . .

She stopped so abruptly her skirts whirled themselves about her body before spreading out as she slipped to the ground. She sat there, legs crossed, and with her hands folded in her lap she said it was difficult to complete this dance. "It has meaning once a year," she said, "when I dance before my gods with a pack on my back. My people are assured then that their Queen is able to move lightly with all the burdens of the state on her shoulders."

Solomon sat on the stone rim of the oil press and looked down at her. She had turned her attention to the surrounding beauty of the sloping land. "If I were the Pharaoh's daughter," she said suddenly, "I would ask to have my gods built here. I would see them rise in fine stone and cedar and the altars before them would be alive with precious gems—" She became silent and pensive. "Why is it forbidden?"

"Because the One we worship has given us ten laws which we must obey," Solomon said. "He has said first of all that he is the Lord our God and no others shall be before Him."

"What does this selfish god of yours look like?"

Solomon felt that he was instructing a child, one who would never understand perhaps. He smiled, "Let us talk of other things—"

"I want to know!"

"How can I tell you? He is not a graven image. We cannot bow before stone and wood and call something made with man's hands an object of worship. Come, tell me more of your land."

"You are afraid," she said, lowering her head and looking up at him with eyes of suspicion. "You are afraid to speak the name of this deity—or is he nameless as well as without body?"

"He is Eternal," said Solomon, "and Nameless."

"Where do you hide him?"

"I wish you would ask that of every man you meet," he said with a smile. "Where do we hide Him?" For a moment he was lost in a thought that moved into the distance and he had to recall it to the present. "He is invisible, yet he is in all things—"

Anger flashed in her eyes. She was very still.

"You ask me to believe that?"

"No," he said in a mild voice. "You asked a question. I answered it."

"You speak in riddles."

"So does God," he said.

"Have you ever seen him—or heard his voice?" She spoke softly, but as her irritation increased her voice became husky. "Why do you hold all this knowledge back from me—when I journeyed far to sit as I am at this moment"—her eyes softened, her voice lost its edge of anger—"when I came to sit at your feet and learn, Solomon?"

He looked into her upturned face and wanted to touch it with his fingers. It was a simple thing to do, to lean forward and caress the smooth oval of cheek and throat, but he refrained. He was no teacher, if any existed who could teach a person into belief. No words could penetrate a lifetime of tradition. She was born as an animal is born and her instincts are still those of the animal. But she speaks to me, he thought, and asks me why we believe as men who were meant to be more than beasts who have no will, and no choice, no sense of right and wrong.

"I heard Him," he said simply. He told her how, after he was anointed King of Israel, he had felt on his back and soul a burden under which no ruler could dance. He had walked out of the palace, through the night-deserted streets of the city and he had wandered out into the countryside, not caring where he wandered. When he looked up from the shale and brush at his feet he had found himself near the high place of Gibeon. A crude altar stood on the top of the hill, for before the days of unity the people worshiped and sent up incense and the fat of sacrifice to the Lord on many hills in the promised land. And it was there, on the moon-pale crest of Gibeon that he knelt and prayed. . . .

He could not look down on the moist, parted lips so eager to receive his words, as if they were food and nourished the same urgency that stirred him to prodigious tasks. He wondered, for an instant, what lay behind the leashed energy of *her* purpose.

"You prayed," she prompted him, "to something—someone—?"

"I prayed," he said. And the words of his prayer seemed to hang before him, in the boughs of the trees, shining through the green shadow laid upon it by the years, cool with a pure humility so easily lost, so carelessly put away . . .

"I said,— 'Thou hast shown great and steadfast love to thy servant David my father, because he walked before Thee in Faithfulness, in righteousness, and in uprightness of heart toward Thee! and Thou has kept for him this great and steadfast love and has given him a son to sit on his throne this day. And now, O Lord my God, Thou hast made Thy servant king in place of David my father, although I am but a little child; I do not know how to go out or come in . . .'" Why had the words stayed with him as they had been spoken on that night at Gibeon, while he had forgotten many others? He was sure he had spoken with more importance on occasion, his mouth had formed words which were written down by others and called Proverbs, words he could not recall—yet all these were written on his heart as if it were a stele of stone incised with truth, and it could be, he thought, that we carry with us the moments of greatness when we face God, and they are held within the ark of our body as the tablets of the law are held in the ark of the covenant . . . He was not sure, afterward, if he gave voice to all these things, or whether he was conscious at all that a woman sat at his feet, listening . . . But it was all in his mind, every word of it: "'. . . Thy servant is in the midst of Thy people whom Thou hast chosen, a great people, that cannot be numbered or counted for multitude. Give Thy servant therefore an understanding mind to govern Thy people, that I may discern between good and evil; for who is able to govern this Thy great people?'"

He was vaguely aware of her leaning toward him, seeing her tongue pass quickly over her lower lip, her eyes shine with the glitter of a small, greedy cat . . .

"Then you heard the voice—or did he appear as a falcon, the sun," she asked, "or speak out of a tree?"

He could touch her then, without desire. She was a beautiful animal at the moment, nothing more. He took her hand and idly touched the blazing stone of the ring on her forefinger. What could he call a dream and know it to be more than a dream? When Ahiah and Zadok knew of what happened on Gibeon, Ahiah had called it an interesting theophany, and Zadok's great eyes had filled with awe at the Voice of God as it came through the rustling of leaves, the sighing of the night birds and whirlwind of sound . . .

"Because you have asked this,"—Solomon heard and listened and remembered now—"and have not asked for yourself long life or riches or the life of your enemies . . ."—because he had asked for understanding to discern what was right, behold, he was being given this wise and discerning mind, and the riches and honor he had not asked for—". . . And if you will walk in my ways, keeping my statutes and my commandments, as your father David walked, then I will lengthen your days."

Her hand grew suddenly cold beneath his, slipped from his hold and as he looked at her she seemed to withdraw her whole body by the gesture.

"You look frightened." He smiled and rose suddenly to his feet, extending his hands to her.

She remained motionless a moment, staring up at him. "If you can't see him how do you know your god exists?"

"You worship the sun," he said, "among other things?" She nodded. "At the moment," he asked, "can you see the sun?"

She looked about her. The sun had gone beyond the trees. She looked back at him, a bit fearfully.

"You can't see it, can you? Does that mean it isn't there? That there is no radiance left of its light?" He pulled her to her feet and she stood beside him and winced from a bright sunbeam visible where she stood and hidden from her where she had sat on the ground. "Now do you understand what I'm trying to say—?" Solomon took her by the arm and they started up the side of the hill. And by her next question he knew she understood nothing at all . . .

"If this god is invisible why do you build him a house?" And other questions tumbled one after another against his ears. Could he take her one day to Gibeon? She would like to see this mountain top for herself. Was it more beautiful than this hillside—would it make a fine high place to build a shrine . . . ?

He had to pause a moment and turn his face away when she asked if it were possible for her to meet Moses. And when he doubted that it could be arranged, she sulked a moment and assured him she would listen with respect to everything the man had to say.

They moved out from the shade of the silver-green trees. They had reached the summit and she grew silent, gazing across the Valley of the Kidron to the city of Jerusalem spread out on the other side; and because she was warm despite the cooling breeze that met them from the west, she breathed through parted lips and slowly unwound the blue veil that held her hair.

"They are leaving," she said quietly.

Solomon turned his eyes from her and looked to the walls and the gate where Benaiah and his aides, mounted on horses, were receiving the labor list and watching the army of workers separate on the road. The boisterous, singing lines were moving in opposite directions, on the road that led northward and the route that led to the south. And women, clinging to a farewell embrace, marched along with their men until the way grew long. Then they fell back in silence, waiting at the roadside until the last wagon swayed out of sight.

"It will not be for long," Solomon spoke softly after those who had started for the mines and those who would join others at garrisons and towns along the way to Lebanon. He had a share in all the aching separation of those who loved. And he wished he could stand outside the suffering of others and be content to pity them; ar at least see them as a mass, a whole without distinct and separate individuality . . .

As he watched, silent groups of women disappeared beyond the walls for a month of waiting. He wished again that he had spared himself the sight. He should have gone into the Tyropoean Valley, on the other side, or invented urgent business in some palace of Mahanaim . . .

Then a woman's voice came up to him, clear and sweet, and another who had waited by the roadside picked up the song that had faded into the north and the south. As the daughters of Jerusalem lifted their voices they went back to the work still to be done. A great pride in them soothed the uneasiness in Solomon. For he was the cause of their separation and the loneliness of their waiting. Overskirts were folded upward to strong waists as they swung scythes to their shoulders and moved into distant fields, golden ripe for early cutting; and others carried hoes and mattocks toward the slopes of later harvest where the crop must still be tended.

But as their song faded from his ears, the echo of it died suddenly within him, for his eye was caught by a piece of rose-colored cloth waving from the sill of the deserted house which was once Adonijah's!

He had been able to pass the sprawling house beyond the trees on the far side many times, with only a faint longing to hear Adonijah's laughter rolling out of the open doors on a summer night; or if he had been intent on a journey of business past the quarters of the guard, Solomon would wish briefly that they would suddenly spring to life with the flashing helmets of his brother's bodyguard of fifty, and he would allow a moment to hear the thunder of chariot wheels and the hoofs of their horses as they went with Adonijah up and down the land—in the sad days when he was joyful, thinking he was to be king . . .

But this bit of rose-colored cloth!

Recognized instantly as the cleaning cloth of a servant, obeying his orders to always keep the house in readiness, it was still a shock. His mouth felt dry and his throat constricted for a moment. He must have uttered some small sound of surprise, for Makada asked what was the matter, why did he stare so at the house across the valley?

It was strange that he felt no reluctance. He spoke as he thought, telling her that for a moment he had forgotten that Haggith was dead. The bit of rose-colored fabric was bright and new, just as the gown Haggith had donned for the coronation feast of her son. And when her son was not anointed king, when the last oxen turning on a spit over the fire had fallen on the deserted ground, and there was no more feasting—the mother of the one who cursed Solomon and fled, was the only one left in the big silent rooms.

"She would not leave the house," Solomon said. "But she went from window to door to window, looking out into bright sun, letting her hair hang wet from winter rain that blew in against her, and her eyes sank deep in her head with a wild look and she kept calling out for her son. She refused to wear fresh clothes and the robe faded, the sleeves were torn and when she leaned over the sill the rose-colored rags would blow in the wind—" The picture was too vivid in his mind. Poor Haggith, calling to Adonijah, but not as he was greeted on that day of fear when he clung to the altar. She had returned to earlier days when he was not yet being hailed as the new King of Israel, back to the days when Absalom and Amnon were still his older brothers. And she called out as if to a child, telling him to come into the house, out of the wet grass, to put aside his war games with a wooden sword, to come now, come into the house, child, and warm your feet at the fire . . .

"When I visited her," Solomon said, "she spoke to me as if I were a child and had been playing some game with Adonijah."

Apparently his story was distasteful to the Queen, for she became suddenly very still.

"Adonijah?" she asked slowly.

"My brother." Solomon apologized: "I have tired you with this story—"

"I should like to meet—your brother," she said.

"So should I," Solomon said. "In friendship. But he has none for me—although I did nothing to forfeit it." For a moment, glancing at Makada, he was afraid she thought he was being false. It suddenly became important to him that she know the truth—that David had given him, Solomon, the blessing he should have given to the elder son . . .

But he could see that this, too, was a mystery to her. She could not know that a command of a king, who was also his father, was still a command. To be obeyed.

"I had no alternative—" he began, then smiled suddenly. "I want to show you Gibeon, if that is what you want to see. I'll take you wherever you wish to go, do whatever you wish to do—everything within my power."

A look of sly mischief clouded her eyes. "There is one thing you cannot do. You are not allowed. Your law, or your god, or your people—something won't allow you to build one of my gods on that spot down there—where we sat near the olive press." She moved toward the other side of the summit, hoping to impress her words with a playful scorn as she pointed below. And Solomon followed her, bemused by her audacious remarks.

Then he saw that she was staring down, far down at the base of the Mount of Olives, where its gentle, fruitful slopes were transformed on the side that faced the east.

She could not speak. He took hold of her arm and it was cold to his touch. A shudder ran through her.

He could not quite understand her horror. Perhaps because he had been born in Jerusalem and felt, somehow, that to cross the brook and rise to the mountain groves of olive was a natural thing. To see beauty and a city of peace—he preferred to see it as a city of hope—and then to look down on the bleak, scarred emptiness of the cliffs that dropped into the Dead Sea, was part of his youth, his maturity, part of his thought. The great hills of Moab and Ammon plunging down into the sea of salt, were a challenge to him, never a towering fear. What was it she saw then, to make her afraid? She was primitive in her soul, and there could be nothing here to strike her with the reminder of bottomless eternity.

He put an arm about her shoulders and they were cold and unmoving.

He took the length of blue veil from her fingers and covered her, and only then did she stir. And eventually she attempted to smile.

"It is like a punishment," she whispered. "It waits down there—like a punishment." Repelled and fascinated, she stared down at the Sea so deep below the level of the Great Sea on the other side. The waters of the Jordan had torn down from the high Lebanons in the north, plunged wildly into winding patterns, and deep into the oasis of Jericho; and here it lost itself—in the lifeless waters with its shore of precipice, marl, and weird forms of salt . . .

"I want to go back," she said quickly, and turned away from the sunless deeps of the rift that seemed to cleave the world in two.

To all outward appearance, that afternoon was much the same as any other in late spring. Still there were those few, particularly two women of the palace basking in the sun of composure, who were disturbed by unseen insect wings of apprehension. It was a faint humming without substance, rising to a high pitch and whining through the veins; something variously heard and instantly killed by cold reasoning. It was too privately and vaguely experienced to merit a spoken eulogy.

Tanis heard it.

She was watching the dark forefinger of a gardener trace a watery furrow between small cones of soil that held fresh seed. And even as she commended him, the tiny channel became the brook of Kidron and by crossing it this day with the Queen of Sheba, Solomon was deserting his city and all those who loved him. It became in her imagination a more tragic exile than David's, when the old King's tears fell in the vale and on the hill of olives as he bowed his head and descended the eastern slope to find refuge across the Jordan, a refuge from Absalom's greed for the throne. And she was shamed by these foolish, exaggerated fears. Angry with herself, she called up the true name of her emotion. Without warning or cause, she knew the pain of jealousy. With trembling fingers she twisted a bracelet into the flesh of her wrist until pain became something to be seen, a blue and throbbing network at the base of her palm. She hurried out of her garden, waving away the servants who would follow her.

She was an infrequent visitor and rarely a solitary one in the courtyards beyond her walls. Like Solomon's mother, she preferred the privacy of her own garden. When they met unexpectedly, their surprise was mutual and quickly concealed by pleasant greetings.

Bathsheba was sitting on the far side of the smooth stonework that circled an acacia tree.

Bracing herself, Tanis looked down into the eyes that saw too quickly through a deception.

"I have only a glimpse of the new blooms from my roof," she said, "and their color intrigues me. Crimson, purple, yellow—I must see them closer . . ."

"Then I'll walk with you." Bathsheba rose with unusual haste.

Tanis need not have bothered with an excuse, for the eyes of the older woman held an inward look, faintly troubled.

They walked, and Bathsheba's disciplined hands made unnecessary motions as she rolled up her handwork. She pushed it with small, savage gestures deep into the bag of fine linen fastened at her waist. She looked up suddenly, fearing that the Pharaoh's daughter would somehow guess that this odd vehemence was also burying unwelcome suspicions. But Tanis was placid, as always, speaking of the healthy branches under which they passed, pausing to touch an exotic vine out of Babylon and wondering if its roots were taking well to strange soil.

Bathsheba was relieved; but her lips would not unlock the taut muscles of her face. An earlier hour of the day had compressed her mouth into a line of firm speculation. She had been at the open window of her chambers, examining the sill for any dust overlooked by a careless servant. Hearing someone humming softly below, she had smiled with indulgence after the woman who sang as she walked along the path leading to the house of Solomon's royal guest. The voice stopped suddenly, as if in fear of being overheard. The woman glanced swiftly over her shoulder and did not continue her song as she crossed the garden. In any other woman the glance would have been modest and self-effacing. On the face of Abishag— who had forgotten how to smile and how to sing—the look was furtive. An admission of some secret guilt.

Only one person could evoke song from a voice grown bitter as an apple of Sodom; only the imminence of that person's return to Jerusalem, or some fresh knowledge of his whereabouts. And if Adonijah were close at hand, the news would be cried joyfully at the gates—if Solomon knew of it . . . Bathsheba stood at the window long after Abishag, with her smile and broken song, was out of sight. Resolution to turn away all small concerns was immersed against her will in a tide of worry. If only another prophet had risen when old Nathan had become a shade! She could go to him and his words would reassure her, would still the senseless fear pounding at the back of her neck, tightening her mouth, holding her entire body rigid as a pillar of salt. It was something she could not reveal to anyone, particularly to her son. He would say look now, how you selfishly begrudge the girl's contentment in serving another queenly woman.

She must force herself to believe that, she had told herself, then hastened down to sit in the garden where others passed by. Perhaps she would hear a bit of gossip and she could face Solomon then with something more tangible than her own formless anxiety. But when Tanis came along, Bathsheba was shamed before such calm dignity. She admitted to herself then, that Abishag was happy once more only because she was more content serving the Queen of Sheba. Nothing more.

Bathsheba turned her head aside, delicately inflated her cheeks for an instant, working her mouth in a circular exercise before setting it in a relaxed smile. She lifted her chin and felt much better, walking beside the Pharaoh's daughter who was superior to the usual woman fears. And Bathsheba was conscious that others looked after them with admiration— two gracious, richly gowned women walking slowly through a tranquil garden.

They reached the bend in the path and paused to exclaim over the soft and heavy purple, the crimson blooms leaping like flame over the hedge.

Solomon's two scribes could be heard arguing before they appeared from the direction of the palace. Ahiah was the first to see the women. He dug an elbow into Elihoreph's ribs to silence him, and bowed.

"Peace be with you," he said, then with a twinkle in his eye he asked Tanis to break off a flower that he might put it behind his ear. "As a reminder," he chuckled, "that I must purchase a new quern in the town for my wife."

Tanis smiled as she plucked the flower. "For such a worthy reason, Ahiah, how can I refuse?"

He looked ridiculous with a flower behind his ear, Bathsheba thought. But then, he was a very learned man. A superior education entitled him to an occasional eccentricity. Although his wife was old-fashioned and ground her own meal, she at least saw that her husband's hair was oiled, his robes were freshly cleaned and he did not let the latchet of his sandal drag behind his heel as the other one did.

Elihoreph kept shifting his weight from one foot to the other, looking somewhat like a bony-branched tree hung with banners, swaying in the afternoon breeze. His farewell, as he moved away with his brother, was as belated and vague as his greeting had been.

When the brothers had gone the two women exchanged understanding smiles. The encounter with the two scribes had put a quietus on their troubled thoughts. Bathsheba was composed now, ready to visit the steward of the household. She went on alone, to make her weekly tour of the palace kitchens and the spice chambers. And Tanis, too, was in a quiet mood. She would go back to her house and lie in a warm bath and open the bottles of new scent, recently arrived, ordered especially for her by the King. There was no profit in hoping too intensely that Solomon would visit her tonight. But she would dress with inordinate care and be prepared. A small sense of triumph lightened her step homeward. She had successfully concealed her qualms from her mother-in-law whose sharp eyes could penetrate the secret of the most reluctant sphinx.

At the fork of the road she smiled as she turned into her private walk for she could hear the mild rumble of Ahiah's disgust as he walked the other way, toward the palace gates.

"Let me remind you of last year, Elihoreph," he was saying. "You went on just such a foolish expedition as you are planning now. To dig up old bones of ancient giants and the pots they cooked in! Your destination was Jericho, not too far away. And when Solomon became worried at your long absence and sent his soldiers—where did they find you? Miles away in the other direction! Living on wild berries and stale crusts, roaming over Mount Sinai as if you were Moses himself! At least he brought down with him Ten Commandments. What did you have? Two blistered feet!"

"This time," Elihoreph answered in a dreamlike voice, "I plan to ride a mule."

When they reached the city it was Ahiah who bargained and paid for the animal. He led it back to the cistern where he had left his brother to fill the waterbags for his journey.

He stopped a few paces away. Elihoreph was engaged in such absorbing discussion with Jehoshaphat he was filling the same waterbag again and again, unaware that it had a large hole in the bottom. Ahiah chuckled softly and went to the stall of a leather merchant to buy a new one. He also stopped at the cheesemaker's. And he bought dried figs and nuts and bread and stored them in the saddlebags on the mule's back.

"My brother," Elihoreph greeted him, beaming. "You are so very good to me."

Ahiah shrugged. "Good to myself. If I thought you were starving in the wilderness—and you are certainly one who could starve on the most fruitful hill—the bread at my table this night would stick in my throat! Now go, leave on this wild goat's journey of yours before the sun sets."

"God be with you!" Elihoreph was cheerful. His long arms hung loosely at his sides and with the mule trailing behind, he made his way through the busy streets.

Ahiah and Jehoshaphat looked after him.

"He bids God stay with *me*." Ahiah shook his head slowly. "How can a man possess such a brilliant mind and so little common sense! Now I'll not have a sound sleep until he has returned."

Jehoshaphat was looking in the other direction. Cries of "Hail, Solomon!" began to fill the air and the crowd about the cistern moved away to join those who were shouting greetings. The King's chariot with Solomon and the Queen of Sheba clattered over the paved streets and disappeared up the avenue leading to the palace.

"It is the first time," Jehoshaphat said, "that Solomon has spent more than two or three hours away from the Temple."

"Then it is time he spent five or six!" Ahiah curbed the irritation in his voice. "Is there any harm in a hard-working man taking his ease for one afternoon?"

Jehoshaphat turned a bland smile on Ahiah. "None at all," he said. "I was only repeating the words of Zadok. He says Solomon's head turns too often after the woman from Sheba—"

Ahiah was about to protest when Jehoshaphat pointed to the flower behind Ahiah's ear and asked what in the name of a dirty Philistine was *that*?

Ahiah turned the flower over in his hand, remembered vaguely that Tanis had given it to him, but forgot the reason. His mind was filled with a strange disquiet. He tossed the flower away. A young girl picked it up and pressed its fragrance into her face. Ahiah and the King's recorder walked slowly up the streets that were beginning to clear themselves of the day's rush of newcomers to the city.

They met the High Priest at the entrance to the forecourt of the tent of meeting. Zadok's arms were laden with small golden censers.

"They were a gift to me from David," he said. "I want to place them in the Temple with my own hands."

And the three of them walked slowly, because Zadok was no longer young and the ascent to the Temple area shortened his breath. Ahiah paused to allow the old man to rest, but he covered his purpose by turning around to survey the sloping land.

"The tabernacle is no longer isolated on a high place, Zadok," he said.

"In David's time, it was the highest. Before he bought the threshing floor up there." Zadok's eyes filled with a shining zeal as he looked up at the Temple. "I was unwilling, at first, to make this change. But the city has crawled up to the tent that David built, and it is right that the house of God should rise on a beautiful elevation. Ahiah—" his face was suddenly seamed with new lines of concern "—I want to ask something of you." He walked to the side of the road and sank slowly to a large boulder. He allowed Jehoshaphat to hold the vessels that would give forth clouds of incense in the holy place, and he mopped his forehead with the back of his hand. "I am the High Priest—the only High Priest since Abiathar conspired with Adonijah to seize the throne. And I am proud to know I carry on the holy office that has come down to me from Aaron through Eleazar. And through me my son's sons—"

Ahiah rubbed the side of his nose and sighed inwardly. Zadok was not one to speak freely of personal feelings. There was some hidden reason for this recital of his history, for he knew that it was common knowledge that the custodians of the sanctuary were of the select order of Aaron since the day of his anointing by Moses. And Levites performed the lesser tasks and were the caretakers and formed a great company who paid no tithes and owned no land, for the descendants of Levi had become an immolation in the eyes of the Lord and were favored in place of the firstborn. Now why did Zadok go on in this manner, drily recounting through his white beard his hopes that the future would bring more civil authority to the priestly ones? Ahiah detected an unprecedented humility in the High Priest. He said he was "only" a priest and this morning as he stood before the veil that concealed the ark he had beseeched the Lord to send down a prophet before a day of wrath descended on His people.

"—And in that moment when I felt only a vault of emptiness and desolation within me, I had a revelation. This is the time of preparation. The earth has been plowed by the Lord and the seed planted and it has thrived and grown strong so that in this spring and summer of our faith the harvest will be rich for all the years to come. It was a golden light I saw and it shone on the face of Solomon our King and on his crown and

I knew then that there would come prophets after us—those who would speak out in a loud voice as no priest can. And then, when my heart was lifted up in thanksgiving it seemed to me a cloud came over the house we are building up on this hill. And the cloud came not from the sky but from the armies of the godless who cast a wicked shadow over the land and trampled the golden grain of summer on our hills; the hoofs of their horses trampled the golden grain of our faith. And in the midst of the healthy full-grown wheat were the tares that could not be told from the good stalks until they were full-grown also, and they were not plucked out in the time of plucking and they poisoned the land. . . ."

He sat with his chin fallen deep into his chest and the tasseled fringe of his robe touched the dust at his feet. Ahiah no longer looked at him as if he suffered from a touch of the sun. Whatever was in the priest's soul at the moment, it was real and pitiable.

Ahiah looked down at him and it seemed that Zadok's posture was symbolic of his stern exhortations. To fix one's eyes on the ground was to blot out the freedom and light of broader paths that allowed others to walk beside you. The High Priest was one who traveled with a foot lamp down the stern and narrow path of ritual, putting vast importance on ceremony. He lacked the wider vision of a prophet who moved always in the center of his own light—and though there was a risk of fanatic brilliance—at least it fell on those who were lost by the wayside.

Zadok was troubled indeed when he allowed the corners of his robe to lie in such a manner. Ahiah bent down and arranged the hem of the old man's garments. When he stood up he saw Jehoshaphat staring at him in disbelief. He couldn't blame him. Ahiah and Zadok had never been the closest of friends. But he was touched by the first indication of helplessness in the priest who always stood head and shoulders over other mortals, his confidence unassailable. He must say something now, if possible, to assuage his despondent heart. Let Jehoshaphat's mouth drop open, drop to the ground if it wished.

"When you speak of tares in the grain, Zadok, you imply that the poisonous stalks thrive in our own midst."

Zadok nodded his head slowly but did not look up.

"Have you forgotten that there are as many different men and beliefs in this kingdom of ours," Ahiah asked, "as—as—"

"Climates?" Jehoshaphat suggested.

Ahiah thanked him with a quick nod and continued.

"If the nation itself has survived in spite of this, then what is it you fear from the outside?"

Zadok sighed heavily. "If there is first barbarism within our walls, if it is allowed to flourish without restraint—there is no longer need for walls. An enemy from without cannot be stopped by towers that have already crumbled. I see cracks in the wall. They appear in the judgment hall when the King does not punish an idolater. They appear in the eyes of the workmen on the Temple when they see the King ride away from his duty with the arms of a pagan woman around his waist. If the King is encompassed by the arms of one who kneels before graven images—" his voice trembled deep in his throat "—then the blood that has spilled over this land in God's name will only give drink to His enemies! Surely our fathers fought for survival, not for the destruction of all the generations of man!"

"You fear for the time to come," Ahiah said. "Do you have so little faith, High Priest, that you see another duration in bondage—would your God and mine place us down in a promised land and then desert us till we are hemmed round by mountains without rainfall and a sea in which the waters would not pile up once more and give us safe passage wherever we go?"

He stopped, a bit surprised at his own words—for he could remember no time in his life when he felt compelled to proselytize to a priest. But now that he had started, it was simpler to continue rather than out-stare the astonishment of Jehoshaphat and the thoughtful burning in Zadok's eyes.

"Perhaps we take too much for granted," he said in a low voice. "In our endeavor to withstand the tyrant at our gates, we become the tyrants. We are attempting too much when we say this tree is planted and here it stands for all time and all storms will bypass its height and its girth. We should be content to nurture the roots, Zadok. The roots. They grow deep and they spread in the warmth of the earth and after pillage and burning and devastation the tree may fall, but who can stop the roots from reaching up, thrusting aside the dark earth and growing tall and strong again in the sun? And there is this, a certainty: If the armies of the godless or those who serve other gods—and I speak not only of the Ashtaroth cults and the Baals, but of gods made of gold, greed, lust and power—if the armies of those sweep over us, they destroy the very wellspring of their own survival! Do you not preach that the Almighty is the God of all men? Then if He is denied, dishonored by the wicked, He will cut them off in total darkness—" Ahiah rubbed the back of his neck and studied the sky to avoid the eyes of the others. And he heard Zadok's voice, slow and thoughtful.

"May He look down with mercy on our mortal defections as men. But may His countenance shine upon us for what we try to be in His eyes—a people who would walk in His ways and partake of His divine nature—to live in His image as we were meant to do."

Ahiah pursed his mouth in the silence that followed and he frowned, anxious to extricate himself from this somber meeting.

"I must return to my house," he said. "It is beginning to grow dark."

"Wait," said Zadok, rising.

Ahiah waited, but Zadok was again ill at ease. He made a great ceremony of taking the golden vessels from the hands of Jehoshaphat.

"I wish, Ahiah—I wish you would speak to Solomon."

Ahiah grinned. "Why shouldn't I? We're not enemies."

"I mean seriously." Zadok's strong face was half in shadow. Its planes and ridges stood out pale and white as stone in the early starlight. "He will listen more readily to you."

"That is a strange admission from his old teacher."

"I told you before—I believe I also told him," Zadok said, "that he learned too quickly. Too much and too soon. And he believed in nothing."

"A long time ago."

"When your opinion of me, Ahiah, has been censorious, oh I know what you think of my scrupulous, uncompromising rules on the observance of ceremony—but when you think of that, ponder for a moment on the state of Solomon's convictions."

Ahiah was beginning to smart beneath the small whip lashes of the day. He made no effort to soften the irritation in his voice.

"His convictions, Zadok, are as strong as your own. His tolerance, to you, is worse than apostasy. And because you cannot condone it, you misunderstand it. As for your precious rituals—and some of them will be changed, mark my word, as surely as the Lord stopped Abraham from killing Isaac and substituted a ram for the sacrifice—who observes the rituals more faithfully than Solomon?"

"You are the one who misunderstands, Ahiah." Zadok's voice had regained its authority. He was once more on sure and solid ground. "If I am overzealous in my observances, it is done because I believe with all my soul in their acceptance by the One I worship. But to attend ceremony, to give it the appearance of devotion without true belief—isn't that another matter?"

A strange uneasiness filled Ahiah. He remembered a question put to him this morning by Eli the physician. He had asked, too casually, how long the Queen of Sheba planned to visit in Jerusalem. And Zadok's question now held more than the argument of Solomon's true belief.

Ahiah started toward the road leading to the palace grounds. He paused, then turned slowly. Zadok was standing motionless, as if he had no doubt that Ahiah would turn back to him.

"Well then," Ahiah said. "What is it you would have me say to Solomon—and I say quickly to you, Zadok, this is no promise. I am no merchant in a stall, passing goods from a man's field to the table of another."

"Let us say," Zadok said, "that I wish to remind Solomon that the completion of the Temple is of first importance. And let us say, that an hour neglected today becomes too easily a day wasted tomorrow."

"You speak as if he were for hire! You would perhaps like me to tie a mason's apron on the King and put a trowel in his hand in place of a scepter!"

"Is he any less a servant of God than you and I?" Zadok's voice had risen and several Levites passing by turned their heads questioningly. Zadok waved them away with a brusque gesture and he lowered his voice. "You are confusing my words, Ahiah. You know full well the meaning of them. I repeat, the structure must be completed before the winter rains. If the dedication is to take place during the Feast of Tabernacles—conjure up in your own head the skill, the time it will need. Above all, above the labor of hands and the united efforts of the entire nation—the leadership of Solomon is most important!"

For a moment neither spoke. Ahiah knew that Zadok's appeal was costing the majestic priest a measure of the dignity he treasured so highly. But he no longer was warmed by the condescension. And he said as much, knowing it would bring Zadok closer to an expression of naked truth.

"You see no harm done, Ahiah. And perhaps you are right. I hope so. But it could be only the beginning. If I must speak boldly of this woman from Sheba—then I speak boldly."

Ahiah wagged his head from one side to the other. "You take an ephah of grain, Zadok, and bake a loaf with too much leaven. It swells beyond recognition. Before Solomon is King, he is a human being. Allow him to be one. Restrain yourself from looking on an idle hour and stretching it to an eternity. Solomon has had many infatuations in his life. Why do you concern yourself over this one?"

"It is not as the others were," Zadok said.

"Before we know it, your fears will run like a fire through the market-places, out of the gates and finally from Dan to Beersheba! Has any voice raised itself against Solomon in reprimand for his many wives—pagan wives? Certainly not. He has saved Israel too many times by taking pagan women as wives—and in time he controlled the pagan country. I know our laws. I know our commandment forbidding adultery. But can you find the most honored mother, the most faithful wife or husband and father who would not condone in Solomon what they would denounce in their own home? He has made it possible for them to *have* homes, preserve their families and raise them in honor and health. His alliances, the ones you would condemn, have spared the blood of Israel's men, saved it for the labors in the field and the yield of the womb. Now I ask *you*, Zadok. Is that not more important than overseeing the work of a building? Which has the more lasting value—walls of wood and stone, or living walls of flesh, blood and spirit!"

"It is of the spirit that I am thinking," Zadok said in a calm tone. "But I am not an unreasonable man. Can you assure me this attachment is nothing more than a passing infatuation?"

Ahiah was grateful for the gathering shadows. He spoke with conviction, with lighthearted tolerance for the useless worry of the priest and assured Zadok it was nothing more than a fever in the blood.

"Or is that something both you and I only remember, Zadok?"

"If she does not leave soon—what is the cure?"

"An ancient remedy—older than the balm of Gilead," Ahiah said. "The fever burns itself out. A loose rein on the patient, and a certain period—in bed." Ahiah saw an expression of relief come over Zadok's face, almost indiscernible in the waning light. Then the High Priest bowed formally to both men and walked away, up toward the next level of the ascent to the Temple area.

"You spoke well, Ahiah," said Jehoshaphat.

They walked toward the palace and in the courtyard they saw Solomon entering the great hall for the evening meal and he was alone.

"Zadok's mind is often too similar to a burial cave," Jehoshaphat said with great sincerity. "It holds the acrid dust of moldy ideas—"

Ahiah opened his mouth to defend the priest. But if he did so, the words would cause one more person to look upon the King with critical eyes.

"Let us go in and eat with Solomon," Ahiah said. And as they made their way to the great hall and the King's board, the insect-wings of apprehension that had stirred the distant air about Bathsheba and Tanis, came closer to the ear of Ahiah and whined until his head began to ache. What an afternoon it had been! He resolved to drain a glass of strong wine first thing, before tasting the roast lamb and the herbs and honey-cakes he could smell. The buzzing in his head would then drown out the unwelcome harbingers of trouble to come.

As the doors were opened for them, Ahiah sighed and hoped fervently that Zadok believed all he had told him. Because *he* most certainly did not.

Solomon was sure that as soon as the night sky darkened and there was little risk of being observed, Makada would leave her apartments and make another attempt to steal past the Temple walls. Tonight she would succeed. The gate leading to the south side chambers would be unguarded at this hour. He had made certain of that.

Imagining her unnecessary scheming to elude sentries who would not be there, he smiled as he finished his meal. He looked up to find Ahiah watching him again from across the table. Solomon thought he recognized the expression. The deep lines of the scribe's face seemed to fill with the dust of worry kicked up by another of Elihoreph's vague wanderings into the past. Then the hearty booming of Benaiah's voice over the hum of conversation drew everyone's attention and the ending of the commander's anecdote provoked a small explosion of hilarity.

Solomon's laughter was the heartiest, for it was good to see his faithful old Benaiah in such high spirits. It seemed so long ago that David had given his permission for Solomon and his friend, Zabud, to go traveling, but only on condition that Benaiah accompany them. And after passing through dangerous country, hunting their own food, narrowly avoiding trouble with the King's enemies—after watching over the son of David and the son of Nathan like a grizzled and lion-scarred uncle—Benaiah's role of bodyguard had ended abruptly. Solomon had been called home.

"He was off with the speed of wind," Benaiah said. "The tail of his horse spread straight out and wide as a bar of hornbeam! And I—" he jabbed a thumb into his massive chest "—I, the one called valiant out of Kabzeel, the fearless son of Jehoiada, was not with him when he was ambushed in the mountain pass!" He exaggerated his sense of futility, spread it as a humble rug before the company but embellished the ridiculous pattern of his guilt till everyone was laughing. And he asked Solomon if he still bore the scars of the bandit sword.

"That and a few more you surely remember," said Solomon. "Also the pain that lives in them when the rains come." He and Benaiah had fought side by side in those very early days of his reign when David was still alive. Before Hadad took refuge in the rocky wilderness of Edom there had been a brief but savage skirmish in the Negeb; and another with Rezon before Solomon had time to fortify the cities which cut out the sting of the thorn in Damascus. Since then the days of peace had lifted Solomon's sword only in tests of skill on the practice field.

The mention of this brought something to Benaiah's mind. He shook a thick forefinger slowly from side to side, dug his elbows into the table and leaning forward, said he had beheld something this day which made his mouth drop open with surprise.

"When Adoniram and I finished the count of men for the current levy," he said, "we accepted an invitation from the Sabaean population—" he glanced quickly in Solomon's direction and corrected himself "—from the Sabaean soldiers and attendants of my lord's royal guest. And I wish to say that next to my own warriors, there are none better!" He praised their skill with all weapons but above all, their horsemanship. "They were getting ready for some kind of feast day, some deity they call Ashtoreth—I didn't bother about the explanation given me. I kept looking at those dark, almost naked bodies mounted on those short-backed stallions and then something happened you'll never believe. The men were lined up—twenty across—and just as their leader shouted the signal for the race to start across the plain, another horse appeared from out of nowhere. It was black and polished like metal and jewels blazed in a headpiece bearing the royal insignia."

"The Queen of Sheba's steed," said Ahiah.

Benaiah nodded. "It came up to the speeding horses, passed them without effort and returned to the starting point with scarcely a bead of sweat on its flanks. And who do you think was riding this horse I would give my arm to own? A woman!"

The question on everyone's lips remained unspoken for a moment which to Solomon stretched into hours of absurd silence. He glared down the length of the table, angry with the eyes so studiously avoiding his. The Queen of Sheba had been with him the entire afternoon. Until the beginning of dusk. He had made no secret of it! What ailed these men, suddenly dawdling over their food, staring blankly through the lamplight? Was this their manner of telling him the swift rider on the black horse could not have been Makada—for she had captured the heart of their King and was now leading him about like a tame beast on a leash?

Ahiah was carefully examining an ink stain on his forefinger, Jehoshaphat tipping a bowl delicately this way and that, watching the light sparkle like rubies on the wine. A few of the visiting governors from the provinces and princes who had recently arrived, appeared to notice nothing out of the usual and continued to reach for the honeyed fruit and the fine cheese being passed by servants. Solomon was consumed with rage that would strike out at everyone; but, unreasonably, it seized on an irritation of long sufferance. If he did not control himself it would certainly be Barzillai here at his side who would know the whip of the King's tongue and the back of his hand. He must sit in rigid silence, tighten his mouth against offending one of the sons of Old Barzillai. He bore the same name as his father, but here the resemblance stopped. Honor, unfortunately was not inherited with a name and had to be earned by each in his own lifetime. This younger Barzillai was a vain one, using his limited talents as a minor official in Gilead to cleverly purloin for his own aggrandizement the results of honest toil by others, giving no word of praise where it was due. Without admiring it, Solomon respected the man's cold audacity but despised Barzillai for thinking it was a secret.

A muscle in Solomon's jaw grew taut as he watched the studied grace of Barzillai's well-kept hand. It was brushing a crumb down the length of embroidered sleeve. Old Barzillai's knuckles had been rough and gnarled from the hard work that had brought him wealth without false vanity. He had been a good friend to David in the days of exile across the Jordan, in the days when the cries of the dying and wounded had drifted with the winds to Mahanaim from the battle in the woods of Ephraim. And David had prolonged his gratitude beyond the grave by commanding Solomon to forever show kindness to the sons of Barzillai. But whenever this one sat at the royal table, this fawning one who held himself to be superior to all men and was scarcely civil in his speech to anyone but the King, then this sacred obligation was at best a burden beyond human patience. The one who only this afternoon had seen manly beauty and dignity in the misshapen body of the silversmith, was touched with nausea by the sallow elegance of Barzillai. It seemed to Solomon that some playful fuller had mixed a strangely pale dye in one of his huge vats and dipped Barzillai into it, skin, clothes, soul and all, and hung him over a thornbush to bleach dry in the sun.

Solomon of a sudden realized Benaiah was speaking. The commander had obviously paid no heed to the moment of silence and if he had, he must have considered it a compliment to the effect of the story he was now trying to finish:

"—And remember that as I said, she had come like a streak of black lightning out of nowhere, from somewhere hidden by the balsam growth, perhaps, in the valley plain. And I was eager—as all men with blood in their veins would have been eager—to see the face of this woman who was complete master of this superior steed. For she rode as a man rides yet her legs were not visible. She wore a garment of great length and a veil dark as the mane of the horse. Then the race was done and she was the first to return to the line of starting. Voices lifted in praise for her swift and daring ride but she looked neither to the left nor to the right. She was like the dark and silent spirit that troubles the dreams of younger soldiers than myself when they are too long in the fields of battle; the vague and faceless spirit of woman—and still, something about that erect posture was formidable. The unrelenting stiffness of the back draped in darkness struck a note of awe within me. Since I have never known true fear, I could not in truth call it fear. Yet—"

"Get on with it, Benaiah!" Ahiah's head was bent to the side, its weary weight resting in the palm of his ink-stained hand. "Kindly leave the detailed exploration of your inmost thoughts to one who has been trained to observe arid landscapes at a distance. I assure you, if this flat and endless vista holds interest worth preserving, I'll write it out in your own words. That is, if there is enough papyri in all of Egypt on which to record them."

Benaiah's busy brows tangled in a scowl. "It is your job to deal with words. Come to the compound of the armory and let me see your skill with shield and sword!"

Ahiah gave him a lazy nod, accepting the rebuke with a smile. "Then proceed without interruption. You were about to say that the woman passed you as you sat on your horse and you saw her face for the first time and it was—"

"I had not yet come to that!"

"Then the telling takes longer than the race. I'm thinking not of myself, Benaiah, for I hang with adoration on each of your words. But surely your eyes can see that our host, the King, is growing impatient and anxious to be gone?"

He had said this without glancing at Solomon. The amiable impudence of Ahiah restored some of the King's good feeling and he was as anxious as anyone now to hear the identity of the mystery woman.

"The name," Ahiah pleaded. "Nothing more. The Songs of Moses, Miriam and Deborah concerned more important events in our history than a horse race. And they were told in less time—"

"So be it!" Benaiah shouted. "I saw the face. Before it disappeared as suddenly as it came. And it was old! Solid and silent as rock." He grumbled and shrugged. "It was the one who has no tongue!"

On second thought, Solomon was not greatly surprised to hear that Vashi had retained the vigor of her youth. But he was pleased, for Benaiah's sake, to see that the others, particularly Ahiah, were frankly amazed.

Benaiah's voice rumbled now with gruff satisfaction. "So now you sit up and take notice, honored scribe who uses a pen for a sword!" He revenged himself by taking his own time answering all the puzzled questions. With both hands he reached into a large copper bowl filled with hard-shelled nuts. As he ground them between his bare fists Ahiah winced as if his bones were being cracked. Selecting the choice nutmeats, Benaiah chewed them vigorously as he talked. "I was told by a captain of the Queen's guard that this woman, this slave, was born of a wild tribe that roamed the desert and far into the wilderness between the seas. And every secret spring, passage and cave touched by the four winds was known to her before she was captured by the Sabaeans. It is said that she knows her way on narrow trails far better than any scapegoat sent into our own wilderness to die with all our sins upon its head. . . ."

As he continued, the supercilious lift of Barzillai's eyebrow was lost as he listened with rapt attention. Then he must have sensed Solomon's eyes upon him. The smirking superiority quickly returned as he faced the King. A corner of his dry mouth curled up in what was meant to be amused tolerance. It said poor Benaiah must be out of his mind—and how fortunate for Solomon that there was at least one in this room whose thoughts and speech could tread the mountaintops with those of the King.

"My lord," he whispered, and Solomon withdrew slightly from the twisted smile. "May I say only your patience excels your wisdom."

The King nodded with mock solemnity. "Of all people, Barzillai, you are the one best qualified to know."

Barzillai beamed with pleasure. His eyes, watery and pink-rimmed from the afternoon's journey against the wind, moved swiftly to assure himself that someone had overheard this praise from the King.

"What a pity," he went on, carefully subduing his voice beneath the rumble of Benaiah's, "how ironic to find that brave men of action, even one who slew a lion in a snowy pit, are so often infants intellectually, enormously impressed by spectacular banality."

Solomon studied the sycophant out of Gilead with a distaste he made no effort to conceal. But the son of Old Barzillai was blind to everything but his self-esteem. It surrounded him like an invisible wall, transmuting crude insult into pure and golden self-deception. Highly pleased with himself, he turned away to share his glory with an envoy whom he had ignored up to this moment. And as Solomon rose, Barzillai was repeating a story which the envoy must have heard a thousand times: How King David, beloved King David, had spent an evening in the house of Barzillai's father. "I was only a child," Barzillai said, and others nearby heard the familiar, tiresome words and quickly moved away from the sound of his voice. "A mere lad, you must remember. But the moment is a shrine in my memory. The King picked me up and I sat in his lap." His voice faltered and became an emotional whisper. "I sat in the lap of David the King."

It is true, Solomon would have added. You sat in his lap. And from the moment your common backside touched the royal knees you considered yourself sacredly anointed. The thought provoked many methods employed by those who protected the seats of their crown. And they overcame Solomon's temptation to insult the son of the old man who had been his father's friend in a time of need.

He left the room while Barzillai was still boasting, while the servants were lighting the fires of hearth and braziers and the guests of the King talked freely among themselves.

Outside he found Tanis waiting for him. She had thrown a thin shawl over a gown of sea-blue.

"She has gone up there!" She stared into the distance where the building on the hill thrust its black shadow against the starlight. "She wore a cloak and covered her head—I would have followed her and urged her to come back, but she disappeared through the south gate and of course—I dared not follow."

"You are much too generous with your sympathies." He pulled the scarf higher on her thin shoulders and smiled. "She is indulging a childish curiosity, nothing more."

"Then you knew she would be up there?"

Solomon nodded. "She lied to me, naturally. She invented an urgent meeting with three of her dignitaries. That was her excuse for not coming to my table." He shook his head and chuckled. "One moment she is an imperious queen, the next a wide-eyed child—"

"And you are hoping the moment is hastened, my lord, when she is a warm and loving woman." It was neither question nor bitter accusation. But they both knew it to be the truth.

"I said she was a child," Solomon repeated and searched the events of the afternoon to prove it. "Take this absurd suggestion that her pagan gods be built on the hills where the olive grew . . ."

He saw a look of disbelief and fright come into the face of Tanis and he turned it to the starlight's reflection in the fountain pool to see more closely.

"I have never before seen you alarmed." He soothed her qualms, speaking slowly, telling her not to worry over Makada's strange defiance of law and custom, but to try and understand it.

Tanis spoke barely above a whisper. "And will you build her gods for all to see?"

He was disappointed for a moment. He had expected something different from Tanis, a wholehearted support of his own emotional balance. It was not in the great hall during that brief interval of secret and critical silence. And it was not here. If such trivial disappointments evoked such anger within him, what would be his reaction to more serious ones?

"How can you ask that question?" His voice was slow and gentle. "She had no idea that she was suggesting something impossible."

There was a long silence in which Tanis seemed to draw within herself and step back into the shadows of the garden.

"I must leave," she said. And Solomon, puzzled, looked after her a moment. He called, asking her to wait, she must not run away until he had allayed the last of her imagined fears. But she had disappeared. He looked up toward the Temple then, walking slowly toward it, wanting to give the curious child her freedom to peer into dark corners and wonder where Solomon's God was built, for she had told him this afternoon that he was full of contradiction about this deity. If men were created in His image then He must be a man. She could not understand his explanation.

And she had thought, when Solomon mentioned the ark, that he spoke of one like Noah's, constructed to battle through heavy seas and never be submerged. And perhaps her simple imagery was full of unsuspected truth. A covenant with God was a sturdy ark that rode the crest of waves that had threatened it for centuries . . . There was a light in the Temple! Solomon stopped on a terrace of the ascent then suddenly realized that the glow of light, now dull and fading as it moved to other rooms, was carried by the High Priest. Zadok had brought up some of the lamps and censers then from the tabernacle and was walking through the shadows of the Temple rooms!

Solomon broke into a run. By the time he reached the chambers of the south side the rooms of the Levites were empty and smelled of cedarwood and the faint scent of frankincense. Zadok was premature in his offerings of sweet odors in the sacred house. But it was to be expected that he would want to sanctify each room and beam and wall as it took its destined position in the house of God. The recessed frames of the narrow windows cast the rooms in darkness and Solomon stumbled over a carpenter's tool lying on the floor. The noise echoed through the adjoining chambers and the voice of Zadok came back with the echo, hollow and full of anger.

"Who walks in the house of the Lord! Who dares to enter the sanctuary of Yahweh!"

At the same instant Solomon was about to answer, he heard a muffled gasp of fear. He reached the pale archway of illumination in two strides and found himself looking into the inner rooms. He moved along the wall, keeping in shadow. Then he saw Makada. She stood as if frozen with terror in the holy place, staring with horrified eyes at what she saw before her, beyond the steps leading into the room where the ark holding the stone tablets of the law would one day rest, shielded by a veil of richest thread. The enormous golden cherubim were bathed in shafts of greenish light streaming down from the clerestory above. The outer wings of each touched the walls and the inner wings met over the empty space reserved for the box of acacia overlaid with gold. But as Solomon watched, the empty space seemed to glow with a wavering light and an indistinct blur became the gold band of a turban and as it appeared out of the shadows it took form. In this ribbon of pale light from above, Zadok's eyes were dark caves moving slowly to scan the darkness of the middle room where the ten golden lampstands stood ready for the kindling of flame on the appointed day. The smoke of the censer drifted upward, coiling about the whiteness of the priest's beard, suspending the face in a cloud. In this light Zadok was a burning-eyed god of vengeance, nothing human, but eerie, cruel-visaged and disembodied.

When he suddenly lifted the oil lamp in his hand, extending it outward to cast a light ahead, Makada backed away. And when she felt something at her back she stifled a cry with both hands, did not look to see that it was only the altar of the shewbread which blocked her escape. She fled toward the archway of the side chamber, with the voice of Zadok screaming after her.

"Daughter of wickedness! Pagan abomination!"

Solomon caught her in his arms and she struggled against him in mute terror, gasping for breath. Not even the sound of his voice quieted her. She was caught in the nightmare arms of demons and she fought with the wild writhing of a serpent. She sank her teeth into his arm and when he recoiled she sprang free, picked up her skirts and ran through the empty chambers, seeking the door to freedom.

Zadok came down into the middle room and held the lamp close to Solomon's face. The King thrust it aside.

"You frightened her!"

The echo of her running feet rushed back at him and he could tell by the soft fading away and the pause, the scurry that came closer and fell away once more that she was too frightened to find her way out. He started after her.

"Solomon!" Zadok cried. "You have desecrated the sacred foundation of all that is holy!"

"Nothing is desecrated!" Solomon shouted back at him. "Until the day of dedication and the coming up of the ark—"

He stopped, listening for the footsteps. He heard nothing, only the terrible voice of doom calling down the punishment of the Almighty on the pagan who had stolen into the rooms with walls of gold overlaid on fine wood, and he raised up his cry to drown out the vibration of Zadok's imprecations.

He called out her name. There was no answer. Then he moved against something pressed against the wall and he found her shoulders beneath his hands and they quivered at his touch.

He picked her up in his arms and carried her out into the night. He walked away from the walls and down the terraces of trees and shrubs and her body was soft and warm. He could feel the violent pounding of her heart against him. He looked down into her eyes and kissed her parted lips. Her arms went about his neck and she pressed her mouth to his. And even as they kissed the knowledge came to him that the fire in his blood enveloped but did not consume. It reflected only its own wild and blinding light. And a sadness broke over him, then a wave of anger and he held her body in a cruel grip as he carried her into the shadows of the trees. Against the earth and the sharp scent of leaves, thick and black in the pale streams of light from the sky, she lay beside him—in passive deceit. Her cloak had been torn in the struggle and lost somewhere in the boundless silence of the walk down the hillside. She was the dark, unfathomable tide of a darker sea, waiting with a curious stillness, withholding nothing from his hands, offering him the outline of love without its substance. With this yielding, deeply breathing flesh he could lose himself here with the smell of the earth and her hair mingling with the tide that would engulf him and out of this dark exultant union she would be the victor.

She gave him nothing if she offered only the gestures of love. There was no shame in her, no conscience, no heart—and even as he spoke these things into his mind, his body denounced such stupid caution. He was bestowing the value of precious gold on something which was his without the asking . . . I know that when I rise from this earth bed I rise poor and shivering from the couch of my only beloved. I clothe myself in costly raiment and I look down at the one who smiles and stirs in her sleep and the rags of my spirit drag in the dust. I have been poor in the past, still falsely rich because I did not know that I was hungry and had never been fed. The darkness of a thousand nights are past and there is only this one. . . .

He moved away abruptly and after a moment he turned back to her waiting, secret smile. He helped her to her feet. She pushed back her disheveled hair and waited for him to speak. But he had nothing to say. He had no fear of the more delicate feelings wounded in others, for Makada shared no such feelings. He kissed her lightly on the lips. "When you love, Makada," he said. And as they started down into the palace garden he knew he should have said, "*If* you ever love."

In her own garden she did not pause to bid him goodnight at the foot of the stairs leading up to her roof terrace. She turned, extended her hand to him with the same smile that held all the secrets of her pagan soul, and he followed her up to the couch beneath the canopy.

Benaiah's craggy face was not welcome so early in the morning at the various doors of the apartments and rooms in the House of Women.

He had gone first to the house of Tanis. But Solomon was not there and Tanis, dressed in a gown of sea-blue meant for the light of evening, was already walking in her garden. Benaiah had the impression she had not slept in her bed throughout the night. Her face was drawn and her head seemed too heavy for her shoulders as she slowly moved it from side to side. "No, Benaiah, your king is not here," she said. And another answered his query with a sullen scowl: "Go away, Benaiah, it's too late, or you are much too early—"

"I am looking for the King!" he shouted. "Is he here?"

The sleepy woman smiled and sighed. "I wish he were."

Grumbling to himself, Benaiah tried again. Before his fist met the wood of the door it was opened from within by a young and buxom wench in calculated deshabille. Her expectant smile faded at the sight of the commander. And she slammed the door in his face.

The one who had been a handmaiden to Naamah was now growing soft with idleness. She appeared at the latticed window at the side of the door and her drowsy eyes, deep and slumbrous, only half opened to peer at Benaiah.

"Leah," he said, "wake up and tell me if the King is with you—"

She was not intimidated by the command. Asleep or awake the answer was the same: a short, whining exclamation of scorn for Benaiah's ignorance. The window was shuttered. He scratched his beard and went in search of Ahiah.

He found the scribe leaving his house, on his way to the market-place with a thread tied about one of his fingers to aid his memory.

"Have you knocked at the gate of the Queen from the South?" he asked.

Benaiah stared at him. "Surely not?"

Ahiah spread out his hands. "Surely *why* not?"

But when Benaiah hesitated near the walls of the Queen's quarters, Abishag passed by, carrying a water jar into the garden. Benaiah did not trust her sly smile as she stood at the gate and said the King was most assuredly within—but could not be disturbed.

"He must be! This is most urgent!"

Abishag answered with a demure smile. "I would not dare convey such a message. Who am I to tell the great wise King that your demands are more urgent than his own?" She disappeared then and when Benaiah angrily started to follow, he was stopped by turbaned seneschals carrying long spears that barred his way. He sat down on the stone bench outside the gate and he muttered beneath his breath, calling down the wrath of all their lascivious gods on the pagan pig-eaters who kept him waiting.

He waited a very long time.

The sun was already beating hot on the stone seat. He was stiff and disgruntled. No doubt Solomon would charge out of this gate jubilant as a bridegroom, victorious as an army with banners. Benaiah's news would bring him down to earth!

"What are you doing here?" Solomon asked as he came through the gate. He spoke matter-of-factly, and he was neither an army with banners nor a bridegroom leaping with new-found joy.

"News of Zabud, sire. He lies in his tent two days' journey to the south and west. His foot is sore with pain and he cannot continue his search for your brother until it is healed."

"How did this happen?"

"His patrol suspect an ambuscade, but there is no proof."

"Of course there is no proof! Who would dare incite my anger by such a foolish move within my own borders—"

"It did not occur within the borders," Benaiah said.

"Where then! He had his instructions to keep himself and his men out of possible danger." Solomon sat down on the bench and beat his knee with a fist. "He was not in command of a company—only a small body of men, Benaiah."

"May I remind my lord that there are such passes and winding gorges in the wilderness, it is possible for a hostile army to camp not too far away without immediate detection—"

"That's why you are commander of the host, Benaiah. But you are wandering away from the subject. Does Zabud need a physician?"

"The messenger rode in during the middle watch and—since I could not find you I took the liberty of dispatching a doctor from the town."

"Not from the court?"

"This one begged to go. He was sitting at the gates of the city when the messenger rode in and he said it was a poor physician who couldn't heal his own inability to sleep at night. Eli is the physician, my lord, the one with the long and worried nose—"

"Then Zabud is in good hands." Solomon rose and walked beside Benaiah. "And perhaps a hard journey will cure the physician. Now tell me the way it happened to Zabud."

He was greatly concerned. Zabud was not a professional soldier, nor much of a captain. Solomon had given him the job of searching for Adonijah because he knew the son of Nathan would not be hasty with a sword. He was in fact named as a priest, arbiter in small civil matters and officially the King's friend. To hear that he and his men narrowly escaped death, in a dry wadi with rocks tumbling down on them from above, sent a shiver of guilt through the King.

Benaiah was still telling his stories as well as he had last night. He saved the most important fact until the end. "Of course one can usually expect a loose boulder or two," he said, "—when passing through Edom."

Solomon groaned. "What was he doing there!"

Benaiah's voice held censure well-covered with respect. "You sent him to look for Adonijah, my lord."

"My brother, yes. But not to stir up that dog, Hadad!" Solomon gave Benaiah a sidelong glance. "And let's not hear that old caution about long-time enemies uniting out of fear when they have a common purpose. Adonijah is not so foolish."

"I hope not, my lord. When I lead a patrol to continue the search I intend to find him without the necessity of battling the Edomites."

"We'll postpone the search," said Solomon. "For the present. Now stop seeing my brother as an enemy lurking behind each bush! If you must be a soldier, Benaiah, I suppose you must act like one. So hunt out those who would stir up trouble. Put salt on the rocks and traps in the trees—" he smiled "—and who knows, you might even catch Zadok!"

"You have no better friend than the High Priest."

Solomon cuffed Benaiah's thick arm with his fist. "I have you, Benaiah. Do you know that one afternoon when the cherubim were being placed in the Temple, I looked at those symbolic guards with their faces of man, and lion-bodies with wings, and I said to myself the one on the left is Benaiah guarding my body and the other is Zadok, protecting my poor soul—in the middle—with his frightened wings."

"And an odd pair we would make!" Benaiah grumbled. "But you could fare much worse."

"Indeed I know that," said Solomon. And they went up to Solomon's rooms where Ahiah was setting out the business matters of the day with Jehoshaphat.

Among the most important of the King's affairs, they suggested when agreements had been sealed and taken away, was the appeasing of Zadok's contentious mood. Something had certainly happened last night to upset him. According to Ahiah, the High Priest had gone about all morning, glum, morose and thundering at anyone who crossed his path. "His anger makes gurgling sounds in his beard," he said, "like wine being poured to the point of bursting an old goatskin."

"I hope I am not around when *that* happens," said Benaiah.

Ahaih gave Solomon a sharp look. "He declines to reveal the reason—" Ahiah paused to re-read a message.

And a good thing, Solomon thought.

"—But," Ahiah continued as he neatly piled the letters for the day, "he made an observation which has its value. He told me for no reason at all —for we were certainly in no position to speak leisurely with masons and carpenters passing all around us—he said that when discipline is thrown off, when a nation becomes lax in the performance of its duty under the law, then moral decadence begins."

Solomon vigorously splashed water over his face and hands and flicked a drop of it off his fingers in Ahiah's direction. "Some other time, Ahiah," he said, rubbing his face dry. "You know very well I recognize the flaw in that statement but I'll not be drawn into one of your discussions today. I've more important things to do." He went toward his bedchamber, taking off his clothes as he walked. At the door he paused and looked back. "I believe Zadok said nothing of the kind."

Ahiah lifted his shoulders in an apologetic shrug.

"Perhaps he didn't. It was my subtle manner of trying to worm some information from you."

"Leave the worming for another day."

"As you say. But I was hoping to make my way from a generality to a certain specific point—without seeming to be overly curious about your personal life."

"Is it possible for a King to have one?" Solomon went into the dressing room and old Benjamin helped him change his clothes.

"I ask only for the good of the court," Ahiah called in to him, "but it may be necessary for me to know how long you plan to be away."

Solomon paused over an untied sandal, and he smiled to himself. Such a sly one as Ahiah deserved a shock. "Six weeks," he answered. And knew by the sound of overturned inkpots that Ahiah had been jolted for a moment.

When he was ready he rejoined Ahiah and the others.

"Six weeks!" Benaiah was stunned. "Who will pass judgment? What will the people say when their King has not observed the Feast of Weeks with them?"

"They will say the King is a scoundrel, a thief, and morally decadent," said Solomon. "So that brings you all back to the subject dear to Ahiah's heart at the moment." He bowed to them with exaggerated courtesy. "I leave you to ponder over these frivolous matters while I spend the day— not six weeks—in my garden outside the walls. I spare you a further task, and will inform Zadok of my plan before I leave. I think he should know that when a King feels the rope of misplaced authority jerking at his collar bones he becomes no better than the stubborn ram who butted the tax official yesterday."

Benaiah slapped his knee. "And that was a sight!"

He was still laughing as Solomon hurried out on the terrace roof and down the stairs.

Solomon had filled the rooms of her house with costly gifts and among them was an ivory game table with cones of delicately fashioned silver. But Makada had no interest in such pastimes and told Abishag to remove it all from her sight.

"Perhaps if I taught my lady the game—" Abishag said, "—she would discover its fascination."

"I have never played such foolish—"

"It is a favorite pastime of the King's," Abishag said softly, obediently bending over the table to remove the gaming pieces.

Makada watched her in silence and when Vashi had finished dressing her hair the Queen picked up a hand glass and studied her reflection.

"You may leave them, Abishag."

Abishag eagerly set out the cones of silver and waited until Makada came casually to the divan and looked down at the gaming table in front of it.

Abishag explained the purpose of the most ornate cone in the center of the board. "The object of this game is to vanquish him."

"Him?"

"A figure of speech, my lady, nothing more." Abishag explained the moves to be made by the Queen, but Makada did not touch the playing pieces. She would not put herself on the same level with the Shunammite handmaiden, concubine, whatever she was. Abishag's face flushed with strange eagerness as she played both sides, naming each move. Then the prize in the center was defenseless and conquered. With a vicious flick of her finger she hit it onto its side. It rolled off the board and onto the floor.

"It is an exercise in patience," said Abishag, staring at the gaming piece on the floor.

Makada glanced at her quickly. "For what reason?"

"To outwit him."

Makada laughed lightly. "When one possesses wit he need not exercise too much patience." She looked closer at the markings of the board. "What is the strategy?"

Abishag placed a few pieces in the area of defense. She spoke slowly, her eyes never leaving the board. "It is well to know which of these can be persuaded to leave his square of duty. Very often one nearest the—prize, can best serve the player who would capture the prize." She looked straight into the Queen's eyes. "Is it clear to my lady?"

"Leave the board, Abishag. Let me study it a while."

Her evasion seemed to please Abishag.

Makada sat on the divan and idly surveyed the gaming board. "You seemed to enjoy playing it alone."

"I have had much practice."

"I should think one who practiced the game so skillfully perhaps has devised a substitute to place in the center of the—deposed cone?"

Abishag's face grew wistful and Makada thought the girl must have been quite lovely at one time. "I play it alone," Abishag said, "but in my mind I am making the moves—for another."

"Then I could never join you in a trial game," said Makada, rising and smiling. "I could possibly learn to be a formidable opponent. And prevent you from winning." She kicked the cone on the floor lightly with the toe of her slipper. "Pick it up." She received it between her fingers, turned it slowly around. "It's a magnificent jewel. One could become very attached to such a rich and costly prize."

"I think not," Abishag said slowly and a ghost of a smile turned her pale lips as she studied Makada. "It would show in my lady's face. I watched closely—and there was no light in your eye, no inner glow—"

Makada raised her brows. Was the girl being impudent, or had she made this observation out of the peculiar, fleeting touch of insight which on occasion illuminates a shrewd but narrow mind?

"One does not always care to wear the emotions of the heart on one's face," said Makada.

"It is not easily disguised, my lady," Abishag said. "One betrays its possession, and cannot simulate the possession if it does not exist."

The girl annoyed her! What did this simpering, curd-faced, boneless little insect know of emotions and the ability to disguise or reveal them! She waved her away impatiently and told her to take the stupid game with her. Abishag scurried away. Makada walked the floor, speaking her thoughts aloud to Vashi.

"The girl is a fool. Without a sliver of sense. It would do her well to be on her guard with me. I could tell Solomon she is an evil little wretch, dreaming, planning to cast him from the throne—" She stopped suddenly, realizing she had been naming her own purpose as evil. She still had the silver cone in her hand. When she looked up to see old Vashi's face move imperceptibly in the faintest of smiles, she flung the silver jewel aside. Picking up her hand mirror, she looked a long time in silence at her face and a look of bewilderment came into it. What did the girl mean? These were the same eyes, the same mouth that had been kissed again and again through the night. Must they look strange to her because of that?

Be that as it may, she did have a face. And that was more than Solomon could say for that god of his. To be frightened into panic by the unexpected face of the High Priest, dim and blurred by smoke and pale light was a natural thing, something to be forgotten. And she would put aside with equal ease any fear of a face she could not see, one that cast no reflection in a mirror as hers did. Still, she placed the mirror slowly on the dressing table. When Abishag had spoken of "another" her face had recaptured a lost beauty. And when Tanis walked in the garden and spoke of Solomon, her eyes had glowed—the "inner" glow, Abishag had called it. What was this elusive thing which possessed women, and was, in turn, possessed by a simple handmaiden and a Pharaoh's daughter in like degree? She wondered if, in the paleness of the night she had missed seeing it in the eyes of Solomon—and if when he took reluctant leave of her this morning his eyes had been searching hers for something he did not find. . . .

The Grand Vizier of Sheba did not stop at his own quarters to wash off the dust of his strenuous journey. He swept past the Queen's carrying chair and its bearers waiting in the palm shade and entered her house. He instructed Abishag to announce his arrival to the Queen and withdraw immediately after doing so.

Makada, with Vashi close behind her, entered quickly from the dressing room. She had been about to leave and greeted him with brisk impatience.

"So you return at last!" She gestured toward the fastening at her throat but as Vashi came forward to remove the Queen's cloak, Tamrin advised against it.

"But I must hear all you have learned!" She walked swiftly across the room to a table bearing reed pens and writing materials. "Vashi can ride with a message to the King."

"It is not necessary," Tamrin said with firmness as she started to write. "I intend to relate only those matters important for your immediate information. The rest can be kept waiting, but not the King! It is wise to meet him at the appointed time—within the hour."

She paused and looked at him over her shoulder. He bowed, pleased that his surprising knowledge of her plans caused the Queen to regard him with new respect. She let the pen fall from her fingers to the table. Then she rose, tossed a blue-fringed cushion on the floor and sat upon it.

"As I rode up through the streets of Jerusalem," Tamrin said, "I encountered King Solomon. He assumed that the return of your humble Grand Vizier would undoubtedly delay your arrival in the garden. But he awaits the Queen's—pleasure." He studied her through half-closed lids and ran the curved tip of a dark-yellow fingernail along the jutting ridge of his nose.

"The King's pleasure." She looked up at him with arrogant candor. "Not mine."

"Excellent!" He was immensely gratified. She had sensed the question implied by his ambiguous words. "You are ruler of your own heart and mind," he went on, confident that he had not only created her perfection but was completely the guiding power of this royal creature sitting cross-legged at his feet. "Soon you shall be ruler of a victorious Sheba! And a supremely rich one!"

"I have already succeeded in reestablishing my country's wealth," she said with quiet pride. "Solomon has assured me the prosperity of my land shall never be threatened by his own trade expansion. My ships will sail once more with full cargo—sit down, Tamrin! To look up the endless length of you gives me a pain in the back of my neck—" She waited till he had lowered himself by slow degrees into the softness of the divan. "There is to be no increase in the levy on our caravans passing through his land into Phoenicia or Egypt—"

"May I ask how this agreement came about between you and the King?"

"Foolish question," she said with soft mockery.

He watched her casually plaiting the fringed corner of the pillow and could not conceal his worry. "I am pleased that my Queen has found great favor in the eyes of Solomon—but that she, in turn, is untouched by his ardent admiration—"

She turned her head to one side and thoughtfully contemplated the strands of fringe. "Not completely untouched, Tamrin. But you have taught me well. I am not stupid enough to confuse the delight of an experience with the one who shares it."

He groaned inwardly. Her heedless surrender was something he had never anticipated. He had been absorbed in teaching her the ways of a monarchial mind and had forgotten she possessed a woman's body. There was little he could say now. It was too late and she would never understand that by her action she had risked the success of this dangerous venture. In a rare moment of complete honesty, Tamrin took upon himself all the guilt. Considering the sum total of his own vast experience in the past, he wished that she had relied on a method of persuasion more in keeping with her sagacity as a queen. But she had been taught, by him, that a monarch of Sheba was not subject to anyone or any law but her own. There was virtue only in the achievement of her duty, and the means by which she performed this duty were beyond question or criticism—by Sabaeans.

But he had neglected to tell her that in this strange and uncivilized land even a queen was subject to the moral restrictions on all women. Indeed, Solomon himself had written that "The lips of a loose woman drip honey . . . but in the end she is bitter as wormwood, sharp as a two-edged sword . . . with seductive speech she persuades him, with her smooth talk she compels him. All at once he follows her, as an ox goes to the slaughter, or as a stag is caught fast, till an arrow pierces its entrails, as a bird rushes into a snare; he does not know that it will cost him his life. . . ." Tamrin sighed heavily. It was at least his duty, now, to tell her he had been remiss. Since no man possessed a constant climate of soul or of the flesh, how long could a woman hold one with the superior sensibilities of the King of Israel! To base a vital alliance on such a capricious emotion. . . .

"I regret that Sami was not here to perform his priestly arts," Tamrin said with a note of despair. "His ancient and elementary form of magic could have been useful." He was well aware that he was locking the vaults after the crown jewel had been stolen.

"My method was more elementary and far more ancient than Sami's," she retorted.

"Nevertheless, incantations over the liver of a frog sprinkled with skull dust is equally effective," Tamrin persisted. "And much more permanent."

He was suddenly aware of having allowed his deep concern to undermine his discretion. He had not seen this icy stillness in her since the day she held the knife stained with the blood of old Queen Belkis and pronounced herself the ruler of Sheba. The true size and shadow of her displeasure was a formidable image, sitting near the hearth. Vashi's powerful hands rested motionless, with palms turned upward, in her lap. Tamrin had once seen these hands close relentlessly about the neck of a slave who had incurred the Queen's anger. He had no fear for himself but he was disturbed by another thought: King Solomon's ardor, already destined to languish too soon, would surely disappear if he discovered his constant danger from the Queen's guardian. There was more here than the appearance of tremendous strength. And Solomon must surely be aware of the violence which grows in the hearts and hands of the most gentle women. Israel's history must have told him that.

When Sisera was the general of the Canaanite enemy and fled before the forces of Israel it was the woman, Jael, who hammered a tent pin through his head while he slept. And perhaps, when the King heard the name Sheba he often thought of a traitor who bore the name: Sheba the son of Bichri, who raised up his hand against David. The host of David pursued the troublemaker and battered at the wall of the city in which he took refuge. And again it was a woman, a soft and peaceful woman in this besieged city, who went to all the people with her plans for saving themselves and the town, and they cut off the head of Sheba and threw it over the wall. Violence was beautiful and terrifying in these women who killed for a holy cause. But Solomon had no way of knowing that in Vashi, violence was not an overwhelming emotion contrary to a softer nature. It was cold duty, unthinking and blind to everything but unshakable devotion to her Queen.

"Your method, my lady," he said to Makada, "was perhaps impulsive but admirably direct." He smiled easily. "My fear was timid and without roots. In my eagerness to give you favorable news of your troops I blew a squeaking trumpet of excessive caution. My Queen's trade agreement with Solomon is certain to stand longer than the walls of his city!"

With consummate skill he soon dispelled the indignation of Makada and with it, the protective hostility of the other one.

The Queen had leaned forward from the waist and seemed to be idly studying the hem of his robe. "Then you will be pleased to hear that the agreement is in writing. In Solomon's hand, and sealed with the Seal of Solomon."

He beamed on her then, but could not understand the veil of caution in her eyes.

"There is a rumor that the patrol searching for Adonijah suffered an ambush." She searched his face with sharp suspicion. "The one with the short body and thick shoulders, the one called Zabud, was injured I am told. In Edom." She paused a moment, staring at him. "When you returned from Bashir's camp, why did you come by way of Hadad's stronghold? Don't deny it, Tamrin, the hem of your robe is red with the dust of Edom."

"I assure you, it was the safer route. I was adequately escorted. We flattened ourselves on the ridge when we saw the patrol passing in the narrow defile far below. To force them to turn back, we sent only two large boulders tumbling down upon them." He waved the significance of the incident into oblivion. "It will be considered a natural rockslide—or if anyone is blamed, it will certainly be the Edomites." This explanation seemed to satisfy her and he then made his report.

From the folds of his robe he drew a slender roll of thin lambskin. It was tightly bound with a strip of raw leather which bore the seal of Bashir, as commander of the Queen's forces.

"This will show my lady where her armies wait, beyond the borders. And the position within them where Adonijah is secretly encamped—"

Makada frowned. "Spread it here on the floor before me, but it will do me little good. You know that a flat surface tells me nothing. My knowledge of the terrain, and consequently our strategy, is not clear. I must see which mountains are high and barren, and which are covered with sheltering growth. I need to see the gullies and watercourses, where rocks and caves provide defense and I must see what manner of land surrounds Solomon's military outposts. I must *see*, Tamrin—"

She looked toward the spot where Vashi had been sitting only an instant before. Now the big slave was entering through a far door. She carried a wide, shallow brazier, emptied of its coals and heaped with clay.

"What has she there?" Tamrin spoke before he recalled a similar service Vashi had performed for the old Queen when pirate companies of Sheba were dispatched to wait in secret places of distant lands and prey upon rich caravans.

"I have only to admire a small thing," Makada said, "such as the frieze of open flowers and festoons of blossoms on this wall, and the next morning Solomon's servants appear with many like it to be added to all the gifts in my store chambers. Every desire of mine, great and small, is of equal importance to him." She watched as Vashi sat on the floor, studied the markings on the lambskin chart a moment, then started to pat and mold the clay between her huge, deft fingers. "This is clay, Solomon told me, from someplace called Zarethan. I remarked on the beautiful castings of the vessels and basins in his palace and in the Temple—" she peered closer at the miniature mountains, stretches of desert and the network of valleys so swiftly appearing on the map before her. "—What is this and why is it marked so?" She pointed to a series of rough gashes which appeared to be impenetrable in the south.

Tamrin leaned downward. He traced the significant locations with the tip of the slender blade with which he had slit the leather binding.

"It is the Negeb," he said. "It is here Adonijah has gathered his men. A perilous, blistered mass of natural barriers. A suitable hiding place when rain has filled the wadies, but now it is necessary to move."

"He will be seen!"

Tamrin shook his head and smiled. The point of the blade moved north and to the east. "I saw for myself. When I was certain I could not be followed I visited the encampment and then I journeyed with some of Adonijah's men—this way. I can tell you later how well organized and strong he has become. How cleverly small groups of his soldiers are being deployed until they will soon meet in full force—here." He jabbed the rocky wilderness of clay so close to Jerusalem and the gesture brought a gasp of astonishment from Makada.

"He is mad to come within this distance!"

"The Philistines did," said Tamrin. "They came up out of the coast and through the low hills and into this country of rock and tree and plain and the valley where giants once roamed. And David went forth to meet them with little time for preparation." He pointed out the site of Bashir's camp, east of the Arabah. And when the time was right, when Adonijah had the word that all was confusion in Jerusalem, that the people were silent when Solomon rode through the streets, then Adonijah would know that within a few hours, Bashir would have possession of the same knowledge and would lead the forces of Sheba to join his. Tamrin felt such an elation within him that he was forced to stop for breath. Makada regarded him soberly.

"In what manner do Adonijah's men move into the Judean wilderness?"

"In safe, ingenious manner." Tamrin sat back on the divan and slowly inserted the long thin blade into a slender sheath of leather almost hidden by his waistband. A fold covered the glittering sun and moon emblem on the silver hilt. "Solomon himself or that wily commander of his could pass Adonijah's army and never recognize them. One group travels by night, filthy bedouins on their way to some filthy camp in the desert. Another travels openly along the trade routes from the sea. They are dressed as merchants, with humble caravans carrying innocent-looking baggage. And I tell you, my Queen, they are cautious! They haggle over the amount of levy with Solomon's tax collectors and grumble as they pay it. They linger about the outposts, begging for favors and even bring out a length of cloth to sell from the bales in which weapons are hidden! I have seen them make such a nuisance of themselves, wanting to camp and set up booths of trade, that they have actually been hurried on their way—each warrior with a sword concealed by his 'traveling' cloak!"

"That is good," said Makada. "In many ways this brother of Solomon has the heart and mind of a Sabaean."

Tamrin chuckled and stroked his beard. "He is worse than the lowest kind of Sabaean," he said with contempt. "When he has served his purpose for us—" He made a gesture as if cutting down the entire kingdom of Israel would then be a matter of moments.

Makada was pleased. "He has great confidence then in my ability to persuade the King to actions unfavorable with his people. Otherwise he would never risk coming so close to the city."

"His belief in your power is equal only to his burning bitterness!" Tamrin quickly assured her without plucking the bloom of flattery that glowed in her eyes. He rose and walked slowly back and forth. "But the prince of Israel whom we are making king is not one to depend on woman's allure—not entirely. He has found several reasons for having the strength now to lead a revolt—no matter, I can expand on these workings of his mind when my Queen is not so eager to be about her duty—"

"I want to hear more before I leave!"

"Very well," said Tamrin. "I can say—we must face this in a clear light—I can say he is wise enough to wait until he is past any doubt that the people will gather with enthusiasm around the standard he carries. He is not such a fool as Solomon who listens to this invisible God of his. Adonijah uses this God for his own gain—as it should be. He will do battle and ride in to a cheering crowd because he sounds the trumpet of good over evil. Mark this. These Hebrews count that above all things. As a nation, as a religion, as the heart of every man, woman and child—so you can readily see that Adonijah's triumph is assured. Yes," Tamrin said slowly, "he moved out of the Negeb because he is ready to appear as the liberator of his people—and because the wadies grow dry in the Negeb. We must admit, my Queen, that even men of alien blood thirst as readily as Sabaeans." He watched her rise, in one fluid motion of her body, and gather her cloak about her shoulders. A little smile of satisfaction still played about her mouth and he warned her about it, with great care. It would not do to suggest she was ignorant of the most effective approach to the man with whom she had spent the night. "I would humbly offer an opinion, my lady, that when you meet Solomon on this day, it should be with a diffidence, modest and becoming, perhaps a shade of fearful hesitation and lowered eyes—"

Makada was both annoyed and amused. "I could never assume such a deceitful expression. How can I convince Solomon I am consumed with love for him, when a little serving wretch could not be deceived! The Pharaoh's daughter and this humble Abishag have a common claim to make them seem as sisters. Their eyes grow soft when they speak of a beloved, they possess a strange devotion, eager to withhold their own desires, to efface themselves in thinking only of the men they love—"

"This Abishag," Tamrin said in a low, sharp voice, "can be trusted. I have the word of Adonijah on this."

"Then you trust her," Makada said abruptly, watching Vashi remove the map and its clay mountains from the floor. "I do not. Adonijah's word is true, I am sure of that. But I confide in no woman so possessed by love. Her emotions govern her clear thinking. I cannot afford to have my work undone by the chance of a light, ecstatic sigh from her lips at the wrong time."

Tamrin was reluctantly impressed by this. It assured him once more of her unassailable purpose.

"You are right," he agreed. "For a moment I had entertained the thought that it could be Abishag who could ride to Adonijah, then on to Bashir with the Queen's ring and the message to march on Jerusalem—"

"You entertained a thought unworthy of a moment! The mother of Solomon watches this girl as a hunter luring a bird toward his net." She looked into a hand mirror and smoothed the small smile of growing triumph from the corners of her scarlet lips. "I can only follow your advice, Tamrin. 'Trust me to trust no one'—but you."

He bowed. "I am honored. Are your plans hastening to that time, my Queen? There is much to do—and urgent need for action!"

"I have already given instructions to the drivers in my caravan. They are preparing to pack—"

"Surely you are not leaving before our mission is accomplished!"

She smiled slowly. "It takes more than a day to prepare my caravan, Tamrin. And my mission as you call it is closer to accomplishment when Solomon believes I am leaving."

She told him they would talk again, when time permitted. In the meantime, he was to pamper himself, bathe, oil his beard, wear his most glittering uniforms—and, if possible, be exceedingly courteous to the people of Jerusalem.

"Particularly to the lowly ones," she added, as Tamrin followed her through the sunlit doorway. "It is part of their teaching in this barbaric land. It is believed that men are known by their actions and their actions toward one another are true measure of their efforts to imitate the ways of their God. They say all men are created by this invisible One and all are brothers—" Her eyes brightened with malice. "When we can persuade all men to look upon their brothers as Adonijah looks upon Solomon, then no nation on the face of the earth will have the strength to stand against us!"

The intensity of her ambition swept over the heights of Tamrin's plans for the years to come. With such a woman ruling Sheba there would be no limit to the power of her Grand Vizier!

"There is already dissension between the King and his High Priest," she said, "because of me. Soon the elders and officials will be divided in their opinions. Their tongues will become harsh cymbals deafening the people to reason. Out of such confusion comes the need for action—and the eagerness to follow any leader who offers a golden promise."

Tamrin spoke with calm reservation, concealing his pleasure over this majestic self-confidence. "You seem to carry the secret of Solomon's power in your smile."

"He tries to mislead me! He says all things, all power and all truth have a single root. The source is a single God. And the beginning of all wisdom begins with reverence for this Lord." Her voice was edged with scorn. "When my flesh crawled at sight of the Dead Sea stretching below, he told me that I was foolish. Nothing prevented me from turning my back upon it. The choice was mine. I could turn around and face the light and not look back into the pit where the cities and nations of the godless would forever perish."

"This surprises me," Tamrin said. "Solomon is not a man who speaks easily of such things—"

"How well I know!" She laughed softly. "I have had to reach high and often for them, as one gathers fruit not to be eaten, only for the pleasure of stripping a bough that will not bend! But it has not all been vexation. I ask many questions. He is amused and chides my curiosity. He tells me anyone can gather these things I wish to know, the lessons and the facts, and write them down and speak of them with a haughty tongue. But it is not true knowledge till the things spoken by the tongue are experienced in the heart." She gave a pretty gesture of having suffered this kind of nonsense. "So now you know why the secret of his power is not in my smile, Tamrin. But my thirst for knowledge has been profitable. I observed him sitting in judgment and heard him denounce Zadok for his iron-bound obsession with the law—and through the Pharaoh's daughter I have discovered how to utterly destroy him."

"My Queen has shown astonishing diplomacy!" All reservation was dissolved into praise. "There is no better way of learning a man's weaknesses—than from his loyal wife."

"The all-powerful Solomon has one weakness that will cause him more trouble than *all* his wives."

"His belief, of course."

"No," she murmured. "His tolerance for the belief of another."

He stood at the garden gate a moment, watching her leave. She waved Vashi aside, told her to stay unless she was sent for. And as the carrying chair disappeared Vashi moved silently into the coolness of the garden shadows.

There were a few things Tamrin could have added to his report: that fear of the common enemy, Solomon, had made friends of old enemies, Adonijah and Hadad of Edom—but all that could wait. It could wait until the Queen had time for these matters. And Tamrin could tell her then that he had wasted no time in the villages he passed through. He had eaten and waited for his horse to drink in many places and tarried long enough to whisper doubt into the ears of righteous men who blamed their poverty on the ills of Solomon's system of governing, but never on their own shortcomings. There were always men in each town too proud to work in fields, never too proud to accept food without payment from the weak ones who listened to anything if it made a loud noise. And these men who shouted their loyalty at the gates were the ones to be told that their King grew rich at the expense of the poor. They were the few whose discontent convinced them they were the leaders of the many.

Tamrin smiled wryly as he thought of this. They were more troublesome within the walls of a city in which they lived, than the undisguised invaders from without. While they shouted of God and high taxes in the same breath, they dressed the sickness of their own sour ineptitude in the raiment of justice. And they brought her to the tables of good men, to sit among them and divide their friendly talk into portions of silent hatred while they broke their bread—

A soft and gentle voice from behind startled him.

He turned. It was Abishag, humbly offering him a cooling drink.

He accepted it and drank slowly. Only once did their eyes meet over the rim of his drinking bowl. She could not conceal the dull flush upon her cheeks, the furtive eagerness in her eyes. He wondered how much she had heard, for the stamp of certain hope was plainly marked on her face. She bowed demurely when he thanked her for the drink. Then he walked away. Before he came to the bend in the path leading to his own house, he looked back. Abishag was still at the gate, looking at nothing, a soft smile on her lips.

Let a woman possessed by love betray herself, he thought, by the light in her eyes. But not others! The Queen was right. Abishag was not to be trusted with an important duty.

When he had bathed and rested he looked forward to walking through the palace grounds and the streets of the town. He was consumed with an eagerness to know if anyone saw the true significance in the hasty departure of Solomon and Makada from the pavilion in the King's garden, outside the city walls. The Queen's message had been brought to him as he dressed. She had written only a few lines but in them he read a subtle purpose. As she had predicted they would, the first preparations of her caravan's departure had struck Solomon into articulate declarations of unreserved generosity. He would do anything to postpone her leaving! She had but to ask. But with subtle diffidence she had said there was nothing she would ask of him. He had bestowed more gifts and joy upon her than she deserved. And he had taught her a valuable precept: that duty to her people came above her personal desires. It was because of this she could not remain longer than the time it would take to gather supplies for the long journey back to the land of Sheba. And the duty was plain. Tamrin chuckled when he read that the Sabaeans were growing restive at the approach of an all-important day, the feast day of Ashtoreth. The Queen had advanced the day of celebration by several moons. And she had told Solomon it was important that it be observed in her own homeland—where the great image of Ashtoreth towered with the visages of Kawim and Jaghuth on the hillside near the royal palace.

During his leisurely walk through the town he observed that the people were not disturbed by their King's impulsive departure for the north. They were absorbed in the business of buying trinkets in the market-place, directing visitors to the fields set aside for the pitching of family tents, and the anticipation of some feast of their own was already filling the air with snatches of song and the smell of fruits and dressed meat brought for some offering on the day to come. Even the scribe, Ahiah, seemed to be unworried as he made his way out of the crowd in the narrow street. He carried a new stone quern under his arm and stopped to ask politely if Tamrin had found "the wonders" he sought on his journey.

"Above the rich yield of the land," Tamrin said, "and the wisdom of its esteemed ruler, I beheld an incredible wonder: each man as a King in the domain of his own vineyard."

Ahiah had small eyes, Tamrin noted, but they looked at one with disconcerting penetration.

"And when you told this to your exalted Queen," Ahiah said, smiling, "I can well understand that she wished to journey into the country to see with her own eyes the same—incredible wonder?"

This Ahiah was a shrewd one, not easily deceived. He must be careful in all dealings with Solomon's scribe. "My information then was in error," Tamrin said. "It is my belief that since we cannot stay much longer in your land of—what is it called, 'land of wine and sweetmeats'—?"

"Milk and honey."

"—It is my belief that your King wishes the ruler of Sheba to behold all the splendor of his land. All she can possibly see before she departs." With a hint of concern, he added: "I hope the King's absence from the city at this time is not a matter of grave importance—"

"Not in the least." This Ahiah spoke too smoothly for Tamrin's comfort. He was saying now that the King often left the city, for weeks at a time—and for less attractive reasons.

"Then we understand each other." Tamrin bowed.

"Perfectly," said Ahiah, returning the bow.

And Tamrin stood frowning after him a moment until he was lost once more in the press of newcomers about the stalls.

In the middle of that night, in the bedchamber of the rooms he maintained in Gibeah, Solomon wakened with a pounding sense of alarm. Before the remnants of dream-ridden sleep dissolved, the feeling of loss became intensified. He rose blindly from the bed and although his hands gripped the edge of a nearby table he had the sensation of stumbling wildly through time and space to seize the elusive creature drifting from mind, eye and the touch of his hand.

Then slowly, as the timid light from the antechamber illuminated the silver of a water vessel before him, as the heavy blooms leaned fragrant and white into the room through the open window, all things became ordered and took their proper form in the half-light. But something was missing, the soft breathing of one asleep in the darkness. He moved toward the squares of gleaming white pillows and reached down to touch the indentation made by her head. The hollow was still warm. He hurried out into the garden that led up to a small latticed house covered with summer vines and beyond this little shelter he saw Makada standing with her back against the trunk of a tamarisk tree. The night wind out of the northwest blew against her and although she must have heard his approach, she did not turn toward him. She was looking out at the height of Gibeon which she had visited at dusk. She spoke only when Solomon's arms had closed over her shoulders, surprisingly warm to his touch.

"Was it a night such as this," she asked, "that you went up to the high place and heard the Voice which gave you wisdom?"

He smiled at her insatiable curiosity. She had climbed like a wild creature, sure-footed and swift, all over the ridge which still held the crude altar where he had prayed on the night of his anointing. And she reached down to touch the weeds and scrape up the soil, dusting off her hands only after she was certain there was nothing unusual in them, no glitter of secret magic.

"It was a night such as this," Solomon said, holding her against him as they both looked at the curve of the hill against the pale sky. But as he spoke it was not the echo of his people rejoicing in the festivity which he heard, nor did he see in his mind the hecatomb of bullocks and rams sending up the smoke of roasting, unblemished flesh on the altar. It was a more gruesome sacrifice he saw: the seven sons of Saul hanging by their necks to appease the Gibeonites who suffered famine for three years, and attributed the punishment to their failure in avenging a former injustice of the sword wielded by mad King Saul. It was strange to Solomon now, that until he stood here with the woman of Sheba, he had never felt the empty gnawing in the pit of his stomach. The high place of Gibeon had evoked only the miracle of the divine gift: an understanding heart. Tonight, with the boughs of the trees swaying in the breeze, the ghosts of the seven swayed from them, hung rotting in a sun darkened by the wings of vultures. As he looked, an uprooted tangle of brush tumbled in an arc across the ridge of darkness and became the wild arms of Rizpah who was Saul's concubine, and who stayed up there from the time of the barley harvest to the months of rain, beating away the birds of the air and the beasts of the field who would devour the dead fruit of her own flesh and blood.

"You are hurting me," said Makada and Solomon touched with his lips the marks of his fingers on her shoulder and arm. And he told her of the shadow that had come upon his happier recollection of the high place, how it had drifted up from the days of his youth and for the moment had seemed to hold more substance than the reality of his own experience. He felt her turn and stare up at him as he looked into the distance. But the vengeance of blood guilt on the house of Saul was to her a remote story. When she shivered and suggested they return to Gibeah's fine rooms for warmth, she assured him the story was less chilling than the wind.

And the next morning, as the servants gathered food and packed the carts and beasts with baggage, Solomon quite forgot the somber picture of the night before. Makada's face was bright as the morning and she wore a narrow fillet of purple around her hair as they ate the first meal of the day near the pool at Gibeon. She was in a teasing mood. She waved away Vashi's small attentions and leaned forward, across the small flat rock serving as a table between her and the King.

"You looked between the trees just now," she said, "to the pool where we bathed at dawn—but you were not thinking of that."

It was a mild rebuke, spoken with a smile. He could not understand his difficulty in answering it in a like manner. He had swept her out of Jerusalem with all the speed at his command, and his desire to be alone with her had overwhelmed a moment of conscience at leaving his supervision of the Temple to Jeroboam. He had forced down the taste of Zadok's recriminations when they met briefly in front of the tent of meeting. He had cast off his annoyance with Benaiah when the commander had said darkly that "the cormorant of Sheba has flown back to roost." But the thought of Makada leaving him had created a panic of denial within him. It was not a new sensation. It had been with him from the moment he watched her leave the throne room on the very day of her arrival. Why then, since he had known her in these nights on her own roof terrace and here in the city which was the stronghold of Saul many years ago— why then did he find it less than completely satisfying to have her to himself? He knew the answer. Even as she offered herself freely to him, something within her became more remote and left room in his thoughts for these more somber memories which he longed to banish.

He spoke slowly. "It was at this pool that the dark treachery of Joab stained the waters with the blood of Abner's men. On one side, Joab's soldiers had pretended to bathe for purification and were lying in idleness when Abner the honored leader of the army left after the death of Saul, brought his men to the other side. And Joab tricked him with an invitation to watch a peaceful test of strength between twelve of Abner's men and twelve of King David's, commanded by Joab—but the men of Joab were armed. They had swords hidden beneath their clothes—"

He was suddenly aware of her body growing rigid, unbending as she continued to stare at him. If the story of Rizaph's wild and frantic despair on the high ground had not chilled her, then Joab's treachery had certainly touched her emotions. And for this he was grateful. It became simple then to tell her more, to reveal to her what he had tried to keep from Bathsheba, from Benaiah, from all those who eagerly sought the entire truth of David's charges to him when he lay dying. The words came easily but he did not tell her they were locked for all this time against the knowledge of others who would goad him into performing his sacred duty.

"I am about to go the way of all the earth," David had said. "Be strong, and show yourself a man, and keep the charge of the Lord your God, walking in his ways . . . as it is written in the law of Moses . . . that the Lord may establish his word: 'If your sons take heed to their way, walk before me in faithfulness with all their heart and soul . . . there shall not fail you a man on the throne of Israel.' You know also what Joab the son of Zeruiah did to me, how he dealt with the two commanders of the armies of Israel, Abner and Amasa whom he murdered, avenging in time of peace blood which had been shed in war. . . ."

Those had been the words of David as he died, his last words filled with bitterness for Joab, putting innocent blood upon the girdle of the King's loins.

"He charged me," Solomon said, "to deal according to my wisdom with Joab, not to let his head go down to Sheol in peace. But my father never mentioned the comely one, the son of his heart, who died of Joab's arrows—he said his name only when he admonished me to deal kindly with the sons of Barzillai—"

"Make no move! Quiet your fingers that twist a leaf!" It was a command not to be ignored any more than the words of David. It was whispered through stiff and terrified lips. From the corner of his eye, Solomon saw that Makada's rigidity when he mentioned the deceit of swords hidden beneath cloaks of peace, had increased for some other reason.

Then one more word, scarcely heard, came from between her teeth: "Vashi!" Makada's eyes were fixed on something not far from the rock between them, a dark serpent slithering to a stop, coiling out of the damp foliage. Its small, evil head rose and moved from side to side. There was a hissing sound and instantly another.

Solomon could not tell which had come first: the poisonous sound or the swift passage of the double-edged knife as it cut through the air and severed the body of the serpent.

Vashi came forward, bent calmly to retrieve her knife.

"I am grateful to you," said Solomon.

She looked at him strangely a moment, then wiped the knife on the grass and stuck it into the belt of her garment and walked away.

Solomon was puzzled. "I must reward her when we return to Jerusalem," he said. "But why did she look at me in that manner?"

"Because you thanked her," said Makada, "for doing what is only her duty."

"Was it also yours," he asked, "to warn me?"

"I was only protecting myself!" She rose abruptly. "You wanted to show me Baal-hazor, Bethel—so many places. I must be content to visit only a few if we are to return in time for the dance of the New Moon."

He was still watching her as he got to his feet.

"Several times during your stay," he confessed, "I had the senseless feeling you wished me evil. But that cannot be."

She averted her eyes. "You seem very sure."

[179]

"I am—now. You saved my life and risked your own—the serpent could have struck either one of us—"

She drew herself up with haughty indifference but her reason did not convince him: "I wear an amulet against such dangers—whether they come from serpents, nature or men."

"And evil kings," he said, laughing. "One you might fear wished to destroy the independence and wealth of your own country—come then," he continued, taking her by the hand. "Say words on those amulets of yours that when we pass through Bethel and Baal-hazor I am a more agreeable companion and have left my dark recollections in Gibeon."

But in neither place was he free from them.

In Baal-hazor he could not rid himself of the feeling that everything he had been, each incident of the past was coming back to him in all its horror; events he had long put aside and buried in the deluge of his task as King of Israel. But coming up to Baal-hazor, he was no longer King. He was a young and mischievous child flicking the bare shanks of his older brothers Amnon and Adonijah as he walked behind them with a twig in his hand, squealing and running as they chased him through the countryside, and finally leaving them behind, to become the first of David's sons to arrive at the house of Absalom for the feast of sheep-shearing. He had grown hot and damp with running and stretched out near the animal pens to catch his breath and he had fallen asleep. He was awakened by the secret voices of a laborer and Absalom, and Absalom was making certain the knife that cut the wool would be thrust into the ribs that day of his brother Amnon who would inherit the crown of David. It seemed an hour that he had lain there, paralyzed with fear. But it was actually only a moment before he ran into the room where the board was set with delicacies and even as he ran to warn Amnon, this son of David by Ahinoam fell in his own blood and Absalom fled to Geshur.

He was sorry he had come here with Makada. There was no sense to it. Other times, he scarcely thought of the past when he visited here, for it had become the property of Adonijah and it had been gay with laughter then. And when his kingly duties took him into the house to sleep for a night before he went onward, he had thought only for a moment of the brother who would surely return one day.

Now the boughs of the vineyard were broken and the psalm that praised their rich green shadow on the mountains and the mighty branches sent out to the sea, became a dirge as he watched a shepherd gather a dead vine for fuel. He made no secret of these things in his heart. And several times when he looked at Makada she was studying him with a faint expression of wonder, as if seeing him for the first time. But these moments were fleeting and only once did she speak in a manner which revealed her thought.

He had found the tough vine which David had given Adonijah as a child. It was rich and had grown and flourished without the loving care it deserved, and the fruit hanging in huge clusters would be ripe in another month. But there would be no song of vintage in this lonely place—not this season. Not during the summer when the first clusters ripened, nor in the autumn during the Feast of Tabernacles. The leafy booths where watchmen once slept, where families came out joyfully to watch their crops, protect them from the little foxes that would spoil the vine—the leafy booths in other vineyards would be full of song and blessing, but not here.

"You seem to long for this brother of yours," Makada said. "Why?"

"Is there a better reason than that he is my brother?"

He parted the thick growth encroaching on a pile of white-washed stones which marked the boundary and also frightened away the jackals. And he pointed to the letter "A" marked in the stone. "It is time," said Solomon, "he came to claim his heritage." He would restore the place, send men immediately to rebuild the walls and prune the thorn hedge of a heritage neglected.

And in Bethel he lay outside the crimson canopy of his tent and looked into the dying fire as he held Makada, asleep, in his arms. It was here, in the place named as the House of God that Jacob had made his covenant with God and set a pillar to his Name. Solomon wondered if Jacob had ever sat like this, with his beloved Rachel's hair fragrant with a touch of smoke from a campfire. And he thought, with a touch of anguish, that as Jacob had loved Rachel, so he loved Makada. He wished he were not a king, that she were a shepherd's daughter.

He looked down at her, wishing with all his heart for the impossible. Having found the one woman who was all woman, his desire was cruelly unsatisfied. She met it with avid and breathless greed and when the earth and sky had stopped trembling and they knew a quiet hour such as this by a fire outside their own bodies, she slept as a beautiful animal would sleep; and he knew he must be content with this exultant, earthly love, even as he yearned to experience a greater one that merged in the gigantic embrace of the spirit. He was too demanding. It came to him that of all people he would be the last one to be pitied by other men. Yet he pitied himself, and reclining now in this star-touched country of Jacob's revelation, he thought differently about the son of Isaac. Jacob had labored seven years in the service of Laban. At the end of the seven years, he was to receive Rachel as his wife. But he was the victim of a crafty trick, and another was his wife, Rachel's sister; and during the seven years of lying with the one who bore his first sons, he closed his eyes and it was the image of Rachel he embraced. And he waited another seven years for the image to become reality. A young and sensual Solomon had scoffed at this, called it a legend, most likely called out of thin air by a sentimental woman. Either that, or Jacob was beyond the temptations of other men.

Solomon felt that now he was a man whose love exceeded that of Jacob's. Perhaps his patience, too. He had waited all his life. And still, here in his arms, stirring gently in her sleep as he pulled a coverlet over an arm, was the body of the woman for whom he had waited. How long, he wondered, would he have to wait for the other woman sleeping within her, the one she could become?

Half asleep, she murmured, "What are you thinking?"

"I was thinking of Jacob and his beautiful Rachel."

With her eyes still closed she whispered, "The one who hid the little household gods in her camel bag—as the old woman with the flour on her face had done—" she yawned "—in your judgment hall—"

An unreasonable elation filled him. She had remembered. Could it be that the other Makada who was all woman, selfless, understanding and warm, the one who wore no royal diadem upon her brow—was stirring with faint life?

He started to speak, softly, urgently. Then he looked down and was silent. Her head had fallen deeper into his shoulder, and she was sound asleep.

During the King's brief absence Ahiah had found it increasingly difficult to work without interruption. He moved his inkpots, pens, stylus and tablets from room to room, trying to escape the fretful inquiries of Bathsheba, the grim face of Benaiah, and the smoldering anger of Zadok.

He eventually found refuge in a store chamber adjoining his house. Waning daylight came through a small opening high in the stone wall. Very soon it would be too dark to work and his lack of accomplishment for the day would at last have valid excuse. He found a clay lamp near the spice bins, blew the dust from it and was looking about for oil and wicks when the door slowly opened, creaking on its hinges. He could not mistake the gaunt length of Elihoreph, the bony silhouette against the pale rectangle of light. Ahiah smiled for the first time that day.

He greeted his brother and as the door closed, guided him to the broad table for Elihoreph was still blinded by the daylight remaining in his eyes.

"You work down here in the darkness of Sheol," Elihoreph said, "when the record rooms are still filled with light from the sky." He groped his way to a seat, coughed and thumped his chest.

Ahiah found a small jar of wine. It was a gift from Solomon and bore his seal on the handle. "This is an occasion," he said. Certain that Elihoreph was still finding his eyesight, Ahiah hurriedly wiped out two wine bowls with the cloth he used to clean his pens. "Now," he said, pouring the wine, "wash out your throat with grapes of Hebron and tell me how it happens you return this early. What have you brought back with you this time—a child's toy or proof of the route Moses took in the wandering?" He watched Elihoreph drink thirstily. "To you, I believe the one would be equally as important as the other." He detected a reluctance in Elihoreph. There was some hesitancy working behind those usually enormous and honest eyes.

When Elihoreph had finished and wiped his mouth with the back of his hand, he seemed on the point of saying something, thinking better of it, and then too-enthusiastically relating the discovery of a new cave in the wilderness.

"It held crude implements unmoved for hundreds of years," he said, "and a primitive worker of the soil was kind enough to leave me his plow. You know, Ahiah, many changes must come over a land with the years. Where great forests grew perhaps we see now only broken, barren land—"

Ahiah was watching him closely. Elihoreph was a clever scholar but Ahiah was ashamed of the awkwardness with which he lied. For once, Elihoreph was not completely absorbed by the shape and material of an ancient plow.

"With such a treasure at your fingertips, Elihoreph, how could you tear yourself away? I should think you would have stayed through the summer, winter, and appeared about the time of the Passover—"

Elihoreph burst out: "I saw Adonijah!"

Ahiah's wine bowl was halfway to his mouth. It stayed there.

"I saw him, I tell you! Adonijah and Joab! As clearly as I see you now across this table." Elihoreph was hunched forward, his great eyes staring through the dimness. "It was only for an instant—when the light caught their faces as they looked out from under the hoods of their merchants' cloaks—"

At this, Ahiah slowly put down his bowl and said with warm patience: "My brother, you have been traveling in the hot sun. Here—"

But Elihoreph raised a hand against the wine jar poised over his bowl. "I knew you would think that. But I must believe what I see with my own eyes."

Ahiah leaned back, his head resting against the cool jars and boxes of household supplies.

"Now Elihoreph, consider. As our father always told us, we both wield the pen but yours is tipped with the ink of brilliant imagination. I envy your facility. But not the traps into which it leads you."

"Then may my right hand lose its cunning! I speak the truth."

"As you did when you spoke of seeing a lake of beautiful water in the middle of the desert. It was true because you saw it with the eyes of fatigue and—the need to satisfy your thirst. It must be so now. Out of our desire to see brothers united in friendship, as we are, perhaps I, too, could see Adonijah returning to Jerusalem, and ignore the sense which told me it must be a lonely goatherd leading his small flock homeward."

Elihoreph scowled and thoughtfully twisted a lank fringe of hair, grown long over his ears.

"Then I have seen an old goat wearing greaves on his legs. Only Joab ever wore those heavy old-fashioned kind—"

"And never without armor and breastplate," Ahiah added. "But you said this—this person you saw was clothed as a merchant."

"That is true," Elihoreph admitted. "And this was no army. They did not see me. They turned their horses into a defile and were lost from sight. Later I saw them disappear over a ridge and there were four others with them."

He still wondered if he should tell the King.

Ahiah thought a moment. "It is your decision to make. I would only point out that when the sun plays tricks on you, nothing can be done. But it is another matter to play one on the King. He could well think his scribe had become irresponsible—"

"May my tongue cleave to the roof of my mouth! It was so real to me I suddenly stopped digging around in the cave and resolved to hereafter look about me and see first the events of the day before losing myself in rebuilding those of the past. I hurried to Jerusalem fearing I would miss the reunion between the sons of David."

Ahiah stood over him, patted his shoulder. "You are growling inside from hunger. Come, let my wife have the pleasure of scolding you for neglecting your health—"

As they came into the late sunlight of the small herb garden Ahiah told his brother what events had taken place, how Zadok was unreasonably disapproving the trade agreement drawn between Israel and Sheba.

"What can he do but protest?" Elihoreph was sniffing the air with delight for savory odors were drifting from the kitchen of Ahiah's house.

"That is what Solomon will think. 'Let Zadok attend his office as priest and allow me to do likewise as King.' That is what he will say." Ahiah sighed. "There is little of a joyful nature I can report to the King when he returns this evening."

"While I was plodding toward the gates, another traveler passed me, with military escort," said Elihoreph. "It was Eli the physician."

"Then you learned about Zabud."

His brother nodded. "That will at least be good news for the King. Zabud is resting well and can soon ride back to Jerusalem. He has started to walk with the help of a stick."

"That will indeed ease the King's anxiety. I shall tell him."

"A second thing," Elihoreph went on. "Why has Jehoshaphat such a long face? He was staring out the window of the record room when I entered, searching for you, and he said there was a cloud of strife coming over the land. Has he lost his wits? Not a cloud in the sky!"

"Now you know why I could work nowhere in the palace. It is something I cannot hold in my hand, a poisonous water that slips through the fingers. It is in the eyes and the thoughts and only by a few words allowed to fall can I gather anything! Jehoshaphat has heard from Zadok that a prophet has come out of the wilderness of Shiloh."

"Is that an occasion for sadness?"

"Not when the rumor was first whispered about. Even the High Priest was eager to know what was said. He seeks reassurance that his worry over Solomon's actions is all in vain. He came to me only this morning and he was trembling with fear. He had the word by way of Abiathar's house in Anathoth; and for all Abiathar's support of Adonijah, and being a descendant of priests of Nob—Zadok knows that this old friend does not repeat false words."

"Doom and devastation?"

"Worse," said Ahiah. "It was heard in Anathoth and down in Jericho that this one with prophesy on his mouth speaks of disunity among the tribes of Israel!"

Elihoreph shrugged. "One of those."

"Unfortunately for me," said Ahiah, "his name is much like my own. I only hope if the whispering spreads through the city I am not credited with such stupid pronouncements. He staggers out of the hills, eyes full of fire, cheeks sunken as yours will be if you don't eat soon—and he babbles from a matted beard from which he never washes the foam of his unholy fits. So far he only shrieks and waves his bony arms in the air against what he calls corruption in Jerusalem, rot in the heart and seed of the King—"

"But that is serious. Solomon will be greatly troubled."

"It takes more than a dribbling lunatic in a filthy goatskin to alarm the king."

"It could stir up the people, this kind of talk," said Elihoreph.

"Solomon will let him talk. Blow out the fire with his own foul breath, you might say." Ahiah was filled with disgust. "I anticipate no disturbance. He is still in the north, roaming the countryside, walking through villages with his fists and eyes raised to the heavens. The kingdom is to be divided, he says. The tribes no longer twelve, but ten and two—and it worries Zadok no less because the prophet does not say when this is to happen."

"Do you think it will?"

"I think the High Priest is convinced of it. As for myself—until I have proof I do not call every wild-haired maniac a prophet."

"Then neither do I," said Elihoreph. "We shall wait and allow events to take their course—" he was silent a moment "—And until I have proof, I do not call every fancy of mine a reality."

"I am seeing the King at tonight's entertainment," Ahiah said. "If you wish me to tell him your opinion and what you saw—"

"No, no! Let it lie in my mind for a time. It is quite possible that under the strong sun, that is where it was created. I love you, my brother, and would talk with you here through what is left of the day—but if I did, there would be nothing left of *me!*"

Ahiah chuckled as Elihoreph disappeared into the house. He heard his wife give a small shriek of surprise, followed by the usual scolding, and there was suddenly the sound of pots being moved about, bowls of food being placed on the wooden bench where Elihoreph would eat his fill.

As he passed the house of the Pharaoh's daughter, Ahiah wondered what kept her in seclusion these past few days. And he wondered if she would be present at the festivity across the Kidron brook tonight.

He saw Tamrin, resplendent in fine robes and jeweled turban, being escorted through the town by lesser dignitaries of the Queen's court. And when the people of the town and the visitors looked upon this glittering little entourage they whispered among themselves and cast curious glances toward the gates where the Sabaean guards were waiting for the command to march and ride up the hillside where preparations had already been made. Small fires were burning on the ridges and levels of the hill. There was much conjecture about their meaning, and one of the merchants tugged at Ahiah's sleeve and asked why the fires burned when the new moon fires of Israel had been seen several nights before.

"This is a celebration of the Sabaeans," Ahiah explained. "They are our guests and have the privilege of observing the new moon rites as they always have: when they actually see the crescent in the sky."

The merchant began to draw the curtains across his stall. His wife waited patiently by the side of the booth until she saw her husband pause with arm lifted and gaze open-mouthed at the Sabaean women moving rhythmically through the narrow street. They wore white garments and had painted their faces and their anklets jingled as they walked. The Israelite wife jerked the last of the curtains over the stall and her eyes pierced her husband's face, and his conscience. Still, as they walked swiftly away, Ahiah noted it was the wife and not the husband who looked back over her shoulder at the Sabaean priestesses.

Dusk fell as Ahiah walked slowly through the town. He was in no great hurry. He had seen the observance of the new moon become less important in the last days of David, and more so in the time of Solomon. It was little more than a reckoning of time now, the first day of the month. He had also seen the new moon observed only when the thin curve of silver could be seen by the eye of the Canaanites. It was usually a harmless affair, perhaps an excuse now and then for too much drinking, but never as wild and licentious as the fast days when the pillars of stone were wreathed with garlands and a frenzy of abandon fired the blood. This would be a clamorous observance, for the Sabaeans did not believe in restraining their voices and their hands and the movements of their bodies. But as soon as the moon made its swift disappearance, the wildness would also disappear and the visiting pagans would go back in orderly fashion to their tents and their houses.

He caught a glimpse of Abishag, muffled by the veils of her robe. She was moving to a place outside the city walls where some of the pious but curious Israelites had gathered to watch the festival—from a distance.

If Bathsheba had seen her, Ahiah told himself, she would certainly have made a protest. She was full of them these days. She had come upon Tamrin and Abishag—quite inadvertently according to her story— and they were engaged in a brief but intense discussion in a corner of the palace garden.

"Now Ahiah," Bathsheba said, "what can those two possibly have in common?"

He wondered himself what they had in common but turned it aside with a shrug. "Indiscriminate taste?" he asked, and Bathsheba had sighed politely with exasperation and left him to wonder again why the visit of the Queen of Sheba had stirred up such an undercurrent of uneasiness within the palace walls.

The moon could be seen, low in the sky, as he crossed the Kidron. With it came the first sound of the drums and cymbals on the hillside. The smoke of meat roasting over fires mingled with incense much too strong for the stillness of the night. The breeze seemed to have paused, too, for this soft beating in the night. A humming murmur of voices came down to him as he climbed the hill. The shadow of the olive trees fell in delicate patterns beneath his feet. He stood for a moment outside the vast, irregular circle of firelight. Makada wore a gown of silver and the diadem on her head, sparkling with light, seemed to be the only bit of motion about her. She sat very still, watching two of the priestesses cast powders of crimson and glowing cadmium, vivid green and blue into the two fires representing the slender corners of a moon. The lines of the crescent itself were being defined by swords. The tip of a blade touched the hilt of the sword laid flat and gleaming in front of it. The Sabaeans, Ahiah thought, were extremely serious in performing each gesture. He saw that Solomon, seated beside the Queen of Sheba, was more interested in watching her face, and scarcely looked at the elaborate ceremonies of preparation before him.

Ahiah moved, still in the shadow of the trees, and as he stood close to the King, he made out the watchful bulk of Benaiah. The body of the commander was massive and still as the tree trunk at his back. Tamrin looked up from his place in the royal semicircle and indicated a seat for Ahiah. The scribe would have preferred to stand but when Solomon, too, smiled and gestured him to be seated, there was nothing else to do.

The swords were all in place. A slow chanting began to fill the air. Musicians appeared beyond the firelight, their bizarre headdresses moving in unison, the movement of their fingers against strings and metal creating a ritualistic pattern of their own. Ahiah narrowed his eyes, peering into the heavy stillness beyond, the green and moonlight silver stillness. And a strange heat seemed to emanate in this vast circle, seemed to writhe and move inward like no warmth of fire on earth. He was vaguely aware that barefooted men, wearing strange amulets and philacteries, had moved noiselessly, with cat-like movements into the inner area and had formed a circle around the moon of sword and fire on the ground. They began to dance. Their feet and arms moved almost imperceptibly but as the tempo of the drums increased, and the chanting grew louder, their bodies began to glisten. And it seemed that the pounding of their heels was shaking the very ground, would any moment cause a gigantic shudder that would send the entire mountain flying up into a thousand pieces.

Ahiah found it hard to draw his eyes from the sinuous, glistening circle. The eyes of others, watching, glittered with a hypnotic, inward stillness. He met the King's eyes and for an instant there was complete recognition between them, as two aliens meeting in a strange land, finding in each other they have understanding and are removed from the strangeness. A slight smile came into Solomon's face. His dark eyes moved back to the spectacle now as if he were a remote observer.

Tamrin had leaned far forward, his eyes half closed, his lips moving soundlessly to the ritual chanted by the Sabaeans. The dignitaries at his left were also absorbed, rocking their bodies back and forth, lifting their faces to the moonlight as a priest emitted a sharp call, then lowering their heads in abject worship.

Ahiah moved back, rose and went to stand beside Benaiah. In that moment of barbaric ritual, Benaiah became a figure of true grandeur. None of his physical feats of strength would ever again match this priceless demonstration of invincibility. In the midst of all this pagan wildness, Benaiah was calmly picking his teeth.

Away from the intense light, Ahiah could see the valley below and the soft glow of moonlight falling over the city of Jerusalem.

He was made uneasy by the sight and susceptible, for the moment, to an illusion more fantastic than the experience of Elihoreph in the wilderness: a flash of gold deep in the darkness brought to mind the narrow gold band which formed the headpiece of Zadok's turban. It was a preposterous thought! Ahiah glanced toward the higher summit of the Mount of Olives. It was there David had turned to his two faithful priests, Zadok and Abiathar, and sadly told them not to follow him into exile with the ark of the covenant they carried. Zadok's fierce pride would never allow him to ascend the hillside for a less memorable occasion.

The male dancers flung their bodies to the ground, rose and disappeared, chanting their adulation for the Queen. She had accepted their homage as goddess of the moon. In this light only the rise and fall of her breathing betrayed life within her rigid stillness. The sheath of silver cloth clinging to her body was a continuation of a graven image, not a sheer covering and something apart from the flesh. Slowly, her people moved into the circle of light. Kept in order by the guards, they walked in single file from two directions, pausing in front of the Queen, then continuing to the opposite side.

The Sabaean subjects stepped carefully, away from the lunate field of swords. With glazed eyes they prostrated themselves before the Queen. Each in turn held out a crescent-shaped amulet, touching it to the Queen's ring which now rested in a filigree of gold on the cushion at her feet. The ceremony became accelerated. One after another quickly touched the ring and scurried away with relief to start feasting with the others. An agitation grew far back in the lines of those who still waited their turn. Whites of eyes rolled in wild despair from the glittering ring to the moon's position. The musicians, also, kept their eyes fixed on the silver curve and as it began to visibly sink toward the opposite hills, their drums were muted. The silence between one beat and the next lengthened. The sound of cymbals grew soft, diminishing slowly. In desperation, bodies pressed forward merging and pulsating until the hillside itself became the breathing breast of some sleeping monster.

Solomon's mouth was a grim line. "What is the meaning of this?" He turned to the Queen, his dark eyes puzzled and angry as they searched her face. Ahiah leaned forward for her answer. She responded without looking at the King: "In Sheba they touch their sacred talismans to the eyes of the moon-god's image. It wards off the evil spirits. To be effective it must be done between the time of the first moon gleam and the last."

Tamrin had moved closer to Makada. He towered behind her now and his eyes were opaque with undisputed authority. "The Queen's people have no moon image to worship during their absence from their homeland. Since the rulers of Sheba are offsprings of the gods, the royal ring serves as the eye of the image of Sheba." After a pause he glanced at Ahiah. "Is it so foreign to your own belief?" He did not seem to expect an answer. Ahiah gave him none. He was thinking how strange it was that all men, even these pagans and their Queen, yearned to attach themselves to an image of divine nature. With this overwhelming need in the hearts of all men, the need to transcend their mortal limitations, it chilled him to see how easily the gods of evil could swarm over the land.

He had no wish to remain and was about to leave when a sudden stillness held everyone frozen in the position he held as the moon's last light vanished. There were seven people remaining. They clutched the amulets a moment, then with dead-looking eyes released them, letting them fall from the chains about their necks. Four of the slaves were men. Of the three women, one was a priestess. Without a word being spoken, the seven formed a circle about the crescent outlined on the ground. Two guards carried away all but six of the swords.

Ahiah looked at Tamrin. The Grand Vizier's mouth turned with suppressed arrogance. He answered Ahiah's unspoken question but his eyes covertly watched the King.

"If the moon descends before all are safe from its evil effects, another form of propitiation must be made."

The cymbals clashed violently. At this signal the seven rushed into the center of the crescent. A giant of a man was the first to pick up a sword, wave it triumphantly over his head and kick himself free from the scrambling mass of legs and arms, fighting over the remaining five swords. A woman emerged with her garments torn, a cut across her forehead. She wiped the blood out of her eyes and her teeth shone in a wild shout of laughter.

"The blades are real!" Solomon rose abruptly, his hands clenched at his sides.

Only one remained unarmed now. The priestess stood in the middle of the circle, an expression of dazed, ecstatic dedication on her face. Her hair had come loose from its binding and streamed over a naked shoulder. The six who carried swords moved in a rhythmic frenzy as the music began; a deafening cry came over the clash of cymbals: "Death to the weak! Destroy! Appease!" The blade of a sword grazed the bare shoulder. Another slashed at her back as the six, intent on propitiating an angry god, avenged themselves on a single victim. Her white garment was stained with blood.

Solomon raised his arms in the air. "I forbid this!" The thunder of his voice was lost in the wild shouting all about him. "Stop! I command it!" He pushed aside those who stood between him and the savage, whirling dancers, crazed by the need of human sacrifice. They were prolonging the death thrust brandishing their swords above the priestess, now sprawled on the ground, barely visible as the circle closed in on her. The six moved shoulder to shoulder, defying Solomon's orders, ignoring his hands which separated them, thrust them apart for a stunned moment.

"They will not stop," the Queen said without emotion. "Unless I give the command."

"Then command them!" Solomon shouted.

The Queen's eyes wavered a moment. She seemed not to understand. "The ritual must proceed. It is the law in my country—"

The victim was a slave, she said, why should Solomon protest when the woman herself was acquiescent?

Over the screaming of those who looked on, over the clashing of the swords behind him, Solomon's voice could be heard.

"She is a human being, with the right to live! So long as you remain here, your people have my protection! Now tell them to stop—!"

Solomon whirled about as the body of the huge Sabaean rose high above the others, his sword poised for the death thrust. The blood pounded in Ahiah's ears. The woman would be killed. There was murder in the glazed eyes of the six who danced. Anyone who stopped them now would also be killed. The giant Sabaean's shoulder muscles glistened with sweat. In the same instant that Benaiah sprang forward, scattering the dancers, Solomon fastened his grip on the wrist of the big Sabaean as it plunged downward. The girl rolled aside as the sword fell to the ground. Bewildered, the Sabaeans looked at their Queen. For a moment her eyes grew enormous with outrage as she stared at Solomon. He was gesturing toward a group of Israelites who had grown bold and careless of their secrecy in the wildness they had witnessed. The King told them to take the priestess away, see that she was properly cared for. Ahiah held his breath. The King was unaware of his own danger. The Sabaean whom he had disarmed stood above him, his big hands swinging at his sides. The others turned stricken eyes to the one who could lift the curse of the moon god from them. The Queen muttered a word, clapped her hands together twice. And her eyes filled with a dark strangeness as she watched them, subdued and wondering, drop their swords and disperse.

Since the moon turned the tide of seas created by God, Ahiah could not censor the uninformed who believed it also cast an evil shadow on the lives of men. Yet he fought against a gnawing apprehension. Perhaps the glitter of triumph in the eyes of the Grand Vizier was only a reflection of the dying fires. If it existed at all it quickly became a look of secretive caution as Tamrin studied the face of his Queen. Ahiah warned himself.

The orgy of the pagans must not seduce his usual detachment. He must avoid groundless fears. He had only to look around him to be assured. It could not be ignored that for a short time this night the pagan fires had circumscribed a rotten spot. But the blemish was now being removed. The hillside was growing still, peaceful once more. The Sabaeans were moving across the Kidron, back to their quarters. The Israelites who still lingered on the slopes were being brusquely ordered back to their homes by Benaiah. The violence was now only a memory, as vaguely remembered as the light of the moon that induced it.

A wordless constraint had fallen upon Makada and Solomon. Without taking her eyes from his, the Queen spoke.

"I would remain, Tamrin," she said. "Alone."

His reply was almost inaudible. "Is it possible the evening's event has caused the Queen to alter—a former decision?"

She turned on him in anger. Then, seeing Ahiah within listening distance, she said quietly: "My plans—for an early departure?"

Tamrin bowed. "I have nothing else in my mind."

She spoke with slow disdain. "Since you find room in it for some doubt, pray be the custodian of my—unswerving purpose." She indicated the ring still lying on the cushion before her. A shadow of understanding passed between the two. "Take it. And be assured."

"I need no assurance, but if my lady insists—" Tamrin took possession of the ring. "For safekeeping." He bowed. The other dignitaries followed him and inclined their heads with respect to both monarchs as they withdrew.

Solomon stood near the spot where the priestess had fallen. He and Makada faced each other as strangers. The trampled ground that lay between them could have been a chasm into which they seemed willing to plunge if it were the simple means of restoring them to each other.

Solomon had not seen what happened shortly after the Sabaeans passed him.

They stopped abruptly, then stepped aside to make way for the august approach of Zadok. He was followed by a worried-looking Jehoshaphat, a few of the Levites, and three visiting elders. It was little wonder the Sabaeans instinctively cleared the way. Zadok was an awesome figure, tall and powerful in his white-bearded age, walking in cold righteousness that would have frozen hot coals if they lay in his determined course. He came as if trumpets were blowing and the smoke of the smoldering fires became the smoke thickening on the top of Sinai when the Lord said He had brought the people of Israel out of the land of Egypt, out of the house of bondage, and "You shall have no other gods before me. . . ." He was Moses striding with the words of the Lord written in stone. The Ten Commandments were written in his eyes and in his hot anger he was ready to pluck them out as readily as Moses smashed the tablets at sight of the backsliders worshiping a golden calf . . .

"Hill of Offense!" Zadok stood with hands outspread and his voice was more terrible as a whisper than thunder on the mountaintops. He became the King's accuser.

"Let all of Israel mourn this night!" Zadok cried. "Let us strike our knees on the ground and throw ashes on our heads to atone for this hill of abomination!"

Ahiah watched and came closer as Solomon's face grew taut with anger. And he saw the Queen of Sheba lower her eyes and wait for the King to speak.

His voice was calm. "You are overwrought, Zadok."

"You have permitted the planting of wickedness in this soil! May the Lord spare us its evil harvest!"

"No lasting harm has been done." Solomon spoke quietly but his eyes were dark and ominous. "The injured woman is being cared for—"

"Let her die in agony!" Zadok's mouth trembled with rage. "May she never rise again to worship on one of our high places!"

"She and all of them are ignorant of our ways." A sharpness in Solomon's voice would have warned a less angry man than Zadok. "It was you who taught me the word of God, saying, 'You shall not curse the deaf or put a stumbling block before the blind!' Have you forgotten His law that we love our neighbors as ourselves?"

"You have made a covenant with them, and to deal with them in commerce will lead to a covenant with their gods. Would you have your kingdom torn asunder, its people scattered over the earth, the nation of your fathers a proverb, a byword among the disbelievers?"

"I have built walls about my cities," said Solomon, "towers and fortresses around the land. But I cannot close out the skills and ideas of other lands, nor shut out their beliefs! If we fear that by looking upon them we lose our own belief, then we are weak and lukewarm in our own. Has all my effort been to this end, Zadok, that I have taken the raw material left by my father and find I build a house to a god of ignorance and roaring bigotry?"

Ahiah felt his chest constrict with an inner anguish. He listened to Solomon and felt that he heard the words as from a timeless distance, reaching into the days and hours of life unborn, when Solomon's views would find a kindly climate in which to flourish. But it was too soon, too soon.

To Ahiah's surprise, Jehoshaphat was speaking and his voice came as a calm between two storms.

"I remember that your father in the days of his power slept near his tent with a sword ready at his hand." His fleshless chins had folded themselves against the neck of his robe and his eyes regarded the King with an upward, beseeching sadness. "He was ready to battle for his God and his people. Perhaps because he was born a shepherd he was closer to the Lord's will than one who is born a King's son—and has never had to fight for his faith?"

Solomon muttered. "I have fought for a country in which that faith can live. Why do you come to me this way! All of you! Did I *ask* to be King?"

"It was your father's command," Zadok reminded him, "and Nathan's prophecy!"

One of the elders found his voice. "You are young, Solomon, and your way is difficult. But consider what Jehoshaphat has spoken. You have the belief and conviction of a strong leader—but your actions must be guided by the weakest of us. If we lose our faith in the One Name, we lose everything. Give us the time to build on solid rock before we look upon the gods who have no breath in them and crumble with time into forgotten sand."

They spoke a truth as they saw it. They were as right, and as wrong, as Solomon.

A shepherd, Ahiah thought, must walk with his flock. He must not drive them ahead, beyond their strength.

Zadok's voice reverberated across the mountain.

"You say I have no sense of justice? You have forgotten the word, Solomon. It is not here on this desecrated hillside tonight. But there!" He pointed a trembling finger toward the city of Jerusalem, shining in the starlight. "There in the eyes and hearts of your people! Their senses have been enticed by pagan drums. Their bodies have swayed to the cymbals of evil. They have looked upon their King whom they revere and have seen him bow down his head in iniquity!" His voice grew hoarse and strained, his breathing labored. "Has your heart grown proud, Solomon? I tried to teach you well. Now I see the shadow of my failure in your insolent eyes. You were my hope, the light of David's dream. When you said to us, 'Cast your bread upon the waters and it will be returned to you after many days'—my heart rejoiced. I thought in my own vanity I was seeing the grains of my instruction returning on waves of wisdom to bathe the land in love and God's mercy. I saw at last a leader of self-discipline. One who practiced our laws of responsible conduct—but you have deserted us, Solomon. You have turned your back on the Lord, because of a strange woman!"

Solomon stood in the midst of them and there was silence. It held them all in a spell, for no one had remembered that the Queen of Sheba sat listening. They all turned to her now and Solomon went to her quickly.

"Benaiah will escort you to your house," he said.

She lifted her eyes, moved them slowly over the group of his accusers. She accepted the King's hand, rose and addressed him in a clear voice. "I have caused you much trouble. I came to learn your ways, but I have failed. With the King's indulgence I shall remain in my house—until the caravan is completely prepared—then I must leave." She smiled with self-effacing delicacy. "It is true I have caused you to turn away from your Lord and your people. I desired only your guidance. I regret that in leading me—you have lost your own way." She inclined her head and walked away.

Solomon's fury had never before known its full power. He had always checked its rise and said only a fool was given to sudden wrath. Now it poured forth as a rain of fire on their heads. He called forth from his memory the laws given them and asked them to remember that *"When a stranger sojourns with you in your land, you shall not do him wrong. The stranger who sojourns with you shall be to you as the native among you, and you shall love him as yourself; for you were strangers in the land of Egypt—"*

"We possess the priceless gift of the true word," he said. "The one law in the one word: love. Out of it came our need and right to freedom. Our heritage is the search for a God who would never have condemned one who would *learn* our ways. In our bones is the memory of wandering toward a home of peaceful living, and in that seeking no hand but the Lord's was extended to us. Look at yourselves! You who tell me I do not follow in His path. Because the hand of no man was held out to your fathers must we withhold our own?" He paused for breath and his voice was barely a whisper: "Where is your faith in God if you have no faith in man?"

"You have given your strength to a sinful woman," Zadok said. "At the end of your life you will groan when your flesh and body are consumed and you will remember this moment, how you despised reproof and would not incline your ear to the advice of your priest and your elders."

"Then as you anointed me King, Zadok, for the rest of my life, I beg you to pronounce me dead—that I may start to live!"

The elders gasped and closed blue-veined hands over their mouths.

Zadok shook his head slowly. His eyes were steeped in sorrow. "You are angry, Solomon, and speak without thinking. Let us not bring calamity upon ourselves and break our covenant beyond healing." He was suddenly an old and exhausted man. He walked slowly to the olive press and sat down on the stone rim.

"You have brought the discord among us, Zadok." Solomon spoke from where he stood. "I once said there were six things which the Lord hates, but seven are an abomination to him: haughty eyes, a lying tongue, and hands that shed innocent blood; a heart that devises wicked plans, feet that make haste to run to evil, a false witness who breathes out lies—and a man who sows discord among brothers!"

He started to walk away, then turned and cried out:

"You have called this the Hill of Offense! Then I will make it so. The gods of the aliens within our midst will rise from this ground, spring up as an orchard of wood and stone. Let the Sidonians and the Ammonites within our borders look upon Ashtoreth and Moloch. And the gods of Moab will grow from the earth that Baal-Peor and Chemosh may remind the foreigners of their homes and the worship they prefer—"

Ahiah closed his ears. Solomon was profaning the air with his anger. In his own confusion and sense of guilt, he had gone far beyond the need to defend himself. Ahiah could not listen to him. Nor could he look at Zadok who should have stayed away. He could blame neither one.

"Zadok," Ahiah said when Solomon had gone, "he spoke in idle anger. Let me help you descend the mountain now—"

"There is no rest for me this night." Zadok's hands were folded in his lap and they trembled. He stared at the ground. "Jehosphaphat," he said, "you know what must be done."

"But I believe, too," Jehoshaphat hurried to say, "Solomon was shocked by what he had seen tonight, angered into unwise statements by what you said—"

"You know what must be done," Zadok repeated in a weary whisper. "Send messengers to all the provinces. Summon the elders of all the tribes—the administrators and those who must form a council. Say to them that they must gather here without delay!"

Ahiah was disturbed by this resolute decision. He argued that it was a hasty one, as ill-considered as Solomon's threat to raise up gods of wood and stone. It was an empty defiance, nothing more.

"He will raise them up," Zadok said in a flat, lifeless voice. "Not out of defiance to me. For love of an evil woman. It is in his voice and in his heart. For her he would do anything, relinquish anything. Even the throne." He looked up, searching each face in its turn. No one denied his words. Even Ahiah feared he had spoken the truth. "Now, send the riders out."

Jehoshaphat still hesitated. "I cannot do it, without an order of the King."

"In this land," Zadok said, "the precedent has been established. Samuel anointed Saul as the first King of Israel. And the Lord repented giving Samuel this word, for Saul had not performed His commandments. And you remember that Samuel said rebellion is as the sin of divination, and stubbornness is as iniquity and idolatry. And because Saul had sacrificed the fat of rams and had not truly offered his heart, he was rejected—as we must reject a ruler who has turned from God."

"This is a greater sin than Solomon's defection," Ahiah said. And he named the blessings that had fallen on the land, its prosperity, the King's fame, the time of peace.

There was no fire now in Zadok's eyes. It had spent itself and become a dull ash of resignation.

"Peace, Ahiah? If it is ever to be more than a temporary calm, a quietness between the times of strife, every man must recognize the moral poverty in his soul."

Ahiah thought upon this and he was impressed, but still it had a familiar sound. And then he remembered. He had been the one who told it to Zadok.

It was very late. Tamrin walked slowly back and forth in the Queen's garden, waiting for her to come down from the hillside.

He pressed his elbows close to his sides as if malicious delight threatened to burst through his ribs and must be physically restrained. Lacing his long fingers over the middle of his waistband he absently patted the slight protuberance made by the ring. He waited now to return the royal emblem to the Queen for he had seen the assuring glimmer of triumph in her eyes when Solomon was being accused. Tamrin had protected the precious stone by folding the soft flap of the leather sheath around it. As he inserted it beside his blade he had watched Zadok unwittingly save the Queen's plans from delay, if not perilous defeat. This knowledge had been as clear to Makada as to himself. He was positive of that. Another moment and Solomon's anger would have been directed at her. But Zadok had appeared, rashly hurling arrows of imputation at the King! At the one man who held this citadel of power in the palm of his hand! How easily it would fall and crumble if those fingers spread out in anger and closed tight over a new cause he thought was righteous. Let the defenders of this upstart nation look on one another with hostile eyes and they would not see the true danger walking quietly through the streets soon to be destroyed.

Tamrin narrowed his eyes, peered upward, through the distant foliage. A light had appeared in the embrasure of the King's quarters. At irregular intervals it disappeared as a shadow paused a moment, then walked past, only to reappear. So Solomon had returned. And since the King's troubled thoughts led him up and down in the solitude of his rooms, Tamrin smiled and could allow himself to rest. The Queen would not linger on the mountainside beyond the time of Solomon's departure. She would be here soon. Tamrin sat down on a bench, leaned the back of his head against the garden wall. He did not allow his eyes to close completely for he intended to be on his feet the moment he caught a flash of silver through the pale light at the gate. He wanted to tell his Queen of the pride he had cherished up there on the hillside.

From Tamrin's vantage point, beyond the periphery of the judgment circle, he had watched Makada rise with unperturbed grace. This being he had fashioned surpassed his loftiest hopes! Her soft-spoken apology was perfection.

When she reached his side, Tamrin had whispered: "No need to remain, my lady. The breach has been created. Now let them dig a deeper pit with their quarreling mouths and fall into it—together." The Queen's body turned in acquiescence, as if to leave; but her eyes remained on the figures of dissension. Her posture became an amusing symbol of female duality. Her chin was poised directly in line with her left shoulder. One eye was a dark slanted shadow in her profile, dimly seen by the starlight sifting through the trees. In that rigid instant of listening and watching, she became an inscrutable figure; one of those lustrous earth-colored paintings Tamrin had once seen on an Egyptian wall. She wished to hear more, she told him, and asked him to wait for her in the garden of her house. "As you wish," he agreed. Then Tamrin had drawn his cloak about him and walked through the town, muffling his face, keeping well in the shadows; and the stillness in the streets, the huddled groups whispering softly, the eyes rolling toward the hill across the Kidron filled him with sublime contempt.

He became drowsy. His chin slowly sank to his chest. The starlight began to fade. From somewhere beyond the trees one of the garden torches laid a mottled ribbon of light across the path at his feet.

Makada entered the garden with little memory of how or when she had descended the hillside. She vaguely remembered the walk through the city. Perhaps she had imagined the unnatural, waiting silence, and the whisper of sandals as small islands of shadow broke apart and quickly disappeared into the houses. The small stone which fell at her feet could have fallen accidentally from one of the rooftops.

She turned a bend in the path and stopped abruptly when she saw the peacock sheen of Tamrin's robes. She fought the impulse to steal away from the inevitable questioning, the relentless probing of his eyes. But if all her unwelcome sensations refused to be vanquished by reason, they would lie in secret on her couch and possibly be discovered on her face by daylight. It was better then to speak with him now, in the shade of night. She walked closer and stopped on reaching the edge of light. The jewels on his clasped hands rose and fell with the shallow rhythm of one who always sleeps lightly—if at all. Makada took a deep breath. The pounding of her heart had almost drowned out the words on the hillside. They had not been spoken for her ears yet they had beaten against all the things she had been taught, had been born to believe. Between the hours up there and this moment of return lay a timeless and chaotic unreality. Hidden in its depths, as if it rose from the very bottom of the sea that held death and corruption, had come the inchoate awareness of right and wrong. And she detested its presence. She had known at once that it had lain dormant, stirring in its sleep now and then, unrecognized and rejected in Sheba, stretching its arm at Gibeon when the serpent crawled; she had heard its faint whisper in Solomon's judgment hall and closed her ears in scorn; it had walked between her and Tanis through the garden of the Pharaoh's daughter, was pushed back into the darkness by the stamping feet beneath the new moon.

And now it was making a stranger of Tamrin.

She could not remember a time when she had looked upon him with his eyes closed. When she was a child she had been certain he never slept and that he was born with the awesome turban of a Grand Vizier on his head. She yearned to recapture, if only for this moment, that complete dependence on his unquestioned authority. She searched his face, and was frightened. It remained austere and unfamiliar. Or had something Zadok called malevolence worn the deep grooves from nose to the bearded corners of the mouth? His sunken eyelids seemed long dead, as if greed for power had smoldered too long beneath them and left a loathsome ash. . . .

"Tamrin—"

He was instantly awake. The swift opening of his eyes, the immediate bow as he stood before her, soothed away some of the fears. She was grateful for his talk, although she scarcely heard the extravagant words of praise, only their whispered intensity. She had this time then to restore at least the façade of the insensate wall guarding her heritage and purpose. Since Tamrin was the architect of this human fortress he called Queen, he would be the first to detect any sign of weakness in its structure.

She was calm once more and could separate his voice from the one she had silenced within her.

"My most profound admiration, my lady," he said, "is reserved for your superb decision!"

He was too engrossed to notice her silence. His nostrils widened as if breathing in the scent of unsuspecting quarry. "I was well aware that your words to Solomon were part of a clever strategy. It was not your serious intention to seclude yourself until the day of departure—"

She evaded his eyes. "How well you know my thoughts."

"How little the King knows them!" Tamrin purred as he recalled the scene on the hillside. "Your words drew the color from his face. He was stricken. The very thought of not seeing you will aggravate his anxiety, urge him to further rage against his critics. It will hurl him into a final act of audacity which will cost him his throne."

A heavy silence oppressed her. She remembered how she could have reached out and touched Solomon as he passed her in the darkness; how she had felt closer to him in that moment than any time with his mouth pressed against hers.

"If Zadok has his way," she whispered, "Solomon has already lost the throne—"

Tamrin's head came up sharply and she told him all that happened after he left. "They sent for the elders of the tribes and officers of the provinces—"

"Then we have very little time!" Tamrin stood rigid, motionless.

She could see no cause for urgency. No need to proceed with the plans for a siege.

"And what of Adonijah?" Tamrin asked. "He had your word—"

"What is it worth? I have been taught to hold others to their word, but never hesitate to break my own." She added softly, "You were my teacher, Tamrin."

"Do you believe the King any more trustworthy? He will soon forget the trade agreement between our countries!"

"Not between our countries, Tamrin. Between Solomon and the Queen of Sheba."

"So much the worse, my lady. The King is famous for many things— but not the constancy of his affections."

"You forget their law, their commandments." She was satisfied, she said, that a sealed treaty was not taken lightly in this land. "They have something called conscience, Tamrin. Since we don't possess this strange treasure, we must take advantage of it."

He was silent a moment. "I have only one question. Is this talk of peaceful negotiation to become a royal decision, or does my lady see the wisdom of thinking no more about it until tomorrow? We can discuss it then?"

"You know I do not make hasty decisions." Her rebuke was mild, deliberately evasive. It relieved the Grand Vizier and he turned his mind to the point at which she had diverted it.

"If only an idol had been worshiped on the hill this night! Then there would be no need for delay. Until the people see a graven image they will waver and listen to the roar of Zadok as if he were a tongue of fire against Sodom and Gomorrah!" He lowered his voice. "You saw how quickly the moon dance lured some of them from the city walls."

"I saw." She did not tell him that the sight of these people had given her no pleasure, that what he called her triumph had left her hollow and empty of feeling. She could not tell him that she would hold herself aloof from everyone until she understood what had happened to her.

"His High Priest believes he will give up his throne?"

She had the impression Tamrin was repeating his question for the second time.

"Solomon would give up everything—for me—" she stopped abruptly. The soft wonder which had held her spellbound on the hill had crept into her voice. Defying Tamrin's searching eyes, she stepped into the pale light, calmly drew her cloak about her shoulders. "It grows cold. . . ." She gave him an inquisitive smile. "You find it difficult to believe he would relinquish his throne?"

Tamrin sighed. "Strangely enough, I believe he would." They walked a moment without speaking. "He would do anything to be with you. But to willingly give up everything—would defeat our purpose. It is important that he remain defiant—in the way we wish him to be: as a king imposing his personal desires against the law—by throwing aside all restraint, to keep you here in Jerusalem as long as he can!"

She felt chilled. No cloak could be drawn against the malevolence she recognized in him now. And if this man had shaped her own being over the years. . . .

"He knows you must return for the feast of Ashtoreth," Tamrin went on with fresh eagerness, "so he will act quickly. We shall see. If we do not hear the sounds of hammer and chisel within the next few days then I must leave immediately with the message to our commander. Your caravan will be prepared by that time—"

"Tamrin," she said slowly, "are we a nation of *false* gods?" She had heard many things on the hillside this night. Or perhaps she only heard them in a new way.

Tamrin chuckled. "*They* are the ones who worship falsely. Not images of stone but still of mortal creation. They have ten commandments. They all begin with an ironic and convenient phrase: '*Thou Shalt Not—*' so everyone can point an accusing finger at his neighbor. Never at himself."

"But they are not the words of man to man," she said. "They are the laws spoken to Moses—" She broke off, sensing the displeasure in Tamrin. She found herself holding back the extent of her information without fully knowing the reason why. There was no point, however, in irritating him with useless knowledge. She had been close to naming the Maker of the laws given to the leader of the people. And she had formed a holy Name in her mind and knew she could not utter it without a whisper of something called the fear of God. The fear that was reverence and love for the ineffable *Elohim*—to Solomon's people. But fear alone to her. Or would she have spoken of *Yahweh* or remembered vaguely hearing someone sing: *"By the word of the Lord were the heavens made"*—or still, hesitated to speak out *Adonai?* And from out of nowhere, unbidden, came fragments of song prophesying the terrible destruction of those whose tongues devised mischief, *like a sharp razor, working deceitfully*: *"He shall take thee away and pluck thee out of thy dwelling place and root thee out of the land of the living"* and from the banquet room or perhaps rising from a field of Bethel—wherever the voices had lifted up—came the cry of *Selah.* . . .

"—But it doesn't matter," Tamrin went on. "Who remembers it was a deity who spoke to *all* of them? Whoever spoke from a burning bush must roar with laughter. These people have sought for centuries—perhaps they always will—to know the true essence of ten foolish laws which they break over and over. They are forbidden to steal. To covet. To bear false witness. To make graven images. Yet a miser can bow down before the weight of silver in his house and not be charged an idolater. They acknowledge a god invisible, thereby saying the supreme value of all things is in the spirit. Intangible. But mark this—are they inclined to punish a thief who *steals* something of that precious spirit, something which cannot be seen? No. It is a doubtful theft, open to question, if it cannot be weighed on a scale of *tangible* values."

She said she did not understand how the weakness of men reflected the nature of their god. Tamrin gave her a swift frown and she knew, instinctively, this was not the time to antagonize him. She asked him to go on.

He waited a moment before continuing. "I am only explaining," he said, "the idiocy of those who pretend to uphold certain statutes by finding devious ways of tearing them down."

His stiff bearing, the lengthened strides, spoke more eloquently of injured pride.

"I believe I understand now," she said. "You were telling me of false values. Not false gods."

"One and the same," he said loftily. "A man may bear false witness and be stoned for it on the same day another is applauded for falsehoods, dressed in the raiment of truth. So you see how useless it all is if a man is allowed to covet with impunity in one generation that which is reprehensible in the next." He gave a short contemptuous laugh. "How can they deceive themselves that they search for truth if they cannot all find the same meaning in the same law?"

She wondered, silently, if the constant searching was not in itself the answer. He would not care for such a suggestion from her.

She was uneasy and Tamrin had confused her.

"They say we are a corrupt nation, Tamrin."

He shrugged. "Naturally. According to their values we are corrupt. Without conscience. But I have given you a few brief examples of the corruption in their *values*."

She did not want to believe him, entirely.

"Has their God the power to strike us down?"

Tamrin whirled to a sudden stop. "He doesn't exist!" He took a deep breath and lowered his voice. "Look at it with the light of your mind. Why do you suddenly ask these preposterous questions! Does your own intelligence not tell you if a being who is invisible created an orderly plan for the stars and sun and earth, then why did he not give his precious mankind more than disordered confusion? No, if he ever existed he lost his power when Solomon became King. His power was not fashioned for a King who prattles of peace. Let him be used as Adonijah will use him. On a standard of war! May I be struck down and vultures pick at my dead eyes if there is a god of peace!"

Tamrin yawned behind skeletal fingers and bade the Queen a restful night.

She brought her eyes from the strangely quiet garden and studied his face. "Weren't you frightened?"

"Of what?"

"That wind—it seemed to come from nowhere—"

"Their laws and their climate," he said with contempt, "are equally stupid."

He bowed low, murmured formal words of withdrawal and disappeared down a branch of the garden path.

For two nights and two days the Queen of Sheba allowed no one into her presence but Vashi.

Tamrin's annoyance surpassed his discretion. He wrote out a message which scarcely veiled the implication that the behavior of a capricious woman could be an irritation; but when she also possessed the authority of a Queen it could be disastrous. So much depended on her progress with Solomon at this critical time, he reminded her. Let her exclude her humble Grand Vizier if she wished, but give him one good reason why she had consistently refused to see the King?

Abishag waited for the reply at the door of the Queen's private rooms. It opened only wide enough for Vashi to pass out the answer. It reddened the face of the Grand Vizier. The Queen was deliberately taunting him! She had written that a capricious woman would *have* no reason and a Queen certainly had no *need* of one. Tamrin stormed out of the house, determined to leave for Adonijah's encampment. Success would have to be risked. From the camp of Solomon's brother he would then go on to where Bashir waited for the word to join Adonijah. Tamrin patted the Queen's ring, still lying sheathed beneath his waistband. The gods were on his side. If they had permitted Makada to behave foolishly they had also clouded her memory. She had not asked about the royal symbol of authority, and he had conveniently forgotten to return it.

Supremely confident, he left the palace grounds. He would occupy himself outside the city walls on the pretext of inspecting the caravan being assembled. He would ride casually up and down, giving orders to the scattered groups of servants, the overseers of the camel drivers and stewards of the royal gifts. And when the time was right, when darkness had fallen, he would surreptitiously move away and ride swiftly to the south.

During this time when the Queen did not show her face, Ahiah became increasingly concerned about Solomon.

The King walked freely among the people, as always, but he seemed to look upon them from a remote distance. Yet when a question was asked of him his eyes would fasten with fierce intensity on the speaker until satisfied the query concealed no censure of him or, most particularly, the Queen of Sheba.

His duties were dispatched with accelerated efficiency. A long-dangling controversy with a peevish prince was illuminated with a flash of logic that blinded Solomon's adversary into amazed agreement.

And in the judgment hall Jehoshaphat whispered that the King's pronouncements were brilliant, but shining cold. "Can it be, Ahiah," he asked, "that justice too can become a habit, as external as the robe he wears for the hearing of petitions?" Ahiah shook his head, too eager to deny such a thought.

There was an unspoken feeling—apparent in the dwindling number of grievances on the following day—that the King's judgment was inclined to favor one side of the scale. An honest dealer in silver received little recompense for goods adjudged stolen by the accused, who happened to be guilty as well as poor.

It was possible for Ahiah to wonder then if Zadok's accusation against Solomon was beginning to fan the King's natural warmth of understanding into an excess of indulgence—toward *all* defendants.

The Solomon who showed this tendency was a stranger to everyone. A pitiable one to Ahiah. The King, it seemed, had withdrawn more completely, was less approachable than the Queen who stayed within her walls. Solomon was seen glancing toward those walls, as if hoping for a glimpse of her. But she neither appeared nor answered his messages.

He had talked freely only on the night Ahiah first visited him, a few hours after the Sabaeans had desecrated the hill with their savage performance. The sandals of the scribe had squeaked up the outer stairs.

When he entered he found the King sitting at his work table with his face buried in the palms of his hands.

Solomon spoke without looking up. "I'll not roar at you, Ahiah, because you are my friend." His voice was flat. "But I'll not listen to the bellowing of big mouths with small minds!"

Ahiah sat down and for a long time the only sound in the room was the idle tapping, end over end, of the pen in Ahiah's hand. The oil in the lamps began to disappear. Solomon sighed. He rested his arms on the table and stared into the sputtering flame.

"Zadok has no doubt summoned the elders."

Ahiah nodded slowly without taking his eyes from the pen. "He fears the threat you made tonight was not an idle one; that it could jeopardize the survival of a united people. He sees pillars rising on every high place in the land, a forsaking of the only Source of strength—and that for all time to come. For who knows when another time of peace will shine upon the land?"

"The people know I would do nothing to harm them!" Solomon rose with abrupt impatience. His chair fell over and crashed softly into the camel's hair rug. "They will understand!"

"They will do more," Ahiah said. "You are their adored leader. They will follow and condone, without bothering to understand. There lies the danger—" He was moved to smile at himself. "Now look at me, sitting here spewing forth words of advice. I have always taken pride in holding myself above the affairs of other men and nations. I have watched them rise in glory and knew the hour they would inevitably go down in defeat. I have been content to sit by and watch the things come to pass which needed nothing but a study of past events to foresee with a clear eye. Ah, it is a great feeling to be a spectator, unmoved, impartial, all-seeing. I hoped never to lose that superior comfort of serving without being involved in the folly of others. At times I thought it almost god-like. I was wrong. I struggled against the emotions that climbed to my lofty window but they crept into my stone-like sleep." He gave the pen a little push across the table, waited as it rolled to a stop. "It took all my courage to come up here to your rooms, to listen to my own voice. But didn't you once say there was a time to keep silent and a time to speak?" Ahiah shook his head in slow surprise. "I never thought I would speak as an ambassador for—of all people!—the High Priest. I have never before seen anything but tyrannical fanaticism in his obdurate views—"

"Then how can you support them!"

"Because for the moment they are right." Ahiah spoke quietly, hearing his own words go out as if they came from a stranger. "There is a delicacy in the times, Solomon. We cannot foresee the future, but we must try to do all that is possible in this passing moment we call our lives that our children's children may *have* that future. Remember David. He knew when he lay dying the only true heritage he could leave his people—"

"Zadok would lead them like cattle to the altar with a whip!"

"The better way is still yours, Solomon. Not to scream and preach. Not with force. But by example."

Solomon absently set the chair upright. Spasms of dying light flickered over his white knuckles as he gripped the back of the chair and leaned forward against it.

"I try to lead them to a field of sunlight where sheep of all breeds, from countless folds, eat of the same grass. But I am accused of leading them astray—into darkness!"

Ahiah ached with futility and sadness. "I know, Solomon, I know. But they are not ready. The sheep are too young, too impressionable. They must first learn the call of the One Shepherd lest in their mingling they are lost to Him forever and for all time."

Solomon turned toward a sudden illumination near the door. Old Benjamin's pale face hovered in the shadows as if disembodied by the bright flame in the bowl he carried. He tottered into the room, bent and uncertain.

"Bring us a fresh lamp," Solomon said, "and more!" He strode across the room, sweeping the shadows with a wide gesture of distaste. "Leave no corner in darkness! Bring all you can find!"

This too was unlike the King. How often Ahiah had heard him gently scold the old man for staying up so late, saying he needed no further light and then as soon as the old·man had disappeared, tending to the need himself. But this night he had allowed the ancient servant of David to make many trips to and from the upper supply rooms and all the while, as the room bloomed slowly into light, Solomon spoke of the insult to the Queen of Sheba. His own humiliation, he said, could not possibly be as deep as hers. He would not sleep until he had made a formal apology. How dared Zadok call her evil!

"Must she account to *us* because her ways are not ours? Would we see our own guilt if *our* eyes had been taught from the first hour of their opening to look without mercy on acts of needless cruelty? Our sin is greater. Because we *know* what we do. A stranger came into our midst and we did not treat her as our own. Zadok has forgotten the story of Ruth."

He talked of the Moabitess who had entreated Naomi not to leave her; that where her mother-in-law journeyed there would she go also. Naomi's home in Judah would be Ruth's home. And when they came at last to Bethlehem, what if Boaz had not taken the stranger to wife? What then, if the gentle Boaz had not taken her to his heart?

"There would have been no child," Solomon said, staring at the shadows until, one by one, they disappeared. "No Obed to beget Jesse. No Jesse to beget David."

It was significant to Ahiah that Solomon did not go beyond the name of his own father. It seemed not to matter to him that there would have been no King Solomon. Deep in his mind then there must still lie a vestige of the feeling that his spectacular achievements were nothing but the need to justify his place on the throne.

Ahiah was on the point of saying this and more. But with the fresh illumination in the room the shadows seemed to have converged in the blackness of Solomon's eyes. They were withdrawn and unfathomable. It would profit neither of them to say there was a vast difference between the gentle young woman of Moab who became a sojourner in the land, and the imperious woman of Sheba who was a foreigner. The delineation did not lie in the submissive devotion of the one who said: "Your God shall be my God." It lay in the smoldering embers of the fires that would never die on the Hill of Offense. It must be stamped out if it took a lifetime; for the Queen of Sheba, without uttering the words, had said: "Look upon the worship of other gods and destroy your own!"

In this first moment of Solomon's withdrawal, Ahiah searched frantically within himself for a wedge to keep open the invisible gates closing between them.

"My brother has returned with news of Adonijah. He saw him!" Ahiah spoke with haste and transient shame. Lending not only the semblance of truth but urgency to one of Elihoreph's daydreams! Then as Solomon turned slowly and faced him, Ahiah's guilt dissolved. He had diverted the King's interest. Perhaps he could prolong it. The opaque darkness did not leave the eyes of the King, but at least he was listening. "Joab was with him. There were others, Elihoreph told me, all dressed as merchants—" That was a mistake. Solomon was giving him a downward, skeptical look. Ahiah chided himself. He should have known Solomon would give no credence whatever to an Adonijah traveling as a common merchant, without glittering uniforms or a resplendent guard. "Elihoreph is of the opinion your brother seeks a friendly reunion with you. Would he enter the city or come so close to it, in anything but the raiment of humility?"

"You don't believe it any more than I, Ahiah. And you know I have no wish to see my brother humbled." Solomon's voice held no inflection, no joy of anticipation. "Incredible as it may seem after all my efforts to find him, this rumor does not stir me. The longing to find my brother is no less than it has always been, I am sure. Still I find it difficult to call up the feverish need. Perhaps it is only overshadowed by my present greater need—or it is gone. Whichever it is, Ahiah," he added with irony, "tell the news to Zadok. Tell him he need not summon the elders for council after all, that another son of David can be found—" He strode across the room. "Tell him to bring my brother into Jerusalem and let a procession of coronation form at the gates!" He grasped the wine goblet that rested in the wall niche near the harp that was David's, and he thrust it into Benjamin's trembling hands. "Polish this wine bowl that bears my brother's initial, Benjamin. Let it shine like a star and replace it with haste so it might welcome the entrance of a new king into these rooms!"

Benjamin shuffled hastily from the room and when the door had closed on his frightened backward glance, Ahiah spread out his hands in a hopeless gesture and let them fall heavily at his sides. It was a trick of the light; it must be. The radiance in the room, reflected from copper lamp-stands, golden bowls and rich fabric seemed to lighten the glossy darkness of the King's hair. The bones of his face, the width of his shoulders, every line of the posture was David's. A young and passionate David on the eve of battle.

"You cannot possibly mean those words, Solomon," Ahiah said. "Wisdom was given you, now I wonder if you are being asked to earn that wisdom."

And he held to the hope—through the meetings of the next day and the judgments of the next—that Solomon would be still in his heart and listen to his inner voice of guidance.

But it came into the mind of the scribe as he approached the tabernacle this late afternoon that Samson too had been given a special gift. He who had slain a thousand Philistines with the jawbone of an ass had lost his prodigious strength for love of the woman of Sorek. Because of Delilah he had to know blindness before he could truly see. Depressed by the thought, Ahiah found himself avoiding the creeping shadow of the tabernacle. Zadok detached himself from a group of Levites working in the forecourt and came toward him. The High Priest listened as Ahiah spoke out his thoughts.

"We must give him time," he said. "Solomon has a unique vision. He sees far beyond the horizons of other men—"

"He forgets his obligations to other men!" Zadok sighed, pressed a thumb and forefinger into the inner corners of his red-rimmed eyes. "He forgets he is no less a servant of God than you and I. It is the pit of evil experience, Ahiah, that separates all of us from our Creator. And we plunge into it with open eyes taking all reason and conscience down into darkness. The King's mother grieves because her son does not heed her warnings. She and the Pharoah's daughter came to me, pleading that I help Solomon and not turn against him." His hands were clenched at his sides. "How can I help a man who turns against himself? There is nothing I can do. Nothing less than a miracle can make him see. But we have become unworthy. I fear we are past the age of miracles—"

He looked past Ahiah and stiffened. Drawing himself to his full height Zadok turned his back on the street, fixing his gaze on the altar being scrubbed in the forecourt. The cause of his sudden anger rode closer on a shining white horse. Sun and crescent amulets jingled from the bridle. Tamrin bowed with an obsequious greeting to Ahiah and said the Queen's caravan was being prepared to his satisfaction. He had just finished inspecting it. He cast a crafty smile toward Zadok's rigid back, then rode on toward the palace gates.

"He is pleased about something," Ahiah said as Zadok turned around. The High Priest was pale. His cloud of white beard trembled as he spoke. "You will know the reason when you walk through the streets." He raised a hand against Ahiah's question and continued. "Every hour of the night was an hour of prayer. I knelt before the veil of testimony—" his voice broke with despair. "I fasted and prayed for a manifestation. But I am not Moses on Sinai. I am only Zadok, in Zion. Still I prayed for a cloud by day and pillar of fire by night to hold the Presence that guided us through another sort of wilderness. Something must strike the fear of God into us! We need a sign, a Shekinah for all to see, exhorting us to wipe the pollution from the Promised Land lest its mountains fall upon us! I pray that the Lord will speak out against our backsliding and abominations in a voice of thunder! And bring our heads to the ground in fear and trembling!" A distended worm of blue vein throbbed beneath the waxen skin at his temple.

Ahiah looked away from his fury to the caretakers laboring in the late sunshine.

"The coming feast day will be the last to be celebrated in David's tabernacle," he said. "I should make some mention of it in the records—"

"Mark it down then as a time of shame!" Zadok whispered. "From sundown to sundown there will be singing and rejoicing—but when it is over, the next day will see the abomination revealed on the Hill of Offense!"

Ahiah could not believe his ears.

"Then go into the town!" Zadok cried. "Hear for yourself the sounds of hammers and chisels. A wall of rough board has risen in the night and within it, artisans and laborers work till they drop. An image of brick and timber is springing up and by the time the ram's horn sounds out for our own feast day, the image of *Ashtoreth* will be complete behind its protecting wall!"

The soft purple shadows lengthened. There was no escape from them now. They touched Ahiah and covered him as he had known they would.

"The King is bewitched," Zadok said. "But still clever. He made haste in its building so he could still observe the cessation of labor required on the feast day. Moreover, he told me an hour ago, on his way down to inspect new chariots out of Egypt, that he will be at my side during the holy convocation—as he always has been. A further concession to his doddering High Priest is his gracious offer to withhold the tearing down of the wall until the close of the holy day—"

Ahiah waited to hear no more. He hurried into the town and in the streets he heard and he saw. A terrible quiet prevailed over Jerusalem.

He met Eli near the crowd at the Horse Gate. The physician said he was on his way to a sick man and had paused to look back at the activity on the hill. Together they watched oxen pulling carts of sun-dried bricks up the slope. The brown legs of burden bearers glistened in the sun as they moved in and out of the trees, carrying supplies up to the laborers inside the wall.

"It is not too large," Eli said, by way of comfort. "I could not restrain my curiosity. It is square with receding courses of brick and timber and a ramp leads to the top. A construction of more speed than beauty. The monolith which will be raised to the top is an incuse figure of some lascivious deity—"

Ahiah scarcely heard him. He did not care whether the shrine was made of emeralds or mud, whether the base was a circle of stones or the pyramidal ziggurat Eli had described.

Feeling sick, Ahiah muttered: "At least the laborers are not our own people."

There was no malice in Eli's chuckle. Ahiah caught an echo of something remotely familiar. Unpleasantly so. He looked at Eli, wondering at this odd and sudden revulsion for his friend the physician. And when Eli spoke, Ahiah knew. It was the echo of his own voice he heard: the soft chuckle of the bystander, the observer peering from the lofty window shuttered from the heat and cold of passionate conviction.

"Within the scaffold is the one young man who could build a Golden Calf itself without a hand's breadth of self-reproach," Eli said. "He supervises the labor. It is only another task to him. Brick, timber and noise. After the silent building of the Temple, how Jeroboam appears to love the noise! Now I must leave you, my friend. I can cure the sick man of his boils—" Eli's voice, Ahiah was relieved to hear, had recovered its anger "—but who can cure the unseen sores that will spread and drip with poison over the length of the land the moment that hideous idol is revealed?" Then he hurried away, taking long strides that carried him from the barbaric hammering on the hill.

A small but solemn delegation rode through the gates. The elders out of Ephraim and Manasseh had journeyed together up to Jerusalem. The fathers of the tribes were beginning to gather in answer to Zadok's summons.

Tamrin entered the Queen's house in time to see a handful of silver playing pieces, hurled from within one of the alcoves, fly out into the main chamber. They hit the glazed floor with a resounding echo. For an instant the clatter drowned out the hissing anger of a woman talking to herself. Abishag swept out of the side room, her cheeks blotched a disagreeable red. Swift as a serpent's tongue the toe of her sandal flicked out from beneath her robe, kicking the most ornate gaming piece in a shallow arc across the floor. It dropped without sound into the deep rug on which the Grand Vizier stood.

"You play a solitary and violent game of draughts," he murmured.

Abishag's brusque movements had brought the soft fall of her headveil over one shoulder. She tossed it back with a reckless shrug. "I have just seen the Queen of Sheba," she said, her lips pinched with fury.

Without a downward glance, Tamrin stepped over the glittering cone, and seated himself in the Queen's chair. She had at last sent for him but he wanted first to hear from the Shunammite. From her manner he feared the worst.

"Your agitation is hardly a compliment to my sovereign." His fingers traced the buds and open flowers carved on the arms of the royal chair.

"For the past three days her desire to be left to herself has increased." Abishag took a deep breath to control the tremor in her voice. "Even her old serving woman spends most of her time packing the personal gifts in the store chambers, or riding that black demon of a horse!"

Tamrin waved aside this information. "You delivered my message, that the royal caravan is prepared to leave at any hour?"

Abishag nodded.

"Excellent," said Tamrin, and glanced toward the niche where the small image of Ashtoreth gleamed above a spiral of incense. "Then you also told Her Majesty that the idol on the hillside was completed this afternoon?"

A spark of malice flickered in her eyes. "She was not overjoyed as you said she would be. She was alarmed to hear the image had risen at all and was relieved only when I said it had not yet been made visible to Solomon's people."

Tamrin adjusted the folds of his robe with deliberation. He was disturbed, but less than he thought he would be. There was not much the Queen could do now to destroy his plans, unless . . .

He smoothed an eyebrow with his forefinger and asked, as if it were only a random thought, if Abishag had informed the Queen of Sheba that the Edomites had joined Adonijah's forces? "You remember I told you some days ago to deliver such a message?" And he held his breath for her answer.

"I remember." Her voice was flat and sullen. The long pause that followed irritated him to the point of outrage. This little fool was no further use to him; still he could not afford her enmity. He spoke with mildness: "Then she knows."

"I did not tell her."

He sighed inwardly and caressed the arms of the chair. Abishag misunderstood his silence. Her face distorted with rage. "Adonijah's cause is destroyed. She thinks only of *Solomon*! It is written on her face—"

A warning glance stopped her. Whatever happened now, this lovesick wench must never doubt his loyalty to the Queen. "Her Majesty has already fulfilled her agreement with your loved one."

A corner of Abishag's mouth turned with scorn. "If your commander receives an order from her it will be an order to return to Sheba. I know it as if she had spoken the words."

Her insolence displeased him because he suspected it held some truth. "I would not dispute the knowledge of your heart for it is superior to your reason. But consider. What does it matter whether Adonijah leads Sabaean or Edomite soldiers into a city already fallen beneath the shadow of an idol?"

He allowed her to search his face carefully for a renewal of hope.

"Have no fear," he said. "The Sabaeans will march against Jerusalem." And he thought, if they do not—if some unforeseen destiny sends Bashir and his soldiers back to Sheba without joining in the siege—the city, the nation and Solomon's power will nevertheless be crushed for all time. So he repeated, "Have no fear."

Her mouth trembled and pressing a fist against it she ran weeping from the room. She was out of his mind sooner than out of sight. He ran his fingertips along the arms of the chair with a delicate, sensuous delight. Authority rising to full power came over him. Like the throne in Sheba, he thought, this chair was better fashioned for his proportions than those of his Queen. Another night and day and he would no longer be bound by the need to control his impatience. These were the last crucial hours.

He rose from the chair. As he started toward the Queen's rooms he looked up and stopped. The great doors at the far end had been opened soundlessly during his reverie. He wondered, with quick reflection and distrust, how long the inscrutable eyes of Vashi had been watching him.

She stepped away from the door as Makada entered. He looked at the face of the Queen. Abishag's instinct had not been wrong; nor his own apprehensions. A knot of fury tightened his chest and he made a longer than usual obeisance to gain a moment's time before meeting the vulnerable, tender expression once more. He doubted if she truly saw him. Her eyes held a new and childlike wonder but for an instant he thought he detected a shred of his perfect creation. Still inviolate. But the moment she spoke he knew he had mistaken self-reproach for a remnant of self-interest.

"We must leave, Tamrin, before we are swallowed up by our own evil." She spoke with breathless urgency as if she had said the words many times to herself.

There were faint shadows of fatigue beneath her eyes. They told of sleepless nights. Her throat and ankles were unadorned. She wore no glittering bracelets and in her hair no diadem. Yet she stood in an elusive radiance.

"If we are destroyed," Tamrin said, indicating the royal chair with a specious gesture of subservience, "it will be by the hand and power of the King."

She shook her head slowly, ignoring the waiting chair. She looked down at the carpet, her hands clasped tightly together beneath her chin. "It came to me when I was no longer able to think. Then many things which had been incomprehensible were suddenly clear. I *knew*. It came over me like a warm and comforting tide. . . ."

She paused and stared down at a shaft of weave struck into silver and ruby brilliance by the last rays of the sun.

"You no longer fear this powerful nation?" He saw her pick up something from the floor. It was the tall cone-shaped gaming piece and she studied it between her hands.

"I fear the power that created this nation."

"You no longer speak as a monarch of Sheba. Yours are the words of a woman—any woman—who loves someone more than herself!"

She looked up at him with slow realization. An inward smile curved her lips. "Humility was hideous to me. A sign of weakness." Her voice was soft as the down of a thistle. Caught up by an aimless breeze it searched into dark corners for some hidden mystery. "It is too soon and too vast to see everything in the first moments of seeing. I thought I lived alone and by my own law. Solomon could have spoken of me when he said there was more hope for a fool that a man wise in his own conceit." She held the gaming piece in her fingers as if it held some secret significance; and as she talked she entered the alcove and placed the tall silver cone in the center marking of the ivory gaming board. "He could have named me as the abomination who fostered discord among brothers."

She was talking rot. Tamrin watched her with narrowed eyes and was caught up in a whirlpool of calculation. And he feared the expression in her eyes. It reminded him of Abishag. Whether it shone on the face of a handmaiden or a Queen it was the renunciation that consumed all identity. It tore through his bones, uprooting his self-control. He had to cross his arms slide his hands up under the wide sleeves to cover their trembling. With a gesture of bowing to her wishes he assured her he was ready to carry them out. He would ride immediately and inform Adonijah. . . .

"You'll ride nowhere," she said mildly. "We have no message for Solomon's brother. He had no true claim to the throne—and that is important to me, now." She walked toward the garden door and paused, looking out. "He is an arrogant man. He would be an evil, pernicious ruler. When he learns we have returned to our own land in peace he'll abandon his plan for a siege, perhaps even his bitterness." She looked over her shoulder and impaled Tamrin with a sharp command: "There must be no bloodshed."

He feigned resignation to her change of heart. "As you wish." And he reached desperately for time, and secrecy. "Then I'll take these orders to Bashir."

"You remain here. Early in the morning, before we depart, we must appear before those who would judge Solomon," she said, "and we must make amends for our wrong-doing. I hope it is not too late." She brushed away the unpleasant ordeal she had imposed upon herself—and him.

"It is not seemly for the Queen of Sheba and her Grand Vizier to suffer humiliation—" he subdued the outrage in his voice "—before a King who will threaten our survival till the day he dies!"

She sighed. "We are the aggressors, Tamrin. Not Solomon. Now we have talked long enough. Let our people be informed that we leave tomorrow morning. We need not send a message to Bashir. He will see our caravan soon enough. My army will escort us back to Sheba."

But not in victory, Tamrin thought, and was startled into caution by her next words.

"Not in defeat," she said. "Perhaps this is a greater conquest than I know."

The room had filled with the first shadows of evening. She asked Vashi to fetch her cloak and Tamrin followed her into the garden.

"I must see the King at once," she said, "while I have the strength to tell him why I came to Jerusalem—"

She paused near an arch of dark foliage, looking out upon the courtyards.

"There is no profit in baring your soul," said Tamrin. "Say nothing. Otherwise you leave him with thoughts of loathing."

"I know," she whispered.

She had thought all this out, in those tortured nights. Her decision was made. A malignant weight turned within him. He stared at the low shimmering back of her gown, at the amber curve of shoulder that rose above it. Delicate flesh and bone standing between him and a greater glory. His fingers stiffened an instant. His right hand moved slowly toward the sheathed knife in his waistband and he felt the blood pounding behind his eyes. Then a sound came up to him on the evening breeze. Clear and sustained, it came through the trumpets of those he despised and would conquer. A blast of deliverance. . . .

Makada lifted a fear-stricken face to the call. "What does it mean?"

A tide of exultation washed over Tamrin. His hands relaxed. "It is only the ram's horn, the *shofar*. It signifies the beginning of their feast." He watched her carefully. It was obvious she had forgotten. He gave a slight shrug. "It need not alter our plans—"

She did not answer. With the first sound of singing her eyes were drawn to the deep-shaded gardens beyond. Courtiers and servants of the palace appeared, straggling in a happy pattern along the paths that merged and led toward the gates. They were on their way to the tent of meeting in Zion. Makada drew back instinctively as Solomon appeared on the star-brightened path. Surrounded by his ministers and his guards and dressed in ceremonial robes, he seemed to walk apart from all men. For an instant he looked upward, toward the rooftop of the Queen's house.

She pressed fingertips against her lips as she watched him move away and in the stillness of the garden her breathing could be heard.

"The King's face is shadowed with unhappiness," Tamrin said, watching her from beneath lowered lids. His face darkened when he saw Benaiah and the captains. The commander of the host sang with the others to the Lord of hosts: "*He maketh wars to cease unto the end of the earth; He breaketh the bow, and cutteth the spear in sunder. . . .*"

The fragrance of fresh-baked loaves drifted into the Queen's garden. They would be waved as First Fruits of fine meal, as an offering at sundown and in the first light of morning. The women followed the men and the songs that held the melancholy of long wandering burst into a joyous noise. Yet there were some who held themselves rigid and somber as they joined the procession. The face of Bathsheba was white and anxious. Old Benjamin lagged behind, forgetting to mouth the words as he watched the others in bewilderment.

As the singing faded away, Tamrin waited silently. Vashi had slipped a cloak over the Queen's shoulders, but Makada made no move toward the garden gate.

"We must wait until their day of feasting is over," she said. She could not take the King from his duties at the tabernacle, and for the first time Tamrin rejoiced over her inglorious mood of submission.

"Your Majesty has made a wise decision," he said.

He left the garden, walking with slow dignity past hurrying groups of exuberant young women carrying garlands. The sound of chanting could be heard once more, coming up from the fields, from the streets of the city. When he was well out of sight he paused and looked around. No one was watching. He swept his cloak about him and walked swiftly toward the stables.

The King stood close by the High Priest at the rites before the altar in the forecourt but at no time during the evening did the eyes of Solomon and Zadok meet.

Through the smoke of unblemished meat offerings, Solomon beheld the multitude of faces, shifting in light and shadow, lifted up in prayer and song. His hands and his words performed their duty and he endured this ceremony as he would endure the service in the morning. He saw everything as in a dream in which the gaunt face of Elihoreph smiled tentatively and Jehoshaphat's uncertain agony kept his eyes fixed on the ground. And the beseeching sadness of Ahiah floated toward him in the shifting smoke but came no closer, as if an invisible wall had cut off the King from those who would help him but could no longer be counted friends. The white beards of the elders and the deep-set coals of reproach in their eyes came to him with more substance out of the darkness. These were the old men, the friends of David, the heads of the tribes who had gathered to hold council at the feast's ending over the son of David. They will say I have forsaken him, Solomon thought. They will say I have forsaken all of them but most of all the God of Abraham and Jacob—because I loved a strange woman.

He stood before the veil of testimony which separated the Ark of the Covenant from the Holy Place of the tabernacle. As Zadok moved to the left and right, as incense mingled with the glow of the candelabrum, Solomon looked at the priest's robe of fine-twisted linen with its tassels and cords reverently tied in the ancient manner prescribed. But it held no meaning. Around the hem, small golden bells and pomegranates were exquisitely wrought. The jeweled breastplate over the ephod of blue and scarlet, gold and purple, was an object of dazzling beauty. Nothing more. The topaz representing the tribe of Simeon, the jasper, beryl and sapphire—all the emblems of the twelve—rose and fell with Zadok's sonorous prayers. In other times the sight of them had renewed the challenge of responsible leadership. Now they evoked a memory of resentment. On the day he was anointed at Gihon these jewels had hovered over him in relentless rows. How proper, he thought with irony, that I look upon them the last day of my reign; for the decision to be made at the meeting of the elders is as certain as the setting of the sun which will mark its hour. . . .

So, as it had been asked by generations who were to look upon the twelve stones set up by Joshua at Gilgal—to commemorate the cutting off of Jordan's waters that gave dry passage into the promised land—Solomon could also ask of himself: *What mean ye by these stones?*

He experienced one vague instant of self-accusation. It came after the morning worship. The people had been reminded that they did not live by bread only and their spirits were lifted up in song: *"Be still and know that I am God,"* they sang. *"I will be exalted among the heathen; I will be exalted in the earth. . . ."* As Solomon distributed cakes of raisins and figs to the passing crowds he saw Barzillai, the sycophant, among them. And it passed through Solomon's mind that all the petty vices of the colorless one could be overlooked in this moment because he held his young son by the hand. This shameless head, so skillfully hinged to bow before any favorable wind, had remembered the days of old as in a song of Moses: *"Ask thy father and he will tell thee, thy elders, and they will tell thee."* Rehoboam should be here, he thought, with his sheaf of wheat or offering of fruit. Instead, he sojourns in Ammon and has not often looked upon the feast days of his fathers. I concern myself with his sensitive nose, care for his body and neglect the food of his soul. We have been enjoined not to reap our fields to the very borders, that the poor and homeless might have food. Have I cut the flowering of my kingdom and left nothing for my son? There should be a statute less easy to forget than the one written on our gateposts. A child should be led in the right path that he might know the way when he becomes a man.

It was his custom to mingle with the people at the three great feasts of the year; to share their bread and the wry humor of their family tales. Too often, on this day, he saw a man look the other way as he passed a former friend; another crossed the street to avoid meeting his neighbor. And there were those who walked the middle of the road, breaking off a song now and then to puzzle over the lack of whole-hearted joy. Then shrugging off the somber thought they rushed toward those ahead who danced, waving flowers in the air, too absorbed in their pleasure to notice anything unusual.

Solomon shook himself free of the undercurrent that would pull him deep into a sea of turbulence. To survive he would have had to struggle upward, to break through the surface. It would grow calm once more but limitless and empty. He didn't want that. If he walked among a people divided it was not his doing. The smallness of their own souls had collected to make the cleavage. His face was stiff with smiling at faces he could name with ease; but they were blurred in his eyes. He remembered wishing, when he ached for those separated by the labor levy, that he could see them as a mass of creatures without individuality. Now he saw them, blending, shifting, moving and converging. With longing and intensity he searched for the only face which still held a meaning for him. It was more vivid and alive in his mind than any of these in the city.

A woman came out of her door to call her children. For a flashing instant the lift of her head was the same as Makada's. He could stand there a thousand days and the woman could never again lift her head in such a manner.

He left them all as soon as they began to seek shade and coolness during the high climbing of the sun. Solomon wandered toward his garden outside the city walls. The pavilion there would be free of servants on this day and he had no wish to return to the palace. Bathsheba would be waiting for him and Tanis would be conveniently sitting near the gate of her garden. He wanted to avoid Zadok, the officers and elders—all those who would have a private word with him before the feast ended and the judgment began. He did not seek peace. To possess its torpid imitation was enough for the moment. He felt suspended in time and space, cushioned against all feeling. Still his awareness of outward things had sharpened strangely into countless, penetrating points. They went out from him, piercing through the wall of isolation in which he moved. But when they were withdrawn, the openings sealed themselves hard against hostile glances, double-edged words, all things stark or sensate that would slide through to stir him. They fell away without sound and left no sign upon him.

He had often imagined his nation as an indestructible shield of gold. On its surface the divisions of twelve were lightly marked, scarcely discernible except in the strong light of justice in times of controversy. If something were cutting deep into those lines, exposing old grievances, he refused to see it. A week earlier the people of two different tribes had joined hands and rocked from side to side as they sat singing around a single campfire. Now the Ephraimites kept to their tents on a grassy knoll and a heavy silence lay between them and those out of Naphtali who had camped close by.

Solomon turned from the sight, pushing it back beyond the barrier he carried in his mind. The shield was gold, not inferior clay. He ignored other cracks which had appeared. They branched out, crooked and wild, separating smaller groups within all the tribes. Those who turned their backs on the wall that hid the idol cut themselves off from those they called sinful and unclean: those who gulped their holy festival wine and ran laughing across the Kidron for a closer look.

Beyond a segment of tunneled steps leading down to a pool, the King saw the green of aspens reaching toward the great tamarisk in his garden. Fists of crimson blooms clutched at vines escaping over the wall of rough and yellowed stone. Down below, a score of army horses were being watered at the brook. Tails switched over shining flanks. Heads dipped into the water and lifted dished profiles with low-set eyes, ever alert to the sight and sound of hazard.

With the crowds swarming over Jerusalem, Benaiah had obviously issued a wise order. He was avoiding further drain on the water supply within the city walls.

Solomon would have hurried away but the commander had looked up and seen him. He was already making his way up the rock-strewn hillside. There was nothing to do but wait.

Sometime during his walk, Solomon had slung his folded cloak over one shoulder. Until now he had not realized that he had been gripping it so closely against his chest. His fingers were stiff. The bend of his arm held lines of moisture and the lighter burnish of yesterday's sun. His eyes swept down the slope. Something was not quite as it should be, yet he had no wish to identify it. A rope barricade for the horses had been strung out between lonely palms. Guards played at dice or slept in the meager shade. A captain's voice rang out with anger. He berated a stable attendant who had allowed a mare, about to foal, to come down with the others to the water. Delighted children were now squealing over the sight of the new-born colt.

Ignoring the cleared path, Benaiah was growling a direct line up through the underbrush and flowering bushes. His massive forearms plowed through a tangle of oleander and for a moment his dark, scarred face was incongruously framed with pink blossoms. At another time Solomon would have burst into laughter. Now he ran a forefinger between his brows, erasing a troubled thought as he noted Benaiah's costume. He no longer wore the splendid regalia suitable for a festival day. Solomon glanced downward again and knew the reason for his earlier, vague discomfort. The officers and guards too wore leather tunics, girdles and shield straps: the apparel of men ready at a moment's notice to pick up the weapons of war. Judging Benaiah's grim expression, Solomon wondered if these, too, stood ready and sharp in the armory.

Benaiah scrambled over a rock and jumped down beside his king. His regular breathing belied the gray hairs in his beard.

Solomon sighed. "I suppose you have a message from Zadok?"

Benaiah hooked his thumbs into his wide metal-studded belt. "Let him ring his own little golden bells! He knows better than to censor you in my presence. I heard him say nothing important. Only a suggestion to the elder out of Issachar. He thought it would be appropriate hereafter that this day of the Feast of Weeks should hear the reading of the law."

Solomon smiled as they started toward the pool. "To caution others, no doubt, who also believe the law was meant to enlighten but not blind us."

"Nothing will come of it." Benaiah walked in silence a moment then broke into sudden vehemence. "You are still the King! And I still command your army. Let's see which speaks louder: the wheels of war chariots or the tongues of old men!"

Solomon shook his head, quieted Benaiah with a pat on the shoulder. "What good is a throne held by force?"

"If you are the one to hold it, the good is spread over all the kingdom!"

"I'm afraid, my friend, your opinion is a lonely one. Once a sword is drawn in tyranny how can it fit the sheath of justice?" He looked into the iron face of the commander and smiled. "I'll miss you, Benaiah."

"What will you do, where will you go?"

"I had hoped it would be to the south," Solomon said. "Far to the south."

The lines deepened in Benaiah's face. "So be it. I'll go with you to Sheba."

"I said I had *hoped*. I'm afraid we'd not be welcome there," Solomon said. "The Sabaean caravan is ready to leave. I am prepared to learn at any moment that the Queen of Sheba has gone."

"That could well be. Her Grand Vizier left at sundown yesterday. Good riddance."

"Alone?" Solomon's heart had turned over. Had the Queen taken advantage of the ceremonies at the tabernacle to cover a swift departure?

"Alone," Benaiah said. "I was mystified when the sentries informed me. But only for a moment. I reasoned that the Queen had commanded him to leave in advance."

"Why?"

"Would you look forward to such a long journey in the company of that ugly old bird of prey?"

Whatever the reason, Solomon could think only of one thing. She would soon be gone. He left Benaiah at the pool and went toward the gate of his garden. As soon as the sun had set on this holy day he would go to her house. No seneschals could stop him. Another bit of information had disturbed him until Benaiah said it was nothing unusual these past few days to see the Queen's old woman servant riding at uncommon hours. The attendants of the Sabaean Queen had extraordinary freedom from duty since the night of the dancing on the hill. The old one who had no tongue had left the city early this morning on the black horse. One of Benaiah's captains had seen her riding southward as if a thousand demons pursued her.

There was no one tending the orchards today; no servants picking herbs for the food in the King's garden pavilion. It was a day of rest for everyone.

Solomon paused beneath the fringed edge of the canopy. Throwing his cloak aside he sank into one of the chairs, stretched out his long legs and sat for a long time in the strange quiet, mindless and walled-in. The heat of the day pressed low and heavy over the trees. The leaves were still.

A light sound came to him, a soft footfall. Someone had entered the garden. He kept his eyes closed. The intruder would leave, surely, as discreetly as he had entered. It must be a servant who had stolen in to rest in the shade of the trees.

When there was no further sound, when the steps of the interloper came no closer, still did not retreat, Solomon knew a flash of anger. Someone was standing, motionless, watching him.

He opened his eyes and turned his head swiftly. For an instant he doubted what he saw. The tricks of the sun and his vivid longing had merged to create a vision of his thoughts. Then his eyes cleared of all images but the one standing in a robe of soft white cloth. His heart leaped the distance between them but he did not move. She was familiar but somehow different; as if the creature who had walked in radiance into his throne room, the child who moved with arrogance, and the woman he had embraced with abandon were now the hidden, lesser ones. And the elusive image he had despaired of finding stood revealed, more beautiful in simplicity, a thousand times more enticing. It puzzled and fascinated him to find the answer more mysterious than the riddle. It brought him slowly to his feet and he stood there without moving and waited.

She took a step closer then hesitated. He was reminded of the many times he had stood rigidly waiting in the hills for the approach of a timid doe. Such diffidence did not surprise him yet it seemed to be a strangely confusing sensation to Makada. Her eyes were soft and imploring. They held no hint of the mockery she had so often and so faintly concealed. As if something were forcing her, she came toward him, walking slowly over islands of green crossed with bars of mellowing light. With a helpless look, she stopped in the most unsparing shaft of brilliance; her hands fell at her sides. As she parted her lips to speak he moved swiftly, caught her to him and pressed the words into silence with his mouth. It was the first kiss he had ever known. The first she had ever given. She drew away from him and searched his face.

"I must tell you something," she said, averting her eyes. "The truth—"

This was not a time for words or for thinking. "You already have," he said and would not let her speak again. Together they walked through the garden and it seemed that the walls enclosed them in a hushed and timeless immortality. As the shadows deepened he found her staring at him from time to time, an expression close to anguish crossing her face. She would look away from him and several times she murmured a meaningless, broken apology. Then she seemed to know from a glance at his face that her words meant nothing. He had no ears for anything but the surging words spoken into memory as if some part of him held the reins of reality and said this moment must be treasured now, fully, before it escaped into the past. He had written phrases such as these in the hours of anticipation. It came to him vaguely that never, during those days and nights of intimacy had the lyrics continued. They had started and ended with the searching; had been forgotten in the lustful nights of Gibeon and Bethel. The fruition was not in these places. It had flown wild and far to find its home. It did not belong here, in the garden of a king. It sought the loveliness of Bethlehem-Ephrath where Boaz had cherished his beloved Ruth. Without knowing why, he had wanted to be with her there; as if the sight of the terraced vineyards and the *long home* of Rachel in her tomb could evoke the bonds of blood and heritage, make them as one, carry them on the powerful tides into the future. For the first time he sensed the full vigor and pride of his roots. They were tenuous when he thought of his mother, unrealized with his father. To be born of these two as expiation for an earlier sin had cast a wandering uncertainty within him. And all the while he had only to seek out the road to Bethlehem.

In the courtyard of the palace torches were being lighted, their long standards planted obliquely in the ground. The feast day was over.

Only a few of the ancients passed through the open door to the hall of judgment. The others waited outside in silent groups, still hoping to be delivered from the task before them.

Accompanied by four of the Levites, Zadok came slowly out of the goat-hair tabernacle of Zion. To those who made way for his melancholy austerity he was more than a figure of forbidding righteousness. He was an old man with a heavy burden and he would carry it up to the palace, into the hall of judgment and die rather than put it down.

A silence hung over the streets of Jerusalem. From a gay and painted wanton, she had become a sober, wide-eyed child. Still wearing the spangles and bracelets of an uninitiated harlot, she sat still and waited with one foot poised for quick and jingling flight to the pleasures that beckoned from the high places.

A few creaking carts of visitors who lived at a great distance—or were too frightened to remain—had long since passed through the gates. Shadowy figures folded the tents scattered on the surrounding hills, saddled their mules, filled their water bags and then sat down around their dying fires.

For hours Ahiah had wandered aimlessly through the town. He sat on the stone rim of a well, his eyes dull and upturned to the grave faces of those who passed by. But the sight of each dark perplexity added a weight beyond the fatigue of his body and he found no rest.

In the Street of Silversmiths he paused to speak with the dwarfed artisan but their conversation soon faded into meaningful silence. With the exchange of a helpless nod they went their separate ways. At the north gate of the city Ahiah kept his eyes averted from the unfinished Temple. He hurried past the deserted Sheep Gate, too, scarcely heeding the swift black horse carrying its dark-robed rider into the city. He was to remember it later when he passed the stables and saw a groom wiping the last of the sweat and lather from the beast. The animal heat exuding from it stung his nostrils, called up all his senses in sharp defense.

He looked to the sunless sky. The hour had come and caught him still unprepared. The wind of this unwelcome evening was already cool on his face. He heard the movement now of people, the whispering and—very faintly—a sound coming up from the streets he had left behind; from the gates—a vague stirring in the air. He listened only a moment, identifying the distant thunder before it broke into the beating rhythm of horses' hoofs and he dismissed it from his mind. It was nothing. No doubt only a wild-blooded group from one of the visiting tribes, galloping down from the hills and up into the silence of the city, to ease the unbearable tension of their own fear.

He hurried away, looking about for someone to tell him where the King could be found. He chided himself for waiting until this late moment to know that he belonged at Solomon's side; not as a supporter of a king's apostasy, but as friend of a man who had made one grave error and the still greater one of excusing it with false reasoning.

Perhaps Solomon would reject his offer of escort. Ahiah could not blame him for that. He was a poor one indeed to walk at the side of the King he now censored. But Solomon must not walk alone to face those who would condemn him. What the night would bring was a certainty in Ahiah's mind. Solomon would not recant. He would be banished. A new king would be chosen to sit on the throne of Israel and Judah. There had been rumors that Adonijah was to be summoned. But that was false. Ahiah had been present at the afternoon gathering of the elders—and he knew it was untrue. Rehoboam was still a child and too young to be named king. Another would be named. But no one spoke it. Ahiah knew why. Until Solomon's own words forced them, the fathers of the tribes would not allow themselves to even think of anyone but this son of David as their king. And later Ahiah had seen their old lips moving in silent prayer as he knew Zadok's must have moved in these last hours before the veil of testimony, asking for his Shekinah, his sign from the Lord that He was in the midst of His lost, bewildered children. . . .

Ahiah moved with little awareness of where he was going. He crossed a clearing, passed through a grove of juniper and found himself near the compound, face to face with Benaiah. The commander had turned his horse over to an aide and was hurrying toward the house of the Queen.

Without a word they walked together. It was not necessary to ask if Benaiah had the same thought in mind. His eyes gleamed and at last he spoke: "My one duty is to protect my King—I made the vow to David. Whether Solomon permits it or not, I walk with him and I stand with him! He is planning to take the Queen of Sheba to the council meeting!"

Without slackening his pace, Ahiah stared at the commander.

"She insists," Benaiah grumbled. "One of my men heard them speak as they came up through the town a short time ago. He said they had eyes only for each other and it seemed not to matter who saw or who heard—"

Then it was to be an open defiance. Ahiah's mouth felt dry, incapable of speech.

Benaiah's great chest heaved a sigh. His gold arm band clashed softly against something at his waist. Ahiah noted for the first time that Benaiah was armed. The son of Jehoiada, the valiant man of Kabzeel, once more wore his sword at his belt.

"We'll find they have just arrived at her house," Benaiah continued. "I don't know why. But at least the pause gives us time to try and change his mind!"

He'll not change it—now."

"If he enters the judgment hall alone there is still hope, for all of us. If that demon of a woman goes with him—"

As they walked a moment in silence they crossed a little-used path.

Glancing to the side Ahiah had a glimpse of Tanis as she looked back over her shoulder at him and then hurried away, taking this inconspicuous route to the main courtyard. Her face had been blurred by the pale night sky but there was no doubt it held deep anxiety.

Benaiah snorted. "Zadok would have sent the royal guard to escort Solomon to the council! As if he would appear any less a prisoner surrounded by his own soldiers!" He brought his body to a halt, turned his head and listened intently. The beat of hoofs was closer now and he, too, was giving importance to the same ordinary sound.

"Come, Benaiah," Ahiah urged him. "We must hurry. You hear only horses coming up through the streets—"

"No," Benaiah said. "Up the ramp, galloping up the ramp—" he strained his ears and half-closed his eyes an instant "—four, no five. It is strange, unless they have reason to expect the King still spends most of his time at the Temple—" He gripped Ahiah's arm. "I believe I know the meaning, but I must make sure." Benaiah was already running back to the compound where he had left his horse. Ahiah watched him disappear, then hastened his steps toward the Queen's house.

As he approached the garden he could hear a woman's low voice, vibrant with tension. He did not believe it was the Queen speaking until he saw that the same warm but anxious consideration shone in her eyes. She was standing in the dim reflection of a garden light and Solomon held her hands in his. Ahiah paused near the break in the trees and felt no guilt as he listened to her soft pleading. Solomon was gentle but adamant.

"You are not coming with me because there is no need," he said. "Do you remember that I once said we were rulers over all things but our own lives? I intend to change that. I must go to the council alone. As a King." He kissed her fingertips. "But I'll leave it as a happier man, and free."

She shook her head slowly, murmuring it was wrong, very wrong. "It is the way I have lived, the way I believed. For myself alone. You taught me I was wrong—"

"I taught you nothing," he said.

"You did more," she said. "You *showed* me. And I learned—please, you must not turn your back on your people. Never. And they must not cast you off!"

"You forget. I have no choice. They intend to denounce me—"

As Ahiah made his way along the wall he heard her say she would talk to them and if she could not find the words to make them see, then her Grand Vizier would know. And she called out to Abishag who came running from the house.

As he watched the Shunammite's face Ahiah withdrew his hand from the garden gate and stepped aside into the shadow to satisfy his curiosity.

The Queen asked her to hurry to the quarters of the Grand Vizier and bid him come immediately.

"But he is not here—" Abishag cut off her words, amended them: "He is not in his quarters."

"Then find him, quickly." The Queen turned back to Solomon and did not see the quickly veiled contempt on Abishag's thin mouth.

Her face was expressionless as she walked toward the gate. A slight glance to the side revealed an inner caution, as if someone in another darkened corner of the garden were watching her. By narrowing his eyes Ahiah could make out the shapeless bulk of Vashi, sitting on the ground. It was difficult to remember that only a short time ago he had seen this calm immensity as a streak of black motion at the city gate. Abishag bowed respectfully as she passed him with downcast eyes. Ahiah entered the garden. Beneath the black hood of her robe, Vashi's eyes looked out at him with opaque indifference.

Solomon came to him with an almost buoyant step.

"Ahiah," he said warmly. "I am glad you're here." He turned back to the Queen. "My scribe and my friend will stay with you until I return—it will not be long. Put the time to good use, Ahiah. Explain to her that it is no great sin for a ruler to step down from a throne—"

"Isn't it?" Ahiah asked and the question was lost in the clatter of hoofbeats against stone paving, the shouting of men and the pounding vibration against the earth as horsemen approached. Solomon was out of the gate instantly, peering past the torchlight, identifying Benaiah as he dismounted and then whispering, "Zabud!" as another eased himself to the ground and limped slightly toward the King.

Solomon moved into the light and embraced the muscular shoulders of the dark young man who was the son of Nathan and Solomon's friend.

"I am overjoyed! You are home, you are safe—" his exclamations were followed by questions, tumbling one after another.

Except for the briefest greeting, Zabud did not smile again. His face was streaked with dust, his eyes troubled.

"I found your brother," he said.

Solomon gripped his friend's arm, his face came alive with pleasure. "I sent you to find Adonijah," Solomon said quietly, "and you found him."

The message seemed to blot out of his mind for the moment the serious hour ahead of him. He could think of nothing but the joy of seeing Adonijah once more. He blessed Zabud for this accomplishment.

"Hear the rest of his story," Benaiah muttered. "Then you will change yours."

Solomon said quickly, "What is wrong—has something happened to my brother?"

"He is marching against Jerusalem!" Zabud said. "I saw your brother without his seeing me. He has raised up an army against you, Solomon."

The heavy tidings sent a wave of sickness through Ahiah.

"We must raise the signals," Benaiah said, and he talked swiftly, sharply, outlining the plans of defense. Adonijah was coming up by way of the wilderness. The others of Zabud's patrol were already informing the men under Benaiah's command of the way the enemy would come. It was a mass of tortured rock, steep ridges and treacherous passes in the deep course of a drying stream. Few level plains where chariots could be used. But in the Valley of Rephaim now—in the Valley of Rephaim where the Philistines came up against the host of David—there was a likely place to meet the foe. Benaiah's excitement grew, he was rising to the challenge —a true warrior. He carried no thirsty sword such as Joab's but a righteous one of defense. Still, Ahiah thought, the weapons and the motions are the same.

Solomon seemed to find a remote amusement in the sight of Benaiah down on one knee, drawing lines in the path, setting a small rock here to represent a mountain where ambuscade must be anticipated, and pointing out the route of David's early victory.

"He was guided by the Lord," Benaiah said, looking up at the faces about him and settling on the lines in Ahiah's face as a target of age most apt to remember the battle. "He was told that when he heard a stirring in the tops of the mulberry trees then he should know that Yahweh had gone out before him to smite the host of the Philistines. And the three armies of David spread round about and went to the rear and the flanks of the enemy and they were utterly confounded—" Benaiah got to his feet, dusted off his knees. "The contours of this siege will be similar, and we'll be ready! We'll double the number of horsemen. Our archers are in the hundreds—what a fortunate thing the companies of javelin-throwers have not yet been sent to Megiddo. If Joab plans a surprise attack at dawn he'll not find us sleeping in our beds, waiting for the walls to be ringed with burning branches! We must prepare at once, Solomon. Go out and meet them—at once!"

"I can't believe it," Solomon muttered. "Adonijah. My brother. Why is he doing this—"

"To seize the throne!" Benaiah shouted. "Simple!"

"But why now? After all this time—why now?"

"What does it matter," Benaiah said, waving an impatient hand.

"He knows my armies are powerful," Solomon continued. "He knows the strength of our defense, our unassailable towers and bastions—"

Ahiah could keep silent no longer. "He has perhaps learned of the weakness within the walls, Solomon. The crumbling unity—"

"Enough of talk," Benaiah said. "There's no time to waste. Do we leave before the middle watch?"

Solomon stared at the ground. There was no question in his mind now of being less than the King of his country. The council would have to wait. "We'll go to meet him," he said slowly, "in peace."

Benaiah's head thrust forward out of his great shoulders. He peered closely at Solomon.

"In *peace*?"

"It's a difficult battlefield also, Benaiah." Solomon smiled at his commander's collapsed face. "The terrain is more treacherous than your rocks and gullies where the horses can easily lose their footing. The field is understanding and mutual faith. The weapons—fair words. You are no expert in these things, Benaiah. Zabud and I go alone. Adonijah knows him as a man of peace. He will listen." He looked toward Zabud and the dark head nodded without hesitation.

Benaiah spat on the ground. "Your brother is within a few miles of the city with a vast army behind him. He is preparing to batter down the walls of your father's city, to lay waste the fields and bring the darkness of the sword on the land—and you talk of peace!"

Ahiah only half listened to him and to Solomon's calm response. He had heard someone take a sharp breath beside him and for the first time was aware that the Queen of Sheba had come close to listen.

"A vast army," she whispered, then her voice was clear and demanding. "What vast army supports Prince Adonijah? That cannot be!"

Solomon agreed. It was another of Benaiah's exaggerations he was sure. Benaiah spat on the ground.

"Do I lengthen the truth, Zabud, so that I might jump on a wooden horse and wave a sword in the air for child's play?"

"He tells the truth, my lord. From a distant ridge I looked across at the encampment as they were preparing to move closer to Jerusalem. Their weapons are of the best and their armor is new. The men count into thousands—"

"No!" The Queen of Sheba took a step forward. "They are not the swords of my country! Not my warriors!"

There was a moment of silence. The men looked at her in bewilderment then turned away from the stricken terror in her face. They did not understand. Solomon took her hand and held it soothingly as he probed for more information from Zabud. The supporting army was out of Edom. Hadad's warriors had joined the small force of Adonijah and Joab.

Solomon gave a derisive laugh. "Now I can sleep well tonight. The whole thing is a touch of the sun, my good friend. The Edomites detest the ground Joab walks upon. Their memories are long. When his sword was young and wilder than it is now, he massacred hundreds of them in the Valley of Salt," Solomon shook his head. "I can think of no stranger alliance."

The Queen withdrew her hand from his. Her voice was low and it trembled. "You do not believe me. You would not call an alliance with Sheba a strange one. You believe my armies have met with your brother's." She broke in as Solomon protested. "It is not true!"

She would not be calmed.

Ahiah looked about for Vashi and found that the old woman had come silently to the side of her mistress and was trying to communicate some comfort with her eyes and the touch of her hands. At one moment she put a finger toward the lips of Makada but the Queen drew it aside.

"It is true that my army waited for my orders to join Adonijah."

She implored Solomon's understanding with a helpless gesture of her hand. Her voice had deepened from the strain and was little more than a hoarse whisper.

[224]

"But I sent no order—I swear it." She looked from one face to the other. No one spoke. Benaiah's mouth was locked in a tight line. Zabud closed his mouth, after the first shock, and studied the ground at his feet. Solomon was staring at her as if he had turned to stone. His hands were rigid at his sides then they curled into hard trembling fists and his face grew pale. For an instant Ahiah thought the King was about to strike out, thrust her from his sight . . .

"When I visited your garden," she said, "I wanted to tell you—everything. Then—somehow I could no longer say the words. I wanted you to think kindly of me after I had gone—" She turned to Vashi with a little cry of desperation. "If you could only speak. You were there when I told Tamrin—" she looked about and asked someone to find Abishag, to hurry and fetch the girl, ask her why Tamrin had not answered the summons of his Queen. Where was he? Where was Tamrin—who could verify all she had said?

Benaiah and Zabud exchanged a look. Benaiah gestured over his shoulder and an aide came out of the far shadows leading a white horse with crescent amulets hanging from its crown piece and the emblem of Sheba on its bridle.

"Where did you find it?" she asked faintly.

"Wandering in the wilderness. We searched for his rider," said Zabud. "We found him. And we followed his trail back to the camp of Adonijah. Your Grand Vizier had visited there and was racing for the south, toward the borders—"

"Then he didn't reach Bashir," she murmured to herself and a flicker of relief came into her eyes. They clouded again and she looked down at her hand. She touched the finger which should be wearing the ring he had kept—to betray her.

"I am glad you captured him," she said to Zabud. "He will be taken back to Sheba for punishment—"

"Your Grand Vizier is dead," Zabud said. "His face was discolored and the eyes—we beat off the birds and buried him beneath a pile of rocks—"

Ahiah heard her whisper something as if she were recalling the words of another. Something about a curse, the denial of God's existence and the plucking out of eyes from the dead by the sharp-beaked birds of the wilderness.

"He had been pulled off his horse and strangled," Zabud said.

The Queen stared at him, uncomprehending. Then she looked down at a leather sheath which Vashi was holding out to her. The flap had dropped open and the ring could be glimpsed, sparkling against the slender hilt of Tamrin's knife.

Makada looked into the old woman's eyes and she began to weep.

Ahiah followed them as Vashi helped the Queen into the garden. At the gate he heard the men mounting their horses. The big silver stallion had been brought for Solomon. He hesitated a moment with his back to the house of the Queen, then leaped on his horse and rode away with the others.

Ahiah found himself wondering what he was doing here, standing in the fragrant garden of the Queen, looking down at the despondent, still figure robed in white.

"Ahiah," she said in a broken voice, "how does one pray? The King has built an idol for me—a huge image on a hill—and it suddenly means nothing. If I knew how to pray to your God—I would pray."

Ahiah sat down beside her. She had always seemed tall with majesty in her jewels and rich clothes. He was surprised at her delicate hands, the slender line of her throat.

He thought back to the psalms and reached for the simplest words to carry its promise of trust and comfort. "There is a song we sing at times," he said, "and perhaps it is the right one. It says: *I will lift up mine eyes unto the hills from whence cometh my help. My help cometh from the Lord who made heaven and earth.* He is your keeper, it tells you. *The Lord is your shade upon your right hand. The sun shall not smite thee by day nor the moon by night. The Lord shall preserve thy soul. The Lord shall preserve thy going out and thy coming in from this time forth and even for evermore.*" He found her eyes searching his face and he smiled. "Did you understand it?" And she shook her head slowly and said she did not understand and wondered if she ever should.

"I believe you understand more than you know," Ahiah said and he urged her to come with him. They would go into the courtyard of the palace. Solomon and Benaiah and the others would be there presently, after they had visited the armory and given the orders for the night. In the compound, in the armory and about him on all sides was the din of preparation for war.

Through the shouting of soldiers, clashing of armor—through all the sad noise of men who laughed as they girded themselves for battle—only the whispered deception of Makada roared like a great tide in the King's ears. *Many waters cannot quench love,* they had assured each other only a few hours ago, *neither can the floods drown it.*

It had drowned with all the other tender exchanges of devotion beneath the tamarisk: *Set me as a seal upon thine heart, as a seal upon thine arm: for love is strong as death.*

The words were as false as she had been. They were strong as hatred!

He called out to his armor-bearer to follow him. Then with Benaiah, Solomon hurried back to his rooms in the palace.

He was only vaguely aware of changing his clothes, of feeling the greaves being fastened to his legs.

"Joab and Hadad will know before dawn they have a wild dog by the ears—!" He scowled at the trash in his hands and threw it across the room. "If you dig out another cuirass and bow," he thundered at the old man, "I'll use an arrow on you!"

But Benjamin's ears were deep inside the clothes chest. He bent into

[226]

it, probing for still another treasure. Benaiah grumbled an oath of disgust and, since Solomon was paying little attention, contented himself by inventing loathsome names for the Grand Vizier of Sheba; bemoaning the dignity of his burial. "He was a bird of prey and he should have been devoured by his own kind," he muttered.

Solomon picked up one of the spears to test its balance. The shaft brushed across the strings of David's lute on the wall and knocked Adonijah's wine bowl to the floor. Neither the melancholy of the one nor the crash of the other affected Solomon. He compared the spears, replaced them and sank into a chair. He lifted one foot shod with new leather and a servant knelt down to score the sole with a knife, to prevent slipping.

The King and the commander exchanged few words. There was little to be said. An enemy was close to their gates and they were going forth to smite that enemy. The situation was unavoidable. Strategy had been established. The tactics were Benaiah's. The usual three divisions, one to come upon the enemy from the west, another from the direction of the Dead Sea and the third. . . .

As Benaiah went over the plan once more Solomon heard fragments of the sounds coming up from below. He had a dim recollection of seeing Zadok and the elders coming out of the hall of judgment as he ran up the outer stairs. They had heard the news then and were waiting down in the courtyard. Over the chorus of turmoil he could hear the words of Bathsheba, as she had spoken them in this room a few moments ago. She had not bothered to rearrange her headveil, half torn as she pressed through the crowds. Her face seemed to have wilted and aged within the hour. And she made no attempt this time to curb her tongue on the charge against Adonijah. She had waited too long. Solomon had borne her unrestrained venom with a patience which surprised himself. Now she was down below, crying out the full sin of Adonijah who had coveted a woman of the King's household, crying out to all who would listen that now there must be no leniency to this enemy of the king, this detestable son of Haggith.

They were words, only words. He stood ready now in leather tunic with heavily studded breastplate and armor. A purple scarlet girdle about his waist carried scabbard and sword. He examined the bucklers and shield held by his armor-bearer. Someone brought his helmet and old Benjamin had found another piece of useless gear in the bottom of the clothes chest and was holding it out to him. Benaiah made a back-handed gesture, meant to discourage the old man from being a nuisance in this frantic moment of departure. But Solomon had caught a flash of white, white linen, and the deep red of ruby set in gold.

"Wait," he said, as Benjamin turned away. Very slowly he took the dagger from Benjamin's hands. It was the palpable link to the happier past, untouched by the bitterness of the years between.

The linen in which Solomon had wrapped it—so long ago—fell to the floor. He paid no heed to Benaiah's urgent pleas. There was not the same hard anger driving him into violence. He turned the dagger slowly between his hands. The lion-headed hilt with its jeweled eyes was still the thing of beauty he had bought for Adonijah in Tyre. He touched the sharp broken edges of the blade.

"How quickly I forgot my brother," he said, feeling somehow that this blade had cut away the brittle shell of resentment, formed so quickly outside the garden of the Queen. He removed the dagger he carried in the sheath on his forearm and into it he slipped the one Benjamin had found in the bottom of the clothes chest. "Thank you," he said to the old man and the bent bones of Benjamin seemed to straighten with pride.

Then Solomon called his stewards, ordered them to make haste and tear off these hateful garments of warfare. "Hurry! I have no use for these things. Get them off me—at once!" And he unfastened the sword at his belt and threw it on the floor.

Benaiah's face reddened with anger. "Have you gone mad? What are you doing?"

Solomon was free of the cuirass, the helmet and the weapons of a warrior king. He touched the sheath of leather and chain on his arm, adjusted the lion's head, visible and bright in any light. "I'll wear this," he said, feeling that surely no King set out for battle with a lighter heart than his. "Adonijah will recognize it—as a symbol of peace. I want him to see me alone—and unarmed."

Benaiah exploded with wrath. He paced up and down and his footsteps were loud as he put his whole weight to the task of convincing Solomon that Adonijah was evil—and evil was a wild beast without understanding, without the speech and ability to reason . . .

"I'm ready, Benaiah," Solomon said and walked toward the embrasure leading to the roof terrace.

Benaiah's anger held him silent a moment. "I'll not order my men to disarm!"

Solomon spoke over his shoulder. "Did I ask that? Do you think I'm a complete fool? I ask only that you let me go forward to first meet my brother, alone. He is the leader of the forces coming up against us. Hadad's men will be forced to follow his decision."

"Your brother is unworthy, faithless. In your own words you told me never to place my confidence in a faithless man in time of trouble. It is like a broken tooth or a foot out of joint."

"Adonijah is no more faithless than I have been," he said. "I paved the road, you could well say, for his army to come battering at our gates. I allowed the gates and the towers to weaken . . ." Benaiah was beside him now and Solomon could see a protest forming on the commander's face. No doubt Benaiah was thinking in terms of stone and mortar and the strength of the walls. "How can I carry a sword against him when the betrayal is mine—all mine." His own guilt of inaction was greater than the Queen's conspiracy. The air was filled with the blast of trumpets. The trumpets of Zion were sounding from the hills. Solomon walked out on the terrace. He looked over the parapet and saw many of the people in the courtyard move and sway as they chanted a song of deliverance. The members of the council were in somber thought and others stared up at him, astonished to see him without armor. He was hoping to see once more the face of Makada. If he could look upon her without bitterness. . . .

But she was nowhere to be seen. Anxiety filled him. He had no time to search her out and he was afraid—he was certain—she would not be here when he returned. Reluctantly he started with Benaiah down the stairs. He must prepare himself for the time of a next meeting, whenever, wherever it should be. He held a mirror to his reason and knew that from the moment she came to him a darkness lay between them, unfathomable and now swept away—by her own impulsive admission. He would have wished it away, or dreamed it into oblivion. Hers then was the most honest revelation—and how strange it would seem to those twelve down there and the High Priest—to be told their erring King had learned his greatest lessons of righteousness from a pagan woman. How he could shock those white beards. He could tell them that the woman they denounced had recoiled at the sight of the sea that held no living thing; that he had seen her first tears shed over an old servant's loyal, murdering hands. He could tell them of the warning at the pool of Gibeon when a serpent's sting could have saved them the distress of gathering to dethrone their King. A thousand memories now clung to the resisting barricade of his proud injury, bending it to the ground.

He saw her come slowly into the fringe of light. She stopped and he saw that Ahiah was with her, gently urging her forward. She looked at the scribe and shook her head. As she turned to go back, Solomon leaped the three remaining steps and the crowd parted before him.

"Do you see him?" Ahiah asked, restraining her flight with a touch of his hand. "Look now, do you see hatred and bitterness on the face of your beloved—turn now and look upon him—"

She saw the King approaching and her own face slowly absorbed the light that reached out before him. Ahiah stepped aside and marveled at the miracle of harmony in God's disparate creatures. There was a shining and fairness upon them. It stirred his blood to see the silent coming together, as if the earth and sky trembled as they did in times of storm and suffered together; as if they reached toward each other to cling in strength against winds that tore loose, uprooting and destroying. He drew away and found that Zadok had come closer. The High Priest wore the visage of the angry wind that would tear the earth away from the sun.

"I beg you, Zadok," Ahiah whispered, "if the words on your tongue are bitter, swallow them. This once." He heard soft indistinct words between Solomon and the Queen and he raised a finger of caution toward Zadok.

It was a strange farewell, a stranger restraint between two who loved. Yet Ahiah suspected he was looking upon the truest of unions. As the earth and the sky are irrevocably joined in our sight and our minds, he thought so are these two who stand apart from each other and without touching appear to embrace.

It was as true with them as with the meeting of sky and sea and a thousand unchanging horizons.

"Wait for me—here in Jerusalem," Solomon said.

She neither promised nor refused. Her eyes glanced over the forbidding figure of Zadok and Ahiah saw the fear and pleading in the glance. He wondered, when she spoke, if the words were meant for the High Priest as well as the King.

"I came to prove you with hard questions," she said, "that much was true; perhaps I came out of envy for your greatness and wisdom. Then I saw it with my own eyes. And now I have heard about and know the power of your Lord. If I have done harm He has cast me down with shame. There is no more spirit in me . . ."

A soft light flickered upon them, blotting out the faces of those who prayed and chanted in the courtyard. The trumpets of Zion sounded again. The silver stallion shook his mane and whinnied, rearing up at the sound of alarm. He was brought to Solomon and the King mounted the steed.

"Wait here—for me," Solomon repeated. And as if fearing her answer he looked around at Benaiah. The commander was riding toward him.

"Solomon," the Queen spoke softly and waited for him to turn to her. "God be with you."

Then she turned swiftly from the light and was gone. Solomon's eyes followed her until the whiteness of her robe was swallowed up in the dark shadows of the garden. Then he rode away.

Ahiah found that Zadok was still looking into the darkness which had enveloped the Queen of Sheba. His brows were heavy with ponderous thought.

"Can it be that she has given us back our King?" he asked with disbelief.

Ahiah felt the frozen rigidity of the High Priest could well do with another moment of uncertainty.

"No," said the scribe and he allowed a long moment to elapse between the word and a deep sigh. "She has given us back another, a better King."

How could a King who had turned his back on God be counted a better King? Ahiah was talking nonsense.

"Solomon never turned his back," Ahiah said as they started to walk. "How can a man turn his back on something if he has never truly faced it?"

Solomon's defections, as he told them now, were not yet known. "Because his faith has never been tested," Ahiah added. "Tonight in the King's garden outside the city, I sat with a pagan woman, Zadok, and she taught me the true meaning of our own faith."

Zadok was silent. He took long slow steps and they approached the palace gates.

"Perhaps it is easier to one who has nothing to unlearn," Ahiah said.

"Have I done the woman a grave injustice?" Zadok asked. It had been difficult to say the words, Ahiah knew. They would be difficult to answer.

"Solomon has given her many lavish gifts," he said. "Her camel train is burdened with riches. If she leaves Jerusalem, if she should leave this very moment without gold, spices, precious stones—she would still carry with her the richest gift of all. A contrite heart. With that alone, Zadok, she is perhaps closer to our God than you and I will ever be."

So it would seem, he explained humbly, that nothing was truly solved for the leadership of Israel simply by her leaving. "The problem is ours," Ahiah said. "It is purely our own. She did us a great favor. She opened our eyes to danger. To sleeping complacency. To the danger of living in peace. . . ." That was the way he saw it. As for Zadok's tardy consideration of injustice, Ahiah thought he had nothing to worry over. "She is taking something back with her, as I said. She knows humility and the true pride in belief. I doubt very much that anyone can do her an injustice hereafter."

They parted at the gates and went their separate ways. Alone, each had a strange, disturbing sensation of having suddenly been plunged into a whirlpool. Their quiet discussion had held them aloof from the pulsating excitement of the town. Now they were plunged into its noise and confusion and all the worry and fears of a country at war.

The host of Israel was going forth. It was a splendid sight, a terrible sight. They poured through the gates, and they rode with their banners flying.

Halfway up the ramp leading to the Temple, Ahiah stopped to rest. He sat on a stone wall and thought it odd that he should have come up here at a time of strife. He was certain of one thing: he was deeply worried. The reason eluded him an instant then burst upon him with full force. Solomon had gone into battle unarmed! He had no idea why he started running down the hill. He was no soldier, carrying arms for foolhardy kings who made targets of themselves. Still, he was not too much use on his knees, mouthing a prayer. But he must do something. He was out of breath when he passed the tent of meeting, but he kept on. He walked out of the city gates and as he turned southward he saw the last of the soldiers disappearing far ahead.

They moved into the meeting of the valleys, turned away from the moonlit road that led to the high slopes of Bethlehem. Eventually their destination would draw them back, not far from the "house of bread" that was David's birthplace; but now they rode in a dry, cautious direction to avoid the danger of ambuscade.

The silver-gray stallion of the King was flanked on one side by the black horse of Benaiah. On the other, Zabud rode with one foot resting in a loop of rope. When Solomon had seen this at the moment of departure he begged Zabud to stay at home. But the dark face of the King's friend had settled into a square of determination. He knew the site of Adonijah's encampment, he argued, he knew the ridges and the high plateaus over which Hadad's warriors had brought the supply wagons filled with weapons. Benaiah had settled the matter by insisting that Zabud go along. Now as they passed through a night-thickened grove of olive trees only the white bandage around Zabud's swarthy leg distinguished the brown flesh of horse and rider.

"Because of Hadad's warriors out of Edom," Solomon said, "I must meet my brother with an army at my back. He'll find that hard enough to believe. Now that we are traveling this roundabout course Adonijah will surely distrust my peaceful intentions."

Benaiah answered without turning his head. "That is better than putting our trust in his." The dark eyes were never still, searching even here for evil in the innocent darkness.

Zabud's voice confirmed Benaiah's decision to take the longer route. It was safer to travel the way of danger: along the high rock ledges of the wilderness.

"If we approached directly, from below, we would be trapped like birds in a snare. His army would come shrieking down upon us like a cutting wind!" And such a wind, Zabud added, took one's breath away. It could snatch even the words of friendship out of one's mouth before they were spoken.

Benaiah's opinion on words of friendship were chiseled deep in the rigid set of his mouth. Solomon knew he was holding it tight over the thought that it was too late for words, too late for friendship, but it was never too late to fight. Adonijah had finally proved himself unworthy not only in Benaiah's eyes but to all who had heard it spoken for the first time that Adonijah had once asked for Abishag and thereby made a bold declaration for the throne. It was no longer a secret or a fact better left unsaid. By this time the echo of Bathsheba's wild maledictions against the son of Haggith was being carried on the lips of those feast-day visitors returning to their homes in the north, or to their fruitful lands that faced the western sea; it was riding the backs of mules along the roads through the villages, fording the brook and the river Jordan; it was being carried up to the great oaks of Bashan.

Solomon turned aside the descending fear that when they had returned to Jerusalem, Adonijah would be reviled; as King Saul's commander and Rizpah the concubine had been reviled. He thought instead of Absalom, guilty of the same sin; and it had rested lightly on David's favorite son. Sin itself was a variable then in the eyes of those who judged. Was a single act of defection in a blameless man—like Abner the commander—more reprehensible because he had not crushed its significance with the vile weight of greater sins?

Solomon smiled to himself. Benaiah and Zabud were still talking, justifying the longer passage. He had had no intention of changing the course of travel. His complaint was spoken only to relieve his impatience. He resigned himself to another hour of this riding before he would meet his brother.

They were coming out of the grove now and the moonlight laid a bar of silver along the proud mane moving before him. He allowed his thoughts to turn back to the last moments in the garden, to the dark eyes lambent with the need to be forgiven. Who was he to withhold forgiveness? He had spoken it at length, with many words which would have been unnecessary if they sprang fullgrown from the heart. She had shaken the gates of Jerusalem, but he told himself they could surely be made inviolate again. Because she had weakened the watchtowers of unity within those gates, Adonijah was confident he could lead an Army—any army—to easy victory and a hearty welcome. And Solomon remembered how he had longed to go with her to Bethlehem and had been mystified by her vehement refusal. Now he knew it covered the knowledge that his enemies were gathering close by. He hoped that he could forget—in time. Time then, the long hours of conciliation that lay ahead for him and Makada would bring him closer to an unquestioning belief in her goodness. It could not be called, in truth, a complete return. He had been conscious from the first that a secret rested in her eyes. Why then should he have been so horrified when it was disclosed? He had not been blind. The fault was his. He touched the blunted dagger sheathed on his forearm and was thankful that the sight of it had dulled, for the present, the pain of Makada's betrayal. Time and more time—it was all he asked. Time for the false forgiving to leave the cold climate of his will and find a true home within him. And the time would come. He would not allow himself to think otherwise.

That is why he had asked her to wait—wait for me here in Jerusalem; wait for the moment I return with my brother whom you made bold to raise up an army against his own city; wait until the elders and the High Priest and all the people look upon him as their rightful king. And I must help him. Those who still cling to the name of King Solomon must be pried loose by Solomon. Their loyalty must be given my brother. Wait until all this comes to pass and none—not even I—can say that you were false. The wholeness of my love is torn it is true, but when I can say no harm has been done, my people are as one, my brother's dream is no longer a dream and all is as it should be—strong and whole—then one day our love too can be whole. So wait for me, wait for me here in Jerusalem. . . .

A sudden awareness of change had invaded the ranks.

They were leaving behind the fields of standing grain, the warm fragrance of the ripening land. The wilderness loomed ahead with its hidden springs and rock caves. It rose in a tangled mass of crags thrust up from brown, bush-covered slopes that caught the glow of the sky on one side and hurled it into the deep abyss on the other. Adonijah had cleverly chosen the most difficult way into Judah. No large army could ever have penetrated beyond the natural fortresses, well-manned, above the defiles. It was little wonder that as merchants in harmless numbers they had been able to converge within a few hours of Hebron, of Bethlehem and Jerusalem.

It seemed for a moment that men and horses became the unmoving objects in the night and the skull of limestone in the distance came alive toward them. The trail, winding upward, seemed destined to pass through the empty blackness of an eye socket. The bleak desolation crept slowly into the rugged faces of the soldiers, narrowed the eyes with fearless defiance. They had been singing. One by one they fell silent. Solomon felt no regret, for the song they had lifted into the air was an old one of David's when the God of the host breathed fire and smoke from His nostrils and bowed the heavens with darkness to consume the enemies of a king: *"For thee I have run through a troop,"* they had sung. *"By my God have I leaped over a wall . . . He maketh my feet like hinds' feet . . . He teacheth my hands to war so that a bow of steel is broken by mine arms . . . Thou hast enlarged my steps under me, that my feet did not slip. . . ."*

Now there were only the sounds of horses' hoofs against the parched earth, the creaking of leather, the soft clash of metal as someone in the ranks drew his elbows close to his body—perhaps to avoid an overhanging rock—and a buckler met the bossed sheath of his sword.

A command was raised, not too loudly; for they would soon be close to the camp of the rebels. Benaiah's order for single file formation was relayed down the length of the ranks.

Horses were reined in, their breathing became one sound. The powerful bodies waited, then turned one by one into the narrowing road. It was not a safe one, Solomon muttered to Zabud as they watched those ahead. Mules were more at home on this loose rock that kept spilling and sliding down the hillside. He saw his own uneasiness reflected on his friend's face.

"The risk must be taken." Zabud spoke with firmness, turning away his face from the light of the sky which revealed his misgivings. "Mules will be of no use to us later. We'll need the speed of mounts such as these, before dawn."

"You, Zabud? You too have doubts." Solomon's voice was edged with a weariness he had not recognized. It had grown with each glance at a soldier's armor and helmet, each strong hand upon a sword. He had been scarcely aware of its beginning, back in the outskirts of Jerusalem where the host separated into three forces. One of Benaiah's captains had taken his hundreds by way of Bethlehem and another had led his men to guard the outpost ridges leading to the city. They formed no pattern of pure defense, circling in this fashion to surround the men under Joab and the Edomite commander. They were too well armed. The supply wagons held the food and weapons of men going forth to war. Solomon regretted now that he had not taken his usual active interest in the plans set out and discussed in hurried council. In those swift moments of decision Solomon had been filled with thoughts closer to his heart. He had not exercised the surprising legacy of strategy inherited with his father's crown. He had listened absently to Benaiah, nodded with indulgence over the zeal of military men whose enthusiasm for the regalia of battle is not dimmed by a peaceful mission. Now the dividing of the ranks, the exhilarated war song and the stolid readiness for trouble in the face of his friend, welled up in him like a sickness. "If you are prepared in your mind for a battle," he asked Zabud, "why isn't your body prepared with a sword?"

"As you and Benaiah have often pointed out, I am not a fighting man." Zabud turned burning, frank eyes on the King. "But if my only portion in your success this night lies in my reputation for good will, then I can pretend to possess it—even toward the red-bearded dogs who call themselves the descendants of Esau."

A tenderness for such loyalty brought a smile to Solomon's mouth. But he knew he could not ride with Zabud by his side when he faced Adonijah. He had no right to impose that risk on his friend. "Arm yourself well," he said, "and stay with the others when the moment comes."

Zabud was dismayed. "But it is arranged! I go with you—the two of us—without weapons—"

"It is better I go alone." And Solomon tried to ease the distress on Zabud's face by saying a companion who shared his danger but not his confidence in a peaceful settlement was a hindrance to his King. Of no help. "Believe me, I am thinking only of my own skin. Should I risk having it split open by one of Hadad's arrows because an outburst from you has antagonized our foe?" He shook his head slowly. "No, Zabud. A man who represses his true anger is unpredictable in a crisis."

It was time to move. Zabud was studying him with skepticism. Benaiah was already following the advance guard. Solomon fell in behind with a fresh annoyance. He could have gone ahead. Benaiah was guarding him too closely. As if the life of a King without a kingdom were precious to anyone!

He leaned forward as his mount began the steep climb. A handful of gravel came sliding down onto the trail ahead of him. There was an instant halt.

Oncoming horses crowded the beasts ahead. An alarm ran swiftly down the line. Weapons were unsheathed and held ready as the ridge above was scanned with suspicion. A small and shapeless object squirmed on the rim, scraping its feet against the slipping rocks. When it began to bleat with fear Benaiah grunted and returned his sword to its scabbard. The figure of a shepherd, his cloak of goat-hair outlined against the sky, appeared on the ridge. He stooped and lifted up the ewe that had faltered, held it in his arms.

Before he turned a bend in the trail Solomon glanced back. The lonely shepherd of the wasteland, patiently tending his sheep in meager pasture, was still looking after the line of soldiers.

Some brutal ungodly hands had reached deep into the ancient bowels of this earth to lift up such endless anguish of rock. The gaping eye socket had been an illusion of purple shadow in a winding ledge of gray stone. It now became the massive lower lip of a mountain thrusting its jagged jaw over a precipice.

The road curved abruptly, narrowed. Up from the darkness of the gorge below came the thin summer dying of a winter torrent. Its rattle over the deep bed of shingle was muffled by thick layers of mist. It was coiling in now from the Dead Sea and sent back the hollow echo of horses' feet, picking their way slowly over the loose rock.

A heavy slipping movement behind him turned Solomon's head at a sharp angle. The horse Zabud was riding had stepped too close to the edge and kicked loose a boulder. One of its legs hung over the edge jabbing at the air for a footing. Without thinking, Solomon urged his stallion quickly, dangerously forward till its muzzle touched the rump of the black beast ahead. He leaped to the trail, flattened himself against the rock cliff and squeezed past the silver flanks. Zabud had swung his foot clear of the rope and the moment the rock gave way had jumped off his horse. Solomon had allowed him room to reach the head of the struggling animal, to grasp the reins and strain back against the wall of the mountain. Solomon seized the improvised rope stirrup and kneeling close to the edge of the precipice, he swung it over the side. It was not long enough to reach the flaying hoof. Solomon stretched his body out on the trail, extended his arm and torso downward. He could hear the loose rock in wild flight striking the ledges below, its rumble fading as it fell into the mist. The sweating flesh of the horse, convulsed with terror, brushed against his face. He did not take his eyes from the loop at the end of the rope, dangling it slowly, then swinging it tentatively toward the savage, pawing hoof. After an endless moment of waiting, with the jagged edge of the trail cutting into his ribs, he was able to anticipate the next frantic thrust of the horse's leg and in the same instant he swung the rope over it. He began to draw it up toward a small ledge of solid rock, solid enough at least for one moment of support. His breathing was suddenly stifled, his vision blotted out by the heaving brown flesh now struggling with new fury against the rope. He held on. When the horse's foot at last struck the solid rock it clambered up, lunged forward to find its balance and Solomon rolled away from its vicious stamping against the rocks of the trail. Its head circled low, its great eyes rolling and shining in the moonlight. As it threw its frightened weight against the cliff wall Zabud dropped the reins and leaped free. The horse reared, the rope hanging from its foot, the reins lifting off the ground. Solomon reached for them and speaking gently all the while, got to his feet. A horse who had been following Zabud's mount began to back up, grow restive and an echo of the disturbance could be heard moving down the line. Without raising his voice

Solomon ordered the rider in sight to dismount. The soldier obeyed, sliding cautiously to the curve of the limestone escarpment, passing the word to those who followed. Solomon eased his hand along the quivering neck of the brown horse. Its breath was hot and swift. He stroked it patiently and when the animal was quiet he examined the leg and loosened the rope. Zabud mumbled a stream of oaths as he took the reins from Solomon.

"You shouldn't be angry with the horse," Solomon said and gave Zabud a sly smile of reproach. "Be grateful he isn't lame. You may need the speed of this mount—before dawn." He walked ahead, leading his own horse.

The sluggish serpent of mist twisted its body in another direction and disappeared around the dark flank of the lower hill. Without speaking, the men inched along the crumbling edge of the cliff, their eyes fixed on the constant menace beneath their feet. The moon rose higher, casting their own shadows before them, blotting out the precarious step ahead. Then the ledge turned abruptly into a passage between steep walls of rock. It spread out into a vast and trackless waste studded with grotesque outcroppings of rock. Scrub and bushes of thorn crawled laboriously past the hollows, reaching for the slopes that went down to the tide of hills below.

A patrol was sent ahead to learn if the stretches of gnarled rock concealed enemy bands, waiting to attack. They returned, shivering with the cold and reported no sign of life. Even the rapacious birds would close their red-rimmed eyes when they flew over such a stretch of desolation. Benaiah's men moved forward. They came into the wide place and gathered there.

Only a long and treeless rise of ground undulating along one side separated them from Adonijah's encampment. The soldiers of Solomon's army moved with caution, subduing their grunts of relief, warning those who would ease the tension of the past hour with bursts of exuberance. It was a questionable deliverance. In the wilderness, safety and comfort were as scarce as vegetation. To move from one part into the next was only to replace one hazard with another. The night air on the barren back of the mountain range pierced the padded armor, brought up metal bucklers and shields of wood laced with tough leather to fight off the wind. But no man unfolded his woolen *simlah* or reached for the cloak of goat's hair strapped to the back of his horse. Some beat their bodies with their arms or found dubious shelter against the rocky mounds where they could still watch Benaiah. They had only one desire: to be unencumbered, ready to move the instant of his command.

Benaiah's shaggy head was thrown back as he studied the sky. Impervious to the cold, his body was still rigid, as if it had sprung out of the very rock upon which he stood. Then he came down moving his elbow in a slow circle to wipe the sweat from the inside of his helmet.

"We wait, but not for long," he said to his officers. He glanced skyward and his mouth cracked with a one-sided grin of satisfaction. "The Lord has sent us a flock of sheep clouds and a wind to herd them across the moon. He covers us with darkness that we may soon cross in safety over the ridge." The men were to line themselves along the base of the dividing spine and be ready to move over to the other side.

Such precaution irritated Solomon but he saw the need of it. Benaiah was only protecting his men. When the commander started to explain, Solomon could have spoken the words for him.

"That camel-headed Joab is old as Abraham," Benaiah said. "But he still has eyes in his head. If he sees a man outlined against a bright sky or catches a glimpse of the moon on a sword, he smites first and learns afterwards whether he killed a foe or his own father!"

Solomon was filled with a pounding impatience to go over the barrier alone and without delay. But he knew that Benaiah would prove to be a more formidable barrier than a mere ridge of rock.

As they moved toward the narrow channel of observation the wind shifted. It tore through the narrow clefts of the rock where sentries were stationed and it stopped the King, lifted his head with sharp concern. He had caught a hint of smoke from the campfires on the other side.

"The horses," he said and turned quickly to Benaiah.

The commander whirled around, giving the order as he moved away. All war mares and stallions were quickly taken down into the broad shelter of the lower slope. In that windless bowl of shale the scent of horses in the hostile camp would not reach them.

Solomon rested on a rock, his hands hanging empty and limp between his knees. He looked into the far distance toward the hidden desert where the Sabaean troops were undoubtedly still waiting for word from their ruler. With a heavy heart he felt the blood guilt that would have poured down upon him if Tamrin had reached the Sabaeans as well as the Edomites.

Benaiah came toward him. "Another moment," he said, "and a clamor of whinnying would have disclosed our position!"

Solomon smiled with irony. "But not our presence." He scraped up a handful of gravel and watched it fall slowly between his fingers.

Benaiah's words were expected and familiar.

"It is best to assume that the enemy knows as much about our movements as we know of theirs—whether it be on peaceful ground or a field of swords."

Solomon sighed. "But you prefer to speak in terms of battle."

"Because I put myself in the mind of the enemy!" Benaiah spread out his hands and his shadow formed a giant oak tree on the ground at Solomon's feet. "If they think in the language of battle, then I too speak that language—until they learn a new one."

It was a convenient belief, Solomon thought as he dusted off his hands. So long as greed for power lived in the heart of any man, it was a belief not easily cast aside. There would be no end to the time of wars, he feared. Those who would be free and live in peace must also be vigilant against those who would destroy them; and still, was there no way but the way of the sword?

Benaiah was still talking as Solomon rose and they resumed their walk.

"I take no risks," Benaiah said. "A small measure of caution, in any maneuver, is the same as leaven in a loaf of bread. If we are content to wait these few moments, then we have a better chance of rising—and alive. It isn't enough to recognize the hand of the Almighty in our affairs. If He sets up a mighty wind to help us we must know how to make use of it."

Solomon glanced at the grizzled profile moving beside him. And he envied Benaiah. Unflinching and fearless of nature's forces and those of man, the son of Jehoiada approached God with the same directness.

They paused at the mouth of the narrow opening, all but choked by the first jagged foothold between the walls of rock and hard earth. Zabud came limping through the entrance. Solomon lifted a hand and eased his friend's jump from the boulder to the ground.

Zabud caught his breath. "I've seen the camp of the Edomites. There are many more than I thought—it is little wonder Adonijah moves against Jerusalem regardless of Sabaean reinforcements—"

"You saw the enemy and no doubt they also saw you!" Benaiah's eyes blazed with anger. "A white bandage gleaming like a beacon light against the darkness of this opening in the wall! Why didn't you shout down to them, tell them we are here and that our other two companies are gathered in the surrounding hills!"

"Only my head and shoulders could get over the last rock of the opening. You can see for yourself." Zabud was not concerned with defending himself. "They are preparing to march down on Jerusalem! At this very moment the order is being given to fight swiftly through the ranks if they meet resistance within the city, but no matter if they are received with rejoicing or burning oil thrown over the wall—the King of Israel must be slain!"

Benaiah cast a harried look at the clouds, creeping too slowly toward the moon. Then he leaped into the opening and climbed upward, pushing his big hands flat against the sides to balance himself.

Solomon looked calmly into the face of Zabud. "Who gave this order?"

"The land is scarcely lower on that side than this," Zabud said, "yet I heard only what drifted up with the breeze. It seemed to rise from the place where the largest tent of Hadad's men was being folded. The voice came from a tall wide-standing man wearing a cloak of purple stuff with a scarlet border. When he turned to answer a chieftain his face was shadowed by his helmet but the dying fire struck his upper breastplate. It was made of dark scales of metal, unlike the armor worn by the others. I saw that much clearly, then the ground mist moved between us and I could no longer see the Edomite commander—"

"How could you know him?"

"Who else would spit such evil words from his tongue?"

The King looked at Zabud a moment in silence, then he gripped his friend's arm. "When we cross over stay in the rear, and take care." He glanced skyward as Benaiah had, then sprang into the crooked fissure of the rock.

Only a short time was left before the bright curve of ridge would be dimmed by the hidden moon. Solomon climbed over the rubble, mistook a dark place underfoot for a shadow and stepped on it. His foot plunged halfway to the knee, between sharp edges of gray rock. He freed his foot, pulled himself up and hurried forward, toward an irregular square of pale light at the far end. Benaiah's head, pressed close against the shadowed wall, seemed made of stone. Solomon flattened himself on the opposite side and looked out upon the camp. It seemed to be scattered to the horizon of the opposite hill. A formidable force, equal in number to the three companies Benaiah had gathered.

Except for the less violent wind, larger protective rock formations and a few trees, the site was similar to the wide place in which Benaiah's men waited.

Solomon recognized the deceptive leisure of a well-trained body of men, each soldier knowing his duty, performing it with unhurried skill. This must have been a brief stop. The stubble beneath groups of horses was not yet flattened to the ground by their restless hoofs. They had not encumbered themselves with chariots but several of the supply wagons were moving down toward the road that led to Jerusalem. The task of breaking camp was in its last moment. The men were girded for war, seemed eager for it; some were already mounted on their swift desert horses. Only a few warriors still buckled their swords. There were boasting shouts from the Edomites who wore the flowing robes of the desert. One of them screamed a victory and fanatically stamped out the coals of a fire with his bare feet. The men who passed by shouted with laughter, cheering him on. From somewhere beyond a bush-fringed hillock a chanting began among the Edomites. Spreading through the camp it evoked a boundary of dissonance. From the wild song Solomon was able to estimate roughly where the location of Adonijah's forces met the camp of Hadad's men. It was an irregular line; but well inside the silent half was Joab. He gave an order to his armor-bearer and passed the wheeled carriage supporting the battering ram. The years had whitened the old commander's beard but they had taken none of the belligerence from his stride. He halted suddenly, seeming to hear the words of the ominous rhythm for the first time. The Edomites sang of King Hadad's valor and glory, of his long exile in the court of the Pharoah. They sang of his return, after David's death, to the red rocks of Edom and outlaw bands who shared his vengeful passion.

A derisive whisper escaped between Benaiah's clenched teeth. "Look at the defiance pushing out the chin of that sly one! He listens for his name to come pouring out of their mouths with the venom of their hearts. They curse every breath he draws. And every sword. They remember its edge slaughtered their people and caused Hadad's flight into Egypt. I wonder if he has the wits to know he is their friend in this siege only and that is why they omit his name in their dirge. Take care, slayer of Abner, killer of Absalom. Soon it will be over and the Edomites will turn on you—" He stiffened and thrust his thick neck close to the outer edge of the wall.

Something was happening below. A subtle change came over the camp. A tenuous urgency, beginning somewhere in the far darkness, crept closer, sent a group of bowmen hurrying to join others. Two sentries came running toward Joab. As they approached they unfastened the shields and bucklers hanging from the straps on their shoulders and drew them over their left arms, ready for action. There was no mistaking the gesture. This was no longer an encampment of men armed for aggression. They were taking positions of defense.

The two soldiers gasped out their message to Joab. A rumbling echo of his harsh commands came up to the King in the narrow, waist-high opening of the cleft. Brisk orders were relayed across the company and the song of the Edomites faded into silence. A hundred men with javelins ready, galloped into the center of the encampment, dismounted and led their horses out of sight beyond the rocks. Others followed.

The head of Adonijah's commander turned in a slow circle, scanning the surrounding hilltops. Solomon and Benaiah flattened their shoulders against the inner walls of the passage and held their breaths until Joab purposefully strode out of sight.

Foot soldiers ran in from nowhere, the bronze arrowheads flashing up and down in the quivers on their backs. They disappeared behind the natural barricades. Horses, wagons and the iron ram's head of the heavy battering log were obliterated by a veil of mist. When it drifted by there was nothing left. Only a breathing stillness. The land had been suddenly deserted by everything but blue shadows that sprawled into uneven patches of moonlight.

Benaiah's eyes gleamed. "They are ready. So much the better. They are well prepared and have the advantage of sufficient cover. They also have an avenue of escape back to their filthy caves. Now, Solomon, do you still wish to meet your brother in peace?"

Solomon looked down at the desolation of rocks and shadow that concealed waiting destruction. His silence was his answer.

"As you wish." A note of asperity came into Benaiah's voice. "Everything is in their favor. I am sure that consoles your sense of justice."

At the moment Solomon felt nothing but an aching sadness. His seeds of defection had tainted the loyalty of his people, brought forth a crop of spies and informers; possibly in his own ranks. He wondered who, other than Abishag perhaps, could have sent out the word to the enemy. Adonijah still had supporters in Jerusalem, embittered by their abortive attempt at En Rogel to wrest the throne from the living David. It could have been the unctuous Shimei who had been enjoined on pain of death never to cross over the Kidron brook. But it could not have entered the mind of the old priest, Abiathar, dozing out his banished days in the sun of Anathoth. Solomon was certain of that. It must have been a disgruntled vassal prince, made spuriously brave by the dissension in the city. Or it could have been one of those merchants, constantly howling over high taxes, who believed the cure for all afflictions economic lay in a change of leadership. No matter. The identity of the informer was of no importance now.

For an instant Solomon considered leaping down from the opening in the cliff, making himself known at once. He feared an impetuous clash between the armies and felt responsible for the safety of his men. His eyes measured the distance. Benaiah read the thought in his mind and vigorously shook his head.

"You could leap twice the distance and you well know it," he said. "But remember, it is Joab down there. Not a holy white-bearded prophet! He prays only for one thing: a final blaze of glory in his last years. A restoration of the power and respect he once commanded. Before you could land on the ground he would thrust his darts into your side, and kill another son of David as he hung between the heaven and the earth! You are worth a thousand Absaloms! Come—"

"First your word that our plan of meeting is unchanged." Solomon looked straight into Benaiah's eyes.

"We are walking into the lion's mouth, but you not only have my word," Benaiah said. "My King commands my hand, my sword and my life."

They hurried back through the channel of rock and when they reached the lower opening on the other side the first clouds were beginning to hide the moon.

The army of Solomon, as one man, moved up the length of the hill. Before reaching the top the men fell flat and crawled over the ridge on forearms and knees.

When Benaiah saw a thick mist rolling between the hostile camp and the barrier-hill he made a swift decision. If enemy eyes detected a bold wavering on the horizon they would attribute it to the shifting haze, at least for a few moments. And that was sufficient. So the horses, too, were brought over in the deep shadow.

Solomon mounted his stallion and moved forward through the grayness, calling out the name of his brother.

There was no answer.

He called again and could not tell if his voice broke from the choking vapor or relief that the long yearning was ended and peace with Adonijah was at hand.

Someone rode up beside him. It could not be his commander for Benaiah was to follow and the armor-bearers were instructed to keep well behind.

Solomon could barely discern the height of the rocks ahead of him. They were much higher than they had appeared from the cleft in the hillside. They seemed to float above the lost and swirling mass searching for its home in the gorge. A gust of wind rose and the mist thinned out, tumbling back toward the hidden ravine. A torch of flaming pitch illumined the face of the rider at his side. It was Zabud; but there was no time to protest.

Solomon curved his hand at his mouth. "Adonijah!" he called out. "It is Solomon! Show your face to me. Put aside your sword and lay your hand upon my own!"

As the clouds began to move slowly past the moon, vague and unmoving figures robed in white appeared on one side. On the other, the darker uniforms of Adonijah's guard were not visible for another moment in the dim light. All carried swords and javelins.

"I demand to see my brother." Solomon addressed himself to a captain carrying a shield emblazoned with Adonijah's insignia. "I come in peace and with a message of good will. I plead with him to send the mercenaries out of Edom back to their land; to spare the blood that will flow this night and for nights to come if he enters Jerusalem without his brother Solomon at his side. He needs no army behind his back—"

"Stay where you are!"

He had moved closer to Adonijah's captain but the command had come from behind the ghostly ranks of motionless Edomites. He halted and turned.

The half-circle of white robes parted to make way for the august, dark-bearded horseman emerging from the rear of the ranks. He wore amulets of gold and emerald about his neck and his eyes were hidden in the leather-brown hollows above his cheekbones.

"You have come to delay us," he said, "with talks of peace when there can be none. Your own people have turned their backs on you. Peace is not yours to give away any more than the throne is yours. Prince Adonijah is taking what is rightfully his own. He has no wish to receive anything from your treacherous hands."

"I have not come to waste time with an officer of renegades! Where is my brother?"

"Your brother wishes first to know the number of your troops."

Solomon was losing patience. "They are here to assure the peace I ask. For no other reason."

The Edomite's voice lost some of its pretentious serenity. "Let them light torches that we may see their weapons."

Reluctantly, Solomon signaled to Benaiah. The base of the hillside was soon aglow with flares of ignited pitch and tow. The Edomite swiftly measured the length of the ranks with his eyes, wheeled his horse and disappeared.

As Solomon looked back at his men he saw that Benaiah's face was grim and his sword bared. Then he heard a stirring in the ranks of the Edomites and the files of Adonijah's men looked toward a flattened area between truncated cones of rock. A ring of mist had settled there. A helmet emerged from it, then broad shoulders cloaked in purple bordered with scarlet. The colors of a king, Solomon thought, and wondered if Hadad himself had led his troops in this latest uprising. Then the clearing moon shed a pale light down upon dark scales of armor and suddenly the entire figure rose up, mounted on a white horse.

Solomon peered at this stranger who had come up like something out of Sheol and sent as forbidding a shade out before him. The sword in his hand was double-edged. His knuckles gleamed bone-white on the hilt. Another sword was fastened to his belt. The face was deeply shadowed by the helmet but the flesh along the line of his jaw was thick and hard; the mouth cruel.

Something intangible smote Solomon's eyes and ears and the sense of knowing. For an instant he felt compelled to release all the words of rejoicing locked in his throat. But this was a stranger.

"I have come to welcome my brother," he said, looking up at the silent figure on the mound. "I have come to plead with him. In friendship. Now I'll say no more unless to his own ears—"

"My lord," Zabud whispered, "this is your brother." And Benaiah behind him muttered that it was in truth the rebellious son of David and looked no different this moment than he had the day he drew a sword against the newly anointed Solomon. "He is unchanged," Benaiah said in a low voice. "You are seeing him now for the first time as he always was—"

"Adonijah." The name sounded strangely unfamiliar as Solomon spoke it. It could not be! Adonijah's skin was not seamed and bitter grey. It was the color of healthy grain in the time of the ingathering. It was the first-fruit of a golden field.

This was the face of the wasteland itself; silent, hard and brutal.

As the moon came forth bright and clear the last doubt vanished. It was a distortion seated on the white horse, a coarse dream dredged up out of nightmare and guilt—but it was his brother. There was something about the eyes and he searched leaning forward, without knowing the nameless thing for which he searched; something more elusive than the longed-for reunion between brothers. He recognized the familiar face beneath the incubus that had grown upon it and for the moment was content with that.

A weariness that was not of the body came over him.

"Let us go back together, Adonijah, and make our peace," he said. "Let us go home." There was nothing more to say.

He was certain of Adonijah's reaction, more sure now than when he had left Jerusalem. Surely during the years bitterness must have distilled an essence of cold reason.

As his brother slowly appraised him, Solomon was sure of this—until Adonijah spoke.

One corner of his mouth was raised in scorn. "So the golden king rides a silver horse," he said.

A jeer came from someone in the Edomite ranks. It was instantly stopped by Joab. Until then Solomon had been only vaguely aware of his brother's commander and companion in exile.

Joab stood beside Adonijah, at the crest of the shallow incline. "If Solomon who calls himself king has come to us in good faith, my lord," Joab said, "we should demand proof."

"Name it," said Adonijah.

Savoring the privilege, Joab rubbed a hand over the stubble of his chin. He walked forward, paused halfway down the slope and with his thumbs, settled the sword belt encircling his waist. Solomon heard Benaiah take a careful step closer for Joab had come within a spear's throw of the King.

"It is extraordinary," Joab said, "for a King to meet his sworn enemies without an armed guard protecting him. But this alone is not proof of his pure intention. It is true Zabud here carries no weapon but this, too, could be one of Solomon's tricks." He gestured toward the King's forearm. "And in combat what worth is a mere dagger with a lion's head of gold and rubies? A royal toothpick, no more. But the lion's head with the scar of the beast on his face is one of another color! Let him stand far back, cover his sword and throw it ten paces aside!"

Solomon fought down his anger. He sensed the fury rising in Benaiah, festering through the ranks spread out at the foot of the hill, gathering with the throbbing force of a boil about to burst.

"This is a matter between two brothers!" Solomon said. "Not between rival commanders or their armies!"

"You weigh my King's actions, Joab," Benaiah roared, "with your own scales of treachery! My mind hears the call Abner made when you drew concealed weapons and slew his hundreds in murderous attack at Gibeon. He called out to you then as we call out now: how long would you devour by the sword?"

The grooves in Joab's face deepened with anger.

"Sheath your tongue in its mouth and your sword in leather!"

Silence and moonlight hung like a heavy cloud over the camp. A wave of revulsion rose up in the King as he turned his eyes from Joab.

He spoke directly to his brother: "Enough of this! Let us return to Jerusalem!"

"Why do you protest?" Adonijah smiled with insolence. "Is it because you dare not make demands without the protection of your commander's sword?"

"If you would see your King live, Benaiah," Joab called out, "then cast your weapon to the ground!" As he spoke Joab extended his arm full length toward his armor-bearer. A javelin was thrust into his hand.

Solomon's men had moved imperceptibly closer, the torchbearers remaining in the darkness to create an illusion of unmoving ranks. A moment later it was detected and the Edomite warriors, with equal skill, closed their ranks flanking the host. At a command from Adonijah or Joab, they could cut off the army. Solomon, his friend and his commander would be isolated and defenseless.

Benaiah had no alternative. After an endless moment his blade gave out a long sigh as it slid into the length of leather at his belt. The bronze studding on the scabbard hit the rocks on the ground ten paces away.

"You have your proof, Adonijah!" Solomon said. "Now are you prepared to enter Jerusalem with our escort and open support, or do you expect the people of the city to sing and open the gates for you?"

"There are still those who would rejoice," Adonijah said. "No High Priest of yours can change that!"

"He will support you as a son of David if I can assure him you come to lead his people in the way of peace."

"A council has formed," Adonijah said, his voice little more than a whisper of mockery. "The elders have gathered to denounce you—"

"And to bring my brother to the throne," said Solomon. "Now for the love of our father, Adonijah, let us be on our way—!"

"A trick! A lie!" The moon cast a trembling shine of madness on Adonijah's eyes. His voice smoldered with rage and his words were firebrands kindling all the heaped-up malice within him. "You came here knowing they would never offer me the throne. They know well that I would demolish your hideous temple and raise up an army with weapons made from its gold! You know they are waiting to receive you as no king of Israel has ever been welcomed into Jerusalem! With blessings, songs of praise, even forgiveness for your sins against them—!"

Solomon shook his head with bewilderment, denying the words of Adonijah, but Adonijah hurled curses down upon him; and cried out that the news had been brought to him only moments before the message that the host of Israel was gathered somewhere in the hills.

"At this very moment Zadok and the elders go about the city telling the populace Solomon will return in new glory, that Solomon is their only true king! You stand there as if I were the one with lies and oil on my tongue! Throw off your cloak of hypocrisy. Admit what I already know. That the Queen of Sheba came to betray you and stayed beyond your departure to let the elders and the priests behold her repentance! Those who gathered to denounce you, Solomon, now pray for your safety. It will do them little good. You asked me to return to Jerusalem and I do return—triumphant and alone. That is my answer—!" He dug his heels into the white horse and with a frenzied yell raised his sword and charged down the incline.

The night instantly burst into earsplitting tumult. Benaiah's sentries on the hilltop sounded the battle horns again and again. The echoing trumpets on the far heights resounded, shattering the air; but their clamor was lost in the shrieks of Edomites as they fell upon Solomon's men who had surged outward in a mass to breach the surrounding columns. The ground trembled with thundering hoofs, the air filled with dust and battle cries as men leaped from their horses and fought sword to spear in the ditches and on the high ground between wedges of rock.

Solomon's horse reared and wheeled, fighting the bridle and reins, straining to rush into the melee. In the delirium of terror all about him, disbelief had carried Solomon beyond fear. He felt nothing but the sick horror that holds a dreamer paralyzed for an instant of time that seems to stretch to the grave. All the writhing shadows swarming in the pools of red moonlight were unreal. They were not his men in this moment of combat, not the warriors of King Hadad or the followers of Adonijah. They were all ghosts fighting other shades in clashing armor and soon they would disappear as jugglers and tumblers, their entertainment ended, vanished at a feast. Only one had a face; pale and real as death. It came up out of purple and scarlet wings and flew toward him on a white horse—

A warning cry from Zabud and Solomon turned his head to see Joab's full weight lunge forward, hurling the javelin with his mighty arm. As the King instinctively recoiled, the reins loosened in his hand. The silver stallion reared, lifted its head and with a terrible noise fell to the ground with the javelin deep in its throat. Zabud pulled a knife from the bandage around his leg and let it fly. The commander howled with rage as it grazed his hand and deflected the second spear aimed at Solomon as he struggled free of the stallion's twitching body. The white horse was close, almost upon him. Adonijah was bent low on one side, the point of his double-edged sword flashing close to the ground where Solomon crouched. The King needed an instant to gauge the distance, to find a better position from which he could spring up and unseat Adonijah, bring him down to the ground and face to face. Through the haze of battle, Solomon caught a glimpse of one of his armor-bearers slashing his way toward him, but there was no time for that. One of Adonijah's men sprawled in a broken position at Benaiah's feet. The commander was fighting with his bare hands against his own sword in the hand of an Edomite. The white-robed figure fell on the weapon, impaled and grotesque. Solomon called out to Benaiah and ran swiftly across, in front of the white horse. Adonijah's sword slashed through the air. Solomon bent low, choosing his own time, waiting for the horse to turn and bring its rider within reach. In the deep blackness of his mind he felt he had lived through this moment before; the crouching, the waiting, seizing the wrist and upper arm, tossing the rider to the ground. But in the dim memory there was a sun in the sky and a meadow of green and the horse was a lame thing, for David loathed horses and feared them. He would not allow his children to seek laughter and play war games on any but the slow, hocked beasts captured from the Philistines.

The white horse wheeled around. Adonijah came riding back, his eyes gleaming as he raced toward his brother. Solomon was ready, bent low. Then someone came at him from behind, flung him sideways and off balance, away from the horse's path. He caught a glimpse of Benaiah's arm band. It raked his neck as the commander reached down across him and wrenched the broken dagger from its sheath. As he got up Benaiah was running beside the horse. As he leaped up to drag Adonijah away, the sight of them was cut off by a white-robed figure. He came at Solomon from nowhere, and with the sound of a great bird flapping its wings. And another fell upon him from the right. Solomon struck out at them, twisted the sword out of one brown hand and turned it into the body of the other. When he lifted it a loop of gold and emerald amulets slid from its stained point. Cut and bruised he stood with Zabud and prepared to meet another onslaught when the air rang out with the trumpets of the companies out of the hills. The hundreds came sweeping down, shouting from the one side and the thousand galloped into the encampment from the other and the Edomites were confused by the numbers and terrified. They called out for the leader, for Adonijah, and someone saw his horse without its rider. They saw what Solomon saw for the first time: that Joab was going away from them, moving away from the flaming wagons and moonlight, losing himself in shadow and leaping on a horse. The Edomites fled with Benaiah's men in pursuit.

Solomon let the sword fall from his hand, wiped his palm against his tunic and walked through the red glow of the battlefield. The Edomites had brought out vats of oil in which to dip their arrows and it had spilled over the battering ram. The thick log would burn for a long time. A dead warrior lay before it, as if worshiping the iron ram's head wreathed in flames.

He walked among the wounded and Zabud walked by his side until Solomon told him to go back with the others, to return to Jerusalem. And when Zabud had gone, Solomon continued to search.

He found Adonijah. He had died with a look of childlike astonishment on his face. His helmet had fallen off and the rising wind stirred the hair across his forehead. And the mark of Cain was upon his own.

Where now was the power and the glory? There was nothing in him but vanity, all was vanity. He had killed his brother. His own blindness no less than Benaiah's hand had buried the jagged blade in Adonijah's throat. He stared down at the lion's head of gold with its ruby eyes. An unweeping anguish seized him because all his days had been days of vanity. And now that an evil one was upon him there would be no other kind. The ruby eyes sparkled in the waning moonlight. He had given Adonijah his gift: a thrust of violence that redder violence might pour from the wound and leave, at last, tranquillity on his face. For the first time Solomon felt the coldness of the wind. He would feel it the rest of his life. The one who was cut down could have lived to behold the sun another day, and he who stood upright in his shame would walk in its light and see nothing but the shadow. Surely at any moment now the glazed stone eyes would stop staring at the moon, the rose-colored sleeves would flutter at the window of his house and Haggith's bracelets would jingle as she called to him telling him to stop his play, to come in, come in now out of the cold. . . .

The moonlight was gone and a time of darkness fell on the land. The men who cleared the battlefield saw how it was with their King and when at last they came to Adonijah they carefully wrapped him in his cloak of purple and bore him away.

Everything but the borders of scarlet and moving torchlight was swallowed up by the night and as Solomon watched, these too disappeared. A jackal cried somewhere in the hills and from a distant slope of a hidden, fertile valley a voice of grieving rose from the throat of a dove. These things of the earth weep for my brother, he thought, even the wind coming up through the clefts in the rocks makes the sound of mourners sighing in the streets—and I stand here alone in the darkness, watching my brother carried to his long home, and I have no words, no hope, no prayer.

He had no recollection of the hours he wandered. When he next saw his commander the sun had come up over the ridges of Moab and cast a golden fairness over the ripening fields of Bethlehem. Benaiah climbed the ridge of vineyard in which Solomon rested. He brought morning-baked bread from the little house below, near the road, and the old people who tilled the soil had sent up figs and goat's milk for their King. But he could not eat. A dead man had no need of food. Benaiah helped himself and chewed the fruit as he gave his report. Solomon paid little attention. Benaiah numbered the Edomites slain and said it would take Hadad a lifetime to replace the weapons left behind; and Eli the physician had come down into the Hinnom Valley to treat the wounded. There were surprisingly few.

"Zabud's good fortune took him back to Jerusalem without a scratch and our friend Joab is dead." He yawned, saying he would go down now and stretch out beneath a tree in the orchard until Solomon wanted him.

"How did Joab die," Solomon asked, "and by whose hands?"

Benaiah studied Solomon with faint wonder. "I pursued him when the Edomites fled but he took sanctuary and clung to the horns of the altar. I came up to you as you stood over your brother's body. I said I could not slay him while he clung to his last refuge unless the King named him the murderer he was—"

It came back to him then, how he had named Joab's crimes along with his own. And he wondered if Adonijah would be alive now if David's charges had been carried out the day they were given.

Benaiah broke off a piece of bread from the loaf while he described the way in which he had slain Joab; then he washed down the bread with a gulp of milk and went down the hill to sleep in the shade.

Ahiah had met the soldiers on this way back to Jerusalem but when he found Solomon in the hillside vineyard neither of them spoke of battle. Solomon's eyes, to the scribe, were like the dark windows of an empty house. And when the King spoke his voice was too controlled, too natural. The deep wound of a soul had to be kept open, cleansed with pure sunlight for slow healing upward from the source. The King had covered the raw pain too quickly.

"I wanted to visit Bethlehem again," Solomon said, "but I had always hoped I would not be alone. Now that I'm here, I wonder why?"

There were some roads each man must travel alone, Ahiah thought. Aloud, he said: "You were lost and your feet led you here—to the beginning." Only Solomon could find his own answer but Ahiah hoped that where all else had failed, the hands of his dead brother were turning Solomon's face once more to God. But who could tell? A man was a greater riddle to himself than any Ahiah had compounded.

Solomon rested his head against a tree and closed his eyes. His face was drawn and pale beneath the sun-bronzed skin.

The sound of a thousand small bells came up to them. Villagers were gathering along the road below to watch the caravan of the Queen of Sheba pass by. She was returning to her land, with all her servants. Solomon looked down upon it without surprise. He was beyond the lesser emotions. Remote and cut off, only the long days ahead would restore him to his people and to himself. He rose slowly when Makada's palanquin came into view but he did not make himself known. As the procession moved slowly away the curtains of the Queen's chair parted and her eyes gravely moved over the faces clustered beneath the trees. The face she sought was not there but perhaps she would one day look upon it again. The hope was written softly on her lips as she withdrew behind the curtains.

"She suffers, too, Solomon. What a pity you could not bring yourself to go down and say farewell."

"From the moment we first met, we knew we were saying good-bye." He looked after the caravan until it disappeared; until its tinkling bells faded into silence.

As they started back toward the city Solomon said, "I am dead, Ahiah. It is too slow and painful to return to the land of the living." But before the sun went down on that day he heard the rejoicing of his people at the gates and his heart was lifted up. He looked into each face with gratitude and his love reached out to all of them. He heard the measured words of the elders and felt the compassionate touch of Zadok's hand upon his shoulder; and during the night when dreams of mist and blood-red moons tortured his sleep he dressed and hurried up to the unfinished temple.

He took the advice he gave the sluggard and went to the ant. A body exhausted by labor could sleep. In time it could regain hope, and he wanted that in abundance to pass on to his people. Memory was not enough to sustain them. A belief such as mine was, he thought, is not enough. It wavers and allows the strides of the godless to lengthen across the earth. He must go back to the beginning of things and find there the fervor of truth, back to the fire and faith of Abraham and Jacob and the zeal of Moses. He must remember that God comes closer to man if man walks toward Him, making of each step an imitation of His ways. . . .

The servants of the household, rising at dawn, saw the King on the hilltop; and the palace, the city streets and the hills resounded with the news that Solomon labored in the house of the Lord. And the word was carried with joy through the length of the land. The leaves of spring turned brown and crimson and after the long heat of summer, fell to the ground. The earth was slowly taking back its own. While the sun gave out its last burning heat for the ingathering, the Temple was finished in all its parts.

Solomon had built the Lord a house of great splendor. On the day of dedication he walked with the elders and the leaders of the tribes as the Ark of the Covenant was taken from the tabernacle and carried up on long staves to its new sanctuary. The silver trumpets sounded, the singing was jubilant: *The earth is the Lord's and the fulness thereof . . . for he has founded it upon the seas and established it upon the rivers. Who shall ascend the hill of the Lord? And who shall stand in his holy place? He who has clean hands and a pure heart, who does not lift up his soul to what is false . . .*

The cymbals and harps and timbrels made a joyous sound and he wished for lightness in his feet, as there had been in David's when he danced before the Ark that held the Commandments of the Lord. But Solomon's transgressions still weighed him down. He entered the doors of the Temple with Zadok and the priests and the multitude chanted their songs of praise in the forecourt; and when the house had been dedicated to the Lord a thick cloud filled the sanctuary. Then Solomon made supplication and spread out his hands and asked that justice and strength live within the walls; he asked that the faith that built them live forever beyond the days of the cedar and the stone and that when a foreigner came from a far country, hearing of the Lord's mighty hand and outstretched arm, and prayed, his call should be heeded that all the peoples of the earth might know His name. He blessed the Lord who had given rest to his people.

"The Lord our God be with us as he was with our fathers," he said and looked out upon the shining faces of the multitude. And he prayed that the Lord would always make His face to shine upon them in the generations of man and he wondered if he had done enough in his own time to incline their hearts to Him. He could say little more, do nothing more but exhort them to walk in the ways of righteousness—*"That all the peoples of the earth may know that the Lord is God and there is no other!"*

As the feasting began and voices were lifted up in song, Solomon felt a great weight within him surge up and dissolve in a strange exultation. He felt the warmth of unshed tears behind his eyes and he wondered why he was moved to weeping. Was it from joy or from sorrow?

Did he weep for himself—or for his people?

001